The Crown and Empire

Ethan R. Divelbliss

Table of Contents

Table of Contents

Table of Contents

Act 3: His Majesty's Most Loyal Government

Table of Contents

I would rather obey a fine lion, much stronger than myself, than two hundred rats of my own species.

-Voltaire

Act 1:

A Lion Among Men

Chapter 1: Amanda

It was nighttime in Colonna City. The rain trickled about in the east coast winds as the dull humdrum of night life in the city buzzed through the air. Engines whirred, heels tapped, and horns honked. Time marched forward. Here in this city, in an unassuming building, on an insignificant street, lay Amanda. Amanda Beasly was a woman not unlike others. Brown hair and equally brown eyes, all enclosed in a slender build and average height.

Growing up in poverty, as too many before her, had led Amanda into pursuing financial stability through the oldest and noblest of professions. Her time on the street found her in the employ of a Pimp who went by the name of "Pump Nasty". Pump was an interesting fellow, as his chosen moniker suggests, he was a bit of a showboat. His real name: Charles Brown, but he only responded to Pump. He was a giant of a man standing six foot four and two hundred and ten pounds of hulking muscle. A board firm jaw and hefty neck to match. Proud of his physique he was often sporting tight fitting clothes consisting of a silk button down and chinos, capped off by dress slippers or designer tennis shoes. As is common for Pimps, he was always adorned in copious amounts of jewelry, gold rings and bracelets littering his skin leading up to a grill crusting his top row of teeth. Amongst the gold Amanda always noticed one piece that stood out. On his left pinky he wore a singular silver ring every day without fail. A silver ring embossed with a sword crossing a trident, covered by a crown and all wrapped within a laurel wreath.

Through the course of his less than reputable career, Pump had come into possession of an old warehouse in Colonna City's Industrial District. This dilapidated cesspit of a building was quickly gutted and turned into a headquarters for his operations. The layout of the building was rather simple. A large open work floor with a set of stairs leading up to an overlook and a floor manager's office. The work floor was filled with cots to house the multitude of women in Pump's employ while the old office was refitted to serve as a private bedroom for Pump himself.

This was where the lord of the castle would take his pick of the concubines in his service, forcing one to serve as his comfort for the evening while the rest stayed below. The cots provided for the working women were hastily constructed heaps of scrap metal crudely fastened together with moth-eaten mattresses thrown atop, courtesy of old porno sets and other less desirable sources. Pump was not a peddler of high-end escorts rather, the lowly members of society with no one else to turn to. He was their lifeline and this fact was not lost on him. Providing minimal accommodation while expecting maximum return of investment was how the great Pump Nasty applied his trade.

The other key factor in Pump's administration was Macy. Devastatingly beautiful by any standard and smart as a tack and yet hopelessly smitten with her master. Despite her best efforts, Pump did not always stay faithful to Macy, preferring instead to dip into the wide selection, both figuratively and literally, placed at his feet. He seemed to prefer the defenseless conquest to the willing participant. Still, she stood by him, unwavering in her devotion. The girls had various theories about Macy. Some thought she was after Pump's money, others suggested she wanted his ear so she could take over his business, others still thought she was just insane and genuinely loved the man. Her true motivations: who could know? What matters is she acted as Pump's bottom girl, overseeing the entire operation by his side.

And this is the situation Amanda found herself wound up in. A poor girl from the street with few other options, brown hair, brown eyes and property of Pump in all but name. She had originally tried to act as an independent agent but unfortunately such things weren't very feasible in Colonna City. The trains may be late, the buses may wreck, but the crime is always organized. Every inch of the city was someone's territory and very little patience was given to strangers siphoning their business.

Certainly, vassalage to a man like Pump was far from an ideal circumstance. Amanda did try to see the advantages, rationalization perhaps, but who wouldn't want to make the best of a bad situation. Pump, in all his acumen, didn't just employ working girls. Also, he had security on his payroll. Perhaps a John didn't feel like paying, not Amanda's problem. One of Pump's goons would merely intervene, and Amanda would receive payment plus restitution. Someone tried to get rough. A quick shout to the street below would see a quick end to any overzealous actions.

Fortunately, this was a rare occurrence in Amanda's experience. Most customers were relatively professional, as professional as one could be in an industry such as hers. Still the backup was good to have when it was needed. One of these such men was Frankie. Frankie was the newest of the guys but had been around for a few months. Big and buff like the others, maybe a little cleaner cut but all in all indistinguishable apart from his bright blond hair. Frankie was very clearly fond of Amanda yet played the gentleman. With his chiseled jaw and his blue eyes, he was always polite and never acted inappropriately. Amanda didn't quite reciprocate his feelings, but she appreciated his trying so she would humor him from time to time. She would go out to dinner with him on occasion, maybe see a movie, nothing too assuming. Mostly it was an excuse to get out of that godforsaken den Pump tried to pass off as a home.

Such was Amanda's life. At night she would go out with the others escorted by Frankie and the security team. Everyone went to their assigned spots and business was conducted. At the end of the night Pump would be given the cash to redistribute, after he skimmed off the top of course, and onward goes the cycle.

When Amanda got her money it all went into a safety deposit box. The farther away from the IRS' clutches the better. That's what it was all about at the end of the day. Along with the stack of saved up cash there was one other thing in the box. A small postcard with a picture of the beach. That was the dream. Save up enough to leave the city behind. Retire to a small house by the beach somewhere down south and never talk to anyone ever again. If there was a heaven; this was about as close as anyone could get to it on earth.

All the girls have their own dreams of course, some want to open up their own business, put money on the street, that sort of thing. Others were just trying to get enough to buy a small place in the city and maybe work for someone more reputable once the opportunity presented itself. Others still were just looking to fund their drug habits. Amanda didn't judge the motivations of her coworkers, after all she was in no better a spot than any of them. She had yet to "make it out" and who knows what the future holds? People that found themselves under Pump's thumb were not the sort who come from a plethora of opportunities. Survival was the order of the day in the dilapidated little warehouse they all called home.

Was it a pleasant life? Not really, no, but it was Amanda's. She trudged on and made the best of it when and where she could. She had a few friends in the group. Tiffany was the one that she talked to the most. Tiffany was just about as polar an opposite to Amanda as you could get. Where Amanda preferred to keep her nose down and hide in the shadows, Tiffany preferred the spotlight. She played up to the trope of the dumb blonde, being loud and flirtatious and about as annoying as a person could be. This was a pretty successful tactic for her. It was the kind of persona that put the men on the street at ease but kept people like Pump at a distance. Amanda admired her for it but could never see herself acting in a similar fashion. It looked exhausting. She much preferred putting on a fake smile during work hours and hiding as much as possible in the off time. This sort of natural balance allowed a bond to develop between the two. Tiffany was one of the ones who wanted to put money out on the street "*Why should the men have all the fun*" she often said.

Amanda couldn't understand why she would want to stay in this city that had done nothing but spat on her but still she thought it was ballsy. Getting into the game in Colonna City was a big deal. The whole city was claimed by various gangs or groups but there seemed to be a relative peace and cohesion amongst them all. Amanda knew there had to be some overarching structure enforcing this, but she wasn't exactly sure how it worked. All she knew was it was hard to carve out a slice for yourself but once you did you were set for life. Personally, she didn't find the idea appealing at all. "*Not worth the trouble*" she thought, much more content to squeeze out a comfortable if humble life somewhere far away from here. When Amanda would be going out to dinner with Frankie or catching a movie to enjoy some peace, Tiffany would be hunting down loan sharks or drug dealers and talking to them about God knows what. Anything to get a foot in the door. Amanda had to admire her tenacity.

This is where Amanda finds herself presently. More fortunate than few, less fortunate than many more. But an interesting course of events was soon to unfold, that would change all of that forever.

Chapter 2: Sandra

Gunshots ring out. *"BANG BANG BANG"* A young officer ducks for cover. She's quite alone outnumbered and certainly outgunned. The dark alleyway before her lit only by the muzzle flashes of suppressive fire endlessly assaulting the concrete slab that she shields herself with.

Safe for the immediate moment, the officer takes the opportunity to replace the magazine in her department issued sidearm. She takes a deep breath. Too dangerous to poke her head out. She concentrates, listening to the pattern of the gunfire. Two assailants on her right, one semi-automatic weapon and one full. One assailant on the left, semi-automatic only.

Another deep breath. The automatic rifle reloaded after twenty-five rounds. The semis, every ten. The automatic gun must be silenced first. She would have about a four or five second window to strike. She must be quick; she must be surgical. The last bullet smacked into the concrete. Go time. She leans out to the right of her cover and fires two shots. She hears the metal clanging of guns falling to the ground. Direct hits!

Quickly she rotates to the left. Too slow. The final gunman gets a shot off grazing her shoulder, throwing off her aim. She returns fire and hears a searing howl from the darkness followed by footsteps retreating into the night. She pursues adrenaline holding back the pain of the slug nestled tightly in her shoulder.

She follows him down the alley. He turns a corner. She follows suit. Turning the corner, she is alarmed to see he has taken a hostage. Her pistol trained on the gunman; the gunman's pistol trained on the temple of a poor woman unfortunate enough to be nearby. The combatants stare each other down. Quickly the officer surveys her surroundings. Suddenly an unseen smile passes behind her stern expression. She begins to relax her arms as if to surrender. Then, at the crucial moment, she quickly snaps back to shoot at a heating pipe on the exterior of a nearby building. The resulting concussive blast staggers the gunman and his hostage, loosening his grip. The officer springs into action, tackling the gunman and knocking him unconscious with a swift strike of her pistol grip.

The next thing she knows, the heroic officer is in a grand reception room. Fellow officers in dress uniforms are lined up on either side, creating an aisleway. Their faces beaming with pride and hands beating out thundering applause. She walks down to the path. At its end lies the Commissioner and the mayor. She shakes Commissioner Helming's hand before approaching the mayor, both men sharing the same pride and excitement as the officers witnessing the spectacle. The mayor holds a box in his hands. He opens the lid to show a dazzling golden medal, the inscription on its surface read *"Officer Sandra D.*

Blewens, For Extraordinary Bravery in Service to Colonna City" The officer smiled with excitement as the mayor prepared to pin the medal on her chest. Time seemed to stand still, then all went black.

Sandra's hand fumbled along the nightstand in the apartment. Blindy grazing the surface of the particleboard, she searches for the snooze button atop the alarm clock, ringing out like the rooster's crow. Her hand finds its mark. The alarm goes silent and Officer Sandra Blewens rises from her slumber.

A woman of thirty-eight years, she was always amazed at how hard it still was to wake up in the morning. She assumed by middle age waking up would come naturally. *"Not quite middle age"* She would mentally correct herself. As long as that first digit was less than four, she was still safe. She sat up in bed and rubbed her temples with the heels of her hands. Gathering enough courage to remove the blankets she got out of the bed, jolting at the sudden temperature change.

She made her way to the bathroom and turned on the shower. Giving the water time to warm up, she began to brush her teeth mercilessly. Yellow teeth be damned if she could help it. A police uniform didn't provide her with much chance to show femininity on the day to day, so at the very least she could keep her teeth white. She knew there were more important things to care about in life but what's so terrible about wanting to feel at least slightly pretty? By the time her teeth were polished and flossed she could feel the steam beginning to emanate from the shower.

The warm water felt good on her skin. She allowed herself to enjoy it for a moment before getting down to the task at hand, water isn't free after all. As she cleaned herself, she thought about the dream she had. The images all replayed in her mind. She wasn't naive enough to honestly believe when she had joined the force that it would be all shootouts and medals, but maybe just one wouldn't hurt.

After all, what did she become a cop for if not to help people? Settling domestic disputes and busting low level stickups was all well and good but it did leave a lot to be desired. If she could only get a good drug trade or a human trafficking ring under her belt, something with some press power. It was selfish to feel that way, she knew it. Of course, she wouldn't wish these problems onto people but it's kind of hard to be a hero when someone else is always beating you to the punch. When she first joined the force, she figured her day would come in time.

But that was fifteen years ago, and her hope was beginning to wane. She had yet to receive a real case. Something of substance. She was more than willing to put her life on the line. She wasn't top of her class in the academy, but she wasn't struggling at the bottom either. What was the hold up? There was an answer that sulked in the back of her mind, but she tried not to think that way. It wasn't 1955 anymore, surely, she couldn't use sexism as an excuse for everything wrong in her life. But still... it was possible.

Done with the shower she quickly attended to the rest of her grooming. Teeth were brushed, deodorant was applied, and hair was pulled tightly back into the regulation bun. Up next came the uniform. Laid out the night before as always, she quickly got dressed and performed one final inspection in the mirror before she decided she looked satisfyingly professional.

She then popped out into the kitchen. As she did so she let out an internal sigh. She never liked her studio apartment. Who wants to walk out of the bedroom into the kitchen? She could afford a nicer place easily enough but there didn't seem to be much of a point. She had a TV, a couch, a bed, a kitchen, and a bathroom. She didn't require much else. It was just her these days after all.

Quickly, she scrambled some eggs and popped some toast in the toaster. Scarfing her breakfast down before heading out the door, she made her way across the parking lot and into her car. One perk of the job, an issued police cruiser.

She moves along the city streets, mindlessly tapping the steering wheel along with the radio. Eventually, she makes it to the station and pulls into her spot. Walking in she was greeted by Clara at the front desk. Clara always made her smile. Sandra always thought Clara got her job as a receptionist and dove headfirst into the role. With her horned glasses attached to beads and overly applied makeup the woman was a walking stereotype of her field.

"*Sandra honey are you doing today?*" She asked with a smile. Not looking up from her computer screen as she did so. Acrylic nails fiercely tapping away at the keyboard. Sandra sometimes wondered if Clara was just sometimes typing on a blank screen to give off the appearance of looking busy. *"I'm alright, how are you?"* Sandra replied politely. *"Oh, you know sweetie, busy and bored!"* Clara responded. Sandra gave her an affectionate pat on the shoulder and made her way into the bullpen.

Today's briefing was nothing exciting. Break-ins, angry ex-husbands, angry ex-wives, vagrants, vandals, and so on into an infinity of boredom. As the Captain gave the briefing Sandra's mind wandered back to the dream she had last night. Recreating visions of heroic shootouts, glamorous medals and everything in between. She snapped back to, with enough time to catch the end of the briefing and nodded, feigning attention. She left the briefing, signed out a shotgun, placed the firearm in the rack on her cruiser, and began her patrol.

She sat and sat. For God's sake could someone at least speed? The day drags on. Minutes feel like hours which in turn feel like years.
Cars go by, people walk along the city streets, and nothing happens. Eventually noon rolled around. Lunchtime! Sandra wasn't really all that hungry. But

she was bored. It's funny how eating becomes something to do when there's no more enticing alternative. She took a break from her patrol and drove off to a nearby fast-food restaurant. Grease is what she needed right about now. Bad for the body but good for the soul.

She orders herself a burger and pulls into a parking space to enjoy her lunch. She took the paper bag and set it into her lap. She found a parking space facing the street so she could still keep an eye on things. She spread out napkins to keep the cruiser clean. If there was one thing she couldn't stand it was a slob. She sat, chewing on the burger, Jesus it was good. Just the thing she needed to keep her spirits up through the second half of her shift.

She sat and she ate, as the cars duly passed. She watched and watched and nothing happened. The life of the city buzzed around her, almost as if it was leaving her behind. But then, when all hope seemed lost, it happened. Sandra was casually browsing the street when a blue Malibu went screaming past her. It had to have been going at least seventy miles an hour. *"Not much, but something!"* Sandra thought to herself.

She sat her burger down onto the passenger seat and turned on her sirens. She pulled out into the street and made her pursuit. Weaving in and out of traffic felt good. For once she felt like she was doing something, anything. She bobbed between lanes as the traffic got out of her way until she had eyes on her target once again. The Malibu thundered down the street, screeching between lanes indifferent to other traffic. Sandra sounded her horn as much as she could to get the other driver's attention, hoping they would swerve out of the way in time.

The chase continued for six blocks. Sandra clutching hard onto her steering wheel. She had radioed for backup, but she worried it would take far too long. She began surveying the streets to find some way to cut off the lunatic in front of her. She was gaining on him, right behind his bumper now. Sandra looked at her speedometer. They were going ninety miles per hour. It was getting too dangerous. They were going too fast for the other cars to react in time. It was only a matter of time before a civilian got hurt. Up ahead she saw her moment. A stretch of road that was empty of other cars. She had a small window in which to act.

The opening was there. She veered off to the side and sped up slightly. Then with one deep breath she rammed her bumper into the tail end of the Malibu causing it to spin out of control and crash into a traffic post. A perfect pit maneuver. Sandra quickly pulled over and jumped out of her cruiser. She ran up the Malibu, her head running through all the possibilities. She hadn't heard any robberies come in over the radio. Whatever, this guy was fleeing, however it had to have been violent.

She walks up to the wrecked Malibu and knocks on the window. It slowly rolls down to reveal a rather underwhelming sight. Before Sandra sat nothing more than a common junkie. Nose dripping, drool emanating from his lip. He was about middle aged, almost bald, and riddled with piercings and tattoos. As his head bobbed in his barely lucid state his mouth was drooped open revealing a golden tooth. Sandra looked down into the window, almost pitying the sight before her.

Maintaining her professionalism, she began her preamble by introducing herself and trying to obtain preliminary information. Her questions were answered with little more than nonsensical ramblings, something about a party and "just having a good time no harm done." Deciding she had enough, Sandra asked the man to step out of the car. As he exited the vehicle, he kept muttering to Sandra something about "Did she see the ring" and continually tried showing her his left hand. Sandra kept trying to ascertain more information from the man asking him if he had taken anything, where he was who he was with, all while constantly having to push away the hand he was so desperately flaunting in her face.

Finally, Sandra decided that diplomacy was achieving nothing and placed the man under arrest. As she was placing his arms behind his back and cuffing his wrist, she noticed what she assumed the man had been blubbering about. Amidst the sea of tattoos, on his left pinky finger was one singular silver ring. Curiosity, getting the better of her she examined the insignia embossed on its surface. It was a sword crossing a trident, covered by a crown and all wrapped within a laurel wreath. Sandra had never seen this symbol before and had no idea what it was supposed to mean. Attributing its significance to nothing more than the musings of an intoxicated brain she informed her prisoner he was under arrest for driving under the influence and placed him in the backseat of her cruiser.

Headed back to the station she radioed ahead informing dispatch that she was returning with a guest. Her passenger had become remarkably quiet compared to the mumbling idiot he was not five minutes ago. Sandra had seen it before. The experience was definitely a sobering one. Some people become radically apologetic, realizing the trouble in store for them. Others go into a sort of shocked stasis. Others go quiet because they know better. Shut up and hopefully the lawyers can work out a deal.

This man was definitely the latter. Glancing in the rearview mirror, Sandra could see the color rapidly fading from his face. His nonchalant attitude quickly turned into fear. Eyes dancing around the cruiser, almost as if looking for any possible means of escape. Soon after, terror turned into despair and resignation to the situation. He hung his head for the remainder of the ride.

When she returned to the station, she turned her prisoner over the holding cells and sat down to begin her report. Fingers tapping away at the keyboard in mundane rhythm. "*Click, Click, Click*"

Chapter 3: Amanda

Pump had been acting strange. Amanda had noticed it for the past week or so, and it all started with the visitor. Pump had had other guests before but usually just his boorish friends. He would show them around to show off his decrepit palace and let them pick one of the girls to take for the evening before setting them up in a hotel. This one was clearly different, however.

First of all, he knocked. No one had ever knocked on the door before. Amanda remembered, probably exactly the same as the other girls, how silent everything went. To any and all of them a knock meant a raid. Everyone held their breath. Pump stood with Macy on the balcony overlooking the floor. Frankie and the guys stood around the door. Hands reaching behind their waistbands. All of them staring at Pump, after another knock, he nodded for them to open up the door.

Frankie walked forward. Placing a hand on the door handle he looked back for one final confirmation. Amanda saw the eyes of Pump’s men narrow as they nodded in approval, clutching the guns in their waists. Frankie cracked the door at first, muttered something Amanda couldn’t make out and then opened the door fully. There in the doorway was, not an army of police or a rival gang, but a lone man in a suit. Amanda knew it couldn't have been a detective. Detectives didn't dress that nice. The stranger was dressed in a deep black pinstripe suit, with a matching vest. Hands covered in black leather gloves and a felt fedora on his head. Like a stock image of a man from the forties, he was tall and trim, his back straight and head held high he crossed into the threshold. Despite his outdated clothes she found him quite handsome.

As he entered the dilapidated brothel, he removed his hat and gloves and held them out to his side. He kept his hand outstretched for a moment and then began to look around rather confused, slightly shaking the hat and gloves in his hand. Pump who had been standing dumbfounded up to this moment quickly snapped to. *"Tiffany"* he barked, *"Were you raised in a damn barn?!? We have a guest, please take his things and make him comfortable"*

Tiffany, just as dumbfounded as everyone else, immediately jumped into action and placed a seductive smile on her face. Slowly she took the visitor's hat and gloves as she placed her other hand on his chest. *"Well hello baby"* She said, *"My name's Tiffany, and I don't need to know yours"* He gently took her hand into his, smiled softly and looked at his feet. *"Another time maybe, right now I have to talk with your boss."* He spoke very politely yet with a twinge of regret in his voice. *"Now if you'll excuse me."* he said as he gently nudged her away.

The stranger made his way to the steps and began to climb. As he walked up the steps Amanda saw Macy squeeze Pump's arm in support. He reached the top of the stairs and greeted Macy with a kiss on the cheek, and the two men gave each other a curt nod. Pump began talking to the man on the balcony and as they were speaking the man placed his hand on the railing. Amanda noticed the glittering of a ring on his forefinger shining against his dark clothes but couldn't make out much more.

Trying desperately to eavesdrop on what was being said above, Amanda inched closer to the balcony. She had no luck. All she could make out was Pump saying something about *"You're supposed to leave me alone."* and the visitor replying, *"maybe better in private..."* With that the two men walked into Pump's office-bedroom and Macy tailed behind them.

Once they all disappeared into the office, the girls all huddled together to discuss what had just happened.

"What the hell is going on?"

"I have no idea!"

"Are we in trouble?"

"I don't think he's a cop."

"There's worse things than cops out there."

"He was handsome though"

"Yes, he was."

"I wouldn't charge him"

"Not if I get him first"

Amanda began to lose her mind. *"God you guys are stupid!"* she exclaimed. *"For the first time ever someone from the outside comes here and you're not even worried!"*

Tiffany placed her hands on Amanda's shoulder. *"Mandy, sweetie, you gotta relax."* she said. *"Whoever that is up there he's clearly not a cop. And if he was coming to kill us, we'd be dead already. There's one of him and six-armed dudes standing right over there. It's probably just some business deal that has nothing to do with us."*

A few of the girls murmured in agreement but Amanda still wasn't convinced. *"Tiff think about it"* She retorted, *"In the five years we've been here, when has anyone EVER come here. Something is up and I doubt it's good."*

Tiffany gave Amanda a friendly smile. *"Even if you're right honey, what are we gonna do about it? There's nothing we can do, so there's no point in stressing. What we can do is hope everything is fine and enjoy the fact that there's a handsome stranger upstairs."* She ended her speech with a sly smile.

Amanda saw the crowd was in agreement with Tiffany. Realizing she was not going to get anywhere, she threw her hands up in defeat. A moment later Pump's door swung open. Out stepped the visitor, straightening his tie as he did so. Behind him came Pump and Macy. Macy squeezed Pump's hand and a concerned look on her face. Pump looked mildly irritated. As the visitor made his way back down the steps Tiffany ran over to grab his hat and gloves. Amanda repositioned herself to get a better look at the man's hand. On his right forefinger he was wearing a ring identical to Pumps. Silver with the same marking, a sword crossing a trident all covered by a crown and wrapped in a laurel wreath.

Tiffany gave the man a smile as she handed him his things. *"I hope you'll come back to see me soon,"* she said. He let out a slight smile before biting his lip to regain his composure. He smiled again, kissed her on the cheek and walked out the door.

Almost instantly the door closed, every head in the warehouse whipped around and looked up at Pump. He returned their stare for a moment before quickly snapping *"The hell y'all looking at?! Go make me some goddamn money"* and with that he turned around and went back to his room, slamming the door in Macy's face as she tried to follow him.

A little dazed, everyone started getting ready for the night's work. Lipstick was applied, heels we slipped on, and not a word was spoken. Once everyone was ready the guys began to escort the girls out of the warehouse and make their way to their corners. During the walk, Amanda caught up with Frankie hoping to pry some information out of him.

"Don't even bother" he said preemptively, *"I don't know anything".*

"Bullshit," Amanda replied. *"If anyone knows something it would be you. He trusts you more than anyone else here."* Frankie muttered something under his breath. *"See, you know something."* Amanda said.

"Sorry no I don't. Let's talk about anything else." He replied.

Irritated Amanda walked away, moving next to one of the other guys and grabbing him by the arm. She heard Frankie let out an exasperated sigh and she smiled to herself in satisfaction.

The rest of the night was pretty routine. Once Amanda had made it to her corner she plastered on her fake smile and waited for the johns to come running. She had an okay stream tonight. A few regulars, a few new faces. Nothing out of the ordinary. After a few hours of bouncing between battered backseats and damp alleyways, she was finally done. This was always her least favorite part of the day. She was tired and she always felt disgusting. She couldn't wait to get to her shower.

All the girls reconvened back in the street. Once the group was reassembled, they started walking to a nearby truck stop. The owner had owed Pump money once over some gambling debt and let the girls have free showers there as part of his payment plan. Once inside Amanda fished through her purse and pulled out her travel soap and shampoo. Before walking into the shower, she gave Frankie her purse to hold.

"You sure you don't want to give it to Bill?" Frankie asked snarkily.

Amanda rolled her eyes. *"I am not in the mood, just take the stupid thing."* she said and shoved the purse into his hand. She instantly began to feel better as soon as she turned the knob and felt the hot water spraying down. She let the water run and soak into her skin for a moment. Nothing felt better to her than a hot shower. Once she was done, she stepped out and changed into an oversized T-Shirt and pair of shorts she brought with her. She couldn't understand how some of the girls were fine just getting back into their work clothes, but it didn't affect her, so she left well enough alone.

Once they all got back to the warehouse Amanda noticed Pump and Macy had both gone to bed. Frankie had gone up and slipped into the room to give Pump the night's profits. Then everyone found their bed and turned in for the night. Amanda lay on her mattress, still riddled with anxiety from the events that happened earlier. She tried fruitlessly to calm herself down, but her mind was running rampant with questions.

"Who was that guy?"

"What did he want?"

"They must know each other; they have the same ring but is that good or bad?"

Eventually her brain could take no more and she passed out from exhaustion.

The next morning Amanda was woken up by the sounds of muffled shouting. It was coming from upstairs in Pump's room. There was shouting and banging, but Amanda couldn't make out what was being said. The ruckus culminated in Macy being thrown from the room crashing onto the above walkway.

Macy stood up and gathered herself, quickly shot everyone below a dirty look before turning back to the doorway. *"This wasn't my fault you know!"* She yelled. *"I told you not to get involved in that shit!"* With that she turned around and marched down the stairs and out the door.

Tiffany wandered over to Amanda. *"How long this time, do you think?"* She said with a smirk.

"I give it two days." Amanda replied. Smiling back.

"Oh, you're way too generous... I give it until tonight." Tiffany countered.

"I don't know, she looked pretty mad. A night to cool off and a day to remember that's her one true love!" Amanda said in a mocking fluttery tone.

"$50 says she's back here by the time we come back tonight." Tiffany offered.

Amanda agreed *"alright I'll get in on that."*

The girls shook on the bet and went back about their business. Amanda was gathering her money from the night prior and organizing it. She liked putting it into her safety deposit box with the small bills on top to make it look like it was less than it was. Better to be pleasantly surprised than disappointed was her line of thinking.

Not long after Pump came bursting out of the office. *"Are we gonna have to do this every goddamn night!?!"* He yelled. *"Get out there and get to work!"* Amanda was getting increasingly worried. Pump always acted like a pig but typically he hid it behind a very thin layer of politeness. His way of telling himself he wasn't a total monster. Whatever was going on however, it had Pump spooked.

Amanda did as she was bid and got ready to go out for the evening. Another day, another dollar. Gross men, gross work, and a shower to make it all better. When they got back at the end of the night, they walked in to see Macy sitting outside the door to Pump's room. Tiffany immediately nudged Amanda and pointed at Macy. Amanda smiled and slid her a $50 bill.

The next morning the situation did not improve. Amanda was brushing her teeth when Macy came up to her. *"He wants you."* Macy said to her coldly and immediately walked away. Amanda spat out her toothpaste with a groan and made her way up the stairs to Pump's quarters. She didn't know why this part of her job bothered her so much. Everyone else seemed to accept it as coming with the territory. *"The boss needs to be taken care of."* That's how it worked. The rusted metal steps creaked as she walked up. Softly she knocked on the door.

Pump opened the door and Amanda stepped inside. She almost vomited. The room was typically never very clean. A bed in the middle flush with the back wall. To the right there was a dresser that doubled as a desk. Clothes would usually be scattered along the floor with dirty plates, disorganized papers and cigarette butts littering the dresser.

However, this time when Amanda walked in it was a disaster scene. It looked as if a tornado had gone through the room. Trash and junk scattered everywhere. All the drawers were ajar with clothes and papers hanging off the ends. The usual faint smell of weed had become unbearable, and bongs were scattered all over the floor along with other paraphernalia.

Amanda looked around but tried to maintain her composure. Looking at Pump close up she could tell he was not well at all. His face was strained and his eyes were beyond bloodshot. Amanda had seen high before, and this was much more than high. Quickly and without a word he grabbed Amanda and threw her on the bed. She didn't even bother to look up. She heard the sound of a belt buckle being undone and braced for what was to come.

She lay silently and still as it was done. This wasn't like him either. He usually liked talking before and during. Some cheap way of justifying this gross abuse of power to himself. But this was a silent separate experience. Thankfully it did not take long. In just a few minutes it was over and Pump climbed off of Amanda. He pulled his pants back up to his waist, walked over and opened the door before sitting down on the bed and placing his head in his hands. Amanda took this as her queue to leave and quickly ran out of the room. As she emerged back out into the main area of their warehouse, she caught Macy giving her an evil glare.

Chapter 4: Sandra

"Another goddamn day" Sandra had thought to herself as she walked into the station that morning. She was sure the previous day's chase would be all the excitement she would get for a month. Back to boring patrol and endless desk work.

She was surprised walking in to see a big crowd huddling around the reception desk. She moved in for a closer look trying to see what everyone was so interested in. She saw Clara in the circle, who happened to turn around and meet her gaze. Clara nudged the officer next to her and nodded her head in Sandra's direction. Suddenly every eye in the room fell on her. Sandra froze in confusion. The huddle dispersed shortly after Sandra's presence was made known, revealing the Commissioner standing at its center. Marcus Helming, Police Commissioner of Colonna City, standing right there. Sandra had met him only once, when she had graduated from the academy. It was doubtful he'd remember her. Clara walked over to her. *"I don't know what trouble you got yourself in here honey"* She whispered. *"But he's here for you..."*

The Commissioner walked up to them. *"Officer Blewens, I take it"* he said, outstretching his hand. His voice was deep and gruff, like a grizzled old soldier from a war movie. He stood there with his hand outstretched for a second before Sandra finally snapped to and shook it. *"Yes sir, Commissioner*

Helming," she replied. *"An honor to see you again sir."*

Looking at him, Sandra noticed he was different from the image she had in her head. Maybe it was all the staged photographs sticking out in her mind but the man before her was hunched, disheveled and looked beaten down. His shirt was barely tucked in and clearly wrinkled. All covered in a long dusty overcoat. She really wasn't sure what to do with herself. This had to be about yesterday, but she wasn't sure whether she was here to be commended or reprimanded.

"I need you to come with me to my office," Helming said calmly and gestured toward the door. Sandra blurted out a stumbled *"yes sir"* as began walking behind him. The Commissioner led her to the station's main exit. Sandra looked back to see everyone staring as they left. They went outside and Commissioner Helming directed her to a car with an officer standing by it. The chauffeuring officer opened the door for Sandra and nodded to her as she got in. Similarly, the Commissioner got on the other side of the vehicle and the trio got on their way.

The car ride was silent. Helming spent the trip going through papers not even acknowledging Sandra. The car ran through the city as thoughts ran through Sandra's mind. She must be in trouble. But for what? She didn't do anything wrong yesterday. Everything by the book. *"This is bullshit"* she thought to herself.

"Risk your neck to do your job and this is the thanks you get. "

The car pulled up to city hall and stopped out front. The chauffeur hopped out and opened Sandra's door. She got out and waited for Helming to join her. *"Home sweet home"* he said sarcastically as he guided her toward the entrance. Helming entered the building with Sandra still following close behind. Their shoes clicked along the marble floor as they walked. A few times people came up to speak to the Commissioner, looking friendly, then their eyes turned to Sandra and smiles faded as they immediately turned away and left the Commissioner to go to his business. Sandra caught a few people standing off to the side glaring nastily at her.
She followed Helming down two different hallways before they arrived at his office. Helming opened the door for her and she entered. He followed her in, locking the door behind him. *"You can have a seat right there."* He gestured to the desk. The office seemed really plain to Sandra. A desk with a few filing cabinets and a computer. Everything was organized, which seemed easy because there wasn't much of anything in there. She didn't really know what she was expecting but this was pretty anticlimactic in her mind.

She sat down at the desk and Helming took his seat on the other side. As he sat, he let out a deep exhale as if the weight of the world had temporarily been lifted from his shoulders. He massaged his temples for a second before looking up at Sandra. *"Listen officer,"* he said, *"Sorry about the cold shoulder routine, I'm not a fan of talking around prying ears."* Sandra began to reply but he held up his hand to stop her. *"I'm sure you have some sort of guess why I asked you here."*

"Well sir, my only thought is it has to do with what happened yesterday." She said, *"Though if I may say so I don't understand what I did wrong."*

"You didn't do anything wrong," he answered. *"That's exactly why I'm taking this risk."*
"Risk? I'm sorry sir I don't follow."
"Tell me something, Officer Blewens. Do you ever hear stories of a man who calls himself The Emperor?"

"I mean he's a local gangbanger, isn't he?"

The Commissioner chuckled for a second before regaining his composure. *"That's one way to put it, sure,"* he said with a smile. He then fumbled with his keys and unlocked a drawer in his desk. He rummaged through the contents before pulling something out and handing it to Sandra.

It was a double rolled scroll, made out of parchment ant tied in the middle with a strand of violet ribbon, fastened by a wax seal. The wax was embossed by something Sandra had seen before. A sword crossing a trident covered by a crown all wrapped in a laurel wreath.

"The guy I arrested..." she said, *"He had this same symbol on a ring he was wearing."*

Commissioner Helming nodded in agreement. *"The Emperor's Sigil"* he stated. *"Go on, read it."*

Sandra untied the ribbon and unrolled the scroll. The ink on it was deep and dark, it had been written with a fountain pen or something similar. The handwriting was beautiful, tight and compact but with long vertical flowing in the lettering.

Dearest Commissioner Helming,

I am writing to express my profound apologies for the incident which occurred yesterday afternoon involving an anointed knight of the Empire. I am well aware that you do not enjoy when I draw comparisons between you and myself... but the fact remains we are both men tasked with the oversight of large consortiums and I know you can understand the impossibility of directly overseeing such vast personnel as they carry out their duties.

As you are well familiar by now, this precise problem is exactly the reason I allow certain members to wear my mark; in hopes that it will expedite any difficulties they have in dealing with governing bodies outside of my Empire. Yet the fact of the matter remains that the individual in question abused that privilege and hoped my band would quietly exonerate him in his blatant disregard of human decency. He was entrusted with a valuable resource, and proved himself unworthy of the charge.

Naturally the duty falls to me to think of the entirety of my subjects. After all, heavy lies the head that wears the crown. My populace must know that they remain safe from your police through the course of their work and that the Imperial Sigil still commands respect in light of what has transpired. To that end, I have arranged with my allies in your District Attorney's office to see my prodigal son returned to me.

I understand, that to a man of your specific moral code, that this will be viewed as a gross miscarriage of justice and a circumstance rather unfair to you in which I would be inclined to agree. The only consolation I can hope to offer you is that upon his return he will have to face the Crown's justice. That, I can vow to you, will be a much more fitting a punishment than that which would have been doled out by your municipal government.

As always, the Crown and Empire desires nothing more than your friendship and will work to continue fostering our bond with the Colonna City Municipal Police Department.

I Remain, Your Humble Friend,
Edward Von Drac
Imperator Rex, Colonna City
All Honorifics etc. etc.

Sandra finished reading the letter and set it back down on the desk. The Commissioner picked it up and put it back in the drawer, locking it shut immediately. *"He's quite the character, isn't he?"* Helming said.

"He has a flair for drama that I can tell." Sandra replied.

"Well, be that as it may, unfortunately everything he said was right. The DA's office instructed me to release your prisoner this morning. And I'd be lucky if only half the cops in this town are on his payroll." He heaved a great sigh. *"Which leads me to why I brought you here... I wanna know why you arrested that man if you saw he was wearing the ring?"*

Sandra shifted nervously in her seat before speaking. *"Well sir..."* she began, *"To be completely honest with you I didn't know what that ring meant. I have never come across it before."*

"Blewens you've been a cop for how long?" Helming asked.

"Almost fifteen years now sir" she replied.

"And you're telling me you haven't come across this before, Drac and his quote-on-quote Empire have been the de facto crime organization in this city for the past six years now." Helming began to sound almost accusatory.

"I mean I've heard of them... sir" Sandra said. *"But have I ever been involved with them? No. If I did something I shouldn't have, I'm sorry I didn't know but if I may sir, judging by that letter it doesn't seem to me like you and this guy are friendly, so I am a little confused."*

Helming paused and took a breath. Another deep exhausted exhale. He started massaging his temples again. *"You aren't in trouble Blewens, excuse my little interrogation. I am just trying to make sure I understand the situation completely before I keep going.*

Sanda let out an internal gasp of relief. *"It's pretty straightforward sir."* she said *"I've never been approached by any of these people. If I were, I would turn it down. I have no desire to be on the take. I don't have kids or a husband. I grew up poor and have pretty simple tastes. I have no use for that extra money or the headache that comes with it. I just want to help the city sir."*

Helming smiled a little as she gave her speech. When she finished talking, he pulled a blank piece of paper from his desk and scribbled something on it with his pen. *"Here, take this and be at this address tomorrow at 8AM sharp. From now on you work directly for me... It looks like your career is going to finally take an upswing. That is... If you're interested in bringing down the biggest kingpin in Colonna's history?"*

Sandra almost snatched the paper out of his hand. *"Yes sir! I'm in"* she exclaimed. The Commissioner then stood up and opened the door for Sandra to leave. He offered her a car but she insisted she was fine with the bus. She kept it together just long enough to professionally walk out of City Hall.

She could hardly contain herself. Finally! Not just an assignment but an assignment that would make her a hero. Taking down this “Emperor” whoever he was would put her on the map. A big middle finger to all the people that looked down on her whole career. This was her chance, and she wasn’t planning on wasting it.

Chapter 5: Amanda

Amanda was getting stressed. It had been two weeks since the stranger had visited Pump's warehouse. Pump was rapidly deteriorating, switching between reclusion and bouts of unbridled anger. She didn't bother trying to bring it up again to Tiffany or the other girls; they wouldn't listen. Frankie was no help either. He just kept telling her nothing was wrong. God how it infuriated her. She felt as if she was being driven insane.

Another night was on the books and Amanda, and the girls had gotten home. She hadn't slept well in three days. As she plopped onto her mildewy cot she was determined to sleep tonight. The insomnia was not helping her worry at all. She lay in bed, forcing her eyes to close. Trying desperately to void her mind of any and all thought. That wasn't working. Maybe a distraction would do the trick. Counting sheep? Nope. Thinking of a movie? Not even close. She got it, her happy place. The beach. She imagined the warm air and the soft breeze. The faint smell of the ocean creeped into her nose. Slowly she felt herself drifting off to sleep...

Tap tap tap. Amanda's eyes shot open. *Tap tap tap*. What the hell was that? *Tap tap tap*. Amanda looked around. No one else seemed to notice it. Everyone else was sleeping soundly. *Tap tap tap*. This was it. She had finally snapped. She was insane now. *Tap tap tap;* and then silence.

A few minutes had passed and Amanda heard nothing else. *"Just go to sleep for Christ's sake"* she thought to herself as she laid back down and closed her eyes again. The beach was back in her mind, the soft breeze and the warm air....

TAP TAP TAP. Amanda shot up again. This time she wasn't alone. *TAP TAP TAP.* Everyone was awake now. Something was banging on the concrete wall outside. *TAP TAP TAP*. Everyone was looking around equally confused. *TAP TAP TAP*. Dust began falling from the ceiling due to the vibrations. Pump and Macy emerged from Pump's room to see what was going on. *TAP TAP TAP*. Macy looked terrified. Pump just looked defeated. Frankie and the guys had come around and looked to Pump for orders, then silence again.

No one was going back to sleep now. Whatever Amanda was worried about, it was happening right now, and all the worrying now seemed pointless because she had no idea what to do. Frankie went over to the wall to investigate. He pulled his gun from his waistband. He placed his ear along the wall where he judged the banging had come from. Suddenly his eyes grew big.

Beep Beep Beep. Amanda heard it too. *"EVERYONE GET BACK"* Frankie yelled. Panic ensued with the girls screaming. *Beep Beep Beep.* Frankie and the guys herded the frantic girls to the corner of the warehouse opposite the wall. *Beep Beep Beep.* Pump's guys had made a wall in front of the huddled girls. Guns trained on the wall. Silence once again fell over the room one last time as everyone stared at the wall. Then it happened. *Beep Beep Bee... BOOM!*

The wall exploded, sending dust and debris flying throughout the warehouse. Frankie and his men opened fire into the smoke, gunshots rang endlessly into the void. Amanda's ears were still ringing from the explosion. There was so much dust in the air she could hardly see anything. Eventually the gunfire stopped. They had run out of bullets. Soon a man's voice rang out from the smog *"Drop your weapons! No one needs to die tonight! You have one chance!"*

The guys looked to Frankie. Frankie looked at Pump. Pump did nothing. Frankie threw his gun down and kicked it away. The rest of the guys followed suit. Through the hole in the wall emerged six men. All wearing black pinstripe suits with matching purple ties. They had assault rifles trained on Frankie as they walked in. Without saying a word, they came up and patted down the guys. After ensuring Frankie and his men were unarmed, the intruders returned to the hole in the wall. Three lined up on each side and they held their rifles to their shoulders as if they were at a military parade.

They stood motionless as a black limousine slowly backed into the warehouse through the hole in the wall. The smell of the exhaust began to fill the room. It stopped halfway through and one of the gunmen opened the rear driver's side door. Out of the limo stepped the mystery visitor from before. Wearing the same pinstripe suit. He stood silently as one of the gunmen opened the door on the other side of the limo. No one else got out.

The stranger from weeks ago cleared his throat and began to speak. This time his voice was cold and emotionless as if it was pre-recorded.

"Now announcing the arrival of his Regal Imperial Majesty, Edward Von Drac, Imperator Rex Colonna City. Anointed Master of the Imperial Convocation. Crowned Lord Protector of the Seven Districts." -He paused to take a breath. - *"First Counselor of the Imperial Diet. First Admiral of the Imperial Armada. Grand Defender of the Street and of the Sea. In his presence, may you bow your heads in unmatched reverence or fall to your knees in repentant shame."*

Frankie bowed his head slightly and nudged the guys next to him to follow suit, they did and the girls picked up the cue and did the same. As they did, another figure emerged from the other side of the limo. First a black cane. Then shiny black boots and then the rest. He was tall but not exactly imposing. He was big, but not muscular and not particularly fat, just filled out. He hunched slightly while leaning on his cane.

The Emperor was dressed in a black tailed jacket with a dark violet waistcoat complete with a silver chain that ran into the pocket. On his right index finger he wore a ring with his insignia on it, though it was visibly much larger than the ones worn by the others. He also wore the symbol around his neck pinned over top his cravat, which was also dark violet to match the waistcoat. The same symbol could be found again on his cufflinks and on the silver head of his cane. He wore a black overcoat draped across his shoulders like a cape and the entire ensemble was topped with a wide brimmed hat decorated with a large white feather.

He stepped out of the limo and into the center of the room. His face looked gaunt and strained. Not old, maybe late thirties but a face that had seen more than its years would suggest. He was clean, shaven and his hair slicked back very neatly. He walked very deliberately into the center of the warehouse, as if each step had been carefully rehearsed. As he hobbled on his cane his eyes shot in every direction, intently studying his surroundings. His face was first one of disgust, but when his gaze fell upon Amanda and the girls huddled in fear it softened. He looked around the room again, finally settled on Pump and Macy up on the balcony.

"Charles - "Pump Nasty"- Brown.... Do you not come to greet your emperor when he calls on you for a visit." The Emperor said with a crooked smile. His voice was coarse and rough, like a sailor's. As he spoke, his tone drastically fluctuated up and down with a hint of an accent, as if he were in a Shakespearean drama. Macy squeezed Pump's arm and led him down the steps. As the pair approached

the Emperor, he extended his hand so they might kiss his ring. They did just that.

"It's Macy... isn't it my dear?" The Emperor said as she kissed his ring. She nodded in confirmation. *"A pleasure to see you again child. Unfortunately, I must insist that you join Master Chesley with the others, for I have come to parlay solely with your beau."* Macy bowed and joined the Emperor's companion as he guided her over to the rest of the group. Now it was just Pump and The Emperor in the middle of the room, all eyes locked upon them.

"Sire, this visit is not necessary." Pump squeaked out, his voice trembling with fear. *"I was actually just gettin' ready to give Cody the money."* The Emperor's malicious smile quickly turned to a scowl.

"I find it fascinating sir," he began, *"That you see fit to use Master Chesley's Christian name as if you were his friend..."* His tone was quickly souring *"Yet when he comes to see you out of friendship and gives you a chance to clear up this matter of back taxes; you throw him out of this cesspit you call an abode in a manner most unbefitting a knight of this Empire."*

The man with the Emperor, Cody must be his name, snickered as the Emperor said this. The Emperor continued his tirade.
"Do you know why we insist on taxation Mr. Nasty?" The Emperor said, placing sarcastic emphasis on

Pump's name. Pump made no attempt to answer *"It is because the multiple facets of this government require money to operate. That protection which you and your compatriots enjoy from the laws outside my own. The weapons and munitions we supply in times of turmoil, The salaries of the hard-working men and women that keep the IRS out of your throat, all these things and more require money sir. Money you seem to feel you are not obligated to contribute. So, I ask you how is that fair to the other marshals, knights, and citizens which sacrifice their hard-earned profits to keep the system that has benefitted us all so much in operation?"* Pump again stayed silent, *"Do attempt to make an answer."* The Emperor said as he cut his eyes.

Pump stuttered a little, fumbling over his words.

"Precisely!" The Emperor exclaimed, cutting him off. His voice was getting progressively angrier. He began speaking faster, *"You have no answer, because what you have done is reaped the benefits of that which you did not sow. You have allowed others to pay the price so you might enjoy the reward. You have stolen food from their mouths, toys from their children... and now, as King and Emperor, the task falls upon me to defend their interests."*

Pump dropped to his knees and began to sob. *"I'M SORRY"* he wailed *"Please don't kill me! I swear I'll pay!"* He grabbed the Emperor's legs holding him like an infant, pleading forgiveness as he sobbed.

Amanda stood in a silent combination of horror and shock seeing how this man who didn't appear very physically threatening had managed to turn a gangster like Pump into a groveling child.

The Emperor bent down and placed a hand under Pump's jaw, tilting his head up so they could meet eyes. His composure regained he once again spoke softly, *"If you do not wish to die then you must tell me, here and now, fully and truthfully, why is it you have neglected your duty to the Crown and Empire?"* Pump calmed down slightly. The news that he might save his life seemed to offer him some solace. *"It was the drugs Majesty..."* he said. *"I got out of control, but I promise I'll quit right now."* He turned toward his girlfriend, *"Macy go up to my room and throw all that shit out."* Back to groveling at the Emperor's feet *"I'll never disappoint you again. I promise. Please just give me another chance."* Macy ran upstairs as she was told and the Emperor smiled once more. He helped Pump get back up to his feet. *"Now now my boy,"* he said, patting Pump on the shoulder, he seemed satisfied with Pump's answer. *"I know you won't... Tell me, was it cocaine? I know that's quite the expensive habit."* Pump, still sniffling, nodded. The Emperor shook his head disapprovingly, like a parent would to a toddler. *"Snorting that confection has taken many a man down to the bellows of financial ruin. But fear not!"* He exclaimed his voice getting strangely giddy, *"I am going to help you overcome this tumultuous obstacle."* The

Emperor suddenly had a gargantuan smile spread across his face as Pump's eyes widened in total and complete terror.

No sooner than he had finished speaking, the Emperor jabbed Pump in the gut with his cane and sent an equally swift blow to his head, knocking him to the ground. Pump began to scream in agony as the Emperor sprung alive, jumping on top of him. Using his knees to pin Pump's arms to the ground, the Emperor reached into his jacket pocket and pulled out a pair of needle nose pliers.

Pumped screamed uncontrollably as the Emperor placed the pliers around his nose and began to twist and pull. It was the most brutal thing Amanda had ever seen. Blood began gushing from Pump's nose as the Emperor pulled and pulled. What disturbed Amanda even more was the twisted, excited wide-eyed look on the Emperor's face, while his entourage stood silent and cold.

Macy came running back downstairs after hearing the commotion. Screaming for the Emperor to stop, but Cody, the Emperor's man, intercepted her and restrained her back to the corner with everyone else. Pump still screaming, blood still gushing. It went on for what felt like hours. Until the screaming stopped and the Emperor had thrown Pump's dismembered nose onto the floor of the warehouse. Amanda was fighting every urge not to vomit.

Pump lay writhing on the floor as the Emperor stood up and dusted himself off. He looked down at the bloodied Pump in disgust. *"Tsk Tsk Tsk."* The Emperor muttered. *"You're losing a lot of blood son. We're going to have to cauterize that wound."* He smiled again as Macy screamed for him to stop. The Emperor bent down over Pump once more and this time pulled out a lighter, flicking it alive. Then the blood curdling screams started all over again as the Emperor slowly melted Pump's flesh back together. The smell alone was unbearable.

When he was done the Emperor got back up once more. Amanda caught a quick glimpse of sadness cross the Emperor's face as he looked down on Pump's limp body, gently massaging his pocket watch within his waistcoat. As quickly as it had come, it had gone. All the adrenaline Amanda had seen in his face a moment ago immediately went as he returned to the calm collected man he was prior to the attack. He looked over to the gunmen.

"Gentlemen, if you'd be so kind as to help this repentant sinner to his feet." He lazily gestured to the barely conscious Pump lying on the floor, suddenly disinterested in the entire affair. Two of the gunmen rushed over and lifted Pump up to his feet holding him up under each arm. Amanda could barely make out his face with all the blood and charred flesh. The Emperor smiled softly and patted Pump on the cheek. *"There now."* he said *"Chemical candy will*

bother you no more... Now just one last thing to take care of..."

He walked slowly over to the limousine. He went into the trunk of the limousine and pulled out a pair of garden shears. He walked back to Pump and tapped him gently with his cane. One of the gunmen holding Pump up took the cue and grabbed Pump's left hand and forcibly extended the pinky finger that Pump wore his Imperial ring on. The Emperor placed the shears around the pinky just below the ring, ready to slice.

"Charles-" Pump Nasty"- Brown," The Emperor began. *"You have been deemed guilty of theft and abuse of Imperial privilege. Through the forgiving grace of His Majesty the Emperor, your sentence has been reduced from death to exile, in hopes that you may cure yourself of your wicked ways. But from this moment forth, you are a part of my Empire no longer!"* and with that the Emperor chopped off Pumps pinky and the finger along with the ring fell to the ground in another pool of blood. The gunmen dropped Pump's limp body back to the floor and returned to their positions by the limousine.

The Emperor took his handkerchief from his breast pocket and gently wiped the blood from his face. Then he bent down, picked up Pump's severed pinky, removed the ring and tossed the finger back to the floor. He cleaned off the ring and walked toward Amanda and the crowd huddled in the corner. He first nodded to Cody who released Macy so she could tend to Pump. Quickly the Emperor blocked Macy's path with his cane stopping her in her tracks. *"He's not to come back here my dear."* He said softly. *"Or it will mean his death."* He then moved the cane and allowed Macy to rush to her lover. The Emperor handed Pump's ring to Cody and then turned to Frankie and smiled warmly. *"Franklin my dear boy you've done very well."* he said as he embraced Frankie in a hug. *"I am sure these derelict conditions are not ideal for a man of your stature. As soon as Master Chesley and I can settle the issue of succession, we can talk about bringing our most valued mole back home."*

Frankie smiled back and made a deep bow in front of the Emperor. *"Thank you Sire,"* he replied. *"I'm just happy I could help."* Frankie glanced back towards Amanda trying to get her reaction to this revelation, but she immediately looked away. The Emperor then turned to the rest of the group, removed his hat, and began to speak softly and solemnly.

"This, I am sure, has been a very trying night for all of you. Do try your best to get some sleep. Tomorrow you may all have the day to yourselves to recuperate. The Imperial Treasury will pay you a day's wages. Then, you shall go back to your profession, earning money, business as usual. The Honorable Lord Chancellor Cody Chesley will preside as your interim governor until such a time that a permanent replacement is selected."

Nobody said anything back to him, he looked around again, disgusted by the state of the warehouse. Looking back to the girls he had pure pity in his eyes. It vexed Amanda how quickly and drastically this man's emotions appeared to change. *"Do not shed tears for those that abuse others."* He finally said, *"Remember that what you have seen tonight was little more than cause and effect in action. Continue to work honestly and the Crown's power shall continue to protect you, as it always does, and always will.*

After his speech, he placed his feathered hat back atop his head, climbed into his limousine, and was driven off into the night.

Chapter 6: Sandra

Today was the first day of the rest of Sandra's life. She woke up promptly at 6:30 AM, no alarm necessary. Hastily she did her morning routine. Shower? Check. Hair? Check. Teeth? Check. She practically jumped into her uniform and ran into the kitchen. She scrambled herself two eggs and scarfed them down in record time.

Out the door and into her cruiser she began driving. The slip of paper the Commissioner had given her instructed her to meet him at the library on 53rd street, in the historic district nestled at the city's center. Odd choice for a secret task force she thought but maybe there'd be some sort of underground bunker. Her mind was racing through every spy movie she'd ever seen.

She pulled up to the library and got out. She walked up to the door. She entered the library and realized she had no idea what she was doing. In her head the Commissioner would just be out front or in the lobby. After walking in she quickly noticed he was nowhere to be found. She wasn't sure how to proceed. It's not like she could go up to the librarian and ask, "Hey where does the secret task force meet?"

She began to browse the books on the shelf. Wandering over towards the history section she loosely combed the shelves. She landed on a large volume, titled *"The Rise of Bonaparte and the First French Empire"* she opened up the book and began to graze through the paintings that were supplied with the text.

She became transfixed on a print of Napoleon's imperial portrait, dressed as Caesar, holding the Scepter of France and Le Main de Justice. Something about the image had completely taken over her mind. Transfixed, she didn't notice the man behind her till he placed a hand on her shoulder. She jumped in startlement and quickly turned around. It was the Commissioner.

"Commissioner Helming sir." she said, *"I'm sorry, you startled me."*

He looked down on Sandra with a look of mild disappointment. *"You're gonna need to be on your toes for what we're about to start."* he said, *"follow me."*

He gestured for her to follow as he turned and walked. Sandra popped the book back on the shelf and tailed behind. She followed the Commissioner down the stairs of the library to the basement. They traversed through a series of hallways until they came to a closed door labeled "Storage".

Sandra took a deep breath as the Commissioner laid his hands on the handle. He opened the door and Sandra's heart immediately sank. In front of her was a conference table with a few disheveled people, and papers scattered everywhere. Along with the chalkboard on the wall that's all this "secret task force HQ" consisted of.

The three men sitting in the room looked up at the doorway as Helming and Sandra entered.

"Gentlemen," The Commissioner said, indicating to Sandra. *"This is Sandra Blewens, the newest member of the task force."* Sandra gave a polite nod and a smile, and the Commissioner proceeded to introduce the rest of the team. First there was Greg Peterson, A tall and lanky accountant. He was the Commissioner's brother-in-law and Helming deputized him solely for this task force. Next was Treyvon Randall, A tough but soft-spoken cop who harbored a grudge against the Emperor for getting his neighbor's son pulled into a life of crime which ended in his death. Finally, there was Keith Walker, a cop who came from money and didn't need to be on the take.

"So, we let brauds in here now?" Keith said jokingly.

"Really man....?" Treyvon responded. He pulled a chair out for Sandra to sit *"Sorry about him.... He's not actually a prick but turns out money really doesn't buy class"* Sandra sat down and shrugged off the joke with a laugh.

"Alright..." Commissioner Helming began. *"Now we're all here... what do we have this week?"*

"Well Marcus...." Greg replied, adjusting his glasses as he pulled a stack of papers from the pile on the table. *"I've been looking through the filings of his museum, but his books are airtight. If he is*

laundering money through there; a federal prosecutor won't be able to prove it."

"I'm sorry" Sandra interrupted, *"Museum?"*

"The Latonya Duchant Memorial Museum and Amphitheatre" Kieth answered. *"The huge place on 5th and Lincoln"*

Greg cut back in, *"Owner Proprietor, and head Curator, one Mr. Edward Von Drac*

"But as we know him..." Commissioner Helming joined in

"THE EMPEROR" all 4 men exclaimed with a chuckle.

"Look Blewens, all you need to know is up until about six years ago Little Eddie Drac was a nobody. Then suddenly he supposedly inherits a whole bunch of money and suddenly became the new darling of Colonna City high society."

"In reality" Treyvon expounded, *"He somehow managed to drive every semblance of organized crime out of this city and consolidate total control of the city's underworld under his thumb. Now he quite literally calls it his empire."*

Greg inserted himself next. *"A pompous bastard to the core."* he said *"He acts like he's some super refined man of art and culture, meanwhile he sits on top of an ill-gotten fortune made from drugs, prostitutes, gambling, and whatever other illicit activity he's got his nose in."*

Sandra nodded in understanding. *"So how do we get him?"* she asked.

"That's kinda what we're all doing here toots..." Kieth answered. *"Trying to figure that out"*

"Our main hurdle right now...." the Commissioner interjected. *"Is the DA is in his pocket, so any evidence we get doesn't matter yet, no one will prosecute him."*

"We get the DA to play ball, we get the Emperor." Treyvon added.

Greg cut back in, *"We assume that Mr. Von Drac has some sort of blackmail over the DA... but we don't know what it is. If we could figure that out, we could leverage that against him, but all of our investigations have borne no fruit."*

The Commissioner patted Sandra on the shoulder, *"Well Officer Blewens, you're pretty much caught up. All in all we have.... not very much. But we know we can trust everyone in this room. So, any ideas?"*

Sandra cleared her throat nervously and ran her tongue along the top row of her teeth. *"I don't know the DA personally, but you guys might... what are his interests, any potential vices that we can explore more in-depth."*

Keith's eyes darted toward Sandra and then back at the Commissioner who met his gaze, Keith began to smile slyly.

"No." The Commissioner said very flatly to Keith.

"Come onnnnn." Keith protested, *"tell me it's not a good plan"*

"What?" Sandra asked. The two men ignored her.

"We're not doing it that way." The Commissioner reiterated.

"Marcus for the love of God you finally bring us an ace in the hole, and we aren't gonna use it?!?"

"WHAT are you all talking about!?" Sandra said again, more sternly this time.

The two men ceased their argument and looked back at her. The Commissioner began to answer. *"A few years ago, a little bit before the Emperor's time, there was an internal investigation about some potential sexual misconduct on the part of the DA.... but the evidence was flimsy and nothing really came of it."*

"We are literally here because we know flimsy evidence doesn't mean innocent." Keith argued, *"The Emperor probably is the one that covered the whole thing up! Got his foot in the door so to speak, Sure we can't prove it now... but with the right bait...If you'll pardon the turn of phrase ...."*

"Jesus Man..." Treyvon groaned *"Can you go twenty seconds without saying something stupid?"*

"No, he's got a point." Sandra interjected, *"A gross point but whatever."*

"We're not putting you in that situation." The Commissioner stated. *"It's not right"*

"We have to do something sir." Sandra replied *"And I'm willing"*

"I didn't invite you to this task force just to throw you up as a sacrificial lamb," said the Commissioner sternly. *"That's not how we do things."*

"At the risk of sharing Keith's questionable views" Greg interrupted, nervously adjusting his glasses. *"If Sandra is willing... At the very least we could cross that off our list."*

The group looked at Treyvon who just shrugged.

"I don't like it..." The Commissioner exhaled, *"It's slimy."*

"Sometimes you gotta fight fire with fire." Sandra said. Keith nodded in agreement.

The Commissioner sighed in defeat, *"Ok"* he said, *"How are we gonna pull this off?"*

Chapter 7: Amanda

It was eerie how little had changed since the Emperor had busted into the lowly whorehouse and thrown a noseless Pump out onto the street. As promised, they were all given the day after to do as they wished. Amanda had gone to a movie, alone. By the time Amanda got back, the hole that had been blasted into the wall had already been patched up. Things just sort of went on as if nothing had happened. No one ever saw Cody. The first night, he and the guys had thrown basically all of Pump's stuff out of that room and Amanda had seen Frankie bring up an air mattress presumably for Cody to sleep on. Other than that Cody stayed up in the room only Frankie went in and out to speak with him.

Frankie kept trying to talk to Amanda, but she wouldn't indulge him. Honestly, she didn't know quite how she felt. She didn't have any great love in her heart for Pump, but how could she trust Frankie now, betrayal is still betrayal. She also wasn't quite sure what to make of the Emperor. She heard murmurings like anyone else on the street of the kingpin that had taken over the city, but she was so low on the totem pole of Colonna City's crime structure that it never really concerned her before now.

Cody seemed more or less normal, even Pump, though a pig, was the kind of pig Amanda was used to. But then there was the Emperor, this anomaly of a man, with his weird clothes and overly exaggerated mannerisms. Amanda wasn't quite sure why they all followed him.

More than anything however, she was just relieved she survived the ordeal. Everyone did, too often people like her got caught in the crossfire of these gangland disputes. She went to talk to Tiffany to see what she made of the whole situation. Tiffany was much more into the whole organized crime thing than Amanda was. Tiffany was more in awe than anything.

"He's really real Mandy!" She said, *"I had heard the stories for sure, but this is proof!"*

"Tiffany, he blew up our home, I mean it's a shitty home but still..."

"So what..." Tiffany replied, *"That's how life is around here. He was mad at Pump and did what Gangsters do.... And now there's an opening."*

"You think they're gonna put you in charge Tiff?"

Tiffany rolled her eyes and smirked *"Nah of course not... but a girl can dream. I'm just gonna keep doing my thing."*

The two women then separated and went about their business. Amanda also noticed the warehouse she called home had gotten progressively cleaner. Each night she would come back and notice less grime on the wall, less dust on the floor and the like. Simple but noticeable changes. Still, she never saw anyone cleaning, and she never ever saw Cody come out of the bedroom-office.

After two days her curiosity overtook her emotions, and she ended her vow of silence with Frankie. She had successfully shunned him up until this point and he eventually gave up and left her alone. As the girls got ready for another night of work and began their walk into the city, Amanda repositioned herself amongst the crowd so that she was walking next to Frankie.

"So what happens now?" She whispered, eyes forward, pace unchanged.

"I'm not exactly sure" he whispered back, Amanda caught him smiling out of the corner of her eye, *"This is a first for me too..."*

"Well..." Amanda pressed, *"What does he talk about up there?"*

"Honestly not much." Frankie replied. *"Just asks how things are going, stuff like that."*

Dissatisfied, Amanda reshifted herself so she was no longer walking next to Frankie. Heels clicking on the pavement as she walked in silence contemplating. Nothing made her more uneasy than an uncertain future. She felt the queasiness in her stomach as her anxiety soared onto the night sky. She hated that feeling, the powerlessness that plagued her her entire life.

Throughout her life on the street, she had learned to make peace with situations beyond her control. When she had nothing and needed an income, she made peace with selling her dignity. When she needed protection, she made peace with working for a man who treated her as little more than a mound of flesh for sale. She had found a rhythm, she had a goal, she had a plan. Then in the middle of the night, a madman in a feathered hat came in with a pair of pliers, and she was once again thrown right back into the unknown.

If there was a God, he must hate Amanda Beasly. She liked to think she was all in all a good person. She didn't steal from anyone. She made her money illegally sure, but it was as honest as she could be. A fair trade of goods for services. What had she done to deserve this? Was it her fault she was born to a pair of junkie parents? Was it her fault that they traded her innocence for a quick fix when she was barely fourteen years old? Her mind went numb for a moment. She didn't like remembering that. Quickly repressing, she shook her head in defiance and returned to her internal tirade. She did not dwell on the past. She did what she had to do. She took care of herself. Was it so much to want a little stability in return? Exasperated, she dropped it. *Que sera sera* and all that. Nothing she could do about it now.

The night dragged on and Amanda's mood was not improving. She was off color and certainly not of a seductive disposition. It had reached about two in the morning when Amanda found herself in the passenger seat of a client's car. She had thus far survived the night by allowing her clients to take the lead and herself playing the role of "the good soldier". Not the ideal method in the customer service lens of the business but it worked in a pinch. Well, most of the time. Presently she found herself in the company of a fat, bald, and altogether odious man only too eager to share his opinions.

"You know you could be nicer..." he said, his breath reeking of cheap bourbon.

"Sorry." Amanda muttered under her breath, her mind elsewhere.

"Well I mean what the hell am I paying for.... I could buy a doll to do what you're doing." The stench pulsating in Amanda's nose.

"Lemme take care of you baby." Amanda replied, though more instinctually than warmly, like a pre-recorded line.

"Whatever screw this..." the man said as he pushed Amanda off of her, *"Pay a slut good money can't even..."*

He continued on his tirade, but Amanda only heard faint buzzing. Who the hell was this pig to judge her? What did he know about what she was dealing with? Let him try degrading himself every night day after day just to get by. She was so sick of these entitled jerks who couldn't even be bothered to treat her like a human being. Over and over again she tried playing by their rules and every time it had blown up in her face. Jesus Christ did it ever end? Her mind was whirring now, circling around itself. The rage was boiling inside of her until she could no longer contain it.

She punched the man right in the throat. He let out a gasp as the wind got knocked out of him. The floodgates opened, Amanda wailed on him as hard as she could over and over and over again. Blood came shooting out of his nose after Amanda landed punch after punch. Then all too quickly she regained her sanity.

"Shit, Shit, Shit!" she thought to herself. The man was hunched over in the car seat, faint moaning the only indication he was still alive. Anger quickly turned to panic as Amanda realized exactly what she had just done.

What the hell was she gonna do now? If it got out that she beat up a client she knew that was big trouble. At the very least she'd be thrown out on the street and could kiss any hope of a better life goodbye. Too much was happening all at once. She couldn't think straight.

She began concocting a story, *"He hit me. I was defending myself."* That could work. Her word against his. Wait. With her luck he would have a dashcam that recorded the whole thing. She searched for the car frantically. Any sort of recording device. She couldn't find one. She was in the clear.

Wait. His phone, was his phone recording? She reached into his pocket and pulled it out. Fumbling with panic, she dropped the stupid thing under the car seat. She reached underneath to retrieve it. Blindly reaching along the underneath of the seat, she felt something.

Pulling it up revealed it was not the man's phone but a knife. A big knife, probably placed there in case of carjackers. Suddenly the plan changed... It didn't have to be her word against his. He could be denied a say in the matter. A John got rough and got what was coming to him, that happens all the time, no one would bat an eye. He was a prick anyway. Who would really be worse off? Amanda looked at the knife in her hand and back at the lump in the seat before her. This was the only way to guarantee she got out of this. After all the world had screwed her enough it was about time she did some screwing. She raised the blade up to strike.

She couldn't do it. She dropped the knife faster than she had lifted it up and placed her head in her hands. This guy sucked but he didn't deserve to die. Defeated, she exited the car. Only one thing left to do. She had to go find Frankie.

She found him at the usual meeting spot making small talk with one of the other guys out with them that night. She ran up to him and practically flopped into his arms. Without saying a word, Frankie followed Amanda back to the car. He saw the man hunched over, face doused in blood and he understood. He looked back at Amanda.

"Just go back." he said calmly, *"I got this."*

Amanda left Frankie at the car and began walking back to the warehouse. The cool night air brushed her legs as she journeyed back. She knew Frankie would handle it. He always seemed to. Still that feeling of hers persisted. Why had she been so stupid? Did she really have such little self-control? It wasn't right what she had done. She knew that. He was a paying customer, and she should have given him the experience he paid for. But no. Like an idiot she lost her temper.

She made it back to the warehouse. No one else was there yet. She got into her cot and laid down. However, sleep was eluding her yet again. Frankie could handle this. Right? That goddamn unknown. Always gnawing at her. She lay there for what felt like hours. Eventually everyone else had returned. Amanda's body stayed still, but her eyes jolted to life. As all the other girls shuffled in, her gaze was locked on Frankie. He didn't look in her direction, instead went straight up the stairs to Cody's bedroom and knocked softly on the door. The door cracked open. Cody didn't emerge at first. Frankie just leaned into the barely open doorway. Eventually Cody came out onto the balcony. Amanda could make out a confused look on his face as she saw Frankie speaking into his ear, suddenly both men turned and looked right in Amanda's direction. She quickly averted her gaze. After a few moments she once again looked upon the balcony. The two men were still speaking in hushed whispers until Cody simply shrugged, shook Frankie's hand, and patted him affectionately on the shoulder before retreating back into the room. Too exhausted to stress anymore, Amanda soon fell asleep.

The next morning, Amanda woke up to murmurs all throughout the warehouse. She sat up in her cot and noticed everyone staring up at the balcony. She followed suit and saw Cody standing there, in his pinstripe suit looking down toward all the girls below. Frankie standing beside him. Amanda jolted to life, jumped out of bed and joined the huddle forming below the balcony. Everyone now gathered below Cody held up his hand and the murmuring died down to silence.

"Thank you all for gathering." he said, his voice was much more down to earth than that of his employer. *"I'm sure the past couple of days have been very hectic for all of you but I think enough time has passed and everyone seems to be adjusting well, so thank you all for that."* Silence from the crowd, Cody cleared his throat.

"Anyway, it's time you all had a real leader again. How we're gonna do this is simple. You all are gonna get about forty-five minutes to talk it over with each other, and then you're gonna write down who you want to be in charge and give your vote to Frankie, silent ballot style. There's gotta be an over

fifty percent majority for someone to be selected and if you can't figure it out.... We'll just cross that bridge if we come to it, no sense in making it more complicated than it needs to be. So, any questions?"

There were a lot of confused faces among the girls but no one spoke up. *"Okay then,"* Cody said with a smile *"You got forty-five minutes to talk then y'all can vote. I'll leave you to it."* He once again retired to the office. Frankie and all the security guys joined him.

At first no one spoke. They all just stared awkwardly at each other. This was a lot to process first thing in the morning. Middle of the night raids, early morning elections, did these guys ever do anything at a normal time?

After about five minutes of silence one of the girls spoke up *"so like, what do we do?"* She asked. More murmuring followed.

"I have no idea."

"Who do we pick?"

"I don't even know where to start."

Amanda was afraid to speak. She wasn't sure if anyone knew about last night's fiasco or not. Eventually, Tiffany took control of the conversation.

"Okay listen up!" Tiffany said, *"We don't have a lot of time and we gotta figure this out. I have a feeling if we don't, we're gonna get another Pump and I don't think anyone here wants that."* Everyone seemed to nod in agreement with that notion. Tiffany

continued. *"Let's start off simple, does anyone wanna nominate a person and we can go from there."* There were a few separate conversations, but the cohesion had once again been lost.

Amanda finally got the courage to speak up. *"What about you Tiffany?"* She said. Silence filled the room again

"What about me?" Tiffany asked

"I nominate you to take over." Amanda replied.

"Me?" Tiffany asked again, her face confused.

"Yes." Amanda reiterated

"Hell no, nominate someone else." Tiffany stated.

"Come on Tiff, think about it." Amanda argued, *"You've always wanted a chance to join the big league. You just took control of the situation literally two minutes ago. Everyone likes you. You've got the leadership qualities. This is your chance, am I right everyone?"* Amanda looked around to see everyone nodding in unenthusiastic agreement.

"First of all," Tiffany began in reply, *"I'm pretty sure everyone more or less likes everyone here so that doesn't really mean shit. Second, I do not want to be in this business at all, no offense to anyone here but this is degrading and I wanna be out of it as soon as possible."*

Everyone now nodded in agreement with Tiffany. *"Useless..."* Amanda thought to herself. Tiffany continued speaking.

"Besides Mandy," she said *"If anyone should be in charge it's you..."*

"Don't even start" Amanda said sternly, *"I don't want that"*

"All of your hunches have been right so far." Tiffany said, *"You could tell something big was going down before any of us, that's the kinda person that should be in charge."*

"I am not a leader." Amanda retorted *"You are."*

"Amanda, you care about everyone in this room like they were your own sister." Tiffany said *"If you were in charge, they'd have someone who actually cares about them watching their backs"*

"So what?" Amanda said *"You care too... don't act like you don't"*

"But you're smarter than me." Tiffany countered. *"You'd do a better job."*

"Tiffany if I was smarter than you, I'd have already convinced you to take the job and we wouldn't be having this conversation."

Everyone giggled a little bit as Amanda said this, *"Shit"* she thought to herself *"not helping"*

"There's gotta be someone here who actually wants the job." Amanda offered. Everyone bit their lips in silence.

"Plus...." Tiffany began again; she smiled as the Ace in the hole had just come to her. *"Frankie likes you, Amanda."* Amanda turned beet red. The girls giggled again.

What does that have to do with anything?" Amanda asked, annoyed and embarrassed.

"Everything!" Tiffany answered, *"A, Frankie is clearly higher up than any of us thought so having him as an ally is perfect. And B, do you really think those guys are gonna just take orders from a lady boss like it's nothing.... But they aren't gonna mess with YOU because Frankie's gonna be at your heels like a guard dog."*

Everyone was now agreeing with Tiffany much more enthusiastically.

"Tiffany I...." Amanda began but Tiffany cut her off.

"Mandy, it has to be you." She said flatly, *"It only makes sense if it's you. If you don't want it for yourself, do it for them."* Tiffany gestured to everyone around them, *"They deserve someone who cares about them and has the ability to actually make their lives better."*

Everyone was staring at Amanda now, almost longingly.

"God damn you Tiffany" Amanda said timidly. She then turned to address the crowd, *"If you vote for me, I swear to Christ the first thing I am gonna do is throw everyone out on the street... pick someone else, anyone else."* A few concerned looks began to be exchanged, until Tiffany shot back.

"No she won't and you all know it." She said *"She wouldn't do that to you all. Do the right thing for yourselves and pick Amanda."*

Not long after, Cody and the guys came out of the office again. *"Well, hopefully you guys have your minds made up."* He said calmly. *"We're gonna pass some pieces of paper and pens around and uhhh I guess just hand them to Frankie then we'll count up and go from there."* He gestured to the ladies, and the security guys began passing out pens and paper, the whole thing took not even ten minutes, that did not make Amanda feel at ease.
She scribbled *"Tiffany"* onto her paper and quickly handed it to one of the other girls going up to turn her vote in. Once Frankie had all the votes, he and Coady sat down and began to count. After some short discussion the two men looked at each other and nodded in agreement indicating they were done.

Cody once again stood up to address the crowd. *"Well good that was easy."* He said cheerily. *"Always nice when things work out..."* He cleared his throat to announce the results.

"It is my official duty to announce that Amanda Beasley will become your new representative to the Imperial Marshals and shall from this day heretofore serve as your immediate leader and guardian. May you all wish her courage and wisdom in this endeavor and that these attributes may be put to use for your benefit."

Everyone began to clap as Amanda's heart sank into her stomach. She looked and saw the hopeful smiles on everyone's face while hope had abandoned her entirely. Tiffany came up to hug her.

"Screw you Tiffany" she whispered. *"You just threw me into the lion's den."*

"Amanda, be mad at me all you want," Tiffany replied with a smile. *"But you know it's the right thing."*

"Yea when that lunatic rips MY nose off, I'll be sure to thank you." Amanda said rudely.

"Oh babes," Tiffany said with a smirk *"Something tells me this Emperor guy is gonna like you a lot more than he liked Pump..."*

Cody called for Amanda to come join him in the office. Amanda went up to see the room was completely barren except for Cody's suitcase and a sleeping bag he had been using. Upon her walking through the door Cody noticed the uncomfortable look on Amanda's face.

"It's okay I'm not gonna bite you." He said with a laugh. *"Come in, sit down, let me get you a drink."*

Amanda smiled politely *"I'm sorry Mr. Chelsey it's not you... This room just has bad memories in it"*

"Oh God please please call me Cody" he replied *"I don't need all that la te da crap like his Majesty, I'm sorry if that announcement was a little dramatic but that's how he likes things done and I gotta do my job."* He handed her a glass of whiskey *"Anyway, what were you saying...?"*

Amanda graciously took a sip and sat down *"It's nothing now I guess"* she said.

"Please tell me... it would make me feel a lot better if you did." Cody replied, Amanda could see the concern growing on his face.

Amanda then recounted how Pump would take the girls up to the room and have his way with them. As she talked, the mild concern on Cody's face turned to disgust.

"Ugh" he scoffed, spitting on the ground, "*So unprofessional. I wish we'da known we would've sent that SOB packing ages ago. But I guess now you've got a chance to turn things around."* He smiled softly at her again.

"From here it's pretty simple." Cody continued, *"You're gonna move all your stuff up here, not to worry, I had this dump deep scrubbed the first day I moved in. As you can see, I threw all of Pump's garbage out... We'll get you a bed or something..."*

"I'm sorry to interrupt," Amanda said, *"But I have no idea how to be in charge, I literally have no clue what I am doing..."*

"Right right right," Cody replied *"Well just about all of your friends think you have what it takes so you must have something. But I'm getting ahead of myself."* He took a deep breath and regained his thoughts. *"I was saying..., we'll move all your stuff up here, get you set up, then this afternoon we'll go over to Reginridge, and you'll meet everyone and learn everything you need to get started."*

"Reginridge?" Amanda asked.

"Oh" Cody said with a chuckle, *"I guess you wouldn't know... Reginridge is what he calls his house... you're getting a personal audience with his Majesty the Emperor..."*

Chapter 8: Sandra

The plan was pretty simple. Greg was friends with the accountant at the DA's office; he would pull some strings and get Sandra a job working at the desk there under the name Stacy May. All Sandra had to do once she was in was lead the DA on, trap him and boom, new blackmail beats old blackmail. A sting operation plain and simple.

Greg had done his part; Sandra's first day was tomorrow. The Commissioner had enlisted the help of his daughter Rosanna to up Sandra's sex appeal. Sandra never really did much with makeup and this needed to be quick and painless.

Sandra and Rosanna were sitting on Rosanna's bed as she taught Sandra the basics. *"So why am I turning a middle-aged cop into a milf?"* Rosanna asked, not looking up from Sandra's lips as she applied the lipstick.

"Well first of all I'm thirty-eight" Sandra replied, *"but thank you for making me feel fifty."* Rosanna said nothing and just continued applying lipstick.

"I guess to answer your question" Sandra went on *"Sometimes good guys have to do bad things to stop bad guys."*

"Whatever you say..." Rosanna returned, having already lost total interest in the conversation. *"Anyway, you just kinda rub your lips together now and voila."*

Sandra examined herself in the mirror. Her face was caked in paint. Her eyelashes doused in thick mascara, blush accentuating her already prominent cheekbones. And her lips; red and fat. She didn't feel very pretty. She just felt cheap. Still, that's probably what the situation demanded.

She really wasn't sure herself how comfortable she was with this whole thing. The Commissioner was right, it was slimy. But he knew what he was doing. She wasn't some naive idiot thinking that the powers that be are beyond corruption. Were they just supposed to do nothing? Of course not. Something had to be done, even if that meant playing dirty.

She woke up the next day and started getting ready for her first day at the DA's office. Rosanna had given her some makeup, and she applied it just like she was shown, mmmmm... good enough. She then went to her closet and selected a nice tight-fitting dress. She chuckled to herself, all those years doing the police department's physical training and the only time it did her any good was keeping her figure to hopefully seduce a potential scumbag.

She made it to the office and got settled, the job was easy enough, answered a phone that barely rang, and directed people to the right office. It took her maybe twenty minutes to get the hang of it. What she didn't know how to do was to accomplish her mission. She never considered herself much of a seductress. She was hoping an opportunity would just sort of present itself.

She could not believe she got an undercover mission as a part of an elite task force and somehow, she was still sitting at a desk wasting the day away. She vowed then and there to have So Close Yet So Far etched on her tombstone. She laughed at the image in her head. And before she knew it her first day was over, never even saw the DA, not once. She was supposed to report to the task force by the end of the week, if the rest of the week went like today it was going to be a pretty short report...

The next day she vowed to be more assertive. More social around the office, make her presence known. There was a little coffee table in the office she could see from her desk. She would wait for someone to go up and casually bump into them. Her victim was Stephen, some accounting something or other she wasn't really listening.

"You're new right?" he asked.

"Yup!" she said cheerily, practicing a flirty smile. *"My name's... Stacy"*

"Nice to meet you Stacy...." She stopped listening again.

Step one done. She repeated the process a few more times and began to enjoy inventing the life of Stacy. Stacy was a former stage dancer looking to settle into a more traditional career. She started getting into it, wooing crowds at lunch with completely bogus stories of touring the country for various shows, throwing in an off-color joke here and there. Over the course of an afternoon, she had become the belle of the ball. Hopefully no one in the office were theatre enthusiasts.

She went home that night feeling much more satisfied. She hopped into bed and dreamt of Stacy and all the adventures she could share tomorrow. The next day was more of the same. She fell into her element gracing the office with fabricated tales of a life not lived. The whole room enthralled with a complete lie. She was shocked how easily it came to her, she never saw herself as much of a deceiver.

It was Friday that her moment came at last. A man walked into the office, and everyone immediately stood up. That had to be him. He didn't look like much. Thin, dark hair, thin glasses, all warped in a charcoal gray suit, all and all... average. Sandra looked for a silver imperial ring, but instead only saw a wedding band.

"Hello Everyone." the District Attorney said politely, *"I've been meaning to come by, but you all know how it goes... I just wanted to introduce myself to our new employee."*

He gestured toward Sandra and smiled. Sandra smiled in return and extended her hand toward him.

"Danny Hamlin, District Attorney" He said kindly.

Sandra went to shake his hand... then remembered her mission and daintily outstretched her fingertips. *"Stacy May"* she replied sweetly, she hadn't quite mastered the flirty smile yet but was steadily approaching passable.

"So" Hamlin said, *"I hope you're settling in okay?"*

"Yes sir, thank you." Sandra replied, forcing herself to stare into his eyes. The District Attorney clapped his hands together.

"Well good!" he said cheerfully, *"My office is just down the hall on the left, my door is always open if you need anything. I'll let you all get back to it."* He then turned around and left the office as everyone got back to work. Sandra returned to her desk, satisfied with her performance. The stage had been set. Now time for the curtain to rise, and for the leading lady to make her entrance.

She gave it all a little time, no need to act overeager. A few hours passed by. She walks over to one of the workers, tapping away at her cubicle. *"This is so embarrassing,"* Sandra said playfully, *"But I have no idea where the bathroom is."*

Her coworker laughed in reply, *"Come with me sweetie,"* she said, *"I can show you."* She got out of her seat and escorted Sandra down the hall in the direction of the restrooms. Sandra made a show of feigning gratitude and assured her she could find her way back. Sandra waited a moment to ensure the coast was clear and began walking back down the hallway.

"To the left of the accounting office." she thought to herself.

Success! She had found it. She took a deep breath, preparing herself. Annnd, action. She opened the door. District Attorney Hamlin looked up from his desk. Upon seeing Sandra standing there his face shifted from friendly to confused.

"Stacy right?" he asked, pointing at her with his pen, *"Can I help you with something?"*

Sandra playfully slapped herself on the forehead.

"I'm such a ditz!" she laughed. *"I must have gotten lost."*

Hamlin stood up from his desk and chuckled slightly in reply. "Not to worry" he said with a friendly smile. He began walking toward her, "We'll help you find your way."

As he got closer Sandra maneuvered herself between him and the doorway. Here goes nothing. She gently rested a hand upon his arm. *"Thank you SO much!"* she exclaimed, that flirty smile was really coming along. *"I am so embarrassed."*

"Don't worry about it." Hamlin replied, keeping a kind tone. He patted her hand gently and went to circumvent her to get to the door.

She was losing him, time to up the ante. Sandra backed up to maintain her spot between district attorney Hamlin and the door. She caressed his arm slowly and gently, up and down, with her fingertips. *"Surely there's some way I can thank you."*

The District Attorney looked piercingly into Sandra's eyes, trying to non-verbally interpret her intentions. Sandra moved in close enough so she would have to look up to meet his gaze, she tilted her head slightly and batted her eyelashes. She had seen that in the movies.

Gaze unbroken, Hamlin gently placed his hand over top of Sandra's, stopping her caressing of his arm, she took the opportunity to squeeze his hand and guided it close to but not yet touching her thigh. She was close enough that he could hear his breathing become labored. She leaned in even closer; she could feel his heart beating faster.

"*What in the hell are you doing!?!*" Hamling blurted out as he shoved Sandra away. *"Explain yourself!"*

Caught off guard, Sandra desperately tried to regain control of the situation. She leaned in again and grabbed the lapels of Hamlin's suit. *"I... sorry I just..."* she stumbled over her words.

"You just what?" Hamlin asked again, backing away from her and raising an eyebrow.

"I just thought you're a hardworking man..." Sandra replied, her confidence quickly waning, *"I thought you might want someone to help you relax."*

Hamlin held up a hand to stop Sandra from speaking, the other hand massaging the bridge of his nose underneath the rim of his glasses. *"I am a hard-working MARRIED man."* he said indicating the ring on his left hand. *"I've said maybe five words to you prior to this.... whatever it is... so what put any sort of idea in your head I don't know."*

"Well.." Sandra replied, delicacy was of the utmost importance now if she was to salvage this endeavor. *"I know sometimes its not always easy being married.... And that some men need appreciation when they aren't getting it at home."*

"Jesus CHRIST" Hamlin said, throwing his hands up in the air, *"This again?!? Listen I don't know who the hell you work for but that ploy was a crock of shit then and it's a crock of shit now."*

Sandra was at a loss for how to proceed, *"I don't follow..."* was all she was able to get out.

Hamlin sighed and sat down at his desk; he looked over Sandra's shoulders to make sure the door was shut before proceeding to explain;
"A while back..." he said, *"A couple of mafia thugs, back when there was a mafia in this town, thought they were some real grade A gangsters, and they were going to be the next Don Corleone by having the DA in their pocket."* He sniggered at his own joke, *"So they fabricated some stupid sex scandal and tried to use it as blackmail..... absolute idiots. Still, it made some trouble around the election that year. People are all too happy to crucify you over baseless gossip.*

Luckily, a friend took care of it for me, so I haven't thought about the whole thing in years.... Till some dumbass just tried to do the exact same thing." He threw his hand rudely at Sandra as he finished his last sentence.

Sandra bit her lip. She was about as embarrassed as someone could be. But she couldn't show it. Her brain began processing all the information at lighting speed. The initial plan was a bust, but something could still be salvaged here. But what to do next? She was in a tight spot, one more wrong move and all was for sure lost. Sandra ran through everything Hamlin had just said, looking for a weak point. But luckily he took care of it.... Perfect.

"Who took care of it?" Sandra asked, feigning ignorance.

Hamlin scoffed and chuckled. *"Wow you really are a terrible criminal."* He said mockingly, He opened a drawer in his desk and reached into it. Sandra stepped back, not sure what to expect. She was relieved to see all he was grabbing was a piece of paper. Hamlin looked up at Sandra, scoffed again and shook his head before quickly scribbling something onto the paper.

"If you want to make something of yourself in the underworld of Colonna." He said, extending the folded paper out for Sandra to take, *"You'll ditch whatever morons put you up to this stunt and call this number. Or don't, I don't care, just get out of this office and don't show your face here again."* He

waved her away as Sandra curtly thanked him and walked out the door.

She went straight from the DA's office to the library. She wasn't sure how Commissioner Helming and the guys were going to take the news. She walked down the stairs and through the hallway to their meeting room. As she entered, she found everyone sitting around the conference table awaiting her arrival.

"Well?" Commissioner Helming said, *"What have you got for us?"*

Sandra bit her lip nervously. Nothing to do but come out and tell them, whatever happens happens.

"Well," she sputtered out. *"I've got good news and bad news."* The Commissioner, Kieth, Treyvon and Greg all looked at her intently as she recounted the story of her interaction with the District Attorney. She ended with handing the Commissioner the note the District Attorney had given her.

Helming motioned for Sandra to sit down at the table. All eyes were on him now. He tapped the table contemplatively as he studied the slip of paper Sandra gave to him. He spent several moments looking at Sandra, then back to the note, then back to Sandra again. After coming to his conclusion, he gently returned the slip of paper back to Sandra.

Helming rose slowly from his chair and caressed his chin. He then pointed at Sandra.
"Well..." He said, *"It looks like Stacy Mae is going to infiltrate the Empire itself."*

Chapter 9: Amanda

Amanda's stomach was again in knots. She was sitting in the back of a limousine taking her and Cody to Reginridge, the home of the Emperor. She must have looked like a total wreck. Conversely, there was Cody sitting opposite calm as could be. She had to admit it. He actually did seem nice.

"I promise you don't need to be that worried." Cody said, trying to reassure her, *"He's all flash and no bang.... He's actually kind of a softie."*

Amanda sat silent, as Cody was talking all she could picture was the sadistic look in the Emperor's eyes as he ripped Pump to shreds. *Softie* was not the first word that came to mind. She still was in shock that she found herself in this position. God Damn Tiffany and her mouth.

The limousine rolled along down the street. They were leaving the city. Amanda saw grass, not little patches barely preserved in front of the multitude of Colonna's many row houses but actual real grass. Sprawling, green, beautiful. She couldn't remember the last time she had left the city, and how serene it was. It was crazy to think this landscape was only ever ten minutes away from her. The smog and grim replaced with flowing fields of light shining on a bright barren green plane. There was a peaceful quality to it Amanda couldn't help but take in. It reminded her of the beach on that postcard she kept in her safety deposit box. She would definitely have to come back here on a better day so she could enjoy it properly. That is if a better day ever came.

As the limousine carried on, they got farther and farther outside of the city. More and more nothing whirred past them. They were about ten minutes outside of the city now. Suddenly the car took an exit. Now they were really in the middle of nowhere. Amanda had enough of the scenery, it was only a temporary distraction anyway.

She looked at Cody, he was writing something on a legal pad, seemingly lost in whatever he was doing. Amanda stared at him as he scribbled away. Eventually, he sensed her gaze. He looked up at her, smiled again, and lifted up a finger indicating he was almost done. Cody finished writing on the pad and placed it back into the briefcase that was sitting next to him. He then clapped and rubbed his hands together looking at Amanda.

"All right," he said with a jovial exhale, *"Let's give you the rundown."* Amanda shifted nervously in her seat and Coady looked at her with sympathy in his eyes. *"You're gonna get through this I promise,"* he continued. *"It's really easy, once we get there, I'm going to lead you into the throne room. You'll wait there 'till I come back with The Emperor. Once you hear the music, you're going to bow your head until he starts talking. He's going to speak to you, when you speak to him the first time you address him as "Your Majesty", after that "Sire or Your Majesty" whichever you prefer".* Amanda was having a hard time keeping

up but Cody pressed on, *"He's gonna ask you questions, you're gonna answer them. He's gonna tell you what he wants you to do, and that's it. Not so bad right?"*

Amanda shuffled nervously. *"No, I guess not."* she politely responded. *"Thank you, you've been very nice."*

Cody reached forward and patted her on the knee. *"Don't worry about it."* He said, *"It's my job... Now, look at those trees there and you'll see the palace."* Amanda jolted up and looked out the window. Through the trees she could make out the top of a building. As the limousine turned a corner into the drive, Reginridge really came into view. Amanda was taken aback at the magnificence of it.

At the end of the long driveway was a building in the shape of a crescent. Three stories high, the exterior was adorned with arches on the ground floor and columns on the floors above that. The two halves of the crescent shape were separated by a massive rectangular tower one story higher than the rest of the structure with a grand arch entryway in its center.

This central tower was capped with a massive copper dome, gleaming in the sunlight, not yet touched by oxidation. Amanda could see a small glass door in the center of the dome that led to a balcony that ran along the entirety of the highest level. The top of the dome housed a large violet banner with the Emperor's sword and trident symbol embroidered on it in gold.

As she got closer, she could see the statues that aligned the roof of the building. Where a column touched the roof of the structure, they were all crowned with statues of a knight holding a sword standing next to a mermaid holding a trident. The free hand of each figure raised up, together holding a laurel wreath. Four arched windows were spaced out on each half of the crescent's ground floor, the second and third floors were slightly indented to allow for a continuous balcony upon the roof of the first story, Amanda could see armed men in all black patrolling on this walkway.

The driveway was long and lined with trees on either side. It ended in a large carriageway, encircling a magnificent marble fountain. Sprinkling water three hundred and sixty degrees around. The fountain was the base for the largest statue seen on the property. Unlike the fantastic atmosphere of the rest of the palace this statue was very realistic. Where the rest of the palace was made of beautiful marble and limestone, this statue was cast from dark iron. It was a statue of a woman, seemingly middle-aged. She was dressed in a 1980's blouse and skirt set with high-heeled shoes. One hand clasping the other in the front. Showing a massive round ring on right hand. Her face was stern and scowling, hosting two large pearl earrings and a double pearl necklace draped across her neck. The details were too great. It clearly had to have been a real person once, but Amanda didn't recognize her.

The rest of the grounds were sprawling green with gardens of flowers placed all along the flowing fields. There were flowers of all sorts, but lavender bushels prevailed everywhere Amanda looked. A sea of purple that coated the fields.

The limo pulled around the carriageway and stopped in front of the entryway arch. Above the arch's keystone was yet another engraving of the Emperor's sigil etched into the wall. A footman dressed in a tuxedo opened the limousine door and Amanda and Cody got out. Cody placed a hand on Amanda's shoulder reassuringly and guided her into the building.

The interior of the building was just as opulent as the outside. The black granite floors of the entryway were decorated with elaborate golden designs, leading up to a grand staircase. At the foot of the staircase there was, of course, yet another of the emperor's sigils incorporated into the floor in gold. A great chandelier hung above the staircase with fifty glimmering electric candles lighting the room.

Cody guided Amanda up the massive staircase, and through a maze of hallways. The place seemed to never end. Everywhere she looked Amanda saw candles, and renaissance style paintings, their heels clicking on the granite as they walked. The whole building was imposing.

Eventually Cody stopped at a large set of double doors. A footman was posted on each side, and they opened the doors up and allowed the pair to enter. Amanda peeked in and saw the room was empty. A long thin violet carpet ran the length of the room stopping at the Emperor's throne. It was elevated on a platform, and the sides and rear were encased in a violet curtain with the same sigil embroidered on it, again in gold.

The chair itself was mahogany with violet cushions on the seat and back decorated with the same sword and trident sigil. Other than that, the room was bare. Electric candles for light but no windows to be seen. Cody guided Amanda up to the right of the throne and showed her where to stand. He looked at her again and grasped her by the shoulders.

"I know you're nervous," he said. *"It's okay to be nervous, it's a lot to take in, but you'll do fine."* Amanda smiled at him sheepishly. *"You remembered everything I told you, right?"* Cody asked her.

"Bow my head until I he starts talking, Imperial Majesty the first time, Sire after that." Amanda responded. Cody gave her a fist bump in reward.

"He's gonna love you." Cody said with a smile. *"Now just wait here and try not to get too worked up. I'll be back soon..."* With that Cody turned and left Amanda alone. Amanda paced around the room. She wished there was something to look at to occupy her mind while she waited. Cody seemed

nice. Men have the ability however to seem nice when they want something. Still, she didn't quite get that vibe from him. If Cody trusted this Emperor man maybe he wasn't all bad? Wishful thinking, and when had wishful thinking gotten her anywhere in life. Better to be prepared for the worst.

Amanda heard footsteps approaching, quickly she darted back to the spot by the throne that Cody had instructed her to stand and waited. The footsteps got ever louder, it sounded like an army marching toward the door. As the volume increased Amanda could feel her heart racing. This is it, sink or swim, now was the time.

Soon she could hear the footsteps right outside the door and then suddenly, silence. Not a sound. A moment later the doors were thrown open and two men in the same matching pinstripe suits Amanda had become accustomed to seeing entered the room, each holding a horn adorned with a purple banner and the sigil embroidered in gold. They stopped on either side of the doorway and raised their instruments. They began to play and Amanda dropped to one knee and bowed her head as instructed. As the horn players blasted their song a group of three drummers and two fifers entered the throne room and began playing in unison with the horns. The addition of these extra instruments swelled the narrow room with noise reverberating off the walls. The music was sharp and rigid. Amanda could feel the vibrations of the beat in her chest.

Amanda remained looking at the floor until the music began to die down until only the drummers were playing rapidly. Amanda looked up to see Cody enter the room, he stopped in the doorway and nodded politely at Amanda before stiffening his back and looking directly forward. The drums ceased and soon Cody's voice soon bellowed into the room.

"Now announcing the arrival of his Imperial Majesty, Edward Von Drac, Imperator Rex Colonna City. Anointed Master of the Imperial Convocation. Crowned Lord Protector of the Seven Districts. First Counselor of the Imperial Diet. First Admiral of the Imperial Armada. Grand Defender of the Street and of the Sea. In his presence, may you bow your heads in unmatched reverence or fall to your knees in repentant shame."

As Cody finished his introduction the band began again in full force, but the song was different. The powerful horns changed to violins. The music was smooth and much more graceful. Amanda shifted her eyes to peek into the hallway but couldn't make out any figures. Slowly but definitely, Amanda could make out a clanking sound growing louder and louder mixing in with the music of the band. She very quickly was made privy to its source.

At first it looked like a faint outline of two men. As they got closer Amanda could make out their distinctions. First, she recognized the Emperor, regally dressed in a similar suit to Amanda saw him last time, holding his cane in his armpit as he walked, other hand placed atop his waistcoat pocket, tapping his pocket watch. Amanda noticed he took large but slow steps as he entered the throne room. His gaunt face bore a slight smirk as he observed the musicians announcing his arrival.

Accompanying him was the cause of the clanking Amanda had heard. What it was could only be described as the stuff of nightmares. It was a man, or at least it had been a man at some point in time. His arms and legs were all manacled together in unnecessarily long and thick metal chains, the weight of which clearly contributed to his poor posture. The pitiful thing was hunched and dressed in rags, tattered, frayed, and held together by the layer of dried blood and filth that coated them.

An iron mask encased this man's head completely save two holes for his eyes. The mask was scuffed and dented, stained with dried blood, the same as his clothes and the weight of it kept his head constantly hanging below his shoulders. This creature could barely stand let alone move, each step being a clearly laborious challenge.

As the two men walked down the violet carpet toward the throne Amanda made sure to look at the ground. Partly because of the instructions Cody had given her and more so because she could not bear to look at the hulking monster by the Emperor's side. The Emperor in turn paid no attention to Amanda as he walked. Instead, basking pleasantly in the music being played in his honor.

As they neared the throne Amanda's curiosity got the better of her and she lifted her gaze for a quick peak. The Emperor's companion was right next to her now, she looked up to see him staring directly at her. His eyes were bloodshot beyond belief, to a point where Amanda wondered if they even still worked. The little bit she could see of his face through the eye holes in his mask was bruised and bloodied beyond anything resembling a human. He looked dead, yet he was moving.

Amanda looked away again, she couldn't stare at him for long. She had now seen the Emperor twice and it seemed that wherever he went, blood and physical mutilation followed. How could anyone serve this man? They must all be scared beyond belief.

The Emperor reached the throne and turned around to face the walkway he had just traversed. He stared back at the door, standing motionless and tall until the violins finished their entrance march. Only once the music faded away did he take his seat. He leaned on his cane as he sat down. Once he was seated, he tapped the cane twice on the granite floor. As he did so, the wretched servant that accompanied him creeped to the floor below The Emperor's feet on his hands and knees. The Emperor kicked the man in the ribs and chuckled to himself before resting his boots upon the man's back as if he were an ottoman. Cody came up beside The Emperor and took a position opposite of Amanda, who was still bowing her head diligently.

"Your Majesty..." Cody said with a curt bow. *"It is my duty to present to you, Amanda Beasly, duly elected by your subjects, her peers, to serve the Crown and Empire as Knight of your realm."* The Emperor slowly raised his eyebrows. He then looked to Amanda who raised her head to meet his gaze. He smiled at her.

"Well, if nothing else she has a healthy respect for decorum!" The Emperor said jovially. *"You may may approach my child."* He gestured for her to come nearer.

Amanda slowly walked up to the throne and was now very close to the Emperor, she glanced down at the miserable creature below the Emperor's feet. He was clearly emaciated, struggling to keep himself upright. The Emperor caught Amanda's gaze and looked down as well.

"Of course, how rude of me," The Emperor said slyly, *"Ms. Beasly this is my valet Mr. Charteris... He looks rather despicable, which he is, but I assure you he won't cause you any harm..."* The Emperor lifted his legs from atop Mr. Charteris' back, placing them back to the ground. He leaned down towards the wretched man studying his warped frame.

"He won't be harming anyone these days...." The Emperor said, his tone became quite callous. He then kicked Mr. Charteris square in the gut with the toe of his boot. Mr. Charteris let out a deep grunt as

he fell flat to the ground. The Emperor cackled and grabbed the back of Mr. Charteris' collar.

"You insolent swine! I should've fed you to dogs years ago!" The Emperor growled. He flung his victim back to the ground. The Emperor grabbed his cane and twisted its head. He tugged and revealed a hidden blade attached to the pommel. He proceeded to run the blade deep into Mr. Charteris' calf. The poor man squirmed but was clearly too weak and exhausted to shout. Blood trickled slowly from the wound.

Amanda looked at Cody who seemed wholly unphased by the whole affair. She put every ounce of energy she had into keeping her composure. Mr. Charteris squirmed on the ground, moaning, like an undead monster. The Emperor was staring down at him shaking his head in disgust.

"Remove this pestilent piece of rotting refuse from my sight." he muttered under his now labored breathing, massaging his pocket watch as he did so. Cody did another curt bow before reaching down and dragging Mr. Charteris out of the room by his legs, the clicking of shoes on the granite floors accompanied by painful groans and rattling of chains, fainter and fainter, until silent, as the Emperor returned to his throne.

The Emperor looked back at Amanda again, studying her up and down. His demeanor seemed relaxed once again. Amanda wasn't sure how to react, so she just stood still, doing her best not to look into his eyes. Finally, the Emperor broke the silence.

"Ms. Beasly... Allow me to begin by saying I am sure this is all very foreign to you. You and I are not familiar with one another; and I can project a rather threatening visage." Amanda caught him smiling to himself as he said this...

"Be that as it may you have the vow of The Emperor; no harm will befall you during your visit to Reginridge today. You are not on trial my dear, so please grant us the ease of honest answers. Am I made plain?"

"Y–yes.. Yes... yes your Majesty." Amanda squeaked out.

"*Good!*" The Emperor exclaimed, clapping his hands together. *"Now let's begin. Tell me child... you come to me as a representative of your compatriots. Yet you do not exude confidence in yourself. Do you actually want to be here?"* Amanda shuffled nervously. No lying her way out of this one. The Emperor was eyeing her impatiently, waiting for an answer.

"Well sir... Sire..." Amanda quickly corrected, *"It's true. I didn't ask to become a leader of anyone. I don't know how to do whatever Pump did. If you really want the truth, I just want to be left alone. I don't want to cause any trouble."*

The Emperor snorted to himself, *"I would think that being unable to behave like that odious rhinoceros would serve you well."* He said with a smile. *"Regardless I thank you for your candor and I do understand your trepidation. Yet for some reason your fellow concubines want you to represent their interests to the Crown."* The Emperor tapped his cane in thought. He rose from his chair and began pacing back and forth. *"It is often said that the best leaders are the ones who do not wish to lead, admittedly not a sensation with which I am familiar."* He giggled to himself just a little.

The Emperor stopped his pacing and turned to face the door. *"Go and find Master Chesley and ask him to fetch Edwina..."* He commanded one of the footmen. The footman bowed and exited the room. The Emperor turned back to Amanda. *"So, Amanda Beasly..."* He pointed his cane at her as he talked. *"You do not wish for advancement in your career. But I cannot imagine you see yourself spending the rest of your life entertaining whoremongers. So, what is it you do want with your life?'*

Amanda mulled over the question. She pictured that beach on her postcard. She could just about feel the breeze and warm sun prevailing through the old stone room she was in now. Screw it. What did she have to lose?

"I just want to retire..." She said to the Emperor. *"I don't want to be involved in anything I just want to keep my head down, stay out of trouble, earn my piece, and get out of here."*

The Emperor smiled softly at this response. He looked down at the floor and massaged his pocket watch, lost in thought. He considered Amanda's answer, seemingly satisfied by it. He looked back up at Amanda again; his face was gentle and sincere.

"A beautiful, noble, and achievable goal." he said warmly. *"Well, I am merely a humble monarch... Far from a God. So, if that is truly what you wish to do, I cannot stand in your way."* His tone had softened considerably, *"But so you are in possession of all the facts... should you refuse this commission, it will be sold to the highest bidder. After all, that is how your predecessor obtained his station... I may be a fair man, but I am not a naive one. I know as well as you what sort of entrepreneur seeks to make their fortune in the flesh market..."* He paused for a moment giving Amanda a chance to absorb this fact. *"You have a chance to spare not only yourself but all of your fellow courtesans of that... rather, unsavory element."* His face contorted awkwardly, as if he were disgusted by his own words.

Amanda knew exactly what the Emperor was doing. But admittedly, he did have a point. Pump was a jackass and more than likely another jackass would take his place. That wasn't really fair of her to do to the girls. But they were also the ones that put her in this position. Goddamn Tiffany and her speeches. Still, she was here now. However it happened, it was now her choice to make.

"If I were to accept, hypothetically..." Amanda began in reply. *"I would need help; I don't know the first thing about actually running a business."*

The Emperor's eyes widened with joy, seeing he was getting through. *"My child.."* he said, placing a hand on her shoulder. *"I don't maintain control of the underworld by mismanaging it."* He looked deep into her eyes and smiled gently. This time Amanda did not see malice, but instead compassion within his gaze. *"If you accept this charge,"* he said, *"the Crown will provide you with every resource to assist in your success."*

At that moment there was a knocking on the throne room doors. The sound echoing through the stone hall. Interrupted, both Amanda and the Emperor turned to face the door. The Emperor became giddy as the footman stationed at the doorway grabbed the handle and opened the door wide. It was Cody, beaming a great smile as he walked in holding something bright white in his hands.

The Emperor looked as if he were the happiest man in the world and he whistled loudly. Suddenly a head popped up from the white bundle in Cody's hands. It was a Peacock. Pure albino from head to toe. Upon hearing the Emperor's whistle, the animal perked up and jumped from Cody's hands to the floor, flapping its wings to grace its fall. It walked right up to the emperor, its magnificent tail dragging behind it as it moved. Once it reached the emperor he bent down and scratched the bird underneath its beak and it leaned into his hand.

"Edwina my beautiful darling!" The emperor exclaimed in a ridiculously high pitch as he scooped up the bird and embraced it joyously. The bird laid its head on the emperor's shoulder almost as if it was hugging him back. *"How has daddy's best little girl been?"*

Amanda couldn't help but crack a smile seeing the happiness of this reunion. This was not the man who beat Pump within an inch of his life. This was a totally different person. The Emperor kissed the Peacock's head and continued whispering adorations at her. The bird reacted as if she understood what he was saying and shared his affection.

Edwina then turned her head and looked at Amanda. At which point the Emperor, though still giddy, recollected himself. *"Ms. Beasly"* he said with a grin, *"I'd like you to meet Edwina, the most beautiful creature Almighty God ever managed to manifest."* Amanda smiled and nodded politely as the Emperor turned back to the bird. *"Alright my pretty precious peafowl,"* he said in a babying tone. *"Daddy has work to do."* He set the bird down and she walked over to the foot of the Emperor's throne. The Emperor took his seat and the bird hopped up onto his lap, cooing as he stroked her back.

"Master Chesley," The Emperor began returning to his stern grovel, *"I believe we have been*

able to convince Ms. Beasly here to rise to the occasion and join the ranks of the Empire." He then looked at Amanda, *"Unless I am mistaken?"*

Amanda looked at the Emperor, his face had gone emotionless. She looked at Cody, who was looking at her in anticipation. Screw it.

"No sire, you aren't wrong." she replied. Cody smiled at this news. The Emperor's face looked flushed with relief. *"I just don't know exactly what I am supposed to do."*

"Fret not!" The Emperor said in response, *"That is our next topic of discussion... I shall leave Master Chesley here to explain the broad strokes of your duties, and I shall insert myself as required."* He dramatically waved a hand toward Cody, signaling him to take over as he went back to giving Edwina playful scratches as if she were a kitten.

Cody cleared his throat *"Well, welcome!"* he said happily. *"I'm glad you decided to take the job... between you me if I had to talk to your old boss one more time I'd have ripped my own nose off."* He chuckled at his joke, but Amanda became visibly queasy. *"Sorry..."* Cody muttered, *"bad taste... Anywhoo. It's really simple, basically you have already been in the business, so you know how day-to-day goes. Make sure the girls get out, do their thing, collect the money, if there's an issue you have the security guys all that there etcetera."*

Amanda nodded her head as he spoke. So far not so bad. *"Here's really all that's different."* He continued. *"You collect all the money made for the week and you divide out 15 percent to give to your marchioness... think of her like your supervisor. You give her your cut as tax along with receipts for how much you made and how much you paid as tax. Got it?"*

Amanda mulled the information over. *"I think so"* she said, *"but who's my marshon...whatever you said?"*

The Emperor interjected. *"Marchioness!"* he exclaimed, *"A lovely woman...she'll be along soon...."* He then returned his attention to his pet.

Amanda turned back to Cody. *"So... if I can ask."* she began, *"I don't really understand how the whole thing breaks down."*

"Yea no worries." Cody replied, *"It is all a little confusing."* The Emperor scowled at this remark. *"Oh, you know it is! Give the girl a break."* Cody scoffed back at him. Amanda was a little taken aback by this display of bravado. The Emperor seemed not to notice and went back to playing with Edwina.

"Basically, here's the hierarchy..." Cody said, turning his attention back to Amanda.
"At the very bottom there's citizens. That's the people on the street, like you were. For security reasons we don't really include them in the inner workings of the whole thing. Too many people to make sure we can trust all of them, you understand. Then, there's knights, that's what you're about to become. People connected to the Emperor, people who run our

various business interests. Amanda nodded again, indicating she was following.

"Next up the ladder are the marshals. The marshals, or marchionesses if they're women, are the people that oversee each sect of our business. There's a marshal for drugs, gambling, girls, etcetera. Think of them as regional managers or something."

Amanda was beginning to understand. *"Okay,"* she said *"So citizens report to knights who report to marshals. It's like associate-soldier-capo from the mafia movies."* Cody winced as she said this and the Emperor groaned audibly.

The Emperor glared at Amanda, visibly annoyed. *"To compare the glory and Majesty of the Empire to some ragtag band of Italian thugs in silk suits is akin to blasphemy."* he said scoldingly.

"I'm sorry." Amanda said nervously. *"I didn't mean to be offensive."*

The Emperor waved her off *"Without ignorance there can be no education."* He replied dismissively before ignoring them once again.

Amanda looked worriedly at Cody who alleviated her concern by playfully sticking his tongue out in the Emperor's direction. He then continued his explanation. *"All the marshals together constitute the Imperial Diet who advise the Emperor and his Grand Marshal."*

"Grand Marshal?" Amanda asked.

"Oh, that's me." Cody replied gleefully. *"Cody Chesley, Grand Marshal and Lord High Chancellor of*

the Empire, at your service." He did a sarcastic, overdramatic bow. Amanda chuckled. Cody chuckled back.

"Noceo est mori." The Emperor grumbled from his throne.

"What's that?" Amanda asked.

Cody's face turned serious momentarily. *"It's Latin,"* he replied. *It means to harm is to die..."*

"It is the central tenet of the Empire." The Emperor interrupted, his voice becoming more and more angry. *"And it must be followed every moment of every day... The Empire provides economic opportunity to many of those whom society has deemed unworthy; we are a people bathed in glory of our own creation. I will not allow that to be tainted by brutish conduct of self-serving degeneracy."*

"Basically," Cody interrupted. *"No stealing, no murder for hire, no rape, none of that sort of thing. Any sort of activity that would cause physical or financial harm to someone against their will, inside or outside of the Empire, needs the personal approval of the Emperor.... And if we find out about anything happening... Well, just don't do it."* Amanda gulped at Cody's sudden shift in tone.

There was another loud knock on the door. The trio all looked on as the footman opened the door slightly and then turned toward the throne.

"Announcing the arrival of Sylvia Jones, Marchioness of the Empire." The footman said as he opened the door.

As the door was opened a woman in a long flowing dress walked into the throne room. She was tall, thin, and beautiful. She had dark hair cut in a bob. Makeup done like a starlet of old Hollywood. Her dress billowed behind her as she walked. She walked with such purpose Amanda found it almost intimidating. She marched up the walk and all the way to the throne; eyes front the entire time. She stopped at the throne and did a deep bow.

"Your Majesty." She said, greeting the emperor, taking his hand and kissing his Imperial Ring. Amanda noticed a touch of southern drawl to her voice. *"How nice it is to be back at the Imperial Palace."*

Edwina hopped off the Emperor's lap as he stood up. Both hands clasping his cane, he bowed his head to Sylvia. *"Madame Jones,"* he said, *"as always Reginridge is brightened by your presence."*

Sylvia, still ignoring Amanda completely, turned toward Cody and outstretched a hand. Cody happily took her hand and shook it.

"How are ya Silvie?" Cody asked, speaking to an old friend.

"I'm doing well darlin', it's good to see you." she replied.

"How's that husband of yours?"

"Ehhh he's a lazy drug pushing sack a shit but what the hell I love 'em anyway."
The pair laughed and Amanda noticed the Emperor's face relax as he watched the interaction. He leant down and scratched Edwina affectionately. He looked at peace.
"Cody," Sylvia said, *"I've been meaning to talk to you... you know those guys... those Republican whatevers, they hit two of our counting houses..."*

"Now is not the time Sylvia..." The Emperor curtly interrupted, becoming stern once again. *"We have other matters to attend to."* Sylvia held her hands up as an apology.

Sylvia turned to look at Amanda. *"So, this is the Amanda I have heard so much about!"* She exclaimed excitedly and gave Amanda a great big hug. *"Baby let me get a look at you!"* Syvlia had a radiant energy of joy about her. Amanda, not entirely sure how to react, stood there awkwardly as the Marchioness held her shoulders and looked her up and down.

"Absolutely beautiful you are baby." she said. *"And what an honor, getting' to join our little family! I hope Cody got you all filled in?"*

"Yes ma'am" Amanda replied sheepishly. *"I hope I do a good job."*

"Ma'am... listen to you, you polite thang. You're gonna do just fine." Sylvia said back with a motherly smile. *"Alright I'm sure you've had a long day, I'm here now... let's get this started."*

"Yes, it's time." The Emperor said and he tapped his cane twice on the ground. As he did, the footmen at the door excused themselves and exited the throne room. Cody ran over scooped up Edwina and placed her on the throne, then ran back to stand next to the Emperor. Sylvia moved herself behind Amanda and placed her hands on Amanda's shoulders. Amanda was facing the Emperor who looked down on her. His face once again solemn.

"Amanda Beasly." The Emperor said, his voice powerful and deep. *"You have been selected by election to serve as knight of the Empire. Do you accept this undertaking?"*

Sylvia leaned forward and whispered the correct response in Amanda's ear.

"I do your Majesty." Amanda replied.

"Do you swear to serve the Emperor as the Emperor in turn swears to serve you?"

"I do your Majesty."

"Do you swear to uphold the central tenet of the Empire, to earn not to take, To defend the innocent and attack the guilty, To turn predator into prey?"

"I do your Majesty."

"Then kneel before your King!"

Amanda bent down on one knee and the Emperor unsheathed the blade hidden within his cane. He placed the blade on Amanda's shoulder *"Pro Corona"* he muttered. He then placed the blade on the other shoulder. *"Pro Imperio".* Finally, he rested the blade on top of Amanda's head. *"Pro Te Ipso".* He sheathed the blade once more and looked down towards Amanda. *"Arise Amanda Beasly.... Knight of the Empire!"*

Chapter 10: Sandra

The task force had decided to have her call the number the District Attorney had given her. The goal was to cut off the head of the snake, irrefutable evidence of the Emperor's criminal activity from the inside. If the DA wouldn't pursue charges, they'd make the evidence public, creating a whole political crisis if they had to.

Sandra had called the number. A voice on the other line simply asked for her name and a location. She once again used the name Stacy Mae and indicated she was at the library on 53rd street. The voice on the other end told her to wait at the corner and then hung up.

Sandra did as instructed. She went outside and found a bench near the corner opposite the library. The crisp fall pierced Sandra's face as she waited outside. It is almost winter now. It took about twenty minutes before Sandra saw presumably the man that was her contact. He stuck out like a sore thumb along the crowd. Pinstripe suit and overcoat, like something out of the 1940s. Sandra pretended not to notice at first. Better to give it a moment and allow things to play out organically.

This guy made no effort to appear inconspicuous, nor did he make an effort to find Sandra. He simply stood across the street, tapping his leg to pass the time. This had to be him. Sandra got up from her bench and cautiously crossed the street, attempting not to seem too conspicuous herself. She made her way across the street and stood next to the well-dressed stranger. Getting closer she could see a ring with the Emperor's sigil on his hand. This was definitely who she was looking for. Sandra turned to look at him. He stayed facing forward. She took the hint and faced forward as well. The pair stood there for multiple minutes locked in silence. Eventually the gentleman next to her looked over at Sandra.

"Stacy??" he asked. Seeming confused.

"Yes. That's me." Sandra replied

"Well what the hell! why did you say anything..." he responded, at first seemed annoyed then amused, snickering to himself. *"Come on walk with me."*

The pair began taking a stroll down the street. The man introduced himself as Cody Chesley but said little else. As they walked, Cody spent a lot of time taking in the old brick buildings of Colonna City's historic district. It was a nice change from the characterless skyscrapers adorning the rest of the city

"I really love this part of the city..." Cody explained. *"My work doesn't get me back here too often."* The walk continued and Sandra found herself looking closer at the buildings as well. Sandra could understand what he was saying. The brickwork did

have an old-world charm about it, at least as close to "old world" as can be found in the western hemisphere.

"So, Stacy Mae..." Cody began, ready to get down to business. *"I take it you're looking for work?"*

"That's right." Sandra replied.

"Well... what are you good at?"

"I can do whatever you need me to."

Cody chuckled. He looked at Sandra with amused mockery. *"Well I'd prefer to do something your good at."* He said jokingly, *"So, let's answer that again."*

"Well..." Sandra said, exaggerating the syllables to allow herself time to think. *"I can fight."*

Cody laughed out loud. *"You fight?!?"* he asked, grinning from ear to ear. *"You look like you just finished a shift at a topless bar for greased up bikers."* He laughed again at his own joke.

Sandra blushed. She forgot she was wearing the dress and all the makeup. She probably did sound ridiculous looking like this.

"I swear..." she said. *"Let me prove it. I can take anyone in the Empire."*

Cody stopped walking. His mild amusement turned to controlled sternness instantaneously. He looked deadpan at Sandra. *"And what exactly do you know about any empire?"* he asked coldly.

"Maybe I'm not as dumb as I look..." Sandra snapped back. She impressed herself with that comeback. Cody looked her up and down. Finally, he

grunted to himself and continued walking. The pair then walked again in silence for a long while.

The pair eventually made it to an intersection where Cody stopped. Traffic whizzed around them. In the midst of the chaos Cody turned and looked toward the street to their right. Sandra followed suit and saw what Cody was looking at.

Towering above the centuries old brick buildings of the historic district, off in the distance was the Latonya Duchant Memorial Museum, the Emperor's front. Columns adorning the outside and a massive dome at its top. It had never really occurred to Sandra before, but it was strange that the zoning board allowed this to be built in this part of the city. Clearly some bribes at the very least. Maybe something for the task force to look into.

Cody turned back to Sandra, who was still gazing at the magnificent building in front of them.

"You know this building?" he asked.

"I do." Sandra replied curtly.

"Well report to the amphitheater tomorrow at 1 PM." Cody responded. *"And we'll see just how well you can fight..."* with that Cody walked off leaving Sandra alone in the buzz of traffic.

The next day Sandra was getting ready. She hated that Cody instructed her to meet midday. She was a morning person. With nothing to do to occupy her mind the anticipation was taking over. As she was getting ready, she was trying her best to be strategic. She knew very little about this Emperor character, but she had gathered that he was a bit of a showboat. So, she opted for tactical boots, and fatigues she had picked up from the army surplus store. He should like that.

She wound her hair tight up into a bun, she was used to that. She looked at herself in the mirror and it was a bit much. Still, she felt more comfortable looking like this than her previous caked on disguise. She was nervous, but not terribly. She could take whoever they threw at her. Probably.

She didn't have a car except for her police cruiser so she would have to take the train. It had been years since she'd used public transit. Luckily her apartment wasn't too far from the station. She had plenty of time. She didn't need to be there for another 3 hours.

She walked leisurely to the station and purchased a ticket. Eventually one of the trains came rattling along and stopped to pick up the passengers. Sandra climbed on with everyone else and found a handle to secure herself for the journey.

As the train clicked through the city Sandra felt a nub on her thigh. She turned around to see an old woman was poking her with her cane. Upon turning around the old woman struggled to stand and proceeded to offer Sandra her seat.

"Please." The old woman said kindly, *"It's the least I can do for a soldier."* Sandra was confused at first but then remembered what she was wearing. She was touched by the old woman's kindness. She politely thanked her and then explained she wasn't actually in the army and she couldn't possibly take her seat. The woman looked confused.

"Why are you wearing that then?" she asked.

"It's just a thing for work." Sandra said sweetly.

The old woman's face turned curious. *"What do you do for work?"* she asked. Sandra didn't answer admittedly because she couldn't come up with one fast enough.

"Oh I see." The woman said her voice more hushed, and her face turning grave.

"What are you talking about?" Sandra asked again.

"I don't judge." The Woman shrugged, *"You guys leave us alone, so it doesn't matter I guess."*

"What do you think I do?" Sandra asked, blindsided by the woman's certainty.

"I'm old dear I'm not stupid," The woman replied, *"I know who wears funny clothes and hangs around this part of the city... But like I said I don't judge."* Thankfully the train arrived at its destination, cutting their conversation off.

Mid-day during the week, there wasn't too much foot traffic in this part of the city. The old buildings of the historic district hosted endless artisan and antique shops that were flooded with tourists on the weekends, towering above them all...the museum.

The Latonya Duchant Memorial Museum and Amphitheatre. It opened its doors not even five years ago. Soon after it began the host location of many of the city's bourgeois parties, fundraisers, and social events. Not exactly Sandra's thing. She had never actually been to visit, all the better now that she knew it was built with blood money. But she heard it was mostly filled with historical exhibitions of old Europe.

The building was even more imposing up close. Marble stairs leading to two great double doors. She entered the building and was immediately caught off guard. The back wall of the reception area was completely covered by an enormous painting immediately visible upon entry. It was a portrait of a woman, slight caramel skin, thick vibrantly red lips poised in a gentle smile. Topped with flowing glossy black hair. She was absolutely beautiful, but the size of the painting made it intimidating. Her piercing green eyes were tearing right into Sandra's soul. It made Sandra uneasy.

Sandra saw a golden plaque next to the painting that read *"In Loving Memory, Psalm 116:15"* She made a mental note to look that verse up later. As she walked toward the reception desk. A tour guide came through speaking with a small group of people. He was very well dressed. Sandra had never seen a tour guide with a tuxedo and matching cane. On his index finger was a ring she felt like she was now seeing everywhere but this one was much larger than the others she had encountered. He caught Sandra out of the corner of his eye. He continued speaking to his audience but never ceased looking at Sandra as he did so. Sandra looking down but keeping him in her peripheral listening in to what he was saying.

"As you can see here..." his voice was coarse and rough, with odd fluctuation. *"Depicted is Mark Antony holding the bloodied robes of Gaius Julius Caesar following his assassination."* He said as he massaged the pocket watch in his waistcoat pocket, eyes still on Sandra. *"See the commoners of Rome worked into an uproar... in their grief they threw weapons, jewels, even their clothes onto the funeral pyre so a piece of them might ascend with their beloved Caesar. And damn to hell vile Brutus and all the senators who plunged their treacherous blades into his heart."* He broke his gaze with Sandra and looked to the ground. This man seemed genuinely upset about the story he was telling, as if he had been there to witness it.

He lifted his head up and continued speaking. Sandra was listening intently now, *"This reaction to the death of Caesar... The subsequent riots and eventual collapse of the Republic. It poses a question to us. Does election run synonymous with consent of the governed? Does being voted in by a democratic system mean you have the people's best interest at heart? Does being an absolute ruler inherently make you evil? For Caesar loved the people of Rome, and they loved him in return..."*

He looked at Sandra once again and politely nodded in her direction. Acknowledging he knew she was listening, then guided the tour deeper into the museum leaving Sandra alone. Figuring out it was time to get down to business Sandra approached the reception desk. A plump friendly woman was sitting behind the counter, smiling politely as Sandra approached the desk, her horned glasses hanging from a beaded string around her neck. Sandra was relaxed at first and then immediately tensed up seeing the brooch on the receptionist's blouse. A sword crossing a trident, behind a crown and all wrapped within a laurel wreath. The Emperor's sigil.

Sandra cautiously asked for directions to the Amphitheatre. The receptionist's face turned from a friendly greeter to puzzled curiosity; she looked intently at Sandra in her combat gear. She then simply jutted her jaw in the direction of a hallway, showing the path. Sandra thanked the woman and went down the hallway.

Cody was at the end waiting for her. He was writing in what looked like a ledger he had rested atop his lap. Upon noticing Sandra enter, he clasped the book closed and stood up. He looked at her outfit and chuckled. *"Well, you certainly look the part!"* he snorted *"He'll like that...."* Sandra grinned to herself. Satisfied, she made the right call.

Cody offered her a seat and sat down next to her. They were on a bench at the end of the hallway. There was a door nearby, she assumed that led to the amphitheater. Sandra couldn't help but notice even this little makeshift lobby was grand. The molding on the wall had intricate scenes carved into them. Sandra traced her finger along one of a man grieving on his knees, an onlooking angel weeping above him.

"All designed by his Majesty." Cody offered, deciding small talk was preferable to silence. *"He designed the entire building, every nook and cranny."* Sandra smiled as she admired the artwork. Regardless of anything else. This was beautiful.

"*Why a museum?"* Sandra asked, still taking in the room around her. *"I've never heard of a museum as a front before."* Cody Scoffed.

"I'll bet you also never heard of a man who runs around calling himself Emperor before!" Cody shot back *"At least not one with an actual army of people at his beck and call..."* Sandra just shrugged.

"His Majesty," Cody continued, seemingly annoyed at Sandra's indifference. *"is very passionate about art and history. He wants to share that love with people... that's why a museum."* he finished his

sentence in a mocking tone, ridiculing what he thought was a stupid question.

"A criminal who likes art..." Sandra mused *"That I have seen."*

"The Emperor is not a....." Cody began, clearly upset. He then regained composure, exhaled from his nostrils and went back to his papers. Not wanting to push her luck Sandra left well enough alone.

After about twenty minutes of silence Sandra could hear trumpets. Faint. Coming from the other side of the door. She also could hear muffled cheering. This must be it. Cody glanced at his watch then jumped to his feet. He snapped at Sandra telling her to come get ready. They both were standing by the door. *"Follow me... and say NOTHING."* Cody ordered. *"I'd tell you good luck... but hopefully you won't need it."*

Cody opened the door which led to a tunnel. Sunlight at the end lit the path. Sandra could hear the music in full force now. Trumpets blasting and drums pounding as they walked through the tunnel. She wasn't sure if it was the insane noise or nerves, but her chest began to tighten.

They stopped about five feet before the tunnel's exit. All Sandra could see was it opened up into a sandy plane. The surroundings not yet visible. Cody looked straight ahead. After waiting for another few minutes, the noise dialed down, and a from the other side called out. *"Now ladies and gentlemen"* it said. *"Escorting a potential newcomer to his Majesty's service.... A Man that needs no introduction..."* Sandra saw Cody straighten his suit jacket and adjust his tie. *"Lord High Chancellor and Grand Marshal of the Empire... CODY CHESELY."* A crowd erupted in applause as Cody's name was announced and the drums and trumpets began again. Cody nudged Sandra forward and the two crossed the threshold.

The crowd was enormous. It had to be almost a thousand people. Positioned circularly around the main level in ascending rows. Cody beamed a great smile and waved to everyone as he walked Sandra along the plane. The main level where Sandra was was a barren flat patch of sand. She saw three other men chained to posts along the opposite wall. They had black hoods tied to cover their faces.

Cody guided Sandra over to the opposite wall bidding her stand in a position where she and the 3 chained men created a semi-circle along the curve of the wall. After he got her into position he ran to the middle of the field. Crowd still cheering, he held a hand up to silence them. An attendant handed him a microphone.

"Friends!" He said into the microphone. His voice reverberated across the entire stadium. *"Thank you very much for your warm welcome."* Another round of applause. Cody smiled at the crowd again before silenced them. *"But I know... there's someone*

you want to see even more than myself!" he exclaimed. Sandra noticed a visible anticipation building on the face of the crowd.

The entire stadium began to rise from their chairs silent as the grave, rigidly upright. Once everyone was standing Cody gestured toward the tunnel, he and Sandra had emerged from not 5 minutes prior. *"Ladies and Gentlemen."* He said, much more professionally now. *"The Emperor!"*

The music played again but it wasn't the same as it had been. A song played that was much more reserved. Violins took prevalence over the trumpets, and the time was slow, the rhythm smooth and reverent. No one said a word. All eyes were on the tunnel.

Two men emerged from the tunnel. Carrying large violet banners embroidered with the Emperor's sigil in gold. Behind them came the man that Amanda had seen giving the tour when she was waiting in the museum lobby. Only now he was wearing an overcoat draped across his shoulders, and a golden laurel wreath on his head. That was the Emperor? Jesus Christ.

Next to the Emperor was a wretched half alive slab of moving flesh, Manacled from wrist to ankle, barely able to move, an iron head casing weighing down his head. He made Sandra's stomach churn. The procession was completed with an additional two banners carried in the rear.

The train moved slowly toward the center to meet Cody, the bannermen marching in step. The Emperor-head held high and face stern-walking in step with his cane, the monster next to His Majesty slumping and dragging his chains alongside his master. As they approached the center Cody knelt down and hung his head. The Emperor gestured to a private box that was right alongside the stadium ground and the bannermen walked over. The Emperor looked down at his slave with scorn and thrusted the heel of his boot into the pitiful man's side. The wretched thing yelped like a struck puppy and scurried over to the box with the bannermen. Now just the Emperor and Cody were left in the middle of the stadium. The music has stopped.

The Emperor looked down at Cody. His face still devoid of emotion. Cody got to his feet and simply uttered. *"Your Majesty..."* The Emperor broke face into a massive smile and suddenly the old friends violently embraced. Squeezing each other with every ounce of strength in their being. The crowd uproared and the Trumpets and Drums resumed again, the mood jovial once more.

The Emperor then proceeded to walk around the perimeter of the stadium. Reaching his hands out for those in the front row to take. The crowd was in a fervor. Gleefully he greeted them in return. Sandra watched as the crowd went insane over this man. Men and women both, acting like a movie star were standing in front of them instead of this oddly dressed crime lord. Sandra did take note of one girl in the crowd though that stood out. Brunette hair hastily combed, she was wearing nice clothes, but they looked scattered together. Shy and unsure of herself she sat quietly among the screeching crowd. As the Emperor approached this girl's section of the stands, she politely took his hand and nodded. The Emperor patted her affectionately on the hand before returning to the middle of the amphitheater. He permitted the crowd to keep cheering but they gradually died down on their own. He took the microphone from Cody.

"My dear darling people," he began. *"How wonderful it is to see you all on such a beautiful day."* he gestured to the sky around them and the crowd murmured in agreement. *"As you all know,"* he continued. *"Belonging to the grand Empire of Colonna, the greatest of honors, may it bring wealth and prosperity and order for us all."* The crowd applauded. *"Building something as beautiful as we have created, is not easy"* his face began to sour. *"There are rules we all must obey. And continually you all make the sacrifices necessary for our continued glory."* The crowd grew hush, as if they knew what was coming. *"And yet..."* The Emperor continued, he was angry now. *"There are SOME who deem themselves above the laws of God and man and believe that the world exists solely to be their plaything."* He spat on the ground and the crowd let out a low deep *"BOOOO."* in unison.

"You all follow the rules!" The Emperor exclaimed *"You do as you should!"* The crowd's anger began to match his. He turned toward Sandra and the men chained to posts *"and these DEFILERS ordain themselves your betters! Refusing to match your sacrifice!"* The crowd now in a frenzy, angrily screaming. *"They have risked our exposure, our honor, OUR GLORY at the altar of their hubris and disregard!"* The crowd was screaming for blood. *"Thieves! Knaves! IDIOTS!"*

The Emperor stopped his tirade, allowing the anger in the crowd to swell. It was then a group of armed men came up behind each one of the prisoners and released them from the poles to which they were fixed and removed their hoods. Sandra's eyes widened.

Two of the prisoners she didn't recognize. But the third. The third was the man she had arrested for reckless driving, the arrest that had started this chain of events. His face was swollen and bruised. He had to be able to recognize her, she kept her head turned away.

"These men were given the same chance I gave every one of you." The Emperor said, his rage replaced with solemness. *"A chance to be a part of a great society, one of fairness and of equity. And they have proven themselves incapable..."* Suddenly he smiled. *"So now they will serve the only purpose they have left... cannon fodder for our entertainment!"* The crowd cheered. The Emperor turned towards Sandra.

"But hold friends!" he exclaimed. *"There is one among these rapacious slugs who wishes to use today's celebration to prove her mettle..."* The crowd *"oohed"* all eyes on Sandra now. *"Madam Stacy Mae has learned of our Empire and wishes to be counted among its ranks! Now we shall see if she is up to the task!"* The crowd cheered and began chanting *"Stacy! Stacy! Stacy!"* It wasn't her real name but still Sandra had to admit it felt kind of good.

"So as our contest begins." The Emperor said. *"Let us see he who would earn his freedom, or she who would earn her place in the sun!"* The crowd cheered again, ready for the show to begin as the Emperor strode to his private box. He sat on a chair placed for him and propped his feet on the kneeling slaves back. An attendant ran up to the box and handed the Emperor a dazzlingly white peacock, who he placed in his lap and began stroking her back. The bird nuzzled into the Emperor's chest affectionately.

Cody, standing next to the Emperor, Reached into his breast pocket pulling out a pistol and raised it high into the air. Sandra looked around. The three other combatants looking nervously at each other, prepped to run. Silence. And then. *BOOM*.

The pistol went off. The crowd cheered as the four spectacles darted from their starting position. *"Okay"* Sandra thought to herself *"be smart about this."*

She did not have time to be smart before one of them came barreling in her direction. A quick jump to the side gave her the much-needed breathing room. Her attacker fell on his face after he missed his dive. She looked over to see the one she knew and the third fighter grappling with each other.

"Good," she thought, *"one at a time."* The crowd hysterically screaming and chanting as her opponent got to his feet, ready to resume his attack. He was way bigger than Sandra, one or two hits was probably all she could take, maximum.

Still, if he was big, she could outlast him. He swung left. She leaned ahead of him. Uppercut. Jump back. Right hook. Duck. After just a few missed blows, he was beginning to waiver. Sandra shot a quick glance at the other two contenders. They were still completely immersed in each other.

Her attention back to the behemoth before her. Punch. Dodge. Punch. Dodge. She could hear his breathing getting labored. Time to counterattack. The crowd roared in amazement as Sandra dealt a low sweeping kick to her opponent's ankle. He staggered but did not fall. Angered by her move. He gathered his remaining strength and charged her full force. She met him with a swift knee to the jaw. He fell forward and groaned in agony.

Writhing atop the sandy surface of the arena floor, another kick to the head knocked him out cold. The crowd cheered frantically. Sandra looked up to see the Emperor clapping gently, a look of smug approval on his face.

Two left. But one of them could expose her. He'd have to be taken care of first. Luckily while she had been taking on the ogre the two others were beating themselves senselessly and were now running on minimal stamina. As they were locked in their duel. Sandra charged.

With the built-up momentum from running Sandra lept into the air and dealt a devastating kick to her former prisoner's side. Already exhausted from fighting, he went down with a thud. Sandra heard a cracking sound. She had definitely broken a rib or two. He would not be getting up. Two down, one to go.

The last one was pitifully easy. Already terrified and beaten, a hook-uppercut combo sent him crashing into the sand. Standing triumphant Sandra turned toward the crowd. They stomped and clapped and shouted. The arena rang out, *"Stacy! Stacy! Stacy!"* emboldened by the praise Sandra beamed and took a theatrical bow. It was an intoxicating feeling.

The Emperor smiled proudly as the crowd carried on. Pushing his slave away with the touch of his boot, The Emperor rose to his feet. Briskly he strode toward Sandra and raised her arm up into the air, canonizing her victory. *"Congratulations."* he whispered into her ear as the crowd roared.

Basking in the glory of the moment, and deafened by the cheers from the crowd, Sandra didn't notice the armed guards approaching the three men lying helplessly in the sand.

"BANG"

What was that?!?

"BANG"

She turned to see guns pointed at the failed champions. *"Stop!"* she blurted out before the final victim was executed, not thinking. The crowd hushed as the Emperor pivoted to face her. His expression was first one of confusion then of intrigue. The executioner looked to his Majesty for a directive. The Emperor gently signaled for him to stand down.

"Stop?" The Emperor inquired. *"Why stop?"*

Sandra had to think fast. But she had been picking up on the way things were done in this so-called Empire. She could get herself out of this.

"Majesty" she said, bowing her head slightly. *"I only meant to say, they are beaten. You have shown them how powerful you are. Shouldn't now you show them mercy ...."*

The Emperor's eyes darted between the last living husk and Sandra. Sandra hadn't even taken the time to notice which one it was. Of course, it was the one she had arrested all that time ago. She would save his life just to sacrifice her own.

The Emperor glanced again. His eyes settled on Sandra. She met his gaze, but the gleam of his golden circlet in the sunlight forced her to avert. The Emperor scoffed at her.

He walked slowly and gracefully to the pitiful man lying in a heap in the sand. The Emperor grabbed him by the rear of the collar and forced him up to his knees. Still woozy from the blow Sandra had dealt he could only remain upright with the Emperor's support. The Emperor stared deep into this man's chest, as if his eyes could peer directly into the soul. He turned toward the crowd.

"Mercy, she says!" The Emperor exclaimed. *"Not even knighted and she is giving council to the Crown!"* The crowd erupted into laughter. The Emperor held up a hand, bidding them to stop. *"Still..."* he said, his voice softening. *"Our savior did preach that we should pity the wicked.... Maybe mercy should be the order of the day."* The crowd immediately began to boo the Emperor in unison. Sandra was taken aback by how quickly these fanatics seemingly questioned their Lords's authority.

The Emperor however laughed in his shrill cackle. Waiving to the crowd they hushed again. *"Yes."* The Emperor said, amused with himself. *"The laws of God dictate we show mercy."* He looked down again at the man whose life was quite literally in the Emperor's hands. *"And as the holy father had mercy and fed the poor... so shall we!"* The Emperor whistled through his teeth and sprinting in came a trio of German shepherds howling and barking ferociously. Stopping at the Emperor's feet they eyed the lump of flesh held at his feet. Sandra's stomach churned as the Emperor cackled, throwing the man to his beasts.

The crowd once again cheered as flesh was torn from bone, piece by piece. Apparently enough life left in the wretch to scream a blood curdling scream as the canines tore him apart. The Emperor watched with glee, standing not even two feet away from the spectacle but the dogs paid him no mind, just gnawing at limbs as blood spurted into the air.

Before long the screaming subsided as the silence of death overtook. The Emperor shooed the dogs away, their coats covered in blood, dripping from their mouths. All that remained was a bloodied mound, nothing that resembled a human being.

Following the events of the arena, Cody had led Sandra back through the museum up to the Emperor's private office. His quarters were not as opulent as the rest of the museum. The walls were plain dark paneling and not adorned with magnificent paintings or engravings. Instead, just a slew of shelves with various books and ledgers hastily scattered about. Alongside the far wall there was a basic rectangular desk. Papers were strewn all around it, the only ornamentation was a small statue with the Imperial sigil sitting atop the desks' corner.

The pair sat at two chairs sitting opposite the desk and waited. If His Majesty had a hobby it would have to be making people wait. It took about ten minutes before the door flung open and in strolled the Emperor, The same peacock which she heard him call Edwina gracefully walking beside him. Cody shot to his feet as the Emperor entered and Sandra followed suit.

The Emperor smiled kindly and waved at them to sit down. Edwina hopped to a perch in the corner of the room as the Emperor removed his coat and tossed it across the back of his chair as he took to his desk. He bent down and Sandra could hear him rummaging through a cabinet. He procured a decanter filled with liquor and three crystal glasses.

"Do you drink?" he asked Sandra, she shook her head no. *"Well, we do."* he responded with a chuckle as he poured a glass for Cody and himself. He and Cody clinked glasses, and The Emperor proceeded to down the entire glass in one gulp. He closed his eyes and had a brief look of pure ecstasy as the alcohol slid down his throat. It had gone as quickly as it had come, and his face returned to its normal shallow and strained state.

"Stacy Mae..." he said cooly, *"Boudica herself bows to your prowess on the battlefield."* He paused for a moment, but Sandra said nothing. He refilled his glass and took another large swig. *"So, what is it I can do for you?"*

"Majesty... am I supposed to call you Majesty?" she asked. The Emperor smiled wide.

"That would be lovely." he chuckled, his face beaming.

"Majesty," Sandra continued. *"I did what you wanted me to do, I proved that I'm capable. All I want is a job."*

"Well..." the Emperor mulled, *"That is what I do, and you clearly do have skill."* He played with the liquid in his glass. He shot a glance at Cody; Cody made no expression. He took another sip of his drink.

"I'm inclined to say yes," he continued. *"I am not one to let talent go to waste.... But I must ask... why did you try to save that heathen?"* his face was inquisitive, genuinely interested to hear her answer.

"I don't know." Sandra said, The Emperor was not satisfied. *"I guess it just felt unnecessary."*

"Unnecessary..." the Emperor muttered. He rubbed his tongue between his upper lip and teeth in thought. *"Unnecessary...."* Sandra looked over at Cody, he began to wince.

"UNNECESSARY!" The Emperor growled, throwing his glass against the wall. It promptly shattered. The impact startled Edwina who leapt into the air and let out a frantic squawk. Cody rushed up to calm the Emperor who was seething.

"Be rational now," Cody said *"She couldn't kno..."*

"Oh she couldn't know!" The Emperor yelled. *"What; do I kill babies for sport!?!?"* He turned toward Sandra. *"I am not a psychotic monster who murders*

without discretion! When I order someone to die you can be rest assured that their fate is well earned!"

"Majesty, I wasn't trying to offend you." Sandra said calmly, years of police work had prepared her for dealing with men of fragile tempers. *"But for all I knew those men were as innocent as I was."*

The Emperor's face managed to turn even more sour. *"For all you knew..."* he said condescendingly as he began caressing his pocket watch, *"I believe you were paraded out to thunderous applause while those three miscreants were bound, gagged and chained to posts. Any idiot with two brain cells colliding could see the disparity in position."*

"Well, what if I had been killed in there?" Sandra asked, keeping her composure, *"Would I have deserved it?"*

The Emperor raised an eyebrow at her. *"What if you had been killed? Perhaps Master Chesley here greatly exaggerated the bravado you displayed on evening last. Or were you not confident that you could defeat three beaten, battered, and barely alive men?"*

"Anything's possible..." Sandra retorted.

"By God your impertinence knows no bounds... IF you had been lying about your abilities and proved unable, I would've stopped it. But the people came to see a show, and I intended to deliver one."

"It seems like they got one so what's the problem?" Sandra said. Cody elbowed to the side. Maybe that last comment *was* a little cocky. *"…. Majesty."* she muttered at the last second.

The Emperor just scoffed and shook his head. He retook his seat and Cody sat down as well. He exhaled deeply through his nose and clicked his tongue. Upon hearing the call Edwina jumped from her perch and waltzed over toward the Emperor, stopping near his feet.

He smiled warmly at the bird as he began to scratch her beak. *"Is this what we did it all for my darling?"* He said, his voice dramatically softened like he was talking to a baby. *"Master of all the land just to be talked down to by plebeians..."* the bird cooed softly as he caressed her.

"Well Ms. Mae..." The Emperor said curtly, not looking up from the bird. *"As I said I am not one to let talent go to waste, corpses or not. You clearly can handle yourself in a battle, I can only pray that with time your attitude becomes more amenable to the Imperial way of life."*

"I will do my best, Your Majesty." Sandra said.

"Well then..." The Emperor said irritatingly massaging his temple, *"I guess we shall need to know your ring size..."*

Chapter 11: Amanda

Amanda stared at the letter on her desk. It had been about three months since the Emperor had placed a blade on her shoulder and christened her a knight of the Empire. She hadn't spoken to him since. Sometimes she thought she may even forget he existed if it wasn't for the gaudy ring adorning her right forefinger. She traced her thumb over the laurel wreath that encompassed the sigil.

Sylvia told her that the sword and trident represented the land and sea, and that the Crown and Empire, the crown and the wreath, lorded over them. It was kind of silly how unsubtle it was. But Syvlia just said it made the Emperor happy, so who cared.

Sylvia was exceptionally nice. She had come back to the warehouse with Amanda and made jokes about how disgusting it was. She took Amanda shopping and helped her get some furniture to make the upstairs area more habitable. She loaned Amanda the money but assured her she wouldn't be charged interest. *"Other members of our little family run that game"* She joked.

Other than that Sylvia came once a week on settle up day. She came and talked to Amanda, she was always pleasant, asked how things were going and so forth. Just all in all-pleasant. Things ran pretty smoothly for Amanda before too long. All the girls already knew what to do, and Frankie lorded over her like a hawk so none of the other muscle gave her a hard time. It was a little patronizing, but she supposed it was a headache she didn't have to deal with so she could be grateful for that.

Her job was relatively simple. She collected all the money at the end of each night and stashed it in a safe. At the end of the week, she took out a cut for herself, for the guys, running the building and for Syvlia. The rest she redistributed back to the girls based on how many clients each had gotten and that was pretty much it. Everyone knew their role, and it was a small operation. Things just worked.

She has set some money aside and had slowly been sprucing up the derelict warehouse, so they weren't all living in complete squalor. One of the guards knew a guy that sold her cheap cots that were a serious improvement over the mildew riddled ones everyone had been sleeping on. It was startling to her how easy they were to get. There was more than enough money. Pump really was one greedy son of a bitch.

All together things were going relatively smoothly, and Amanda was settling in well. Not too long after she had been knighted, the Emperor had forced her to go to this insane gladiator match that was meant to punish some people who had made him angry. She really did not like it; it was not her thing. But there was this woman that was there fighting, Amanda had to admit, she was magnificent to watch. The way she seemingly effortlessly obliterated the other men forced to fight, Amanda wished she could do something like that. The Emperor had given her a kind smile at the event, but he didn't speak to her. She hadn't heard from him at all, until today when this letter bearing his seal found its way to her room.

She sat, debating whether or not to open it. She knew she would have to eventually. But things were going well, what if it was bad news? Why break the silence all of a sudden if it weren't bad news. She remembered what happened last time she saw someone get direct correspondence from his Majesty. Taking a deep breath, she took the scroll and broke the wax seal, unrolling it to read its contents.

My Dear Child,

As far as I have been made aware you have been settling into your new role quite well. Marchioness Jones has nothing but compliments to share on your regard. You will find that those under the banner of Imperial Protection frequently see their loyalty rewarded. As it happens, Master Chesley and I are attending a banquet tomorrow evening at my museum. We would be beyond honored if you would join us as our valued guest.

Regards,

Edward von Drac
Imperator Rex, Colonna City
All honorifics etc. etc.

Amanda had mixed emotions about the invitation. It seemed like a genuine gesture, but she wasn't quite relaxed around the Emperor. The evening would be stress inducing. She couldn't understand him. Those close to him, like Cody and Syvlia seemed totally unafraid of him at all. But she has seen his temper in action. The psychotic look that formed in his eye when he got violent, hidden beneath his thick aristocratic veneer.

"What's that?" Frankie asked her, Amanda hadn't even noticed him walk into the office.

"It's nothing." Amanda said, placing the paper into a drawer on her desk *"just an invitation to some party.... What did you want?"*

"Nothing." Frankie replied, *"Just checking on you."*

"Well I'm fine thank you." She said she knew he was trying to be nice but sometimes it was annoying. She pulled out another paper from her desk and proceeded to pretend to be busily studying it.

"Well if you're all good..." Frankie said, a twinge of disappointment in his voice as he began to walk away.

Amanda started to feel guilty. *"Wait Frankie,"* she said, he whirred back around. *"You never told me how you met him..."*

Frankie's face lit up as he quickly took a seat in the office. *"Well"* he said, *"Right place right time I guess, or wrong place wrong time."*

"What do you mean?" Amanda asked, genuinely curious.

"Well I grew up on the street like a lotta people" he explained, *"and I had this crew of me and a few guys we did small jobs, nothing crazy just thinking we were badasses. Anyway, one night we were hitting this corner store near the residential district, stupid shit. We checked to make sure no one was around, slipped the lock, busted the safe made out with the cash and whatever else we could fit in our arms."* he chuckled to himself as he recounted the story. *"We were walking out and we didn't even see them at first."*

"See who?" Amanda asked.

"These guys all in black, came out of the shadows like Ninjas, beat the ever loving hell out of us." Frankie told her, *"We didn't stand a chance, they were pros, broke at least three of my fingers."* He caressed his left hand as he spoke. *"They tied us up and threw us on the corner and just stood there silently. It musta only been like twenty minutes but it felt like hours, no idea what was going on. Then outta nowhere this limo pulls up and who gets out but the Emperor, fancy suit, cane, everything. His goons did the whole bowing and scraping thing like you've seen and he came up and crouched down to us."*

Frankie paused and looked down, lost in thought trying to recollect. *"He started saying something, one of his droning speeches, I can't really remember what it was I was so piss scared. But at the end he had his men cut us loose and told us we had a choice. He said we could put the stuff back and come with him or we could continue being thieves. I froze, I was so terrified and thank God I did."*

"Why?" Amanda asked.

"Because my boys took off and bolted. They made it about two seconds before he snapped his fingers, and my friends were chased and beaten unconscious right in front of me."

"Jesus" Amanda gasped. Frankie chuckled in response.

"Yea it was a lot to see." he said, *"anyway after that he turned back to me and reached a hand out to me and helped me up. He put me in his limo, took me back to Reginridge and gave me a job cleaning with the maids."*

"Cleaning?" Amanda asked, biting her lip to try not to smile.

"Go ahead and laugh." Frankie smiled *"It was ridiculous. But he had me work and he fed me and I had a bed. Then one day, after a few months, he took me down to the basemen... have you ever been there?"*

"No." Amanda answered. *"I've only been in the big hallway and I guess his throne room."*

"Ah," Frankie said *"Well the basement is his dungeon, just lined with old iron cells. Whole place stinks like death. I doubt they clean the corpses out of there more than once a year. Real horror movie type stuff. Anyway- he took me down there to one of the cells and inside were the guys I used to run with, beaten, starving, barely alive. It was disgusting. He said I had done well working at the palace and I was free to go, but to always remember what happened to thieves."*

"What happened after you left?" Amanda asked, *"How did you wind up back here?"*

Frankie smiled. *"I never left."* he said, *"I had nowhere to go, nothing to do. So, I asked him if I could stay instead and keep working for him. Maybe something a little better than hall boy. He looked me up and down and handed me a gun. He told me if I wanted to stay and serve the crown, I had to prove all old allegiances were null and void..."*

Amanda's eyes widened. *"You didn't..."* she whispered.

Frankie just shrugged. *"They were dead anyway..."* he replied softly, almost reassuring himself more than Amanda. *"He let me work as hired muscle, gave me a salary, more money than I'd ever made before, gave me different jobs, mostly just walking around people and looking scary. Then Pump came on the scene, and the Emperor didn't like him at all. So he sent me here to keep an eye on things, and here I've been ever since."*

"How well do you know him?" Amanda asked.

"I don't know," Frankie mulled. *"Better than some people, but I wouldn't say we're close. I don't know if anyone besides Cody is actually close to him."*

"Well, what should I do about this?" Amanda asked, showing him the invitation. Frankie took the paper and read it over.

"What do you mean?" he asked. *"You should go, it'll probably be fun."*

"But I don't know how to act." she replied. *"I don't know what he wants."*

"Just act like yourself. He won't care." Frankie replied.

"He doesn't seem like the kind of person who doesn't care about things." Amanda shot back.

"Trust me," Frankie said. *"It's not a test. He's weird and loves the pomp and circumstance and all that but he's just trying to do something nice."* He handed the invitation back. *"But if you're that worried about it. I can go with you, so you have a friend in the room."*

"No, that's okay." Amanda said, *"I'm sure Sylvia will be there, and she can help me out, I guess. Plus, it'll be better if you're here since I'm going to be gone."*

Frankie got up from his chair, annoyed. *"Alright"* he said. *"I gotta go get ready for tonight. Have fun at your party."*

It was the day of the Emperor's party. Amanda didn't have time to get a new dress. So, she dug up an old cocktail dress from back when she would entertain the occasional high end client. It would have to do. She looked at the black silk that had felt like a lifetime ago though it had only been a little over a month. It was insane how much things had changed. Even the room she was in now. Two months ago, she dreaded walking through the doors and into Pump's clutches. Now it was where she felt safe. She hoped the other girls didn't hate her for her new position, but she didn't think they did. How could they? They were the ones that put her here. But still she wanted to do right by them. They were her friends.

Sylvia offered to give her a lift since Amanda didn't have a car. She came promptly at seven in the evening. Amanda was always impressed by how Syvlia stunned everywhere she went. The warehouse had been improving but it was still a derelict building. Yet somehow Syvlia threw the door open her flowing royal blue chiffon dress billowing around her arms and a giant smile as she entered, greeting all the girls on the main floor. It brightened the whole place up. Her energy was infectious; she stopped and talked to everyone asking how work was saying if they kept it up there'd be room in her club for more dancers soon. She managed to lift everyone's spirits even

Amanda felt her nerves settle when Sylvia was around. Amanda came down the stairs, heels clicking on the concrete floor as she stepped.

Syvlia threw her arms up at the sight of Amanda. *"Look at you darlin'!"* She exclaimed. *"You'll be the envy of every woman in attendance!"* Amanda blushed and Sylvia came up and gave her a great big hug, the metal of all her jewelry cold on Amanda's skin. *"Well let's get to the car sugar plum, we better not keep all the boys waiting."* Syvlia blew kisses to all the girls on the floor as Amanda waved goodbye. They all seemed happy, a relief.

Syvlia guided her outside to a car that was waiting for them. A man in a tuxedo was waiting to open the door for them. Amanda quickly noticed an Imperial ring on his hand. *"Amanda Beasly, I want you to meet Mr. Harold Jones."* Syvlia said with a big grin as she jumped almost on top of him and planted a big kiss right on his mouth. *"My husband."* Harold gave Amanda a polite nod and shook her hand before opening the door to the backseat for her. Syvlia climbed into the front and Harold sat behind the wheel.

As the car drove along, the radio softly hummed some pop song Amanda hadn't heard before and Sylvia swayed her head to the music, occasionally playfully nudging Harold with her elbow. Feeling awkward in silence, Amanda tried to make conversation.

"So how long have you guys been married?" she asked.

"Five years in May." Harold responded. His voice was very deep. He took Syliva's hand and kissed it gently. *"Still the best decision I ever made."* Syvlia smiled at him affectionately.

"He was so shy about it, too the big baby." Syvlia joked. *"I had only been giving every sign I could think of to get him to ask... thank GOD he finally did."*

"I'm not good at that sorta thing." Harold replied. *"The whole time I was thinking I'd ask and she'd say no and I'd lose her forever."*

Syvlia turned in her seat to look at Amanda. *"Honey, we had NO money back then it was crazy. I was a two-bit Tallahassee whore, and he was selling dime bags of weed for pennies. We musta been the saddest couple you've ever seen."*

Amanda smiled *"Knowing you Sylvia, I really don't believe that."* She said,

"You'd be absolutely right." Harold added, *"Even back then she was an absolute ray of sunshine. I worked for this absolute dick dealer, and it sucked, I took home barely any money, the Emperor had just taken over so things were in complete chaos. It was a mess. But Sylvia made it all worth it..."*

Sylvia frowned, remembering. *"It was a rough time, I mean you know for girls like us it always is..."* She looked at Harold again. *"But then he would hold me and..."* she closed her eyes remembering the feeling. *"He'd hold me and all my problems would just vanish if only for that moment."* They kissed again.

"It was just us against the world for a little while..." Harold said *"We had this ratty apartment in the eastern part of the city. Enough money to eat and a bed.... Then as things went on his Majesty made some changes and we wound up here, fancy people with titles and money and cars and all the rest of it."*

"And I wouldn't want it any other way..." Syvlia said, placing her head on Harold's shoulder for the rest of the drive.

They pulled up to the museum where an attendant was waiting to take their car. Sylvia took Harold by the arm, and the pair entered the building with Amanda following behind. Amanda had never been to the Emperor's museum before, but his house had prepared her for the grandiosity of it. It was all overwhelming the marble floors, the opulent columns, the art that adorned the walls. Amanda felt like she was walking through a fairy tale. People were everywhere and Sylvia knew most of them. She and Harold worked through the crowd greeting people and thanking them for coming. Amanda followed awkwardly behind. Thankfully, before too long a concierge found them and guided them toward the banquet area. *"I'm sorry we didn't introduce you to anyone."* Harold whispered as they walked. *"If they were anyone worth knowing we would have."* he gave Amanda a playful slug on her arm.

They were led into the banquet hall which was set all with tables looking toward a stage. They were directed to a table at the back of the room where Cody was waiting for them. The Emperor was not there. Hands were shaken and cheeks were kissed as everyone sat down. Wine was brought to the table.

"So Amanda," Cody began, *"How are you settling in?"*

"I think things are going well." Amanda replied, taking a sip of wine. *"I hope Sylvia agrees."*

Sylvia rolled her eyes overdramatically. *"My God this one is modest!"* Sylvia exclaimed *"Cody you remember what that dump looked like before you should see it now... and hounding that pig for money I think that was taking years off my life."* She caressed, imagined wrinkles as she said this. *"Mandy is doin' great!"*

Cody lifted his glass up to Amanda. *"To success then,"* he said. The others followed suit and took a drink. It was then that the woman Amanda had seen at the gladiator pit came up to the table. She was wearing a dazzling red dress, almost giving Sylvia some solid competition. Cody introduced her to Amanda as Stacy Mae, the Emperor's new bodyguard. Stacy politely took Amanda's hand and announced to the table that the Emperor would be arriving shortly.

Amanda was curious about Stacy. She had seen her completely dominate in the arena. But here she was not in combat attire or at least combat attire of a different nature. She was beautiful. Not the bubbly full of life beautiful that was Sylvia but a stern, reserved, powerful beauty. She scared Amanda a little bit. As the table talked around her and the general buzz of the room commenced, Stacy sat silent and statuesque, eyes locked on the stage at the head of the banquet hall.

The lights began to dim and the conversations slowly started to hush. A spotlight shone toward the stage, illuminating its center. The room filled with applause as the Emperor stepped out onto the stage waving toward the crowd. His suit was more toned down than usual, but still unique enough to be the most audacious man in the room.

As the crowd applauded, he alternated between bowing, waving, and putting his hand over his heart. Amanda chortled to herself, God this man loved attention. As the crowd simmered down, The Emperor approached a microphone placed on the stage.

"Wow!" He exclaimed, gesturing out like a game show host. *"The richest men in Colonna and they give so much applause for a poor peddler of history."* The crowd laughed as he said his quip. *"We have with us here tonight, land developers, bankers, tech moguls, whatever those are."* another bout of laughter. *"And other great captains of industry.... And*

of course, me... who's going to try and rob you all blind!" One final round of laughs. *"In all candor though,"* The Emperor said, calming the crowd. *"The Latonya Duchant Memorial Museum has been able to educate tens of thousands of visitors on the history, art and literature of worlds long left behind. And it is thanks to all of you. "So please enjoy a nice dinner, a lovely concert and dig deep into your generous pockets."* As the Emperor finished his speech, an army of waiters emerged into the dining area with silver trays delivering everyone their meal. Smoked salmon with a salad.

The Emperor approached the table with a grin. Everyone rose to greet him as we warmly shook Harold's hand and gave Sylvia a kiss on the cheek. He glanced over at Amanda and dipped his head into a bow. *"I am so glad you were able to join us this evening."* he said.

As he took his seat between Cody and Stacy, Cody affectionately patted the Emperor's arm. *"Very well said sire,"* Cody offered.

"Oh, I agree," said Syvlia. *"Another successful fundraiser seems on the horizon."*

The Emperor raised his glass as the table followed suit. *"If these spoiled pricks have to have money, let's at least get our share."* Sylvia, Cody, and Harold laughed as everyone drank the Emperor's toast. *"You see Ms. Beasly..."* the Emperor said, placing his glass on the table *"you are surrounded tonight by nepotism made flesh."* he gestured to the large room of wealth around them. *Here we sit the brave and noble few, drowning in a raging sea of daddy's money."* he chuckled at his own joke.

"I am very grateful you included me sire." Amanda said sheepishly. *"But I shouldn't judge anyone here."* The Emperor smiled politely but had a look of disappointment in his eyes. He muttered something under his breath, but Amanda couldn't hear what it was.

"That's very wise..." Stacy added while sipping her wine. *"No one truly knows anyone's full story."*

The Emperor, who had been cutting his salmon slammed his knife into the table. He exaggeratedly shot his head in Stacy's direction. *"Do you find joy in making me angry?"* He asked sarcastically. *"To have an underling contradict me at every turn. And that I should tolerate it...."*

Stacy smirked, Amanda bit her lip but noticed Coady, Syvlia and Harold were all trying their hardest not to laugh.

"I am merely asking your Majesty if you honestly think that none of these people are here of their own merit..." Stacy offered, *"though of course if I have offended you by asking a question, I do apologize."* As she finished speaking, she looked smugly back to her plate and casually placed a piece of salmon into her mouth.

"Are you so easily fooled by shiny shoes and an expensive handbag?" The Emperor retorted,

glaring at Stacy. *"These people are all here solely because they profited from the work of others. Maybe they've acquired their own fortune, but it was only possible because they were given education paid for by another, or as they were forming their enterprise, another took care of their basic needs, allowing them to pour themselves into their work. They are no more cunning than the lowliest of gutter rats, merely born into more prosperous circumstances."*

"So then how come you were able to do it?" Sandra asked, still looking at her plate. *"Do you not count yourself among these fortunate few?"*

The Emperor chewed his food for a moment, contemplating Stacy's question. *"Allow me to reverse your question."* he finally replied, *"If their system is so honest and equitable; why did you have come to me for sustenance?"* He continued chewing. His last remark stuck in Amanda's mind.

Cody chuckled triumphantly at this reply. *"I think he's got you there."*

"Alright enough!" Syvlia exclaimed lightheartedly, *"We could be listening to the music but instead I can only hear bickering! Now we're all here, we got dolled up, let's just try to have a nice time."*

"Now there's an example you may want to follow." The Emperor said, gesturing toward Sylvia. *"Of course we shall Madam Jones."*

The table fell silent again, Amanda was relieved. She took a bite of the salmon, it was delicious. A steady diet of takeout had made her forget what a real meal tasted like. On the stage there was a band with a singer. The music was slow and sweet. Amanda caught herself swaying gently with the rhythm.

She looked around the room to see everyone happy in each other's company. Some couples were dancing. Others are just content to sit in each other's presence and watch the show. How easy their lives seemed in this moment.

"Oh, I love this song!" Syvlia exclaimed as the singer began the next selection. *"Harold Jones, you get your bald ass up and you dance with me this instant!"* Harold chuckled as Sylvia practically dragged him to his feet. It was then that Syvlia looked at Amanda and smiled softly. *"You know Cody,"* she said. *"As much as we all love His Majesty's company... I bet Amanda could do with a dance herself."* Cody blushed as the Emperor scoffed to himself.

Sylvia cocked her head and raised an eyebrow. *"So how about it?"* she asked.

Cody exhaled. *"Screw it, why not."* he said, *"If Amanda wants to..."* He stood up and held out a hand to Amanda.

"Sure." Amanda said, gently taking Cody's hand as he guided her to her feet. *"Why not."*

"Oh Goodie!" Syvlia said as she clapped her hands together. *"I love to see people having fun!"*

Cody turned toward the Emperor. *"I'll be just over there sire, if you need me."* He said.

The Emperor placed down his fork and waved him off. *"No, no you kids go have a good time."* he said. *"I trust Marie Antoinette here can keep an eye on me, for which she is handsomely paid."* He jabbed a thumb rudely in Stacy's direction. She made no reply.

Cody rolled his eyes and patted the Emperor on his shoulder before leading Amanda out to the dance floor. *"I promise I'll make this as painless as possible."* he said to her. Amanda just smiled politely following his lead.

Amanda noticed how the crowd had silently made room for him as he led her onto the floor. They found a spot where he spun her to face him and placed a hand upon her waist. Together the pair swayed gently with the music. Cody was being kind and patient to her.

"I'm sorry I'm being so stiff." Amanda blurted out. *"I don't know what's wrong with me... you'd think by now I could dance with a man."*

Cody didn't reply at first, just continued gracefully guiding her through the music. *"I'm not a client,"* he said finally. *"And you're not in that line of work anymore. If you're feeling uncomfortable, we can go back."*

"No." Amanda replied, leaning in closer. *"You don't make me uncomfortable at all... all of this... it's*

just so overwhelming." They continued swaying. *"I just don't get it. Any of it."*

"To be honest." Cody said. *"I don't either a lot of the time. But it makes him happy, so I'll do it."* He glanced back at the Emperor's table as he spoke. Amanda looked too, to see the Emperor, watching Harold and Syvlia dance, he was smiling, the first time she'd seen him really smile all night.

"He really means a lot to you." Amanda observed.

"He means a lot to a lot of people... and they mean a lot to him." Cody answered. *"But yea, he does mean a lot to me. So, if he wants to be called Emperor and have galas like this, I'm all in."*

"How did you two meet?" Amanda asked.

Cody just smiled. *"Let's just enjoy the song."* He said, pulling Amanda closer and spinning her with the music. She found herself relaxing as the song went on. She felt safe in Cody's arms. There was something about him. She was no stranger to men being nice to her. But they always wanted something in return. Cody, Cody just seemed genuinely nice. She leaned into his chest as the music played, enough to hear his heartbeat. He gently placed his cheek against hers. Together, they danced.

Before Amanda knew it, three other songs had passed, and they were still on the dance floor. Cody's head shot back towards the table. *"We better go back."* he said abruptly. *"Just to make sure he hasn't stabbed that poor bodyguard yet."*

Amanda laughed at his joke. *"She's newer than me, isn't she?"* Amadna asked. *"You have to kind of admire her courage to talk to him the way she does."* Cody smirked.

"I don't know." he mused. *"Part of me wonders if she doesn't know exactly what she's doing..."* He led Amanda back to the table where the Emperor and Stacy were sitting.

"Amanda my child," The Emperor said. *"I hope Master Chesley was as graceful with his feet as he is affairs of state."* He took a big swig of wine from his glass.

"He was very kind sire." Amanda replied sweetly. *"It's nice of you to worry."*

"What do I do anymore but worry." The Emperor moaned, finishing his glass. He placed it toward the edge of the table as a waiter quickly rushed to replace it. *"But to worry is my responsibility. I'm glad you were able to find some merriment in the evening."*

"I'm sorry sire, if I seem ungrateful." Amanda said. *"It's just all these new surroundings; it's a lot to take in."*

"You have nothing to apologize for!" The Emperor hastily responded, his words beginning to slur slightly. *"The grandiosity of our way of life is new and foreign to you. But soon you will grow*

accustomed to it..." He placed a hand gently on top of Amanda's arm, and he looked at her with that soft caring gaze she had seen power through his sickly exterior before. *"As you have every right to."* He said, withdrawing his hand and returning to his plate.

It was then that one of the guests approached the dinner table. He was young with suave hair. Chest puffed out and shoulders rigid, he marched to the table with such confidence it had caught Amanda off guard.

"Eddie!" He exclaimed as he walked up to the table. The Emperor, completely disinterested, lackadaisically stood up and shook the man's hand. Cody followed suit.

"Amanda," The Emperor said, *"This is Harmon Martin, one of the most up and coming corporate lawyers in Colonna City..."* He side eyed Stacy and smirked, *"...following in his father's footsteps."* he added. Stacy rolled her eyes.

Amanda stood up and greeted the Lawyer. *"I'm pleased to meet you"* she said, outstretching her hand. He took her hand and pulled her in close to shake. She wasn't certain but she could faintly feel him sniffing her hair.

"The pleasure is all mine." he said as he kissed her hand. *"Any friend of the Emperor is a friend of mine."*

The Emperor cleared his throat. *"I haven't the faintest idea to what you are referring sir,"* he said through a forced smile *"I am merely a humble purveyor of the past."*

"Right" Mr. Martin answered, tapping his nose. *"Of course." "Anyway, Mr. Von Drac, I won't keep you. I just wanted to thank you for your invitation and for a delightful evening. My fiancée and I have had a wonderful time."*

"Fiancée?" the Emperor inquired, *"When did this happen?"*

"Oh, a little while back." The lawyer answered. *"I'm getting to be that age and dad said it was time to settle down..."* He turned toward Amanda. *"But I'm not married yet..."* he whispered as he slipped his hand down and squeezed her buttock. *"Hopefully I'll see you at the bachelor party."*

Amanda jolted in surprise. She heard a clanging and turned to see the Emperor violently holding Cody's wrist to the table. *"Well Mr. Martin as you said, you don't want to keep your fiancée waiting."* The Emperor said calmly with a smile. *"It was very kind of you to say hello."*

"Of course you're right." Mr. Martin said, adjusting his tie. *"Goodnight Eddie."* with that he turned and walked away. Amanda quickly sat down. Not wanting to appear phased she just paid attention to her plate. Glancing from her peripheral she could see the Emperor and Cody locked in a silent argument. The Emperor's eyes have taken on that psychotic look Amanda had become increasingly familiar with. She looked at Stacy for some kind of

guidance but all the woman could offer was a soft smile full of pity.

"I'm sorry that happened." Cody muttered once he and the Emperor had finished. *"It wasn't right."*

"Oh, it's nothing." Amanda replied, attempting to laugh the entire situation off. In all seriousness it hadn't bothered her that much, she's experienced far worse. *"Really I'm not worried about it."*

"It's very far from nothing." The Emperor said Amanda wasn't sure if he was talking to her or to himself. He was angrily scratching his pocket watch. *"Impropriety of the highest degree, the gall... and at my dinner table...."* he trailed off until he snapped his head in Stacy's direction. *"You see?"* he said sternly gesturing to the entire crowd. Stacy held up her hands in defeat.

Exhausted by the whole affair and not wanting to make it worse, Amanda turned her head to watch the crowd. Syvlia and Harold were still on the dance floor. Her royal blue dress billowed and furled dreamily as Harold spun her on the dance floor. Amanda looked on with longing, swaying her head to the music that filled the hall.

Chapter 12: Sandra

Everyone walked silently to the Limousine following the gala at the Museum. Cody and The Emperor in the back, Sandra up front. They argued like children the entire ride home. Cody had been livid about that lawyer copping a feel on that girl Amanda. Sandra had felt bad herself. It was obvious the poor girl was in way over her head. Hell, she felt like she had gotten in way over her own head.

She didn't know why she was naturally so obstinate with the Emperor whenever they spoke. It was beyond counterintuitive to her task. Yet at the same time, he never punished her for it. He'd make some snark comment about *"insolence!"* or *"the effrontery of it!",* she imagined his ridiculous mannerisms in her head, it made her chuckle, but he never actually did anything. She wasn't the only one either. She noticed how his closest confidants continually made fun of him or argued his ideas, where the lower ranks were sycophantic in their admiration for the man who called himself king. On paper it seemed like the wrong course of action, but it felt right.

When they returned to Reginridge after the Gala the Emperor stormed through the front door, Sandra had to walk briskly to keep up. She was surprised to see an entirely separate party happening at the Imperial Palace. Not refined or sophisticated, like the event at the museum, but a nightclub rave.

There were strobe lights, loud music, people were drunkenly swinging each other around in the entrance hall. Completely juxtaposing the silent, grandiose, overbearing demeanor the house typically presented.

Party or no, footmen in full dress were still attending each doorway in anticipation of their Monarch's return. Upon entering the hall, a footman had run to the Emperor and peeled back his plain black overcoat, replacing it with an intricately embroidered violet one, and a feathered hat to match, much more similar to what Sandra had grown used to seeing him in.

Still fuming, the Emperor did not break pace as this was happening, instead forcing the poor footmen to run behind him as they facilitated his change of attire. After he was dressed the Emperor was handed a cane. Once the transformation had completed the Emperor finally stopped, he ceased atop the landing of the main staircase in the central hall, Shoulders propped up hat cocked back, glaring down at the festivities before him. His arrival was not announced in its standard fashion, and with the loud music and raging atmosphere, no one had even realized he had entered the house.

He stood silently staring at all of them. Slowly they began to become aware of his presence. The music was turned off, the flashing lights halted, and the dancing ceased. Standing dutifully beside the Emperor, still in the red dress he had provided her for the occasion, Sandra looked out to the crowd, there had to be at least one hundred people staring back at them, almost in awe. She glanced back at the Emperor who was sternly meeting their gaze.

"You all must be hungry." noted coldly. *"Pizzas will be here within the hour... fifty should do."* The crowd cheered and the party resumed in full force. The Emperor turned sharply toward a nearby footman. *"See that it's done. Then you all can retire for the evening."* he commanded before marching up the stairs, opting to use his cane instead of the railing for balance. The footman scurried off to fulfill his emperor's request.

Sandra began to follow the Emperor up the steps when she felt a hand grab her wrist. She twirled around to see it was Cody. He simply shook his head and nodded for her to follow him down a separate hallway. She took one last look up the stairwell. The Emperor was far enough up to be engulfed in shadow, she could only make out the silhouette of his coat and hat. As he neared the top. There was another silhouette waiting for him. Frail and shaking, poor wretched Mr. Charteris. Sandra saw the Emperor give him a swift backhand before dragging him down a hallway, out of sight.

She followed Cody through the corridors of the house. Far enough away that the deafening rave had become a soft rumble. He led her back into an office and plopped himself on the desk. *"Pull one of those chairs up"*. He said, *"take a load off."* He leaned over until he was practically laying on top of the desk, trying to reach a drawer on the opposite side. He fumbled around until he procured a crystal decanter of whiskey. He poured himself a glass and went to pour a second before he stopped himself.

"Oh that's right." he smirked, placing the decanter on the desk, *"You don't drink."*

"I don't know how you drink all day." Sandra said. *"Between the two of you, there's enough alcohol to kill an elephant."*

Cody chuckled and shrugged. *"Practice I guess,"* he said as he took a sip. *"Well can I get you anything?"* he asked. *"I'm sure I can scrounge up a soda somewhere in this castle."*

"I'm fine." Sandra replied. *"But if I could take my heels off that would be nice."*

"Yea yea, sorry sorry." Cody choked out, waving her off. *"Of course, please no one's gonna come in here and I don't care."*

Sandra loosened the strap that held her shoes to her ankle. Sweet freedom. Cody followed suit and unbuttoned the wrists on his shirt and rolled his sleeves up. *"Well Stacy Mae,"* he said, raising his glass. *"Here's to you."* Unable to return the sentiment, Sandra awkwardly flicked Cody's glass to mimic the clinking sound.

"What exactly did I do?" she asked awkwardly.

"You ma'am have solved one of life's great enigmas in record time..." Cody said, taking another swig. *"making the Emperor trust you."*

"Trust me?" she asked, *"I'm pretty sure he hates me much less trusts me."*

Cody rolled his eyes. *"You can stop playing stupid now,"* he said. *"You've been here just over a month, and he already has you glued to his hip... And your little combative attitude, we can all read it for what it is."* He lifted an eyebrow at her accusingly.

"I'm sorry what?" Sandra asked, *"What exactly are you talking about?"*

"You're flirting with him." Cody said bluntly. *"I'm not judging. You aren't the first one to try it, but I will say so far, you're the best. Still, it isn't going to work."*

"I am not flirting with him or anyone." Sandra said sharply. *"When I am speaking to him, I am just expressing my opinion."*

"Suit yourself." Cody said coolly. *"It doesn't matter, that's not what I wanted to talk to you about. The point is he trusts you."* He pointed a finger at Sandra and beamed a grin like an artist who had just found his missing paintbrush.

"Okay let's entertain your logic for a second." Sandra replied. *"You just said it wasn't going to work so what do you mean he trusts me?"*

"I mean..." Cody said condescendingly *"He definitely is intrigued by you. But he'll never give you what you want. You work for him."* He stood up and squared his back rigid. *"And such a thing would be a disgraceful abuse of power for a King-Emperor."* he said, mocking the Emperor's voice and demeanor.

"And what is it I want Mr. Chesley?" Sandra inquired in reply.

"Please..." Cody said sarcastically. *"The same thing they all want. You see the money and the prestige, and you think if you can play it jussst right he'll give you a ring besides this one."* He fronted his Sigil ring and tapped it with his thumb. *"Then everyone will be scraping and bowing to you just as much as him."*

Sandra scoffed. *"I have a set of skills"* she retorted *"and this is where my skills will reap the most benefit. That is why I am here, nothing else. Anything else is just reflective of some deep seeded cynicism of women on your part."*

Cody seemed wholly unphased by this statement. *"Only the ambitious ones..."* he replied softly. *"But stop distracting me for a moment and listen. I... we need your help with something."*

"Whose we?" Sandra asked.

"The Imperial Council and I." Cody replied. *"Normally the Emperor will listen to our advice, but there is one issue that he has been unusually obstinate about, and it's becoming a bigger and*

bigger problem the more he ignores it. I think you're just the person to get him to see reason."

"What problem?" Sandra asked, leaning forward in her chair.

Cody got up to his feet and started pacing. *"There's a group out there..."* he began to explain, *"they call themselves the Republican Regiment... They started out as just a gang, a couple guys doing small time hits, nothing we couldn't handle. They'd rob a shop under our protection, stupid shit like that. The Inquisitors would hunt them down; we'd execute them and think that was that."* He turned to face Sandra. *"Except we'd never get them all, and they just keep coming back...."*

"I'm sorry..." Sandra interrupted. *"Inquisitors?"*

"Yea the Royal Inquisition." Cody said, almost shocked that Sandra had even asked. *"Wear all black... look like ninjas... hunt down enemies of the Empire... super culty and scary?"*

"This whole operation is a little culty." Sandra remarked.

"You know they've got a bone to pick with you." Cody said slyly. *"Before you came along, they were in charge of the Emperor's security."*

"You don't scare me Mr. Chesley." Sandra replied, refusing to take his bait. *"Now continue the story... the Republican Regiment."*

"Right right right." Cody said massaging his forehead. *"So, the Inquisitors would hunt these guys*

down, but one or two would always get away and they'd hit us again. Eventually the rumor mill got to work and now there's a group that's able to challenge the Empire's position and live."

"Just barely." Sandra grunted.

"Sometimes just barely is all you need..." Cody mused. *"This probably isn't a shock to you, but there's a lot of criminals out there who don't like the Emperor's rules, Now these people have a beacon to flock to."*

"So what's the Emperor doing about it?" Sandra pressed.

"Therein lies the problem." Cody said, Sandra could see him getting visibly upset.

"He won't do ANYTHING other than sending the Inquisitors after them and the problem has passed that point." he took a deep breath *"Look, I'm asking nicely, and it's not just me, it's Sylvia and Harold and all the others. Just talk to him, see if you can talk him into taking more aggressive action before this whole situation gets completely out of hand. He won't listen to us but maybe he'll listen to you."*

Two days had passed since the Gala. Sandra had not found an opportunity to bring Cody's request to the Emperor's ears. He was always wandering around the house, talking to someone in hushed tones. Whenever Cody was with him, he would glance in Sandra's direction but all she could offer was a defeated shrug to Cody's annoyance.

It was not for a lack of trying. She followed the Emperor everywhere, trying to gather information. He had become increasingly agitated by it, nothing new when it came to Sandra. She simply dismissed it as her job as his bodyguard. As diligent as she was, the man was just never alone. He was with Cody most of the time, whispering about something. But in between he would wander to various parts of the house. He would go to the kitchen and declare to the cook he *had to escape to some sanity* and work from there for an hour grumbling to himself. Then he would get up and go to the courtyard and go to the great hall, where footmen and maids were cleaning. He'd proceed to talk to them about cleaning products for another hour.

Both days at lunch he would have his chauffeur drive him to the museum. He always insisted on giving the midday tour in person. He had put his foot down on Sandra coming with him to the museum claiming *her looming was too distracting* and that the patrons deserved his undivided attention.

When he would return, he would go right back to his routine of switching between business with Cody and socializing with the staff. When evening came, they would all sit down to dinner. Sandra had seen many bizarre things since infiltrating the Empire, but dinner had to be the strangest.

The Emperor's dining room matched the grandiosity of the rest of his house. A long mahogany table covered in a purple velvet runner and lit with candles. His Majesty refused to eat alone and always had a multitude of guests, but they varied in quality. Always there was the Emperor, sitting in full dress at the head of the table. Jacket, waistcoat and cravat neatly pressed in his standard regal fashion. But around the table there was a mixed collection of men and women, some dressed up, some not. Some try to mimic his manners, others not. It was never the same group of people twice. The Emperor, however, was completely unbothered by any of it. He was always sure to be the last to join the table and the first to leave. He did insist that everyone stand as he came into and left the room. Other than that, and the fact everyone ate on silver plates brought out by staff, the dinners were very similar to a family reunion at Grandma's house.

The Emperor would go around the table and ask people about their interests. He would feign disapproval declaring *"Such things are beneath the dignity of a monarch!"* and then immediately proceed to ask more questions. It was also the one time of day he was not consistently berating Sandra, albeit mostly because he was distracted. She found the whole thing sweet in a weird way. His Majesty was without a doubt a cold man, habitually in a bad mood. But during these private dinners a faint yet clear warmness broke through. A genuine interest and concern that was rare in Sandra's experience with the criminal element.

The whole thing was massively frustrating. Cody said he trusted her, but Sandra had yet to see the Emperor do anything even remotely illegal. The closest thing was the hours he would spend pouring over his ledgers which Sandra knew were for illicit activities. But the Emperor wasn't stupid enough to put anything substantive in writing, and of course the money was all laundered through legitimate businesses anyway. She had sent word to the Commissioner about the Emperor ordering the men at the arena killed. But she didn't know what they had done with the bodies nor would anyone present even think of testifying. It was borderline useless information. Hopefully this Republican Regiment business would prod his Majesty into more overt action that Sandra could use as evidence.

The following day was when Sandra's opportunity came. She was wandering around the palace, almost resigned to defeat. Until she glanced out of a window, to see the Emperor strolling through the garden, his only company Edwina the peacock. She bolted down the stairs and out the door, not wanting to miss her chance.

She slowed down as she got close to the Emperor. He had not yet become aware of her presence. He walked slowly through the field as his bird kept pace. He looked out to the lavender bushes and softly grinned. He had reached a stone bench where he sat down, admiring the view. His faithful companion right alongside. Sandra walked up cautiously, the Emperor paid her no heed. He sat and rested both hands on his cane. Edwina jumped and flapped her wings to fly up onto the bench.

"Look at this treasure my darling." he said, nuzzling the peacock. *"This Xanadu we have created together, you and I…"* Edwina cooed softly. Without looking up, the Emperor's face turned to its traditional scowl. *"Yet even now they will not give us peace…"* he said, gently closing his eyes. *"What is it you want Ms. Mae?"*

Sandra cleared her throat. *"I was sent to your Majesty with a request…"* she eked out. The Emperor smirked. He scratched Edwina on the head before scooping her up off the bench and placing her on the grass.

"Go on, my darling." he said to the bird. *"Daddy has business to attend to."* Edwina turned her head toward Sandra. Her black eyes almost pierced into Sandra's soul. It made Sandra uncomfortable, as if the bird could see through her facade. The bird approached her cautiously. Sandra froze, unsure of how to react. Edwina then nuzzled her leg and wandered off into the field.

"You may sit." The Emperor said curtly, looking off into the distance as opposed to Sandra. She took a seat next to him on the stone bench.

"You're very fond of her." Sandra observed.

"And why shouldn't I be?" The Emperor shot back sharply. *"If this house burned to the ground, all my wealth and fortune gone to dust, Who else would I have but her?"*

"I'm sure that's not true." Sandra replied. *"What about Cody?"*

"Master Chesley is an honest and true man." The Emperor mulled, massaging his pocket watch. *"But he has his own life and motivations, just like you all do."* he let out a deep sigh. *"I am your priority only so long as I provide tangible value." And who knows what the future holds..."*

"I think that's why most people start a family." Sandra suggested. *"Why don't you consider that?"*

The Emperor reached into the breast pocket of his jacket and quickly produced a small revolver. *"If you're here to pry into my personal affairs..."* he said calmly, gun pointed at Sandra's head. *"I can shoot you now and save us both the time."*

Sandra exhaled slowly as she placed a hand atop the barrel of the gun and gently lowered it. *"You don't need to be so dramatic, we're only talking."* she said as the Emperor returned his firearm to his pocket. *"That's not what I wanted to talk to you about anyway..."*

"Well spit it out quickly." The Emperor growled. *"While there's still a chance I can salvage my free afternoon."*

Ignoring his rudeness Sandra adjusted the strap of her dress, she was still getting used to wearing dresses all the time. *"I was sent on behalf of a few of the Marshals."* She said, *"They wanted me to talk to you about this Republican Regiment thing."*

The Emperor scoffed and leaned into his cane. *"I'm sure they did."* he said mockingly. *"They aren't very happy with me on that front."*

"Can I ask you something?" Sandra asked.

"You seem to be incapable of anything else." the Emperor said. *"Go ahead."*

"You're clearly no stranger to violence." Sandra noted. *"And here you have people openly defying you... it doesn't fit your usual MO."*

"My modus operandi?" The Emperor chuckled. *"Are you building a psychological profile now?"*

Sandra froze momentarily, realizing silence would only make her more suspicious; she quickly blurted *"just answer the question."*

"You aren't false in your claim." The Emperor said calmly. *"Violence is a very effective tool, but also a volatile one."*

"What do you mean?" Sandra asked.

"Fear will keep people in line." The Emperor elaborated. *"But there must be order..."* He stood up and began to pace. *"The second an undeserving person gets hurt on my orders; fear turns to paranoia. Suddenly no one cares about following the Empire's rules because that no longer is a guarantee of safety.*

It's the surest way to lose any power I may have accumulated" He turned to look Sandra in the eye. *"Not to mention..."* he continued. *"I wouldn't be able to live with myself if I willingly hurt an innocent person."* He looked to the ground and continued walking in the garden...

"I have no choice but to trust the Inquisitors." he said. *"I despise these hopeful usurpers every bit as much as my council does."* he spat on the ground. *"But I will not invite chaos in an attempt to preserve order. I will not harass and abuse those that have given the crown their loyalty..."* He turned his back toward Sandra. *"They deserve better than that from their king."* he muttered almost to where Sandra couldn't hear.

"Okay." Sandra replied. *"I understand your trepidation, but there has to be SOMETHING we can do. You aren't stupid, this needs to be stopped before it gets out of control."*

"We?" The Emperor remarked. *"There is no we. I am Emperor, and I will handle the situation how I see fit."* He paused for a moment, massaging his pocket watch. *"But I will take your words into account."*

Sandra stood up slowly and gave a short bow. *"Your Majesty."* she said, excusing herself. She turned away and began to walk back to the house.

"Stacy," The Emperor called out softly behind her.

"Yes sire...?" Sandra responded, turning on her heel.

"That girl Amanda that you met at the Gala..." The Emperor said, running his hand through the lavender bushes. *"How do you think she'll fare here, with us?"*

"I didn't speak to her much..." Sandra replied, *"but with you to guide her, I'm sure she'll be just fine."* She said with a smile. Sandra saw that hint of warmness come across the Emperor's face again as she backed away.

"Get UP! Get UP!" Sandra felt someone violently shaking her. She jolted awake. She looked at the clock next to her bed and saw that it was 10:30 PM. She looked up to see the Emperor looming over her, still fully dressed. *"Honestly woman."* he scoffed. *"Whose asleep at 10:30 at night?"*

"Someone with their priorities straight..." Sandra mumbled as she wiped her eyes. *"What do you want?"*

"We have work to do." The Emperor replied. *"Get up and get dressed."* He snatched the silk blankets from atop her. *"I've taken the liberty of selecting something appropriate."* Sandra heard the clanking of chains as Mr. Charteris limped into the room, his manacled hands bearing folded garments. He hobbled to the Emperor's side, back hunched and chains dangling from his wrists. The weight of his iron

mask always forcing his head to hang low. Bearing the clothes while he was draped in rags, Mr. Charteris used all of his strength to look up at his master.

The Emperor turned to his tortured servant. *"Just place them on the bed and remove yourself cur."* he said while rolling his eyes. *"Or do I need to instruct you on how to breathe as well?"* Looking back to the ground, Mr. Charteris did as he was bid. Placing the clothes on Sandra's bed and turning to leave. Slowly yet desperately labouring toward the door, he did not get far before the Emperor discreetly used his cane to trip Mr. Charteris onto the floor. The clang of metal crashing into the hardwood floor sent a shiver down Sandra's spine. The Emperor merely chuckled as he reached down and grabbed the chains that bound Mr. Charteris' ankles.

"Don't take long, we have work to do." he said to Sandra. *"I'll be waiting outside."* He then tightened his grip and strode out of the room, dragging his victim behind him. Sandra quickly got dressed. The Emperor had selected a blouse with jeans and boots. A far cry from the elaborate dresses he usually had her wear, but far more comfortable. She laced up the boots and headed out into the hall. The Emperor was standing there, Mr. Charteris on the floor at his heels, struggling to breathe. A mixture of pity and unervedness swelled up in Sandra's stomach.

"Ah good!" The Emperor said, clapping his hands upon seeing Sandra *"dressed for battle."* He eyed her up and down pure delight on his face. He

turned toward Mr. Charteris. *"We'll be leaving now. You may go."* he said as he mockingly shooed Mr. Charteris away. Mr. Charteris gave his typical painful moan in response and attempted to move away. The Emperor over exaggeratedly rolled his eyes. *"Faster than that, you fool!"* he scoffed, picking the decrepit man up by the yoke of his rags. He heaved Mr. Charteris down the stairs. Sandra winced each time the chains clanged against the marble steps until the long fall ended with him motionless at the base. The Emperor grinned maliciously.

"Jesus Christ..." she muttered under her breath.

"What?" The Emperor asked. Beginning to walk down the stairs. His cane tapping the marble as he walked.

"I just don't understand you." Sandra said, following him down the stairs.

"Well, it's a good thing I don't require you to understand anything about me other than the orders that ring from my lips." The Emperor replied.

"Why are you so cruel to that poor man?" Sandra asked. *"No human being deserves that."*

"How astute you are Ms. Mae." The Emperor answered. *"Indeed, no human being does deserve it. It's a good thing Mr. Charteris has devoid himself of all humanity."*

"I've seen you show a lot of love to people." Sandra argued. *"You treat everyone in this house like*

they're your flesh and blood. You're clearly capable of a great deal of love."

"Flesh and blood are arbitrary things that people place far too much emphasis on." The Emperor retorted curtly. *"Every member of the Empire is my family and I their patriarch, I love them accordingly. It's that love that sees Mr. Charteris treated the way he is."*

"You love every member of the Empire?" Sandra inquired sarcastically. *"You wouldn't know it the way you treat some people. Me for instance...."*

The Emperor made no reply instead quickened his pace to place distance between them ending their conversation. Sandra followed him out of the palace past the large statue fountain in the drive and to a small separate structure she had never noticed before, tucked behind a cluster of trees. Two inquisitors in all black stood guard at the entrance, a large garage door. They gave the Emperor a deep bow as he approached and proceeded to pull on a rusted chain and pulley system that opened the door.

Inside there were two vehicles. Sandra immediately recognized the Emperor's limo, sleek and black, the Imperial sigil adorning the hood. Next to the limo was a van. It was blacked out and beaten up. It looked like anything someone could find on the street, save one thing. A hood ornament identical to that of the limo. Glistening and polished.

The Emperor reached into his pockets and procured a set of keys. *"I trust you have the ability to drive."* he remarked as he tossed the keys into Sandra's hands.

Sandra quickly caught the keys. *"You can't drive?"* she asked with a smirk.

The Emperor promptly scoffed. *"I am King and Emperor."* he replied as he opened the passenger door of the van. *"It does not behoove a monarch to drive, ability notwithstanding."* he said, climbing into his seat.

Sandra took the driver's seat and started the van up. The engine roared to life and the lights glared into action. She pulled the vehicle slowly out of the garage and onto the drive. *"It would help to know where I am going."* she said.

"You and your incessant inquiries!" The Emperor scolded. *"Get to the city and I will tell you where to go!"* He folded his arms in disgruntlement *"Honestly..."* he whispered to himself amid angry mumblings.

The van pulled away from Reginridge and headed toward Colonna City. The ride to Colonna was quiet. Sandra focused on the road in the darkness. The Emperor sat silently beside her. Hand in his waistcoat pocket, caressing the watch within.

"Why do you do that?" Sandra finally asked.

"Do what?" the Emperor asked, glaring in Sandra's direction.

"Rub your pocket watch like that." Sandra elaborated, still focusing on the road. *"I see you do that all the time. What's it about?"*

"Why do you always ask moronic questions?" The Emperor grumbled, quickly rescinding his hand from the pocket and folding his arms. *"Just drive."*

The van carried on into the night. Soon the bright skyline of Colonna City was visible. As they entered the city limits The Emperor began giving Sandra instructions on where to go. Before long they ended up in the entertainment district. The Emperor guided her through the streets, winding up at a nightclub. Neon lights illuminate the surrounding area, showcasing a sign that read *Madame's Mansion.*

Sandra pulled into a parking spot. *"This... this is a gay bar."* she observed. The Emperor opened his door and began to climb out.

"Technically it's a Drag Queen Show Palace," he retorted. *"I DO like that they call it a palace...."* he remarked with a smile as he walked toward the door. Sandra hopped out and ran to catch up with him. *"I just find it surprising that we're going to a place like this."* she said.

"Oh dear..." The Emperor sighed. *"I had no idea you were quite so intolerant."*

"I didn't say anything bad." Sandra argued. *"It's just surprising for someone of your sensibilities."*

"My sensibilities as you say...." The Emperor replied. *"They lie with those who are loyal to the Crown and Empire. How they choose to express themselves in their private lives is of very little consequence to me."* They had reached the door. The

Emperor placed his hand on the door handle. *"So do try and keep your mouth shut while we're inside."*

The Emperor opened the door to reveal the inside of the establishment. There was a large dim area with lounge tables all facing toward a stage. To the right of the building was a bar. Smoke filled the room. Partially from the burning cigarettes of patrons but also smoke machines Sandra noticed at either end of the stage. Directly inside the door was a massive bouncer.

"IDs..." the Bouncer said rudely, not looking up. The Emperor simply leaned onto his cane and cleared his throat. The bouncer looked up and his face turned to immediate horror. *"Majesty!"* the bouncer declared, stepping into a frantic bow. *"Please excuse me, you honor us with your presence."*

"It's quite alright." the Emperor snorted. *"If my booth is open my companion and I will be glad to see Madame DuBois' show."*

"Of course, sire." The bouncer replied. *"I hope you and your date have a nice time."*

The Emperor blushed at this response. *"Date is a strong word,"* he said coldly. *"But I thank you for your hospitality."* He then strode off into the building without a word to Sandra who had to run after him. The club was buzzing with loud music and flashing lights. Sandra followed the Emperor to a table tucked off into the corner but closest to the stage. He sat down and placed his hat upon the table.

Sandra sat down beside him and flattened her pants. She noticed how he continually winced at the music. His movements were subtle and restrained but he was still visibly uncomfortable. His eyes darted around at the neon and the scantily clad personnel. It was clear he missed his cold marble floors and imposing stone walls.

As a waitress in drag came up to the table The Emperor snapped together and instantly looked relaxed. An instant transformation. *"Majesty,"* the waiter said with a smile, leaning over the table. *"Isn't this a pleasant surprise. Should I tell the Madame you're here?"*

"Oh no no no." The Emperor scoffed, waving the notion away. *"I'd hate to interrupt the show; we can just keep it a pleasant surprise I think."*

"Well, she'll be glad to see you." The waitress replied. *"And who is this beautiful thing?"* she asked, turning toward Sandra.

"This is my new bodyguard, Stacy Mae." The Emperor answered, gesturing in Sandra's direction. *"A fiercer fighter you'll never find."* Sandra smiled politely and nodded in recognition.

The waitress eyed Sandra up and down. *"I'm sure..."* she muttered with a sly smile, adjusting her wig, and giving the Emperor a sideways glance. *"Well here I am talking, not doing my job... I'll be right back with your drink sire. And what about you sweetie?"*

"What about me?" Sandra asked.

The Emperor heaved a great sigh. *"What do you want to drink, you imbecile..."* he groaned massaging his temple.

"Oh I don't drink." Sandra said politely to the waitress. She looked at she confused, unsure of how to proceed.

"Just get her a soda before I shoot her right here and now." The Emperor growled.

The waitress giggled and rubbed the Emperor's solder affectionately *"I'll be right back."* he said as he walked away, heels clicking on the floor. He looked back and flashed Sandra a quick wink.

"You don't have to be so mean all the time." Sandra scolded. *"What are we even doing here anyway?"*

"We are HERE to meet with a Marshal of the Empire." he replied, massaging his pocket watch.

"Here?" Sandra asked. *"Were meeting a Marshal of the Empire here?"*

"Well seeing as she... or he... whichever, owns the establishment it would make sense." The Emperor answered.

"Wait, let me get this straight." Sandra prodded. *"One of the Marshals of the Great Empire, ordained by God and moon and June and pomp and circumstance and all the rest of it.... Is a Drag Queen?"*

"That would be correct." The Emperor said, tongue in cheek. *"Now do be quiet because here she comes."*

The lights inside the bar dimmed, spotlights shone towards a sequin curtain covering a stage. The music turned down and the talking hushed. A feminine voice came over the speakers.

"Ladies, gentleman, and everything in between." It said, *"You've paid your money. You've had your drinks. Now put your hands together for the main event.... Introducing MADAME DUBOIS!"*

The bar erupted in applause as Madame DuBois emerged from the curtain. A red velvet gown and black heels. Her makeup done in the typical comically overstated fashion of drag queens. A large wig gave her elaborate red curls. Pop music blared over the speakers as he went into his routine. As the song livened up, backup dancers came onto the stage and Madame DuBois ripped the gown from her body revealing a form fitting red bodysuit. Sandra looked over to the Emperor who was watching the show, his face bearing an expression of polite amusement.

The song and dance finished to ravenous applause from the crowd. Madame DuBois gave gracious bows in every direction thanking the crowd for their adoration. She turned in the Emperor's direction and saw him and Sandra at the table. She froze on the stage with widened eyes. Her hand went up moving the crowd to silence, her eyes locked on Sandra and her table.

"Well bless my soul..." Madam DuBois said into the microphone. *"All the way from Reginridge his*

Majesty the Emperor deigns to visit my humble home."

The Emperor waved in his typical fashion and blew a kiss to the stage.

"Ladies and Gentlemen, our gracious patron has taken time from his busy day to come and see the show. The poor man hates this nightlife, but he comes anyway because he loves us. Let's give him a hand!"

Applause filled the room once again as the Emperor stood up beaming a great smile, waving to everyone in attendance. Sandra, staying seated, smirked. *"You just can't help yourself, can you?"* she whispered as he sat back down.

"If they're happy to see me, who am I to scorn?" The Emperor replied smugly.

A stagehand came running toward the stage. In his hands was a folded piece of violet cloth. Madame DuBois quickly took it and unraveled to reveal a silk dress, deep purple and the bust adorned with the Imperial Sigil.

"Alright guys and gays lets classy this place up." she exclaimed as she performed her impromptu costume switch. She snapped her fingers and the music faded from pop into an orchestra. Adjusting her new dress, Madame DuBois once again took hold of the microphone.

"For you, exalted Emperor." She said with a deep bow. She then delved into a rendition of a song in perfect French. The Emperor's eyes were closed

and he swayed his head gently with the rhythm. His fingers tapping his watch to match the beat of the song. Sandra wasn't absolutely sure, but she thought she spotted a tear roll down his cheek. She couldn't blame him. The song was beautiful.

After the song had finished the Emperor sprang up from his seat and gave a standing ovation. The crowd followed suit. He proceeded to jab Sandra with his cane and gestured for her to follow him. He led her to an area backstage. Sandra heard the muffled sounds of Madame DuBois announcing a brief break. It wasn't long before she came bursting backstage as well, wig in hand scratching her scalp. Seeing her up close Sandra noticed she wore her Imperial Ring on a necklace as opposed to on her finger.

She approached Sandra and The Emperor digging in her brazier, eventually pulling out a cigarette. *"So what did you guys think?"* she asked.

"Absolutely enchanting as always." The Emperor replied sweetly. *"You give Sylvia herself a run in the beauty department."* He took the lighter to light the Madame's cigarette for her.

"Oh I don't know about that." Madame DuBois replied. *"Sylvia's gotta be the most beautiful woman I've ever met.... Present company excluded"* she offered halfheartedly to Sandra. The Emperor snorted.

"Where even are my manners?" she continued outstretching a hand to Sandra. *"By day*

they call me Steven Grenner. But by night I am..." she quickly put her wig back on and gave a little twirl. *"The Illustrious Madame DuBois."*

Sandra took her hand. *"It's nice to meet you... ma'am?"* she said, unsure of her answer.

Madame DuBois laughed heartily in response to Sandra's awkwardness. *"Don't worry about it baby you won't ever catch me on a picket line, you can call me whatever you want I don't care."*

Sandra exhaled a sigh of relief. *"So what is it you actually do for the Empire?"* Sandra inquired.

"You mean you can't tell?" Madam DuBois joked. *"Honey I'm the best arms dealer in the state. Come on, follow me."* She showed Sandra and the Emperor out a back exit which led into an Alleyway. In the dark there was a large green commercial dumpster. *"You picked a perfect time to come."* Madam DuBois said, *"We just got some great new hardware."*

She snapped her fingers and one of the bar's employees walked over to the dumpster and lowered the front panel. The entire thing had been rebuilt to act as a display case for firearms. Shotguns, Handguns, Rifles, all handcrafted, shiny. Sandra was impressed. *"So, what interests you?"* Madame DuBois asked.

The Emperor smiled wide. *"Oh, it all interests me."* he remarked, caressing one of the shotguns. *"But today I'm picking up my bulk order.... No this is for my security."* he pointed to Sandra. *"Go ahead,"* he commanded. *"Pick out whatever suits you best."*

Sandra's eyes got big. This was way higher quality than anything she had access to as a cop. She combed through the options. The cheapest gun here had to be worth over $1,000 and that was assuming one was buying it legally. She finally settled on a 20-gauge sawed off shotgun. Mahogany finish, with silver trimmings.

"Excellent choice." Madame DuBois remarked. *"Portable yet packs a punch... Majesty, if you give Elena your keys she can pull your van around and we'll load your order."* The Emperor obliged and reached his hand out to Sandra who handed him the keys. He tossed them to the employee who ran to get the van. Madame DuBois began closing up the dumpster display case when the Emperor interrupted her.

"Perhaps you might gift wrap that for me." he said, pointing to a small silver .380 handgun. *"I know someone who could make some use of it."* Madame DuBois gave the Emperor a curt bow as she picked up the gun he selected. Soon after the van was being backed down the alleyway. The back doors swung open and an army of drag queens began loading multiple wooden crates into the cargo area.

"Jesus," Sandra noted. *"Are we arming a militia?"*

"Not a militia..." The Emperor replied. *"A Grande Armée."* The crates were loaded and the door

slammed shut. The Emperor turned and kissed Madame DuBois on the hand, handed her a massive assortment of cash and walked toward the van.

"Stop the bastards!" Madame DuBois called out as Sandra started the engine, holding a hand over her heart like a mother watching her son leave for war.

"Oh I intend to...." The Emperor whispered, but only Sandra could hear.

The Emperor had directed Sandra through the city to their next destination. Sandra spent a lot of time glancing down at the new weapon The Emperor had just gifted her. It's polished barrel gleamed in the city lights. The Emperor caught her gawking. *"I'm glad you like it."* was all he had to say.

The pair stopped at an old office building in the finance district. The outside was unassuming, any typical office space. Though Sandra did notice the Imperial sigil etched into the wall near the door. Inside there was a different story altogether.

The inside of the humble building held more money than Sandra had ever seen in her entire life. Mounds upon mounds of bills. There had to be enough money in this building to fund a small nation. Workers were moving frantically in yet the most streamlined fashion. The process was well regimented even upon first glance. Movers ran the money to counting machines. Men operating the counting machines recorded the numbers in extensive ledgers. Once counted the money was stacked and wrapped into concise packaging. Once stacked and sorted there was another team stacking the money into boxes, presumably for delivery. The organization was impeccable, yet the sheer volume was inviting chaos.

"It's something isn't it." the Emperor commented, full of pride.

"There's no way." Sandra remarked, aghast at the scale of what she was seeing. God if she had a camera right now. *"And this is just one counting house?"*

"Alas I wish it were so." The Emperor answered. *"But I had all of the Empire's revenues routed here this week, to be accounted for."*

"But that's insane." Sandra observed. *"All of your money in this building that's hardly defended... You're basically inviting an attack."*

"Precisely." The Emperor responded with a smug grin. *"This Republican Regiment.... These radical rebels. They only know greed. Once word of this treasure trove got out of course, they will come."*

Sandra absorbed the Emperor's words and remembered the crates of weapons in the back of the van. *"You're baiting them."* she said. *"You want them to come."*

"Now you're thinking." The Emperor said. *"The sad part is how easy it was. Any idiot would be able to discern that this was a trap, but these fools so*

consumed in their lust for my property they won't be able to resist." He flicked the barrel of Sandra's weapon, *"Do keep that new toy of yours close,"* he said. *"I am sure you will need it before long."* Sandra tightened her grip on her new shotgun.

One of the money counters came up to the two of them. *"Sire."* he said with a bow. *"Thank God you're here. Some of the guys were getting anxious."*

The Emperor placed a hand on his shoulder. *"Benny."* he said, *"How many years have you known your Emperor, and when has he ever let you face the enemy alone."*

The man called Benny put his hand atop the Emperor's *"Of course Your Majesty..."* he responded confidently.

The Emperor rapped his cane on the concrete floor to get everyone's attention. The work ceased as the horde of men running the operation flocked around their leader. Sandra noted a yearning present in their eyes. Eager to sop up any wisdom their lord had to offer.

"Ladies and Gentlemen." The Emperor began, straightening his back and propping his shoulders in regal fashion. *"You all know the importance of what is to take place tonight. The enemy marches against us. They are sloppy, they are disorganized, but they are also ruthless and therefore must not be underestimated."*

"Tonight you guard the entirety of the Crown's treasury. The barbarian hordes will come for it, and

we shall drive them back into darkness. You will be defending not only the fruits of your labor but that of all who call the Empire their home..." The Emperor picked up one of the packaged money boxes. *"It seems unfair I know..."* he continued. *"That you shall have to face the fury of the Hun and others do not. Therefore, once the enemy is routed every one of you will be taking one of these parcels home in addition to your standard pay... a small gift from a grateful nation."* Cheers rang out as the Emperor tossed the box into the crowd.

Quickly everyone got to work unloading the weapons crates and arming themselves. Magazines loaded, bandoliers of bullets were adorned. Suddenly a group of money grubbers became a militant force beyond reproach. Middle managers became lieutenant colonels directing their squadrons to cover all potential entrances inducing air vents. Quiet fell over the building. Everything was ready, all that was missing now was the target. All the newly minted soldiers were crouching behind cover ready for action. In the center of the room, standing tall, was the Emperor 9mm in one hand, his cane in the other.

"Remember soldiers," he said. *"We need one to interrogate.... But only one."* He leaned down to Sandra, who was ducking behind an upturned table used as a barricade. *"Do try to survive,"* he whispered. *"I've started getting used to having you around."*

Sandra smirked back at him. *"Someone will still have to keep your ego in check after this is over. I guess I have no choice."*

"Here they come!" shouted a sentry keeping eyes on one of the windows *"I count six cars, maybe more. Be ready for a fight!"*

"Take cover everyone!" Benny yelled. *"FOR THE EMPIRE!"*

The main door was kicked in and the gunfire started. Shots whizzed all around the room. Sandra held her fire. Amid the initial chaos no one could see anything right now. This was suppressive fire, best let the automatic weapons handle that. The force of the bullets sent money flying into the air, sprinkling down like confetti, obscuring everyone's vision. Sandra took a deep breath, keeping her cool.

Her eyes darted continuously between the windows and any vents a human being could fit through. If these guys had any level of tactical thinking the frontal assault had to be just a diversion. Her suspicions were realized when she saw a vent grate kicked from its casing on the ceiling. She lifted her gun and fired. A body came crashing to the floor, lifeless in a pool of blood.

"THE VENTS!" Sandra screamed out as she kept scanning. They were coming in faster now, multiple vents at a time. She fired as fast as she could but could not cover them all. Luckily a few

imperial soldiers heard her cry and turned to provide her cover.

She ducked back behind her table as she refilled the magazine on her shotgun. While she was ducking, she heard the shattering of glass. They must be coming through the windows now. She took a deep breath and emerged from her cover. The defenses were still holding but they were pouring in from all sides. She saw the Emperor wrestling with an assailant who had charged him. The two grappled with the Emperor at a clear disadvantage physically. His attacker on top of him pressing a knee to his throat. Sandra moved over to help but before she could get there the Emperor reached out for his cane, extracting its hidden blade and stabbing his would-be assassin clean through the throat. Blood spurted as the attacker fell dead on top of his Majesty.

The Emperor shoved him off and retrieved his gun. He turned and lunged toward Sandra. *"GET DOW.... AGHHH!"* He had shoved her out of the way just in time. A splash of blood shot out of the Emperor's back near his shoulder blade. Sandra turned quickly and unloaded two shells into the shooter. The Emperor collapsed to the floor. Sandra rushed to his side. *"NO NO!"* He ordered, waving her away with one hand clutching his shoulder with the other. *"I'll be fine, protect the men!"*

Sandra did as she was commanded and continued scanning any points of entry. All of the windows and vents were littered with dead. The men guarding the main entrance had been pushed back. Sandra slid further up the battle line. Heavy gunfire was still coming in. She ducked and waited. They would have to reload eventually. Then there it was, a brief silence. She quickly emerged and began unloading shells. 4 shots, 4 bodies fell to the ground. The remaining attackers bolted back out the front and scrambled into their cars. The gunfire ceased. The battle had been won.

Sandra whipped around to see two men helping the Emperor to his feet. With the support of his cane he was able to stand on his own, but blood still seeped liberally through his shoulder. *"Where's Benny ?!?!"* He growled, gritting his teeth through the pain of his wound. *"I need a casualty report!"* Sandra ran over and took his arm trying to help him walk. He shoved her to the ground with a surprising strength for someone who has just been shot *"I said I'm FINE!"* he roared. *"Now where is Benny ?!"*

The room grew quiet as Sandra realized what had happened. Sitting up against a wall of the building was Benny, one bullet hole in his cheek, another in his abdomen. The Emperor rushed over to him but fell in the process. Sandra once again ran to him, lifting him up and assisting him with moving. This time he did not fight her. She walked him over to where Benny sat dying.

"Ma.. Ma.. Majesty." Benny choked, blood pooling in his mouth. *"I failed you...."* The Emperor knelt down with Sandra's help and sat on the floor. He drug Benny off of the wall, placing the dying man's head in his lap.

"My dear dear boy." The Emperor said with a solemn smile. *"It's I who has failed you... Go now my son, your new master is waiting.... And he's far more deserving of your loyalty than I have been."* With a final sigh Benny heaved his last breath and drifted off into eternal sleep. The Emperor gently closed Benny's eyelids and placed his forehead against the now deceased underling's. *"Please tell me we at least got one."* The Emperor whispered, his eyes closed in mourning.

"Yes, sire we did." A voice answered. *"He's just over here."* Laying Benny's corpse down softly onto the ground the Emperor reached out a hand as Sandra helped him to his feet. They were led to the captive.

The prisoners' wounds were all superficial. He was being restrained by two Imperial soldiers. He was covered in blood, but basing from his wounds it was not his. As the Emperor approached him, he spat in the Emperor's face. One of the soldiers swiftly socked him in the gut in response. The Emperor took his handkerchief from his breast pocket and wiped the spit from his face. All he really achieved was smearing blood across his cheek as the handkerchief was bloodied from his wound. *"His hand..."* The Emperor said. *"Give me his hand."*

The two men restraining him obliged and forced forward the prisoner's hand. The Emperor promptly took the blade from his cane and sawed through the prisoner's thumb. The screams were agonizing. The knife was not serrated so the process took multiple minutes. Sandra suspected the Emperor preferred it that way.

Once he was done the Emperor commanded his men to let the prisoner go. He promptly fell, writhing in pain. Using his cane to steady himself, the Emperor kneeled beside him, flicking the prisoner's severed thumb back in his face. *"You have ten more extremities I can cut."* The Emperor said, his face turning to that characteristic fanatical rage. *"And the next one won't be a finger."* he tapped his blade on the prisoner's crotch. *"So, I suggest you talk."*

"What are you going to do?" The prisoner snarked back, "*Chain me up like that beast you keep in your little castle? Put me in an iron mask. Kill me. Enslave me. I don't care; I won't talk."*

"Hmmmm." The Emperor mulled. *"You still have your spirit. That can be remedied."* He rose to his feet unassisted. *"Take him to Reginridge."* The Emperor ordered. *"We'll pull some answers out or all of his teeth... either way I'm satisfied."* Two soldiers did as they were ordered and began to drag the prisoner away. *"Oh one more thing..."* The Emperor interjected. The two soldiers froze. *"He won't be*

needing this where he's going." The Emperor then slammed his blade right into the prisoner's groin repeatedly. The prisoner wailed as blood pooled in the front of his pants and ran down the pant leg. *"Bandage him and get him out of here."* The Emperor said, wiping his blade clean against a nearby table. *"Unfortunately, we need him alive..."*

As soon as the soldiers turned to leave with the prisoner the Emperor collapsed onto the ground again. That stunt had taken the last of his energy. Sandra knelt down and began opening up the layers of his clothes. *"We gotta fix this."* she said, pulling his shirt back enough to expose his wounded shoulder.

The Emperor grabbed her wrist. *"Do you know what you're doing?"* he asked, staring her directly in the eye.

"Unfortunately, you've got no choice..." She responded, meeting his gaze. *"You're going to have to trust me."*

The Emperor let out a weak chuckle as he released Sandra's wrist and turned his head away, submitting himself to her care. Luckily the bullet passed clean through his shoulder, and the round was not big at all. She found a first aid kit and carefully bandaged the wound. Once she was done, she fixed the Emperor's shirt and helped him up.

He hobbled toward one of the soldiers. *"You all have performed beyond admirably."* he said. *"Clean this up. Take two boxes each for your trouble... Send four boxes to Master Chesley with a note about our fallen comrades, he will see to the rest. I would stay but I have one more urgent errand to attend to before the night is out ....”*

“Your Majesty, I really think we should just go home.” Sandra said as she drove. The Emperor was once again giving her directions to another stop he insisted they make that night.

“I would love nothing more.” The Emperor scolded *“Unfortunately my regal duties don’t reorganize themselves in accordance with my convenience. So drive.”* He directed her to the residential district. Past all the slums and to the nice Victorian homes on the North End. One home was lit up. With cars lined across the street. Some sort of party.

The Emperor told Sandra to pull off away from the house, covered by shadows. He pulled out his pocket watch. *“Ah just in time,”* he said excitedly. *“Now...”* he continued, reaching under his seat and procuring a burlap bag. *“I was going to handle this personally, but I presently find myself..... indisposed. “*He gazed at the wound on his shoulder. *“So, here’s what I need you to do....”*

The Emperor instructed Sandra to scale the wall of the house and secure a vantage point on the roof. She was then to dump the contents of the bag onto the crowd below. Once she had done that she was to return to the van as quickly as possible without being seen.

"Hasn't there been enough bloodshed tonight?" Sandra groaned, reluctantly taking the bag. *"Can't we just go home?"*

"Who said a word about bloodshed?" the Emperor snapped, thrusting the bag tightly into her arms. It was surprisingly light. *"Now go do as you're told..."* Sandra left the van and began walking toward the house. She looked back to see the Emperor straightening his hat in the sun visor mirror, purely content with himself.

Scaling the wall was easy. The house had a lattice along the side for plants to grow. That and the windowsills provided simple climbing steps. The window curtains were all drawn so there was little chance of her being spotted. Not sure what to expect, she did a quick scan of the roof once she finished her climb. She was alone.

The bulk of the noise was coming from the backyard of the house. Sandra crept slowly across the roof to the edge overlooking the backyard. She peered out to see a large gathering of people formally dressed. One woman in an elaborate white gown clued her into exactly what sort of celebration it was.

The reception was lavish. String lights illuminated the backyard. Waiters circled the guests' carrying trays of finger food. The women were huddled together as the men smoked cigars. Sandra could just imagine the Emperor up here with her.

"What an utterly common affair" she could hear him say. She chuckled at the thought.

Before long she saw one of the men swoop in and twirl the bride. Dipping her down into a kiss. It must be the groom. It was difficult to make out from such a distance but he looked familiar to Sandra. Peering closer she recognized him to be Harmon, the lawyer who had come up to their table at the museum gala. Sandra remembered the fury on the Emperor's face when he groped that girl Amanda. Admittedly it had irritated Sandra as well. She looked down at the burlap bag and took a deep breath.

Unsure of what to expect she dumped the bag over the edge of the roof. She heard no sound of anything falling but didn't wait around to see what she had done. She booked it to the other end of the roof and began to climb down. As she was climbing, she heard a mixture of gasps and laughter which soon all melted into yelling. However, the yelling sounded angry, not terrified. What had she just done? She ran back across the street and jumped into the van.

"Did you do it?" The Emperor asked.

"Yes." Sandra said with labored breathing as she started the van. *"What was it?"*

"Excellent!" The Emperor gleefully spurted out. He burrowed smugly into his seat.

"So, you're not gonna tell me what I just did to that woman's wedding?" Sandra asked again.

"Oh, I am sorry." The Emperor chortled as he leaned forward and opened the glove box. He began digging around until he pulled out a handful of photographs. *"Who knows, you may have just saved her from a lifetime of misery. But who cares that wasn't quite the aim."* He handed the photographs to Sandra. Sandra thumbed through the photos as she drove. They were all of Harmon. All of him with different women. Some looked potentially innocent, others much more compromising.

"Oh you are evil...." Sandra remarked, she was trying not to smile. *"At his wedding!?!"* The Emperor merely shrugged.

"He violated an anointed knight of the Empire. I am the Emperor...." He looked both ways, as if he were ensuring no one else was with them in the van. *"Fuck him..."* he cursed. Sandra snorted with laughter upon hearing the Emperor swear. She can't remember him ever using a vulgar word before. There was a childlike innocence about it.

"There was one other thing." Sandra said, sensing the Emperor was in a good mood.

"What is it?" The Emperor asked.

"Thank you."

"For what."

"You saved my life tonight." Sandra explained, she hadn't forgotten how the bullet in the Emperor's shoulder was previously destined for her chest.

"Some bodyguard you are." He said gruffly. Sandra exhaled through her nose but said nothing back. This man was incredibly frustrating.

"You're welcome." The Emperor finally said, sensing her irritation, *"Though don't get in the habit of thanking me for doing my duty. It takes up too much time."* Sandra smiled, she had finally won an argument.

The last stop of the night was a quick one. The Emperor detoured Sandra to the industrial district. They pulled up to a dingy looking warehouse. The Emperor had her turn the lights off so as not to wake anyone up. He grabbed the gift wrapped .380 he had purchased earlier from Madame DuBois. Quickly he scrawled a note and placed it with the gun at the warehouse's door. Sandra caught enough of a glimpse to see what it read:

Amanda,
Justice has been delivered tonight, my child. Always shall I watch over you, but in my absence may this provide you some security...
Yours Truly,

Edward Von Drac
Imperator Rex
All Honorifics etc. etc.

He placed the gift at the door and quickly hopped back into the van. Finally, the night was over, and they could go home.

Chapter 13: Sandra

"Blewens... you've been there for weeks. What have you got for me?" Commissioner Helming's voice rang cold over the phone.

"Nothing yet sir." Sandra lied. *"I'm still working my way into his confidence."*

"Keep on it." The Commissioner replied. *"The second you see him do something illegal you call me."*

"I will sir. Of course." Sandra hung up the phone.

There. Now they were even.

The best argument against democracy is a five-minute conversation with the average voter

- Winston Churchill

Act 2:

Wilting Laurels

Chapter 14: Amanda

"Pretty good haul this week I think." Tiffany said as she wrapped up another stack of bills. She and Amanda were sitting in Amanda's bedroom office. Counting out the week's profits. In the time since Amanda's transition into boss. Tiffany had become her unspoken right hand, helping her out as needed.

"I think so." Amanda answered, wrapping up a stack herself. *"How are the girls doing? Do you guys need anything?"*

"Nah." Tiffany replied. *"Nothing outside the usual stuff. Toilet paper, toothpaste, you know...."*

Amanda counted out $250 *"here."* she said handing Tiffany the money. *"Get whatever you need and if there's change... buy them something fun I don't know."*

"Thanks Boss!" Tiffany said with wide eyes as she gladly accepted the cash. *"But you know..."*

"Tiffany I cannot have this conversation again." Amanda said with an exasperated sigh.

"I'm just saying," Tiffany continued ignoring Amanda's plea *"give me the seed money. I can go out and get you a 25% return. Just loaning it out. No guns, no mess, no nothing. Why can't we use all this money to make more money?!?"*

"It's not that I don't believe you Tiff." Amanda said, *"But things are going good right now and we're*

making money... Other people handle money lending. We don't want to piss them off."

"It can't be that big of a deal..." Tiffany pouted. *"Pump used to let me do it...."*

"Well, I'd rather not end up like Pump." Amanda shot back, instinctively tracing the bridge of her nose with her middle and forefinger.

Loan sharking had been a sore topic between the two for weeks now. Tiffany wanted nothing more in the world than to be a big-time lender. To her that was the definition of success. Amanda felt for her friend. She wanted to help Tiffany get there, but God was she impatient. Amanda had to get her own feet on the ground first before she could start doing favors. Silently the two continued counting. What did Tiffany expect? Was Amanda supposed to be promoted and then the next day just calling shots to everyone else? She was there the night Pump was attacked. Did she not understand that this wasn't a game?

"Sorry." Tiffany finally muttered out.

"Tiffany," Amanda began. *"I promise, I will help you get where you wanna be. But right now, I need your help. I didn't ask for any of this and it's scary. I can't do it without you."*

"I know you're right." Tiffany sighed. *"For what it's worth... you're doing a great job. Everyone agrees."*

The two finished counting the cash. Amanda set out a portion for taxes and placed it into a paper bag for Syvlia. Sylvia had called her earlier in the week and asked if she could deliver the cash this time. She said it would be good for Amanda *"to get out a little more."* but Amanda suspected she just didn't feel like making the trip.

Amanda had finished packaging the money. She reached into her desk drawer and pulled out a small handgun. The Emperor had left it on her doorstep a few nights ago. She had no idea how to use a gun, but she felt like she was supposed to carry it around. Thankfully it was small and could be tucked into her handbag with little trouble.

She examined herself in the mirror before leaving. Heels, jeans, a blouse, and matching handbag. A far cry from the overly tight cocktail dresses she used to wear. She hardly recognized herself.

"You look great." Tiffany offered. *"Like a boss ass bitch!"*

"Thanks." Amanda said as the two shared a reconciliatory hug. Amanda popped her shoulders and walked out of the room. As she made her way to the door, Frankie stopped her.

"Where ya goin'?" he asked.

"Out on business." Amanda replied, not breaking her pace.

"Need an escort?" he pressed.

"Sure." Amanda replied, she thought about how the Emperor always had people flanking him, maybe an entourage would boost her confidence.

The two left their warehouse home and ventured down the street. The address Sylvia had given her was a chemical plant in the Industrial district. Amanda and Frankie walked to the nearest bus stop. She was going to have to get a car. Until now she never saw a need for one.

"So what's this business?" Frankie asked as they sat on the bus.

"Nothing." Amanda replied. *"Just a delivery."*

The bus rolled along through the industrial district. Their stop had come with Amanda and Frankie being the only two that exited the bus. People looked on as the pair got off the bus. Some with curiosity, others with scorn. The chemical plant was a short walk from the bust stop.

They approached the complex. It was a tall, towering building surrounded by a security gate. Amanda walked up to the gate and found an intercom box.

"Can I help you?" a voice rang out from the box as Amanda pressed the button.

"Uh yes, hi... We're here to see Sylvia." Amanda answered.

"Identification." the box commanded.

"I uhhh..." Amanda looked confused. She turned to Frankie who pointed at the Imperial Ring on her finger. *"Oh"* she said as he held the ring up to the camera on the intercom. A loud buzzing emanated

from the gate doors as they rolled back, allowing them to enter.

Inside was a massive network of narcotic manufactories. Chemistry flasks and cook vats littered the area. Men and women buzzing around the place, individual cogs in a massive machine. Some scraping the phosphorus off of match heads, others overseeing indoor greenhouses. The scale of the operation was unlike anything Amanda could have possibly imagined.

She wandered around the plant. In awe of all she was witnessing. Assembly lines moved batches of products from one production stage to the next. A cheery voice called out Amanda's name, and she turned to meet it. Syvlia was waving her over to the packaging station.

Amanda approached to see Sylvia, Harold, Cody, and the Emperor all huddled together. The Emperor was holding an amphetamine crystal in his hands, inspecting it with a jeweler's glass.

"Magnificent." he muttered as he spun the crystal in his fingers. *"Absolutely magnificent."*

"I'm glad your Majesty is pleased." Harold said, *"Our new distillation process has allowed for a much purer sample."*

"My dear man." The Emperor said removing the glass from his eye. *"We are going to make a fortune!"* He patted Harold on the back. It was then he noticed Amanda's presence.

"Majesty, what a pleasant surprise." Amanda said with a polite curtsey.

"Indeed, it is my dear." The Emperor replied with a nod. *"How did you like your gift?"*

Amanda withdrew the pistol from the bag. *"It's very pretty."* she said. *"Though I have to say.... I have no idea how to use it."*

"Well." The Emperor said, rubbing his chin, *"We can fix that soon enough. But another time. For now, matters of state require my attention."* He nudged Cody and motioned it was time for them to leave.

"Um sire..." Cody began *"I was wondering if maybe....?"*

"Oh God this again." The Emperor groaned. *"I have the fireman's ball tonight."*

"Stacy can go with you." Cody answered. *"It'll be more intimate just the two of you."*

The Emperor scoffed and rolled his eyes. *"Stay if you want,"* he grumbled. *"You animals enjoy yourselves..."*

Cody and Harold beamed big smiles and gave each other a silent fist bump as the Emperor walked out of the building. Sylvia shook her head slyly at the boys. *"You hurt his feelings, you know..."* she said to Cody.

"He'll be fine." Cody scoffed with a dismissive wave. *"Why do all this work if we can't have a good time now and again... he understands that."*

"No arguments there." Syvlia agreed with a big smile. *"Amanda honey!"* she exclaimed. *"I'm so glad you came!"* She gave Amanda a giant hug. *"Ooooo and with a bodyguard."* she gestured toward Frankie. *"Look Harold, I didn't know we had the Queen of Shiba working for us!"* the group laughed and Amanda blushed.

"I'm just messing with you sugar plum." Sylvia said, *"No need to be embarrassed, it's always good to play it safe."*

"I have the money for you." Amanda said, desperate to change the subject. She reached into her purse and pulled out Syvlia's cut for the week. *"Another good week this week."*

"Oh aren't you such a gem!" Syvlia exclaimed, taking the money from Amanda's hands. *"You make sure those girls of yours are getting plenty of rest now... we aren't slave drivers after all."*

"Anywayyyyy...." Cody smirked, cutting Sylvia off. *"That's enough business. Time for a little fun."* he rubbed his hands together maliciously.

"Fun?" Amanda asked.

"Well, we just finished a new batch today." Harold explained. *"And on packaging day we have this little tradition."* Sylvia clapped her hands excitedly. *"Call it... quality control."* Harold said with a grin. *"We have pretty much anything you could want."*

"But only if you want." Cody interjected. *"This is just for fun. If it's not your thing you don't have to."*

Amanda looked around. There was everything from weed to heroin. Mountains of all of it. *"Screw it."* Amanda said. *"Gimme a joint."*

"That's the spirit!" Syvlia shouted as she tossed Amanda an already rolled joint from a nearby pile and picked one up for herself.

Harold ushered them all into a separate room. Inside. were couches, chairs and a big central table. *"Welcome to the employee lounge,"* he said, offering Amanda a seat. He then walked over to the liquor cabinet and poured two glasses of whiskey. *"Perhaps a drink Lord High Chancellor?"* he said with a mischievous sarcasm. Cody took a glass and did an exaggerated bow.

"Oh Marshal Jones, you honor me sir." Cody replied jokingly as he tossed Harold a dime bag of cocaine. *"Big boy! you want anything?"* Cody asked, looking at Frankie.

"I better not." Frankie replied curtly.

"Come on Frankie." Amanda ordered. *"We're safe here, let down a little."*

"Alright" Frankie responded. *"Just a beer though."*

Harold quickly snorted a line of cocaine off the table. He then ran over and practically tackled Sylvia. *"For you... mi amor."* he said as he procured a lighter for Sylvia's joint. Sylvia quickly kissed him on the cheek.

"Te amo" she said as she leaned into the lighter's flame. The smell of marijuana quickly filled

the room. It put Amanda at ease as she lit her own. The smell reminded her of simpler days, a young girl eeking out a living making men happy. Those days seemed so long ago, and yet, what was different?

The smoke filled her lungs. That familiar sharp sting of the initial hit. She exhaled. It hadn't even kicked in yet, but already she felt more relaxed. Harold turned on some rock music as he loosened his tie. *"To us!"* he shouted, raising his glass.

The party lasted for hours. All the while everyone became more and more intoxicated. The music roared as everyone danced, smoked and snorted their problems away. Amanda felt herself cutting loose. She swayed and spun with Cody on the makeshift dance floor. He had a surprising amount of moves.

Eventually Amanda's head was spinning faster than she was and she had to sit down. The others feeling the same soon followed suit. The music was turned down to dull background noise and the conversations began.

Harold was recounting a story for the group from years ago when he was first starting out. He explained how he and the Emperor were trying to simplify the processing of meth. Neither of them being chemists all they managed to create was a massive meth lab explosion. *"I thought we were both dead."* Harold chuckled. *"Then next thing I knew he was shaking me awake."* Harold explained the Emperor was yet to have the political connections he had now. *"He practically drug me to his car so we could bolt outta there... a beat-up old Taurus at the time. All I remember was fading in and out of consciousness. Opera playing on the radio."*

"Oh my god I remember that!" Sylvia interjected. *"He drove you to my apartment. He helped me wrap up all of your burns. Jesus Christ I was so scared for you... but he just kept assuring me you would pull through and telling me what to do. And eventually you woke up."*

Harold laughed and then sighed. *"I almost miss those days,"* he lamented. *"There was more thrill in it ya know?"*

"Not me." Cody scoffed. *"This shit was a nightmare back then."*

"It was different for you though." Harold argued. *"You came in after D-Day. And you already knew him..."*

"What's D-Day?" Amanda asked.

"D–Day...." Harold explained *"Was the day it all changed for chumps like me."* Syvlia looked to the floor and nodded in agreement. *"I told you before I think, I used to work for the mob. I was a corner dealer.... Small time crap trying to work my way up like any dumbass thug was. Then, April 20th came. D-Day."*

"I don't follow..." Amanda questioned.

"They all died." Harold explained. *"All of them."*

"All of who?" Amanda asked, already having an idea of the answer.

"Anyone who thought they had any sort of pull in Colonna's underworld." Harold continued, *"Italian, Black, Asian, Russian, Hispanic, Irish.... All of the heads of all the crime rings, dead in a 24-hour window. Shit was absolutely insane."*

"How did they die?" Amanda asked.

"Poisoned, shot, beat to death." Harold answered. *"You name it, it happened... The news couldn't keep up with it fast enough. And since everyone got it no one knew who was responsible."*

"The Emperor..." Amanda mused, taking a draw of her joint. Harold tapped his nose in conformation.

"Slowly but surely, he came around to all of us one by one." Harold explained, *"Basically staying we could join the new order, get out of town, or die...."*

"He's really a character." Amanda noted. *"I wonder where it all came from?"* Everyone else in the room almost subconsciously looked toward Cody.

"Well." Cody began, taking a sip of his drink. *"As to how he got the way he is, I don't know for sure. But I am the only one here that knew him back when he was just Eddie Drac."*

"Really!" Amanda exclaimed. *"What was he like?"*

"Honestly, he was relatively normal." Cody answered *"We were paper pushers together in a government office. Well, I was a paper pusher and he was my supervisor. But we were close friends even outside of work. He was always nice to me, generally friendly to everyone."*

"Well, what happened?" Amanda dug.

"To tell you the truth I really don't know." Cody answered. *"He was always a little strange. He always had the ego and LOVED history...but it was a lot more toned down back then. What I do know is that he had some serious money troubles. Student loans, mortgage, you know that sorta stuff."*

Cody paused to take another sip of his drink.

"Anyway, one day he just disappeared. It was weird because we talked almost every day. I didn't hear from him for probably a year. Then one day he shows up with the hat and the suit and all of it and says he's got my ticket to the good life. That I deserved it more than those privileged a-holes... whoever he meant by that... I've been his right-hand man ever since."

"Hmmmm." Amanda replied. *"The more you know."*

It wasn't long before everyone had decided the party was over. Harold took Sylvia home and Cody offered to drive Amanda and Frankie back. When they arrived back to the warehouse Cody insisted on walking them inside against Frankie's protests. *"Thanks for always being so nice to me."* Amanda whispered to Cody as they walked towards the door. He simply blushed and left the two to go home.

"That guy is such a poser." Frankie huffed as the pair entered the warehouse. He shut the door behind him. Amanda frantically waved at him to be quiet, gesturing to all the sleeping girls in the cots around them.

"What do you mean?" Amanda responded softly, removing her earrings. *"I think he's nice. It's been a crazy couple of months, and he's always gone out of his way to make sure I was alright."*

"Yea." Frankie snorted. *"Only because he wants to get between your legs..."* Amanda's face turned sour; she quickly pivoted to face Frankie.

"And so, what if he does?" she snarled. *"Or are you only nice to me because you're such a gentleman..."*

"Amanda..." Frankie began but she paid him no attention and stormed up the stairs, entering her room, slamming the door shut behind her.

Chapter 15: Sandra

"Well, it's a start." Cody said across his desk to Sandra. She was in his office at Reginridge recounting the events of the skirmish at the counting house. Sandra gave him every last detail from their encounter with Madame Dubois to the final retreat of the Republican attackers.

"But some of them got away." He observed, *"Damn."*

"All things considered I would say it was a successful operation." Sandra countered.

"Hopefully we get some intel from that prisoner." Cody noted before standing. Clearly, he had something else on his mind.

"Am I interrupting something?" Sandra asked with a raised eyebrow.

"No not at all." Cody reassured, *"This is more important."*

When the knock came at Cody's office door, he completely disregarded his last remark to Sandra and pushed past her to open it. A footman stood in the doorway.

"Ms. Beasly has arrived sir." The footman explained, *"She claims to come to Reginridge at your invitation."*

"Yes, that's correct." Cody confirmed, *"Please tell her I'll be out in a moment."*

"His Majesty is keeping her company." The footman told Cody, *"They're in the great hall sir."* The footman then excused himself.

"There's nothing more we can do about this right now anyway, right?" Cody asked Sandra, obviously seeking her validation. She merely shrugged and got up to follow him out of the office.

In the entrance hall of Reginridge masses of people were flooding inside for what to be another one of the Emperor's raves. His Majesty stood by the door greeting the guests with Amanda beside him. Sandra imagined he would stay downstairs long enough to say hello and then disappear to his private chambers. The Amanda girl seemed much more at ease than the first time Sandra met her at the gala. The Emperor would occasionally take time away from greeting guests to whisper something into her ear. Sandra even caught the girl beginning to crack a genuine smile.

Cody and Sandra approached the Emperor and Amanda at the entrance. Sandra noticed Amanda blushing as Cody walked up, Cody blushed in kind. It made Sandra bubbly. It was cute. That made it all the more surprising when Amanda came up to her instead of Cody.

"It's Stacy, right?" Amanda asked her taking Sandra aside from the Emperor and his Grand

Marshal, Sandra nodded in the affirmative. *"I just wanted to say I saw you that day at the arena, you were awesome!"*

"Thank you." Sandra chuckled, *"Really it wasn't anything."*

"Well actually," Amanda began *"I was wondering if you could teach me some of that."*

"You want to learn how to fight?" Sandra asked, crocking her eyebrow.

"I was thinking we could start with just shooting. I just wanna know the basics" Amanda elaborated.

"Well sure I can teach you." Sandra agreed, *"I'm mostly just here. Come over whenever you have the time and we can start."*

"Oh, thank you!" Amanda exclaimed, seizing Sandra in a great hug. Initially caught off guard by the girl's affection, Sandra's body seized up but soon relaxed and returned her embrace. Standing there in the cold and drafty palace, Sandra felt warm. Much too soon for Sandra, Amanda peeled herself off and ran to join Cody, a slight spring in her step. Sandra happily watched the girl skip away for a moment, and then she went to join the Emperor.

"Was that a hug I saw?" The Emperor slyly asked Sandra as she took her place beside him.

"Just because your Majesty does not like me doesn't mean I am unlikeable." Sandra returned with smug satisfaction. The Emperor chuckled.

"I don't need you this evening feel free to do.... whatever it is you do." The Emperor said as the last remaining guests wandered into the hall. Seconds after the last one arrived and the doors closed, he marched up the grand staircase and out of sight.

Sandra could not sleep. The music emanating from downstairs was way too loud. Did anyone of these people actually sleep at night? The pulse of the rap songs blaring kept her from any sort of relaxation. As much money as the Emperor had, one would think he would spring for soundproof walls. She got up from her bed and looked around her room. She had realized it before but now she was finally appreciating how much nicer it was than her apartment in the city. At home she would walk around barefoot but here the frigid marble floors required the use of slippers. She ran her fingers along the silk sheets. Looking over at the mantle, it was adorned with vases that each had to be worth more than her entire apartment, and this was just a spare room that was empty in the house prior to her arrival.

As Sandra was taking this all in, she could not help but remember that every room the Emperor considered private, his throne room, his office at the Museum, they were all barren. What a strange and contradictory man he was. Were he not as rich as a king, everyone would likely write him off as insane. But the fanaticism with which everyone followed him, that had come from somewhere. She saw it that night when he held Benny dying in his arms. The guilt that plagued his face. And these parties, she knew he hated them. That's why he hid in his room, still every weekend he opened his house for all these people. Who was this man? She was beginning to feel that her interest went beyond solely her mission.

Accepting the fact that she was not going to sleep tonight, Sandra left her bedroom and entered the upstairs hallway. Surely this massive place was worth exploring, criminal activity or no. She had seen most of the downstairs, it was mostly open, and that's where the party animals were. But the upstairs was still foreign to her outside of her bedroom.

She walked around the dark halls, but really there was not much of anything, endless rows of empty bedrooms, presumably belonging to attendants of the party below. She felt weird continually walking into bedrooms, so she decided to continue her search elsewhere. Returning to the grand staircase she looked up to the third floor of the house. She had only ever seen one man walk that far up.

Slowly she crept up the stairs. It led to another stretching hallway on either end. Though she did notice this far up she could not hear any noise from the party below. Down the hallway she could see a door that was guarded by two royal inquisitors clad in all back on either side. That must be where the Emperor was. She walked up to the room. The Inquisitors stood silent as she approached. Even as she stood directly in front of them, they stood frozen like statues.

"Is he in there?" Sandra asked plainly.

"You would think His Majesty's bodyguard would know his location." One of the inquisitors said back coldly.

"I was being polite." Sandra snarked back, *"I meant is he awake or asleep."*

"His Majesty doesn't sleep very much." The Inquisitor answered, *"he's awake."*

"Good." Sandra stated as she reached for the doorknob, they made no effort to stop her. She turned the knob and gingerly entered the room.

The room was, not wholly to Sandra's surprise, rather barren. It was split into two halves. On one side there was a large four poster bed with velvet curtains running along the perimeter, the Imperial Seal embroidered upon them. On one side of the bed there was a large mahogany nightstand, and on the other side lay a large, cushioned dog bed, a nest for Edwina.

The other half of the room was where the Emperor was located. He sat at a large dark wooden desk, scribbling into a ledger with a pen, he had a monocle placed over his right eye to better see the figures inside of the book. Edwina lay dutifully at the foot of the desk, her head gently resting on the floor.

On the desk, aside from the mountain of books and papers, was a gold phonograph which let out a soft hum of classical music.

The Emperor did not look up from his work as Sandra walked into his room. Edwina, however, perked her head up and looked in Sandra's direction. Seeing Sandra enter, the peacock rose from her resting position and walked over to her. She nuzzled her head onto Sandra's thigh. Sandra gave Edwina an affectionate scratch on the cheek. The bird cooed happily before waltzing over to her bed and laying back down. Still the Emperor scribbled in his ledger.

"What is it?" The Emperor asked dryly, still not looking up.

"Nothing." Sandra mused walking closer to the desk, *"I just couldn't sleep."*

"The Library is two doors down." The Emperor informed her, *"Feel free to find a book to occupy your time."*

"Oh, I don't read." Sandra told him.

"How little that surprises me." The Emperor scoffed in reply. Sandra rolled her eyes at him; his insults affected her less and less as time went on.

"Do you need any help?" She asked, ignoring his rudeness. Finally, the Emperor stopped writing and set the ledger down.

"Help?" He asked, annoyed.

"With your books." Sandra explained, *"I do have a brain you know."*

"Feel free to begin using it at any time." The Emperor snarled, returning to his ledger.

"Well, you fiddle with those things all day." Sandra noted, *"Maybe you need help."*

Realizing she was not going away, the Emperor placed the ledger on a pile of similar books on the desk. He then got up and removed the phonograph's needle, ceasing the music that filled the room. He reached into a drawer of his desk and pulled out another crystal decanter, pouring himself a glass of whiskey.

"Why are you here?" He asked again, taking a sip of his drink.

"I told you I couldn't sleep." Sandra reiterated, *"The party is too loud."*

"You are welcome to join them." The Emperor replied coldly.

"That's not my thing." Sandra explained, *"I prefer the quiet."*

"Then stop talking." The Emperor said, he resumed the phonograph's music. But before he sat back to his desk he walked to the corner of the room and pulled a spare chair over so Sandra could sit opposite of him near the desk. Without another word he retook his spot at his desk and began again analyzing his ledgers, making notes as he did so. Sandra noticed he began massaging his pocket watch as he was writing.

The gentle piano music coming from the phonograph gave the room a peaceful and serene feeling, the scratching of the Emperor's pen blended almost seamlessly with the music, enhancing it's atmospheric quality. Sandra watched as the Emperor traced each line of the ledger with a finger, mouthing words to himself and scribbling notes, occasionally scratching them out and rewriting them. Her mind was filled with the sight of him in the skirmish at the counting house the other night. Ordering soldiers around a battlefield and taking fire. She wondered which part of his job he felt more at home with or if it was both.

"Amanda and Cody seem to be getting along." Sandra noted aloud, breaking the silence. The Emperor hung his head in irritation causing the monocle to fall from his eye. He paused the phonograph again.

"What concern is it of yours?" he asked rudely.

"I'm not concerned." Sandra explained, *"I think it's sweet."*

"There you are then." The Emperor exhaled.

"Alright, I'm clearly annoying you. I'll just go." Sandra said clearly, he wasn't in the mood to talk to her.

"You're on your time." The Emperor said, *"You can do whatever you wish."* Not exactly an invitation to stay... but not an overt order to leave either.

"Well, I wish to stay then..." Sandra stated matter of factly, The Emperor nodded and went to

resume his phonograph, but Sandra stopped him. *"... and talk to you."* She finished. The Emperor groaned.

"Answer one question for me and then I'll sit quietly." Sandra offered, The Emperor accepted her deal.

"Is it all worth it?" she asked.

"Yes." The Emperor answered quickly and without hesitation.

"Really?" Sandra asked, *"You seem so stressed out and unhappy all of the time."*

"Come with me." The Emperor said flatly, springing from his chair and grabbing Sandra by the arm. He drug her out of the room. He moved with such purpose Sandra was struggling to keep up. He marched into the hallway and down the grand staircase. Onward he charged into the main level of the house. Sandra could hear the bustling of the party again.

The Emperor stopped them halfway down, just enough that they could see the celebration below without being spotted themselves. Sandra watched the frivolity of the dancing, drinking, and smiles. They all seemed so happy. People who had one chance to let loose and they determined to make the most of it. She saw Amanda and Cody, moving in each other's arms, unthinking, flowing with the sway of the music. They existed in a vacuum, the world around them was not present.

"What do you see?" The Emperor asked.

"I see people." Sandra answered, *"People enjoying life."*

"What do you think of these people?" The Emperor pressed again.

"I don't know most of them." Sandra conceded, *"I don't think much of anything."*

"I know them, each and every one." The Emperor mused, *"They are that which society has forgotten, not because they are lazy or dishonest, merely victims of circumstance, children of paupers, abusers, and whatever else, people with nowhere else to turn."*

"What's your point?" Sandra asked him, *"Everyone knows life isn't fair."*

"Life is only unfair because those with power are content to let it be so." The Emperor growled, *"I have no such complacency. These people, they are loud and they are obnoxious, just like the rest of the world, but now finally they have a place in it, thanks to my efforts."*

"That's why you do what you do?" Sandra asked, *"For them."*

"Don't think for a moment I don't benefit also." The Emperor said, *"But yes, I give opprotunity to those who have been denied it by the customs of man, that they too should be able not just to survive, but also to earn a rightful place in the sun. That is my life's work."*

Sandra turned around to look at the Emperor, his face was filled with pride as he watched the debauchery happening below them. *"That's very sweet Your Majesty."* Sandra said, eying him skeptically, *"I'm starting to see why they love you so."* The Emperor relaxed his grip on Sandra's wrist; she took the opportunity to interlock her arm with his. Together, from the great stairwell, they watched the remainder of the party.

Chapter 16: Amanda

"Are you enjoying the party?!" Cody asked. The music was so loud Amanda could barely hear him.

"Yes!" She shouted back; the pulsating strobe lights had turned the world around them into a blur. All she could see was Cody, and feel his hands on her waist, it made her chest pound. She was no stranger to being touched, but this sensation was different. Her whole body vibrated. When Cody pressed himself closer to her, her breathing became labored, it all overwhelmed her senses. There were hundreds of people around them, but Amanda could not register their presence. She turned around and as the feelings bubbling at her surface erupted, she kissed him. Grabbing the collar of his shirt she pulled him even closer, feeling his hand on her lower back only fueling the fire burning within her. When she finally let him go, both were exhausted.

"Should we go upstairs?" Cody asked her, his breathing labored now as well. Amanda looked to the staircase. It was almost deserted, but she saw the tips of a familiar pair of boots standing beside the hem of a glittering red dress.

"Not yet." She responded, *"but later."* The pair continued dancing.

Amanda's eye's crusted open. Her head was killing her. She lifted herself to a seated position in the foreign bed. To her right, Cody snored, sound asleep. She gently brushed his hair before getting out of the bed. Cody's room was similar to the other bedrooms of the house. Mahogany finishes on everything, violet rugs, and artwork adorning the walls.

Cody woke up as Amanda was shuffling around the bedroom. Lazily he stretched himself to life as Amanda returned to the bedside. She smiled down on her lover as his eyes adjusted to light. *"Good morning."* She said to him softly. He gave her a smiling yawn in reply.

"We should stagger our entrance downstairs." Cody groggily suggested, *"no point in giving people something to talk about."*

"Sure." Amanda replied, the same thought had been in her mind. *"I have to get back so I'll go first."* Not necessarily true, but she was hungry. She crept to the door and peeked her head out into the hallway to make sure no one was around. The coast was clear. She opened the door and prepared to make her exit before Cody called out to her. Turning around quickly, the Lord Chancellor blew her a kiss. Amanda blushed.

She ventured out into the hallway. Cody's room was on the second floor of Reginridge, along with plenty of others. A few of the Emperor's footman patrolled the halls carrying breakfast trays but none of them paid her any attention. Amanda trudged on toward the grand staircase. As she descended the smell of bacon filled her nose. She followed it until she found a closed door guarded by two of the Emperor's mystic inquisitors. Hesitantly, she walked up to the door. To her surprise, as she approached the inquisitors silently stepped aside, allowing her to pass. She felt a slight surge of power rush through her as these trained killers made her a path. It scared her how intoxicating such an insignificant event was. Still, she might start having her own man stand guard outside her room back at the warehouse.

She heard muffled conversation through the door, but couldn't understand what they were saying. Still, she was able to recognize one of the voices. The characterized hoarse yet elegant tone of the Emperor. She cracked the door open.

"..... And THAT's why we must consolidate around the entertainment district." She heard the Emperor say as she entered the dining room. The Emperor was seated at the head of a grand table. Next to him was his bodyguard Stacy, and around the table were a cluster of people Amanda did not recognize. The Emperor was carefully cutting his bacon with a fork and knife, slowly placing bite sized pieces in his mouth. The others ate it like normal. Hearing the door open the Emperor froze his fork and looked up, seeing Amanda his eyes widened.

"Amanda darling!" He exclaimed, *"I wish you would have said you were spending the night. I would*

have had cook prepare you something." Amanda awkwardly stood in the doorway while Stacy whispered something into the Emperor's ear. He nodded as she spoke.

"How true." The Emperor mused as Stacy whispered to him. *"Amanda."* He said returning his attention, *"Master Chesley appears to find himself indisposed at breakfast time. You would do us an honor if you took his place."* He gestured to an empty chair at the table which had a full plate in front of it. *"No sense in it getting cold."* The Emperor reassured her. Amanda politely nodded and took the empty seat. On the plate was fired eggs, slabs of bacon, and toast. Around the table the men and women accompanying the Emperor ate like they were at a diner that charged by the minute. His Majesty, however, had a napkin placed gingerly in his lap slowly cutting each bite and using his fork to eat delicately.

Amanda took the folded napkin by her plate and flapped it open, placing it in her lap. She noticed Stacy eyeing her cautiously while the Emperor beamed. She picked up her fork and knife. Stacy whispered something else in the Emperor's ear, he waved her off this time, annoyed.

"Did you sleep well dear." The Emperor asked Amanda.

"I did your Majesty thank you." Amanda politely replied as placed a bite of egg into her mouth.

"And what about Cody?" One of the other men at the table asked. The table collectively snickered until the Emperor slapped a hand on the tabletop.

"Don't mind them." The Emperor told her with a soft smile, *"Those who go without tend to be of an irritable nature."*

"That would explain your Majesty's awful moods!" One of the other attendants joked. The table laughed again, even the Emperor chortled a little.

"Enough you fiends!" The Emperor growled through his poorly concealed grin. *"Did I become Emperor just to be denied a civil breakfast?!"*

The laughter slowly died down but the mood remained light as everyone ate their meal. Amanda did her best to mimic the Emperor's mannerisms, but it was so good she could hardly contain herself. The fact that someone was able to work such magic over the most basic ingredients was surely an art form.

"Sire this is delicious!" Amanda announced, *"What does the cook do to them?"*.

"I haven't the slightest idea." The Emperor replied as he held a bite of egg in his fork, examining it closely, *"But I do always make note to thank her on my morning constitutional, you're more than welcome to join me."*

"Thank you, Majesty." Amanda replied, gently slicing a piece of toast for herself, *"I would like that."* The Emperor stuck his tongue out at Stacy, she eyed him angrily, but it made Amanda chortle.

Once everyone had finished eating the Emperor rose from the table. As he stood up so did everyone else in the room. Paying them no attention, the Emperor pursed his lips and blew a sharp whistle, Amada heard a squawk and the rustling of feathers as Edwina jolted to life beneath the table and stretched her long neck.

"Come my precious dear, time to exercise those legs." The Emperor fawned at the peacock. She followed close at his heels. The people at the table remained frozen as the Emperor marched toward the dining room door. As he reached the threshold he snapped around and turned to Amanda. *"Coming?"* He asked bluntly. Amanda hastily scurried to the Emperor's side.

Clutching his cane tightly, the Emperor led Amanda through the maze of Reginridge to a back stairwell that led to the kitchens. Inside there was a frantic staff all being ordered about by a massive woman wearing a stained apron. Barking commands and waving her arms she directed her assistants all about the kitchen, hastily making preparations for lunch.

"Majesty!" the cook jumped, startled at his appearance in the room. Her sudden cessation of yelling had caused the entire kitchen staff to halt in their tracks and dip their heads low in the Emperor's presence. He nodded at them politely allowing the bustle to continue. *"Was something wrong with breakfast?"* the cook asked indignantly.

"Cookie darling when has that ever been the case?" The Emperor replied slyly, the cook merely eyed him skeptically.

"That's what I thought." She huffed back before returning to her duties.

"Cook dear." The Emperor said cleared his throat, *"I want you to meet Ms. Amanda Beasly, Knight of the Empire."* He gently pushed Amanda in front of him, *"She wanted to compliment the chef, so to speak."* He ushered Amanda forward. Cook eyed her annoyed, presumably at the interruption to her work.

"Go on then." Cook huffed at Amanda, *"I ain't got all day."* She picked up a bowl and began stirring its contents.

"I'm sorry I didn't realize I was interrupting." Amanda sheepishly offered up, taking a large gulp of air. *"But it really was delicious I had to say thank you."*

"Well, you said it... now take that man!" She thrust her spoon in the Emperor's direction, *"And get out of my kitchen so I can make lunch!"*

The Emperor beamed a large grin, clearly tickled with himself. He took Amanda by her shoulders and led her out of the kitchen. As they were walking away Amanda glanced over her shoulder to see the cook grinning herself and she stirred the bowl in her arm. She was humming to herself.

The Emperor led Amanda through the lavender fields that ran along the eastern half of Reginridge's sprawling grounds. He walked slowly and methodically, basking in the breeze that rustled through the lavender stems. Edwina remained just a few paces in front of them, occasionally brushing up against the plants to groom her feathers. The sun infused a calming warmth into Amanda's skin. It was so peaceful in the garden. The faint chirping of birds offered a pleasant atmosphere for their stroll.

The Emperor said nothing during their walk, merely admiring his plants and enjoying the breeze. His boots made a soft crunching noise on the ground beneath him and his cloak frayed gently in the wind. His cane left a small imprint on the ground with each step he took. Amanda watched as the sunlight reflected off the various bits of silver that adorned him and his clothes. Normally, he looked aged and sickly, but here in the garden, wrapped in the sun's rays Amanda saw radiance.

"Your Majesty?" She asked him, breaking their silence.

"Yes child?" He replied softly, reaching to stroke one of the lavender blooms.

"How do you do it?"

"You'll have to be a bit more specific dear." The Emperor smirked, *"I do quite a lot."*

"You're responsible for all these people...." Amanda explained, *"They follow you...."*

"How do I make them follow me?" The Emperor asked, crocking an eyebrow.

"I guess so."

"I don't." The Emperor answered flatly, *"They follow me because they choose to."*

"I guess what I'm asking is how do you make them love you."

"Oh, I wouldn't say that." The Emperor chuckled, *"Most of them tolerate me at best."*

"I don't think that's true." Amanda observed.

"Why are you asking me about this?" The Emperor pressed, regaining control of the conversation. *"What's on your mind."*

"I just see how you are with everyone, in your own way...." Amanda thought out loud, *"And I think about myself and..."* her words trailed off.

The Emperor stared at her and smiled gently. He stepped over to a nearby stone bench and sat down, patting the bench for Amanda to sit next to him. *"It sounds like you're tired of hiding."* The Emperor said softly. He placed both hands on his cane's head and rested his chin on his fingers.

"I want to be powerful." Amanda whispered, *"like you."* The Emperor leaned back on the bench and let out a hearty laugh.

"I assure you dear you do not." The Emperor said once he regained his composure. *"It's nothing but headache... however if you would allow an old monarch to give you some advice?"*

Amanda said nothing, just nodded.

"Don't be so afraid of the world." The Emperor told her, *"I wish someone would have told me that when I was your age,"* He took a breath and began looking out to the clouds. *"You will find it's mostly run by the inept and the infirm... They're not difficult to outmaneuver."* He smirked to himself.

"I will try your Majesty." Amanda answered meekly.

"You're doing fine." The Emperor reassured her, *"And if you ever need help you know where to come."* Amanda nodded, she did indeed know, but it was affirming to hear.

Edwina soon came up to the bench and began squawking incessantly. She paced around in circles fanning her elegant tailfeathers. *"I'm sorry!"* Amanda exclaimed jokingly as she gave the bird an affectionate scratch, *"You want to finish your walk!"* The bird squawked again in reply, playfully nipping at Amanda's legs.

"Oh, you prima donna!" The Emperor laughed as he hoisted himself to his feet, *"God forbid I give anyone else the slightest bit of attention!"* Now that they were both standing, Edwina sheathed her tailfeathers and began stalking down the path once again. Amanda and the Emperor followed close behind her, side by side, laughing with each other as they mocked the peacock's jealous behavior.

Chapter 17: Sandra

"Okay now Amanda all you wanna do is keep your arm nice and relaxed." Sandra instructed, guiding Amanda's arm as Amanda brandished her new pistol. Sandra had found the girl sneaking out of Reginridge a week ago and reminded her of their planned lessons. She was pleasantly surprised when today Amanda had returned to palace, asking for her instead of His Majesty.

"That's it." Sandra continued, *"nice and calm.... Now look down range at the target."* The fields of Reginridge were washed with a crisp breeze keeping the air nice and cool. It was a beautiful day. *"Keep an eye on the target and take a nice deep breath in."*

Sandra heard Amanda inhale as she leaned over the girl's shoulder. *"Good. Good. And Three.... Two... One..."*

BANG

A branch on a nearby bush collapsed to the ground.

"Oh my God I'm so sorry!" Amanda exclaimed in horror.

"Don't even worry about it!" Sandra chuckled. *"You got closer that time!"*

"But the bush...." Amanda groaned.

"It'll give the poor gardener a little excitement in his work." The Emperor exclaimed as he approached the two of them. *"Now let's see it again."*

he said, *"Take your time, listen to Stacy.... She knows what she's doing."* Sandra glanced over at the Emperor and let loose a slight smile. It wasn't very often he gave her a genuine complement.

"I'm gonna back off this time." Sandra said to Amanda. *"Don't overthink it. Just see the target, point aim and shoot."* Amanda nodded before focusing back on the target. Sandra stepped back next to the Emperor; his eyes locked on Amanda.

"She's gonna get it this time." Sandra whispered to the Emperor.

"I know she will...." The Emperor whispered in reply, his gaze unbroken.

Amanda once again raised her pistol. Sandra felt the Emperor squeeze her hand in anticipation. He quickly withdrew, as if correcting an involuntary action. He cleared his throat nervously. Amanda sighted in the target.

BANG

The upper right corner of the target exploded as the bullet just barely made contact. *"I DID IT!"* Amanda exclaimed, jumping up and down in triumph. The Emperor clapped his hands together in admiration.

"That you did my dear and wonderfully done!" he jovially expressed. He walked up and placed a hand on Amanda's shoulder. *"Before long you'll be a better shot than even me."*

"Is his Majesty a good shot?" Sandra said coyly. *"I'd love to see a demonstration."*

The Emperor turned his head to face Sandra, maliciously cocking his eyebrow. *"Then I shall be all too happy to oblige."* He whistled sharply using his fingers. Moments later Mr. Charteris lumbered across the field toward the trio, his chains making a trail in the grass behind him. He took his place beside the Emperor. The Emperor in turn strolled to a nearby tree and plucked a fruit from one of its branches.

"Place it atop your head." the Emperor commanded. Mr. Charteris did as he was bid with his standard moans of agony. He gently set the fruit atop the iron mask encasing his head. *"Do be still...."* The Emperor said, half-jokingly as he walked forty paces away. He turned to face Mr. Charteris, reached into his breast pocket from which he produced his own revolver. Taking aim, he fired, exploding the fruit atop Mr. Charteris' head much to Sandra's relief. The Emperor then shooed his monster away who lumbered heavily back to the house.

"Not bad...." Sandra said playfully.

"Oh, you think you can do better?" The Emperor scoffed. *"I'd love to see it."*

"Sure." Sandra replied nonchalantly. *"Toss me one of those fruits."*

The Emperor walked back over to the tree and plucked another fruit. He tossed it into the air in Sandra's direction. She quickly brandished her own handgun and shot the fruit mid-flight with a perfect hit. The Emperor nodded in respect.

A footman approached the group and took the Emperor aside. Sandra saw the Emperor listen intently as the footman whispered into his ear. He frowned and nodded as he absorbed the information being relayed. He sent the footman away with an affirmative tap on the shoulder before coming back to Sandra and Amanda.

"Matters of state I'm afraid." The Emperor announced to Amanda. *"But you keep at it my dear, you're doing splendid."* He turned to Sandra and opened his mouth to speak, something glimmering in his eye, but he chose instead just to walk away with the footman close in tow.

"I couldn't tell you the last time I saw a man so into a woman." Amanda said cheekily, *"No offense but especially at your age."*

"Hey!" Sandra retorted playfully *"I'm young enough to be your older sister... besides your way off base."*

"Come on." Amanda groaned *"I was a whore for a lot of years.... I know it when I see it."*

"Don't say that about yourself sweetheart." Sandra replied with a softened face. *"You're so much more than that."* She didn't know why the girl insisted on constantly belittling herself.

"It's not a good or a bad thing." Amanda mused. *"It's just a fact. That's what I was."*

"I guess so." Sandra replied half-heartedly.

"Anyway...." Amanda said with a grin. *"He's definitely into you."*

"I don't think anything is exactly what it looks like when it comes to that man." Sandra argued.

"He's still a man." Amanda shrugged. She picked up the pistol and raised it again at the target. *"And as far as men go, he is weird, but you could do worse."* She fired again, *BANG,* her accuracy improving.

"Maybe I don't want a man bossing me around all the time." Sandra stated as she adjusted Amanda's grip *"try that"*

BANG, closer to the bullseye

"Don't be stupid he doesn't boss you around." Amanda argued. Sandra laughed so hard she snorted.

"Are you crazy??" Sandra scoffed in retaliation. *"He's the bossiest person I ever met!*

"To the rest of the world maybe." Amanda countered *"But I've only ever seen two people tell him no and get away with it. Cody and you."*

"Why are you advocating for him so much?" Sandra asked. *"What does it matter to you?"*

"I don't know..." Amanda pondered, *"He's kinda grown on me."* She set the gun down. *"I was scared of him when I first met him... how could you not be. But all that crazy shit... it's always directed. If that makes sense."*

"It does." Sandra said. *"And I know he's really fond of you."*

"He gave me a life." Amanda reminisced. *"He took a chance on a gutter rat and turned me into a person."*

"No honey he didn't." Sandra replied. *"You gave you a life. He may have helped but you did it."*

"Thanks." Amanda smiled. *"If my real parents had been more like you guys, who knows how my life woulda turned out."*

"Alright enough of that." Sandra blushed, waving her away. Something about the way Amanda just referred to her sent her stomach into butterflies. It was then another footman approached the pair.

"Ma'am." he said, directed toward Sandra. *"His Majesty has requested that you join him in the dungeons."*

"Ooooooo" Amanda teased. *"Kinky."*

"Oh Stop!" Sandra said playfully, shoving Amanda. *"I'll be right there."* She said to the footman. The footman bowed and walked away.

"I have to get going anyway." Amanda said, *"It's almost dark, gotta get everyone ready for work tonight."*

"Take care of yourself please." Sandra said as Amanda was gathering her things.

"I can now thanks to you." Amanda replied, waving her gun before placing it back into her purse. Amanda looked around to make sure no one was looking. When she was confident, they were alone she reached in and gave Sandra a big hug. "*Really Stacy..."* she whispered. *"Thank you."*

"You're welcome" Sandra replied warmly, returning the hug. *"Now go kick ass."*

Sandra made her way back to the house and through the maze of staircases and hallways. She had yet to actually visit the dungeon but if movies had taught her anything she figured as long as she kept moving down, she was headed in the right direction. As she descended the various staircases the air became heavier and heavier. There was no ventilation down here. The beautiful limestone of Reginridge was soon replaced with decrepit cinderblock as she reached the subterranean levels.

The bottom of the staircase yielded to yet another massive hallway. It was eerily lit and the smell of mildew was now so pervasive that Sandra had to keep a hand to her nose. As she walked, she saw a small doorway cut out of the wall on the right hand side. This must be it. She turned into the doorway only to find she was mistaken. It was the entrance to a small hollowed out room, no bigger than a walk-in closet. In one corner there was a pile of rags hopelessly clustered together to form a makeshift mattress. The only light was provided by a solitary candle on the stone floor. In the opposite corner there was an old bucket full of water and a straw. Here sat Mr. Charteris desperately trying to suck the liquid through the small hole in his mask. He was startled upon realizing Sandra's presence and fell back. His chains echoing against the stone walls. He flung his hands up in fear as Sandra entered the room.

She tried to calm him down but to little avail. The best she could manage was to kneel down and assist him back to his water straw. This seemed to soothe his fear slightly. He relaxed enough to drink. Sandra peered through the eye holes in his iron casing to try and catch a glimpse of his face, but couldn't make out any features. Only crusted blood and bits of mangled flesh.

The commotion must have alerted an inquisitor to her presence because one rushed into the room. *"The Emperor is this way ma'am."* He said politely. The inquisitors had been kinder to her since word had spread about her actions at the counting house. *"You can follow me."* He helped Sandra to her feet and guided her back to the doorway. He promptly turned around to face Mr. Charteris and his whole demeanor shifted.

"You know the rules." the inquisitor growled sharply to Mr. Charteris. Mr. Charteris had resumed his cowering. *"You aren't to bother any of his Majesty's associates."* He stepped over to Mr. Charteris and swiftly knocked him out with the butt of his rifle. The inquisitor returned to Sandra and gestured to her to follow him.

"He didn't do anything you know." Sandra quipped as the two walked down the dungeons hallway. The inquisitor just shrugged.

"I don't think the Emperor really cares, just likes an excuse to give him a beating." He replied curtly.

"What did he even do?" Sandra asked.

"No idea." The inquisitor answered, *"But the Emperor wants him beat and that's enough for me."*

The rest of the brief walk was silent. At the end of the hallway the corridor split off to the right. This is where the Emperor was, standing tall with Cody and a second inquisitor alongside him. They were standing over a prisoner sitting along the cinderblock wall. Getting closer Sandra could see he was chained to the wall by both wrists. It was the man they took alive from the raid on the counting house. He sat beaten and blooded, barely conscious. The Emperor looming overtop of him sneering at his captive. Sandra noticed he was missing a few fingers and toes, they had been replaced with bloodied nubs.

The Emperor turned his head as he heard Sandra approach. *"Oh, good you're here."* he said, *"Our guest is finally ready to speak."* Cody gave Sandra a simple wave. The Emperor snapped his fingers, and the two guards heaved the prisoner to his feet, he moaned and rolled his neck back and forth upon being moved.

"Alright now pal." Cody said. *"Everyone is here."* He placed a hand upon the prisoner's soldier. *"Save your life man."* he said gently *"Don't die a needless death.... Tell us what you know."*

The prisoner coughed up some blood. *"I said..."* he began struggling to speak, *"I said I would speak to the Emperor."*

"And so you are..." Cody answered coolly, gesturing to the Emperor standing beside him *"Now speak."*

The prisoner cackled meekly, blood drooling from the holes in his mouth previously occupied by teeth. Using all of his waning strength he lifted his head to look Cody in the eye. *"I have nothing to say to the Emperor's dog..."* he spat, then turned to face Sandra *"Or his whore...."*

"You son of a bitch." Cody griped. He raised his hand to hit the prisoner, but The Emperor caught him at the wrist. The Emperor gave Cody a stern look and Cody placed his hand back to his side. The Emperor smiled in appreciation.

"Now young man." The Emperor said, taking over the interrogation. *"If you make another insolent comment, honor will demand that I cut out your tongue."* His face turned into one of sarcastic concerns. *"And if I have to cut out your tongue..."* he continued, *"You will no longer be of any use to the Crown.... Needless to say, what happens after that."*

"I'm not afraid to die." the prisoner retaliated.

"I can change that." The Emperor retorted just as quickly, his eye flickering with the signature psychotic glare that gave his words truth.

The prisoner hung his head and nodded in defeat. *"Good."* The Emperor said sweetly. *"Now be a good man and answer the Lord High Chancellor."*

"The Republican Regiment has gathered its strength." The prisoner began. *"Leadership feels now that they can face you out in the open. The attack will come soon. And once it starts, it won't stop until you are all dead."*

"Where are they planning to hit first?" Cody asked.

"I don't know." The Prisoner replied. *"All I know is they said to me one time - if you can't cut off a snake's head, start with its tail..."* The Emperor did not look amused.

"Describe your forces." The Emperor commanded *"What are their arms? What are their number? Please provide detail."*

"Your Majesty has a made a great many enemies." The prisoner replied, blood dripping from his lip. *"Our estimates say the organization outnumbers you two to one. Every single one is armed to the teeth, assault rifles, shotguns, enough firepower to end your tyranny."*

The Emperor scoffed *"My tyranny...."* he muttered to himself.

"Your Majesty has had an iron grip on the underworld of Colonna City for far too long." The prisoner said. *"Too many people want the old days, where we were all free to do as we pleased."*

"Free to rape and pillage you mean." The Emperor scolded *"And such it is, a thief would betray his masters so quickly."* His temper was quickly flaring up. *"Yours and the chaos you invite are that which I have spent my life combatting."* He grabbed the prisoner by the scruff of his shirt. *"And I will crush you and your pestilent pretenders under my imperial boot!"*

Sandra cleared her throat and the Emperor ceased his tirade and recollected himself.

"I betray no one Emperor." The prisoner continued between heaving and labored breaths, *"All I'm telling you is that your days are numbered. You won't be able to stop the tide that comes for you."*

The Emperor heaved an annoyed sigh. *"Well, we shall see when blows come to pass who emerges the victor."* he said massaging the bridge of his nose. *"But for now... unlike your putrid overlords I am a man of my word. You have provided what was requested of you and so you shall be set free."* He gestured to one of the guards who quickly excited the room.

"There is just one small matter to clear up before your release." The Emperor said, *"I can't have you free just to rejoin the ranks of my enemies."*

"You promised to let me live." The prisoner muttered, desperate but powerless to resist.

"I did and I meant it." The Emperor said. *"You will walk out of here a free man."* The guard returned to the room. In his hand was a metal pole with the Emperor's sigil on one end. It was glowing bright red

from the heat. *"But your friends must know you've been our guest."* The Emperor said coldly as the inquisitor handed him the branding iron. The two inquisitors held the inmate to the wall as his eyes widened in fear. Blood curdling screaming ensued as the Emperor slowly and gleefully forced the brand onto the prisoner's squirming cheek.

"There." The Emperor said, satisfied as he pulled the iron away, a large Imperial sigil burned into the prisoner's cheek. *"Return to them now and let them be aware of your treason. Or disappear into the void for all I care... You are free to leave."* The guards proceeded to unlock the chains, holding the prisoner to the wall and escort him out of the dungeons.

"Master Chesley," The Emperor said, turning to Cody.

"Yes Sire?"

"Summon the Imperial Council." the Emperor commanded, rubbing his temple. *"I would speak with my Marshals."*

"As your Majesty commands." Cody said, giving the Emperor a bow before leaving to carry out his task.

The Emperor crocked his head in the direction of the doorway before storming out of the room, cuing Sandra to follow. He strode down the hallway with such conviction his cane slamming the ground as he marched. Sandra had to jog slightly just to keep pace.

The Emperor's coat billowed on his shoulders as he walked. Sandra's dress flowed similarly in the manufactured breeze. *"How dare they..."* The Emperor muttered to himself. *"What have I not given... the fools.... Damn them,"* He stormed up the stairs from the dungeon, Sandra close behind. Up the stairs through the hallway that lead to the entrance hall of Reginridge. Footmen opened the main door as the pair exited the house. The Emperor's limo was already waiting for them in the driveway.

"Can I ask you something?" Sandra blurted out. Finally breaking the silence of the Limo ride.

"I don't see how I can stop you." The Emperor answered, looking out the window, watching the trees of the city outskirts fly past.

"Why did you have me stay by your side?" Sandra asked.

"What are you talking about? The Emperor asked in turn, a slight crack came into his voice.

"When I first came on." Sandra elaborated. *"You have bodyguards already, the inquisitors. So why me?"*

"You came to me needing help." The Emperor answered. *"You proved your abilities in combat. What else do you need?"* He reached into a compartment inside the limo and withdrew a small decanter and glass and poured himself a drink.

"I just mean..." Sandra continued. *"You have all sorts of people that do physical work. You could have sent me to be an enforcer somewhere or something. Not to mention you don't fraternize with anyone. It's just strange that you kept a complete stranger by your side."*

The Emperor became visibly irritated. *"I fraternize with plenty of people."* he scolded. *"But I'm not their friend. I'm useless to them if I can't command their respect, so I am required to keep a distance."*

"You're changing the topic." Sandra pressed.

"Fine." The Emperor said coldly. *"If you're unhappy with your current posting, speak to Master Chesley and he'll find something else for you to do."*

"I didn't say that..." Sandra began.

"Then what are you saying?" The Emperor interjected. *"What is it you are trying to pull from me like teeth from the gum"*

"Never mind." Sandra said, crossing her arms *"Forget it... I just thought you could be honest."*

"If you have a charge to lay, then lay it." The Emperor snapped back. *"Otherwise, I am slightly preoccupied with the fact that my domain faces an open insurrection!"*

"Fine." Sandra said with feigned dismissiveness, *"I'll drop it."* Amanda's recent words played endlessly in her head.

The Emperor opened his mouth to continue speaking but decided against it.

The limousine arrived at the museum. Sandra caught a glimpse of the amphitheater on the eastern flank. She pondered how much had happened since that day when she met the Emperor. Cody was standing outside as they pulled up to the entrance. *"Not everyone is here yet, Sire."* Cody said as he opened the door for his lord.

"Just as well." The Emperor replied, helping Sandra out of the car. *"I seldom get the opportunity to enjoy this place. I think I'll walk around for awhile yet."*

"Of course, your Majesty." Cody replied with a nod of his head. *"I'll send a message once everyone's here."*

The Emperor proceeded to walk around to the side of the building and entered via an employee entrance, Sandra following close behind. The pair opened the door into what appeared to be a break room. There was a small group of museum staff sitting around, talking jovially. One was sneaking a cigarette. They all turned toward Sandra and the Emperor as they heard the door close.

"Sire!" one of the employees said, all rose to their feet. *"We didn't know you were coming."* The one who smoked offered The Emperor a cigarette.

"Oh no thank you." The Emperor said holding up a hand *"haven't the time... but I hope you all are holding up well."*

"Word on the street is people are making moves against you." another of the employees offered. *"Must be suicidal."*

"Must be indeed." The Emperor said gleefully. *"Luckily your liege lord is happy to accommodate."* The group all laughed.

"Don't get too worked up about it your Majesty." said another, *"We all stand behind you."*

The Emperor placed a hand on the employee's shoulder. *"It's your faith that keeps the Empire from total dissolution."* he said. *"Without it I am nothing."* the group nodded with appreciation.

"Don't let us keep you Majesty." one of them said, *"We know you're busy."*

"Very true." The Emperor groaned. *"Our enemies may destroy themselves in time, but I am afraid it's my job to expedite the process. Carry on with your break... God knows you deserve it."* The group took turns taking the Emperor's hand and sent him and Sandra off with affectionate waves.

"You're pretty popular." Sandra commented once they left the room.

"Being popular is not difficult when people know you have their best interest at heart." The Emperor replied quickly before continuing into the museum. *"Though many seem to find it difficult...."* he continued down the museum halls. *"Like this oaf."* The Emperor scoffed, stopping at a portrait of a man in a red royal uniform.

"Who was he?" Sandra asked.

"George IV of Great Britain." The Emperor stated. *"A fat, whore-mongering, unscrupulous waste of flesh... but a waste of flesh who happened to be son of the King.... and therefore, he gets a portrait, and the peasants he lorded over and stole from get nothing, No one remembers their names, no one sings their praises. Just because they were born to the wrong parents."*

Sandra stood silent for a moment. *"You know."* she finally offered, *"For a man who calls himself Emperor you hate the idea of monarchy."*

"I don't hate monarchy." The Emperor replied, rolling his eyes but still looking at the painting. *"Monarchy is a beautiful institution. It gives people something to look up to, to hold in esteem... Something grand and majestic that they can strive for in their daily lives..."* he turned to face Sandra. *"No, my quarrel is with the idea that anyone can simply inherit a crown. There must be an aristocracy... that is the natural order. But an aristocracy that has earned its right to rule and not one that merely expects it."*

"Isn't that democracy?" Sandra asked.

"Of course not." The Emperor scoffed, *"Praising democracy as egalitarian is one of the great sins of the western world."*

Sandra gazed at the puzzlement of the Emperor.

"Who is in charge in the democratic system?" The Emperor asked, seeing her confusion. *"Any democratic system."*

"Whoever wins the election." Sandra answered.

"Exactly." The Emperor continued. *"And how are elections won?"*

"Well, you run a campaign, get your message out there and hope it resonates with people."

"Right," said the Emperor. *"And doing all of that, travelling the country, kissing babies, all the nonsense, what does that require?"*

"Money." Sandra answered. She realized where he was going.

"Money." The Emperor repeated, almost disgusted with the word. *"Either you have copious amounts of money that you can spend on such an exercise or you find people that do; to fund your adventures and you in turn become their puppet."* The Emperor shook his head in disapproval. *"Either way, the ruling class remains unchallenged. "He* muttered.

"So, what's the answer then?" Sandra asked.

"That... I do not know." The Emperor said awkwardly. *"There are a great many injustices in this world that I can only recognize. "But those I can solve, I will do so with all tenacity."*

The pair continued their walk through the museum. It had been closed down, presumably because of the meeting that was about to take place. Sandra was intimidated by the building when it was empty. The few times she had been inside the past few months it was bustling with activity. Now it was quiet, she was dwarfed by the exhibits. Portraits and statues of great men and women all looming over her. The Emperor must have been able to sense her uneasiness.

"Don't be afraid of them." The Emperor said surprisingly affectionately. *"Like I just said; most of them are only spoiled spawns of privilege... very few are actually people to behold."*

They reached the lobby. Inside was the giant portrait of the brunette woman. The first thing Sandra ever saw upon entering the Emperor's world.

"What about her?" Sandra asked, pointing at the painting.

The Emperor stopped in his tracks. He turned toward the painting and stalled. He walked up to it and placed a hand gently on the canvas, he barely stood half the painting's height. He looked up at the subject's face and Sandra noticed a tear developing in his eye.

"I'm sorry." Sandra muttered. *"Were you and her... You know?"*

"Oh nonono." The Emperor said dismissively while wiping his eye. *"But I'll take it as a compliment. She was beautiful, wasn't she?"* She was indeed beautiful. He walked over to waiting bench and sat down. Sandra sat down beside him.

"Latonya Duchant was my friend. Just my friend mind you." The Emperor iterated. *"But without her none of this would exist. There would be no Emperor."*

"How do you mean?" Sandra asked.

"You may be surprised to learn," The Emperor began *"I did not burst through my mother's womb reciting Latin and assaulting deadbeats."* Sandra chuckled at the image which made the Emperor smile in turn. *"No, I was once an ordinary sort of person."* he continued. *"I fell on hard times like plenty of people do."* Sandra nodded in understanding.

"I was a member of the capitalist machine," The Emperor carried on, *"unblessed with riches by my progenitors so I worked, and worked, and worked."*

"I know the feeling." Sandra added.

"And you also know the feeling of refusing to accept your station." The Emperor added.

"Huh?"

"You're a criminal..." The Emperor explained, *"Same as I. The system was pitted against you, so you went against the system."*

"What does this have to do with your friend?" Sandra asked, desperate to change the Emperor's train of thought. He was stressful when he was making sense.

"Well, when I first decided to engage in that sort of activity I knew nothing." The Emperor explained, *"I had a vague idea of how things went but I didn't have any real connections into this world."* He removed his feathered hat and rubbed his forehead. *"At the time I worked moonlight shifts as a bartender to try and keep a roof over my head."* He pointed at

the painting. *"Latonya was a bartender at the same establishment that's how we met."*

"And?" Sandra asked.

"And..." The Emperor continued, *"she had the connections I didn't have. In addition to bartending, she was a stripper and, in that capacity, rubbed elbows with the exact kind of people I needed to meet."* The memory made him smile fondly, *"She made the introductions for me and my foray into criminal activity began in earnest. Culminating in little Eddie Drac's ascension to Emperor."* he closed his eyes, *"She was such a sweet girl."* The Emperor muttered. *"She took a kid she barely knew and vouched for him, because she wanted to see him succeed."*

"So what happened to her?" Sandra pressed.

The Emperor thrust his tongue into his cheek. He turned from Sandra and looked at the ground. *"She was kind, and she was sweet, but she wasn't smart."* The Emperor mulled, his voice turning bitter. *"Around the time I was starting out she had this beau. She adored him of course, but he was a useless vagrant. I worked with him sometimes because of my friendship with Latonya, but I knew he was swine."* The Emperor let out a deep sigh *"One day he had lost some money his employer had trusted him with... probably squirted the entire amount into his arm, who knows..."* The tears began swelling in the Emperor's eyes again. *"He could've just paid it back and taken the beating....”* his voice was becoming choked.

“What did he do?” Sandra asked.

“He blamed her.” The Emperor growled. *“My dear sweet friend, he threw her under the bus to save his own wretched hide.... Said she gambled the money away and there was nothing to do.”* Tears were now rolling down the Emperor's cheek. *“I tried to hide her, but she insisted she would be fine.... It was a week later I heard how they shot her in some piss infested alley and dumped her body into the coast.”* The Emperor buried his face into his hands desperately trying to regain his composure.

Sandra gently took his arm. *“That wasn't your fault... surely you have to know that.”*

“Of course I know that!” The Emperor snapped back, pulling his arm free. *“I knew who was responsible and I never forgot what he had done!”* The Emperor took a deep breath and calmed himself. *“Appropriate punishment was handed down.”* he said coolly.

“I can only imagine what you did to him...” Sandra said under her breath. Thinking of the various colorful ways she had seen the Emperor administer “justice”.

“But you already know what I did to him.” The Emperor replied. *“I found him. I beat him within an inch of his life. But death was too merciful a sentence, so I bound him in irons, covering his*

wretched face in an iron mask and forced him to live the rest of his cursed days as my servant."

"You mean...?"

"Lionel Charteris killed my dear friend." The Emperor coldly interrupted. *"And now she is immortalized in this beautiful place as the beautiful spirit she was... and he laps water from a bowl in a dungeon, until I see fit to end his cursed life."*

The Emperor leaned back into the bench. *"But it won't bring her back."* He said to himself, exhausted. Sandra took his hand again. This time he did not pull away. Instead, he leant onto Sandra's shoulder and closed his eyes.

"Majesty! They're ready!"

The Emperor's head popped up as Cody came running down the hall.

"The Imperial Council is an assembled sire." Cody blurted as he approached Sandra and the Emperor sitting on the bench.

"Right!" The Emperor exclaimed, springing to his feet. *"Let us end this threat once and for all."*

The trio marched down yet another hall in the expansive labyrinth, up a spiral staircase that went for several stories. Sandra could feel herself getting winded, but the Emperor pressed on with a face full of conviction. The top of the staircase yielded to the top floor of the building. On it was one solitary room concealed by a door. Sandra approached the door to open it for the two men, but the Emperor stopped her.

"We may be facing a crisis..." he said. *"But proper decorum will still be observed."* He stepped to one side and began straightening the lapel on his jacket as Cody entered the room alone, leaving the door cracked. Sandra could hear muffled conversation come to a hush as Cody walked inside.

"Ladies and Gentlemen, Marshals of the Empire." she heard him say. *"The Emperor."*

Sandra could hear shuffling as everyone rose from their seats. Violins began playing over a sound system inside the room. The Emperor gestured for her to enter as he followed behind. Inside the room everyone stood silently, faces toward the floor in reverence. The room was opulent, like the rest of the Museum, portraits hanging along the walls, the floor only adorned with a large dark wooden table. Identical chairs placed all around except for a larger on at the table's head. The table was covered with a violet throw embroidered with the Imperial Sigil in gold.

Sandra looked around the table and saw a few faces she recognized. Sylvia and Harold were sitting side by side, on the other side of the room was Madame DuBois the arms dealer. There were a few others she did not recognize but luckily the name plate filled in the gaps.

"Kurt Stevens: Marshal for Financing" a middle-aged balding and bespectacled man nervously fiddling with his ring.

"George Samerson: Marshal for Gambling" he was scarily thin with slicked back hair and a pencil thin moustache.

"Please be seated." The Emperor said as he took his chair at the table's head. Sandra and Cody remained standing, flanking him on either side. No chairs were placed for them.

"Well my friends." The Emperor began. *"We all know why we are here. Enemies of the Crown and Empire have united in opposition to our hegemony. They seek to usurp our order. And they now feel that they have the ability to graduate from guerilla tactics into the open field."*

"If your Majesty would allow me..." Stevens raised a finger. The Emperor gestured for him to speak. *"Sire,"* Stevens began *"Do we have accurate figures on their numbers?"*

"No." Cody answered. *"Our intel isn't good enough to make an accurate estimate. But for now, I think... and his Majesty agrees, that it's best to assume they outnumber us by a staggering amount. Prepare for the worst."* The table nodded in agreement.

"Regardless of their strength..." The Emperor interjected. *"They are undisciplined and disorganized. They may have spirit these rebels and they may have numbers.... But they lack the*

infrastructure to wage war. Which grants us a serious advantage."

Harold cleared his throat. *"I don't mean to argue with your Majesty."* Harold squeaked. *"But what exactly do we have in terms of infrastructure?"*

The Emperor laughed at the question. *"We have you all."* he answered. *"Your realms of the Empire are all well organized and efficient. We merely need to convert our assets into a militant course."*

"How?" Harold pressed.

"Well..." The Emperor said, *"first we need to create an army. My royal inquisition is a good start but they cannot be expected to face this alone."* He withdrew a small pad of paper from his breast pocket and began reading from it. *"Madame DuBois."* said the Emperor, *"by mine and Master Chesley's count, we have around fifteen hundred able bodies in the Imperial ranks. We shall need them to be armed. Can you see it done?"*

"Your Majesty asks a lot." Madame DuBois replied, itching under her wig. *"Can it be done? Yes. But it'll cost us."*

"I am afraid I have to agree." Stevens interjected. *"What you are talking about will be a huge expense. Perhaps if we had everyone pay for their own...."*

The Emperor held up his hand and the room became silent. *"Ladies and gentlemen. We are here in this room as persons of power, because we undertook a duty to protect those that serve us. They pay their tax to us and we in turn provide security. The Crown is willing to cover half of the expenses with the remainder being split among each of the people that deign to sit at this table.*

"But if your Majesty will just allow me a moment." Stevens tried again *"the cost you are talking about incurring."*

The Emperor held up his hand again. *"We are fast approaching war."* He said calmly. *"Financial stability must come second to protecting that which is ours. As I said I will meet my obligation and finance half of the expenses, if you are all willing to do the same."* Murmuring ensued around the table, but ultimately the council was in collective agreement.

Madame Dubois gently raised a hand. The Emperor acknowledged her inquiry. *"Your Majesty, this is all well and good."* she began. *"But I can only procure the weapons. I don't have the means to disperse them to everyone. Having everyone come to one of my storehouses all at once is sure to attract negative attention."*

"I can see to that." Harold interjected. *"My distribution network should be more than adequate... and needless to say, they excel at being discreet."*

"Excellent." The Emperor remarked. *"We create a grand Imperial army, ready to fight at a moment's notice. And we drive the enemy back to the rocks."*

"Ahem." Syvlia gently cleared her throat.

"Madame Jones." The Emperor acknowledged. *"You have concerns?"*

"I...." Sylvia began, *"admire your call to the people's patriotism sire. And I have no doubt that the men of the Empire will stand firm in the defense of our realm. But I must advocate for women. Are we really expecting them to take to the streets?"*

"It's their fortune too at stake." The Emperor replied calmly. *"I see no reason why they cannot take up arms against forces that threaten the crown."*

"Sire, be reasonable." Sylvia continued calmly. *"Don't ask them to fight. They're frightened; they'll just get in the way. Spare them please."*

"Have you no faith in your fellow sex?" The Emperor questioned.

"My job is not to have faith in them but to protect their interests." Sylvia countered. *"And they are not soldiers. I will gladly go myself if you need me to prove my loyalty."*

The Emperor leaned back in his chair. Crocking his head he smiled at Syliva. *"How can I argue with such devotion?"* he beamed. He turned to address the table at large. *"The women of the Empire will not be subject to conscription in the Grand Armee, but volunteers will be welcome. Is there an objection?"* The group looked to each other and sporadic murmuring took place but no objection was presented.

"Alright then." The Emperor said, *"There is one last matter in this army business. I will not have*

those who have stood loyally behind us thrust into battle unprepared. We are not rabble. My security forces will oversee a training regimen for all of the Imperial conscripts headed by Ms. Stacy Mae. You all have seen her prowess in combat. I am confident she can turn citizens into centurions. That is... if she is up to the task?" The whole room fell upon Sandra. She stood awkwardly at the Emperor's flank. Eyes of the marshals piercing into her soul.

"I will do what I can to keep everyone safe." She clumsily blurted out.

"I have every confidence." The Emperor said calmly, and for once, unsarcastically.

"Okay everyone." Cody interjected. *"Next order of business...."*

Once the meeting was over Sandra and the Emperor returned to Reginridge in a silent car ride. Upon returning to the house the Emperor and Sandra ascended the grand staircase to their separate rooms. At the top of the stairs was Mr. Charteris, nervously waiting for his master. Sandra looked down to the groveling monster, she knelt down gently and placed her hands onto his shoulders. The story the Emperor recounted at the museum was fresh in her mind, seeing the wretch in a whole new light. She proceeded to shove Mr. Charteris, causing him to fall down the stairs. As Mr. Charteris' agonizing screams echoed in the staircase, his metal casings clanging on the marble floors, Sandra turned and looked to the Emperor. The Emperor was staring into her eyes, his face that of pure delight. She returned the sentiment only for the Emperor to quickly squeeze her hand and leave her in the stairwell. Yet as he left Sandra heard the faint sound of his Majesty singing gleefully to himself.

Chapter 18: Amanada

"This is serious, you know…." Cody said as he fumbled in the bedsheets. It was not long after the party at Reginridge that he began sneaking into her warehouse. It was an easier location to rendezvous.

"You think I don't know that?" Amanda responded, pulling the sheets up to cover herself. *"But we can't do anything about it right this second. So let's just enjoy the moment."*

"You have that gun right?" Cody asked, *"Like you keep it with you?"*

"Yes." Amanda said, rolling her eyes. *"And Stacy taught me how to use it."*

"Okay good." Said Cody satisfied, *"If something happens to me you stay close to her, she'll keep you safe."*

Amanda smiled and kissed Cody on the cheek. *"I can look after myself. And besides, the big guy has everything under control."*

"I hope he does." Cody mulled sitting upright in bed. *"Christ knows I trust the Emperor with my life, but he's not perfect, it's possible he's missing something."*

"Well like I said…" Amanda interjected, nuzzling into Cody's chest. *"There's nothing we can do about it right this second. "So, forget about our problems with me for a second."*

Cody leant down and kissed her on the forehead. Amanda closed her eyes and allowed all the troubles of the world to fade away as she pulled the bedsheets over the heads once more.

There was a loud persistent knocking at Amanda's door. The rapping of metal caused Amanda to jolt awake. *"WHAT?!"* She exclaimed groggily.

"Amanda it's me." Tiffany's voice rang out from the other side. *"We just saw Sylvia's car pull up."*

"Oh shit okay." Amanda shouted back. *"I'll be there in a sec."* Amanda quickly shoved Cody awake and explained the situation. The pair leaped from bed and hastily got dressed. They managed to fumble out of the door just as Sylvia walked into the warehouse below. Graceful and radiant as always, Sylvia's flowing gown billowing behind her as she marched into Amanda's building.

"Grand Marshal Chesley, what a surprise!" Sylvia exclaimed as Amanda and Cody descended the stairs to greet her. *"What would the Lord High Chancellor be doing..."* she looked the pair up and down. *"Ohhhhh"* she giggled to herself.

"Syliva..." Amanda began to explain but Sylvia merely took Amanda by the shoulder.

"Honey there's nothing to explain." Sylvia said jovially. *"I don't judge, what you kids do is your business."* Amanda nodded appreciatively. *"Be that as it may."* Sylvia continued, *"I do need to talk to you darlin' so Cody you run along and let the girls have girl*

time." Cody promptly did as he was instructed and scurried out of the building, with all the girls in Amanda's service giggling as he did so.

"Mmm mmm mmm." Sylvia chuckled. *"Girl you are naughty."* Amanda opened her mouth to offer a defense, but Sylvia cut her off again. *"But anyway, it's not important."* she said. *"I have good news sweetheart."*

"Good news?" Amanda asked, *"With everything going on I figured it'd be months before we got some good news."*

Sylvia laughed. *"God, you sound just like the rest of those stuffy men I have to sit with every day!"* She joked. *"Nothing makes them happier than an existential crisis to fawn over. Thank God the Emperor started bringing his little friend to the council meetings just so I can have another woman around to see the reason..."*

"Sylvia, what's the news?" Amanda asked.

"Right right. Sorry sweetie, you know my brain's a constant clutter." Sylvia responded. *"Where's that little one Tiffany that works for you. It's about her."*

"Oh!" Amanda exclaimed, having a guess what Sylvia was going to say. *"Let's talk upstairs. I'll bring her with us."*

Sylvia smiled in agreement and began walking up the stairs to Amanda's private room. Amanda followed close behind. As she walked, she locked eyes with Tiffany and jutted her chin in the direction of the stairwell, signaling for her to follow. Tiffany jogged to meet up and the three women entered Amanda's room with Tiffany shutting the door behind them.

"Here she is!" Syliva exclaimed, embracing Tiffany with a giant hug. *"Here is the numbers girl Amanda is always telling me so much about!"*

Tiffany awkwardly returned Sylvia's hug. *"It's nice to meet you.. Uh ma'am."*

Sylvia stepped back. *"Oh no, that Ma'am thing won't do."* She said with a sarcastic sternness. *"It makes me feel old. Sylvia will be just fine."*

Tiffany looked to Amanda for direction, but Amanda just shrugged and smiled. Sylvia began to sit on the bed but then looked to examine the displaced sheets, chucked to herself and stood back up. *"Honey, I wanted to meet you."* She said, turning her attention back to Tiffany. *"I wanted to meet you because Amanda goes on and on about how smart Tiffany is and how she doesn't want to work in the pleasure business anymore..."*

"I swear I wasn't trying to...." Tiffany began nervously but Sylvia hushed her.

"Calm down sugar you aren't in any trouble." Syvlia responded in her signature calming tone. *"No, just listen for a second."* Tiffany stopped blubbering.

"In my position as Marchioness of the Empire." She dramatically flashed her ring and placed her hand on her forehead for comedic effect. *"I have*

the distinct pleasure of being in constant contact with lowlifes from all over the city." She placed a hand on Tiffany's shoulder. *"In our last meeting I pulled aside The Emperor's Marshal of Finance and explained to him that we have just the smartest, hardworking girl who was forced into the life of a concubine, but who really wanted to work in the lending business."*

Tiffany's eyes widened, *"What did he say?"* she asked.

"Well I don't know if Amanada has spoken to you all yet but currently our little gang is in a bit of hot water." Tiffany nodded in understanding; Amanda had prepped her crew the moment word came down to her about the impending attack.

"Anyway Mr. Stevens told me, not right now mind you, but when all this ugly business with the Republicans is settled, then he would be happy to take you on and get you started on a career with his people."

Tiffany jumped up and down in excitement. *"Thank you thank you thank you!"* She exclaimed, hugging Sylvia for real now. *"You have no idea what this means to me!"*

"Oh honey yes I do." Sylvia said sweetly, returning the hug. *"None of the people who wear the Emperor's ring started off as people of means. We know how to look out for each other."*

"Well thank you anyway." Tiffany reiterated. Sylvia gently pushed Tiffany away from her and pointed her in Amanda's direction.

"I wasn't the one who spoke on your behalf." Sylvia softly reminded.

Tiffany bottled over and hugged Amanda. *"Thank you..."* she whispered.

"You deserve it." Amanda replied. *"All I did was state facts."*

"Now like I said." Sylvia interjected, *"that's only after this insurrection is over and his poor Majesty can go back to his typical maniacal self."* Sylvia walked over to Amanda's door and opened it. *'And I do have something else I have to discuss with Amanda in private."* Tiffany thanked Sylvia again and scurried out of the door, bubbling with excitement. Sylvia shut the door behind her and her typical cheery expression turned more somber.

"Mandy, he's making an army." she said coldly.

"What do you mean?" Amanda asked.

"The Emperor wants anyone who can carry a rifle to join the cause." Syvlia explained, *"I tried to keep us and our girls out of it but he insisted any women volunteers would be accepted."*

"Okay." Amand said, slightly confused. *"I mean it makes sense to me so what's the problem?"*

"Honey I can't, in good conscience, send those poor girls out to fight while we sit back and

watch. So I have to insist that you and all the other knights under me join up."

"Oh...." Amanda said, *"Well to be honest with you I haven't thought about it much, but now that it's in front of me.... I don't mind going."*

"It's gonna be dangerous." Syvlia said, *"And I'm not talking dangerous like some handsy John... I mean you could die. We could die."*

"I understand." Amanda said, *"Honestly... I agree though. It's the right thing."*

Sylvia took Amanda into her arms. *"Oh baby, I wish it was different."* she said, tears beginning to well. *"When you came on, I was so happy for you, I thought you were gonna have the same grand old time I did."*

Amanda released herself from Sylvia's grip. *"It's not over."* Amanda said. *"This is just a bump in the road. They happen."*

"You are so right." Syvlia said with a smile. *"I'm glad you understand honey. This leadership gig has got some great perks. But you gotta show up when it counts."*

"Yea." Amanda said, kind of quietly.

"What's wrong?" Syvlia questioned. *"Why the change in tone?"*

"Nothing." Amanda answered meekly, *"It's not my place."*

"Mandy..." Sylvia pressed

"Well it's just..." Amanda began, pausing to collect her thoughts. She remembered what the

Emperor told her about not being afraid. And this had been weighing on her mind. *"Before me, when things were how they were. How come you didn't do anything about it?"*

Sylvia looked to her feet. Her face soured. *"You probably have no idea about this."* Sylvia said, *"But that night when the Emperor came here, and when he threw Pump out onto the street. When he left, I got called to Reginridge."*

"So?" Amanda inquired

"He must have screamed at me for six hours." Sylvia laughed nervously. *"You know how he can get when he gets worked up. Once he saw how you all were living he was so mad that I let any of that happen to you girls. He threatened to kill me, though I don't think he ever actually would've done it."*

"He said to me that if I didn't care about what was happening to those who I led, I had no business being a leader at all. And then he got real quiet."

"Why?" Amanda asked.

"He sat there and started breaking out into tears. The only time I've ever seen him do that." Sylvia explained. *"He started saying he was just as guilty and that he was no better than the rest of them... who them was I have no idea, but he was a wreck."*

"None of this answers my question." Amanda pressed.

"Why didn't we do anything?" Sylvia repeated, *"We got careless. The money was coming in and everything was quiet and we didn't bother digging any*

deeper until the money stopped. I wish I had a better answer for you sugar but I don't we did wrong by you."

"But that's not good enough!" Amanda scolded, her emotions bubbling to surface. *"You can't just say you're sorry and that's it! All that pain and hurt happened! And just because you were only caring about money!"*

Sylvia smiled softly, her typical calming Sylvia smile. *"You are absolutely right."* She said, *"There's nothing anyone can do to take that away. But why do you think the Emperor paid off that man you beat up? He felt guilty."*

Amanda froze, it had been ages since she thought about that night in the strangers car, the first time her fury had been unleashed. *"The Emperor paid him off?"* Amanda asked.

"You think that just magically went away?" Sylvia laughed, *"Yes his Majesty paid the man off... and forced me to cover half as my punishment."*

Amanda elected not to respond.

"Try not to hate me too much darling." Sylvia said, *"And especially don't hate him. He already hates himself enough for it."*

"I don't hate you." Amanda replied, *"I'm sorry I got angry just..."*

"Don't be sorry." Sylvia interjected. *"Just be better than me. One day the Emperor and me and Harold and all of us will be dead and gone, then it'll be your turn."* She affectionately shook Amanda's thigh. *"Now enough of this morbid shit lets go get*

some dinner." Sylvia jolted back to life and practically floated out of the door. Amanda couldn't help but smirk and rush after her.

Sylvia drove Amanada to a nearby diner. *"Are you sure this is a good idea?"* Amanda asked as Sylvia pulled into a parking spot.

"Oh, I'm not going to be hunkering down like some doomsday prepper." Sylvia shot back. *"Living in fear is no way to live."* The pair walked along the sidewalk of the city from the parking lot to the restaurant. As they approached the door Sylvia slid her Imperial ring off of her finger and gestured to Amanda to do the same. *"Keeps everything less tense."* she explained.

As the pair sat down a waitress came to take their order. Sylvia ordered a water to drink and Amanda followed suit. *"Mmmmm"* Sylvia said *"What are you thinking?"*

"I don't know." Amanda responded, perusing the menu in front of her. *"What about you?"*

"Oh its going to be a salad for me." Sylvia said playfully. *"But don't let that stop you, I just save all my fun eating for when Harold's around."*

Amanda giggled at the explanation. *"Why's that?"* she asked.

"Because the idiot thinks this..." Sylvia ran her fingers up and down her waist. *"Happens all on its own... men really are the dumbest things, I don't*

know what." The pair laughed as the waitress brought their drinks.

Before long, their food had arrived as well. True to her word Sylvia only ate a salad while Amanda ordered a cheeseburger. The next hour was one full of laughter and peace. Sylvia always knew how to put Amanda's mind at ease. They ate, they drank, they shared stories. Glasses clinked as the ladies forgot their woes and merely enjoyed each other's company.

The waitress returned one final time with the bill which Sylvia insisted on paying. Amanda procured some loose bills from her purse to cover the tip. Both thanked the waitress as they left and emerged once again on the city street.

"Oh thank you lovebug I needed that." Sylvia said gleefully, nudging Amanda's shoulder as the two walked back to Sylvia's car. It was late now and the sun was beginning to set. *"Sometimes it's nice to forget the rest of it and just be girls, you know?"*

"I definitely do." Amanda replied in turn. They were nearing the parking lot. *"All this stuff has got me so stressed out."* They entered the parking lot and approached Sylvia's car.

"Not much we can do now babes." Syliva said *"All that's left is..."*

THUD

They had reached Syliva's car. Amanada had her hand on the passenger side door when Sylvia stopped mid-sentence. Concerned she ran around the other side of the vehicle only to see Syliva lying on the pavement. A small trickle of blood emanating from a hole center of Sylvia's forehead. Her eyes still open, but all life instantly vanished from them.

"Oh nonononononono." Amanda panicked. Sylvia motionless on the ground. Her eyes wide open but any vestige of life in them had gone. *"Nononononono"* Amanda repeated to herself as she knelt down to examine Sylvia's head. She quickly darted her gaze to the surrounding rooftops. It was too dark she couldn't see anything. Tears were beginning to swell in Amanda's eyes. She cupped Sylvia's lifeless head in her hands, tears now streaming on her face onto Sylvia's forehead.

"Jesus Christ." Amanda whispered internally. She leaned forward and pressed her forehead against Syliva's. What just happened? Two seconds ago, they were laughing and now she's just gone. How? Why? What?

PING

A bullet went into the door of Sylvia's car. Shit. The shooter was still there.

PING

Another bullet. Closer this time. Amanda fell to the ground flat. Army crawling, she dragged herself under the car. The bullets kept coming. Chunks of asphalt exploded near the car as the shooter fired shot after shot in Amanda's direction. With her watered eyes she could barely see. Shot after shot continued smashing the ground inches away from her.

What was she to do? She wiped her eyes clear. Her vision returned and she looked to Syliva's corpse. No pockets on her dress. No purse. She must have left the keys inside of the car. Amanda reached into her own purse. She withdrew her pistol. All the good it would do. She had no idea where the shots were coming from.

Still lying under the car Amanda slowly wriggled herself to the passenger side of the vehicle. Shots still raining down onto her. Once at the edge of the vehicle she rolled from underneath it and crouched behind the door for cover, wary to make sure her head did not stick out above the window.

She poked her head around the bumper, and she could see nothing but the tip of Sylvia's motionless head and the pool of blood that was ever growing around it. She snapped back behind the safety of the passenger door. She reached for the handle, locked. Damn. A few more shots exploded into the asphalt by the car. Amanda fell flat again. Crawling back under the car she inched over to the other side once again. The shots had stopped for now. Slowly she reached a hand out toward Sylivia's limp body. Sylvia had a clenched fist lying on the ground. Amanda dug into it. She could feel the metal of keys but couldn't get ahold of them.

Another shot rang out. Amanda quickly recoiled her hand. It took a moment to gather her courage again, but she reached out once more. Slowly she pulled back Sylvia's fingers one by one, releasing the keys. Once they were free, she grabbed ahold of them. Her hand was now stained with Sylvia's blood. The feeling of Sylvia's lifeless fingers made her stomach churn. She wriggled herself again to the passenger side of the vehicle.

Carefully she reached up and fumbled the key into the door lock. Another shot. Amanda could tell by now they were coming from the other side of the car, she did not lose her nerve, finally she heard the click of the door unlocking. She popped the door open and began to climb into the car, careful to keep her head low. She placed a hand down on the seat, only to find that one of the shots had shattered a window, broken glass dug into her hand. She bit down on her tongue to keep from screaming in agony.

She finally positioned herself into the driver's seat, head tucked between her knees. The engine roared to life as she put the key into the ignition. A series of shots slammed into the car door, shaking the vehicle on impact. Amanda slammed the car into gear and cut the wheel. She felt a bump as the car whirred around. *"Holy Shit"* she thought to herself, realizing what it was. No time to worry about that now. She made it onto the street proper and floored the gas pedal.

Amanda did her best to keep the car straight while her head was tucked, after about 20 seconds she figured she was clear and looked out onto the road. Thank God the traffic was light. She let out a big exhale. Time to focus. The immediate danger was over. She had to get to Reginridge. Sylvia was dead. God. Sylvia was dead.

The car began rumbling. The steering wheel began pulling to the left. What the hell was going on? One of the bullets had to have hit the tire. Great. Of course. She was still in the middle of the city. There's no way she could make it to Reginridge like this. She pulled hard on the steering wheel to keep the car level. Only one place she could go.

She screeched into the street by her warehouse. Frantically she exited the car and rushed inside. Slamming the door behind her caused everyone to turn and look. Disheveled, and covered in blood she drew concern from everyone inside. They all came rushing over to her. Her security men pushed their way to the front of the crowd.

"Jesus boss," one of them said *"You just went to eat what happened??"*

"I..." Amanda began. *"Well, I...."* she was trying to hold back tears. *"Can you fix a tire?"*

"What?" The guard asked, confused.

"Can you fix a tire?!?!" Amanda blurted.

"Yea Yea, take it easy," he replied. *"Me and the guys can fix it for you."*

"Good." Amanda muttered while she closed her eyes and took another deep breath. She handed the guard a large roll of cash from her purse. *"I don't care what it costs, just as soon as possible. It's right outside."*

"You got it." he said, leading the others outside to begin work. The girls will still huddle around Amanda.

"None of you are going out tonight." Amanda said to the group. *"You're all staying right here."*

Murmuring sprung out across the group. Clearly, they were not satisfied. *"What's going on?" "What happened to you?" "Are we in danger?" "Is this it?"* The voices were circling around Amanda, pounding through her ears and into her skull. It all turned into ringing.

"SHUT UP!" she roared. *"FOR GOD'S SAKE SHUT UP AND JUST DO WHAT I TELL YOU!"* She shoved her way into the crowd. And climbed the stairs into her room. Shutting the door behind her she collapsed onto her bed, the tears finally loose and streaming down her face.

A soft knock came at her door. *"Go away."* she said, not even rising from the bed. She heard the door creak open. *"Am I not in charge around here?!"* Amanda snapped as she sat up in the bed.

"No no you definitely are." Frankie said as he inched into the room. *"You just seem like you need to talk."*

"If I needed to talk I would say that." Amanda said curtly. *"Now get out."*

"Fine, if that's what you want." Frankie said, shrugging. He turned to leave.

"Hang on, wait a second." Amanda said, her voice full of exhaustion. *"That was rude of me."*

Frankie turned back and approached her. *"What happened?"* he asked.

"I can't talk about it right now." Amanda replied. *"Just, I'm sorry I snapped at you."*

Frankie walked closer still to bed where Amanda was sitting.

"You know you can tell me." he said. Amanda sat up on the bed.

"Thank you, Frankie, really," she said. *"But I need to be alone right now."* Frankie's face began to sour. He mumbled something under his breath.

"What was that?" Amanda questioned, halfway wishing she had just chosen to ignore it.

"Just thinking if Cody was here you'd talk to him..." Frankie grunted.

"What the hell are you talking about?" Amanda pressed. *"Actually nevermind, I don't even wanna know just leave me alone please."*

"I just don't understand how I've been by your side since day one. And then this dude comes out of nowhere and you throw yourself at him."

"I do not throw myself at ANYONE." Amanda said. *"Now Frankie please leave my room."*

Frankie didn't even react to her response. He paced around as if he were in the room by himself. *"It's just not fair."* he murmured. Amanda suspected he was talking to himself more than to her.

"Frankie." she said again. *"You need to leave now."*

Frankie stopped pacing and turned to look at her. *"I love you, you know."*

Amanda hung her head in frustration. *"Frankie, now is not the time for this conversation."* she was becoming increasingly more annoyed. *"I don't know what you're trying to achieve here right now but please leave."*

"I told you before he just wants you for your legs." Frankie said, ignoring Amanda's request. *"I would treat you so much better."*

"Frankie, I am not talking about this with you." Amanda reiterated. She was so exhausted.

"I just don't see why you won't give me a fair shot." Frankie groaned. *"I could make you so happy."*

He reached out a hand, but Amanda slapped it away.

"Frankie, I am not going to tell you again." she said one final time. She did her best to sound as threatening as possible. *"Leave my room."*

"No." Frankie said, *"Not until you listen to me."* He stepped uncomfortably close. Amanda

moved to stand but before she could Frankie put his hands on her shoulders.

"You motherfu..." Amanda began but was cut off when Frankie forced a palm over her mouth, pinning her down onto the bed. Amanda wriggled and squirmed, but she could not get herself free, Frankie was too strong.. She tried shouting for help but all that came out was muffled nonsense. She thrashed and kicked but Frankie was unmoved. With a hand over Amanda's mouth Frankie used his forearm to pin her down. His other hand lowered to Amanda's waist and began pulling at her pants. She felt her waistband fall down to her knees. She continued squirming but to no avail. She could hear the sound of a zipper being undone.

It was then she remembered. Her purse. She had tossed it on the bed when she came into the room. She could feel Frankie tugging on her underwear. She was exposed now. She closed her eyes and held her breath. She needed to stay calm. She couldn't turn her head, but she knew the purse had to be there. She reached around beside her. Nothing. She felt Frankie's hand on her breast. *"Stay calm."* she reminded herself. She reached again; she faintly felt the strap of her purse. Violently and with all her body weight she lunged her arm to the side and grabbed her purse. Before Frankie had a chance to react Amanda withdrew the gun from her bag.

BANG

Amanda felt blood spatter all over her face. Frankie recoiled in pain and lifted himself off of her, though he did not fall. He stumbled back and forth clutching his jaw. Blood pooling into his hand and seeping through his fingers. Amanda quickly redressed herself and sprung to her feet. She took the pistol and struck Frankie across the face, causing him to drop his hand. Dropping his hand showed his cheek had been ripped open and his jaw dislocated, dangling on the left side.

Amanda fell back in shock, giving Frankie time to fling open her door and run out. Amanda started after him. On the balcony overlooking the warehouse she chased him. The girls below looking up with a mixture of confusion and fear. Amanda chased him to the staircase, as Frankie reached the stairs he fell, rolling down the stairs until he reached the bottom, a trail of blood in his wake. Amanda stopped her chase. Once Frankie reached the bottom, he picked himself up. Once again, he removed his hand to steady himself, The sight of his dislocated mouth caused the girls to scream, and panic erupted in the building. Frankie quickly recovered his face and left the building slamming the door behind him.

Chapter 19: Sandra

"God, I feel like a plebeian." The Emperor grumbled as he shifted in his seat. The city stadium cheered as a baseball game commenced on the diamond below. In the stadium sat the Emperor, no feathered hat or fancy garments, just slacks, a collared shirt and a simple ballcap.

"Hey!" Sandra snapped back at his comment, *"I went to the boring ass opera with you last week and I didn't complain. This week you said we could come to a ball game."* She had hoped to be in the stands, but the Emperor insisted on a private box, a detachment of inquisitors surrounding them. Still, it was a concession on his part.

"I remember very well thank you." The Emperor responded, darting his gaze at Sandra, *"I just don't understand why we couldn't go to the opera again, you seemed like you enjoyed it."*

"Because." Sandra groaned, rolling her eyes. *"Sometimes I just wanna feel like a NORMAL person."*

"Why in God's name would anyone want that?" The Emperor mumbled under his breath. Sandra pretended not to hear him. She instead just focused on the game. She would be lying if she said she wasn't beginning to enjoy her time with the Emperor but so much had changed so fast. She frequently found herself jealous of the people who were more removed from his Majesty's circle. The

Emperor would host those raves at Reginridge for the street level guys. They always looked like fun. The Emperor consistently would encourage her to join them, but she never did, mostly because his being annoyed was much more entertaining.

Instead, she sat with his Majesty in his study. He would sometimes listen to classical music, sometimes sitting at his desk working. Most of the time both. He never spoke to her much, but she knew he liked having her there. When everything was accounted for, he was quite a sad man, always nervously rubbing his infernal watch. But people looked up to this madman, and he loved them. She had never seen anything like it. And as the time went on she too found herself increasingly under his spell. But she wasn't quite ready to give it all up just yet.

Her mind returning to the present, she glanced back at the Emperor, he was constantly shifting in his seat, clearly uncomfortable. She placed a hand atop his. *"Thank you."* she whispered into his ear. He did not reply but color flushed in his cheeks.

"You'll excuse me a moment." The Emperor said at the conclusion of the fourth inning. He abruptly rose from his chair and wandered off into the stadium. A few minutes later he returned to their box, one hot dog in each hand. *"This is part of the experience I believe."* he said, retaking his seat and handing Sandra a hot dog.

"Wow, look at you getting into the spirit." Sandra said playfully. *"But I like mustard on mine."*

"Oh, I'm sorry" the Emperor fumbled, *"I didn't..."* he stood back up again.

"I'm just messing with you." Sandra chuckled, taking the Emperor's arm to sit him back down. *"Its perfect just like this."* The Emperor smiled sheepishly and sat back down.

"You know.." he said, in between bites of his hot dog. *"They sometimes have fireworks at these events."* His voice was hopeful, like a child's.

"Yea I'm pretty sure there's fireworks after the game tonight." Sandra replied.

"Oh." The Emperor remarked gleefully *"This might turn out to be a nice evening after all."*

"Oh I'm so glad for you." Sandra shot back sarcastically. *"I didn't realize you liked them so much.*

"They remind me of field artillery." The Emperor said with a grin. *"It takes me back to happier times."*

"You're one strange man." Sandra remarked.

"I know.,," The Emperor replied, leaning smugly into his chair, *"but I am rich..."* Sandra turned and smacked him across the cheek.

"Ow!" the Emperor exclaimed, massaging his cheekbone. *"What in hell did you do that for?"*

"Just shut up." Sandra snapped back. *"Sometimes you talk too much."* She folded her arms, annoyed at his implication.

"There's no talking at the opera...." The Emperor retorted, his face slowly contorting into a smirk. Sandra tried to restrain herself but wound up laughing through her nose. She leaned into the Emperor's shoulder, and the pair watched the remainder of the game in silence.

Sandra slowly pulled the van down the driveway to Reginridge. She had insisted that they not take the limousine much to the Emperor's chagrin. However, the Emperor did manage to hide one of his standard eclectic suits in the van and had managed to change his clothes before they arrived back to the house. *"If they saw me like this, they'd never respect me."* He said, referencing his casual outfit.

Sandra parked the van and as they walked toward the house, Edwina rushed in the Emperor's direction. *"Ah there's my precious darling."* The Emperor exclaimed as he knelt down to scratch the peacock's neck. *"It must be two hours past your dinner time, you poor thing."* Edwina, however, began honking feverishly at the Emperor. The Emperor recoiled, surprised at the bird's attitude. *"What's wrong with you?"* he asked as if the bird was going to start speaking English. Edwina honked again and began trotting towards the front door.

"Hmpm." The Emperor grunted in confusion as he stood up.

"You don't think she's sick, do you?" Sandra offered up. *"I've never seen her not want to be glued to your hip."*

"I don't know... I'm sure she's just hungry." he said dismissively. *"I better go feed her, the poor thing."*

They continued walking toward the door. It was late and all the staff had gone to bed. Sandra found the mansion imposing enough when it was bustling with activity, but when the grounds were vacant as they were now, it felt haunted. Ghostly nighttime winds bellowed through the expansive field, The Emperor opened the door and Edwina honked again, rushing into the hall and up the staircase. Soon lost to the faint sound of her claws tapping on the marble The Emperor shook his head in confusion at the bird's odd behavior. He turned to Sandra.

"Stacy..." The Emperor began sheepishly. He began fiddling with his pocket watch. *"I am a man who.... Well, I mean that in my life I...."* Sandra rolled her eyes. She took his hand from his pocket watch,

"Skip the speech." she said, *"just say what you wanna say."* She had a feeling she knew what it was.

The Emperor recoiled his hand and began again massaging his watch. *"What I am trying to say is.."*

"YOUR MAJESTY!!"

Sandra and the Emperor turned toward the sound and saw a footman sprinting down the hall. *"YOUR MAJESTY!"* the footman screamed again. He got to Sandra and The Emperor panting from exhaustion. *"Thank.. God.. You're back."*

"Why... What's wrong?" The Emperor asked, placing a hand on the footman's shoulder. *"Come on, spit it out."*

"It's Ms. Beasley Sire..."

"What do you mean?" Sandra pressed. *"What's wrong with Amanda?"*

"Madam, she's here." The footman gasped. *"Upstairs.... in his Majesty's study."*

"But I don't understand." The Emperor said. *"Is she hurt? What is the urgency?"*

"Sire she came to Reginride about an hour ago... Madam Jones' car... bullet holes."

"Oh God." Sandra whispered.

"She insisted she would only talk to you sire." The footman said. *"We assumed you'd approve of us letting her up. We couldn't reach you."*

"Of course." The Emperor said softly. *"You've done your duty for the Crown and Empire my son. Go fetch Master Chesley and then go to bed."* He patted the footman's shoulder *"send him directly to my quarters."*

"Your Majesty." The footman said with a bow before rushing back down the dark corridor.

The Emperor took Sandra by the wrist and began rushing up the stairs. Together they sprinted up the three flights of stairs to Reginridge's highest level. The black halls were just barely illuminated by light shining under the Emperor's door. The Emperor stopped them at the doorway. He paused and took a deep breath. Sandra took his hand. *"Come on."* She said, *"She needs you."*

The Emperor placed a hand on the doorknob and slowly twisted it open. Inside his study was Amanda, her face was buried in her palms. Her clothes were torn and dirty and Sandra could see several spots of dried blood blotted all over her. She heard Sandra and the Emperor enter the room and lifted her head. Edwina lay dutifully beside her, cooing softly in a vain attempt to provide comfort.

Sandra rushed over and Amanda collapsed into her arms. *"Sylvia's dead."* Amanda blurted out. Sandra helped her to her feet.

"What?" Sandra asked. *"What do you mean dead?"* She looked at the Emperor, his face was grave, staring at Amanda's disheveled form.

"We were out at dinner..." Amanda began, choking on her tears. *"There was some sniper I don't know. She's DEAD".* There was a knock at the door, Cody entered the room. Upon seeing Amanda his eyes widened in shock and he rushed over to her. The Emperor caught him by the arm before he made it.

"Keep talking child." The Emperor commanded, no emotion in his voice. *"What happened?"*

Amanda proceeded to recount the events of her fatal lunch with Sylvia earlier in the day, pausing periodically to catch her breath or wipe her eyes. Sandra held her close while she told the story but once she was done The Emperor released Cody's arm and he rushed to Amanda's side. Sandra left Amanda with Cody and returned to the Emperor. His face was blank, but she could see anger swelling in his eyes. *"Keep it together..."* she whispered in his ear. *"Not now."* The Emperor squeezed Sandra's hand but said nothing.

"Jesus..." Cody said, cupping Amanda's head in his hands *"What did they do to you?!?"*

"Nothing." Amanda reassured, *"I didn't get hit or anything."*

"What do you mean nothing??" Cody exclaimed. *"You're bruised all over, look at your wrists!"*

"Oh that." Amanda said, instinctively covering her wrist with her hand, *"No that's nothing."*

"Something else happened." The Emperor said sharply. *"Before you got here something else happened... What was it?"* Cody turned back to Amanda waiting for an answer.

Amanda turned and looked away facing the corner of the room. *"Nothing."* she repeated softly.

"Alright leave her alone you two." Sandra said before anyone could press her again, *"She's been through enough."*

The Emperor began pacing, for just a moment, then he stopped. He walked toward Amanda and Cody. Sandra went to stop him, but he held out his arm in defiance. *"Master Chesley, if you'll give us the room just for a moment,"* he said calmly. Cody started to protest but the Emperor held up his hand. *"Just for a moment."* he repeated to Cody. *"Wait outside."* Cody got up and made his way to the door.

Once it closed behind him the Emperor knelt down to meet Amanda's eye level, she met his gaze back with teary eyes. The Emperor gently took her hand and looked at her wrist, examining the bruises. *"Who?"* he asked.

"I don't want to talk about it." Amanda choked.

"Would you please jus..." Sandra began before the Emperor waved her off dismissively.

"Just tell me this then..." the Emperor said, *"Did you get him?"*

Amanda said nothing at first but nodded. *"In the jaw..."* she eventually let out.

The Emperor smiled. *"In the Jaw??"* he asked, his voice rising in pitch. *"God, that must have been some shot."*

"I told you I have been getting better." she laughed frailly.

"Yes, you have." the Emperor said as he pulled Amanda in close. *"You have been so brave today."* Sandra heard him whisper. Amanda leant in returning his hug. He stayed there, on the ground, holding the girl tight. *"I'm sorry..."* Amanda let out but the Emperor shushed her and held her closer.

"I have to go." he finally said, releasing Amanda. *"But you stay here tonight where Stacy can keep an eye on you."* He gently set Amanda down and used his cane to return to standing position. As he turned to face the door Sandra saw the softness in his face flushed away by anger.

"Please God don't do anything stupid." Sandra said as the Emperor marched to the door.

"Later perhaps I will..." The Emperor replied coldly. *"But first... a Marshal of the Empire has died, and we must bury her."* He stormed out of the room, slamming the door behind him.

Sandra had helped Amanda into a bath. Even the bathroom at Reginridge was nicer than Sandra's apartment in the city. Gloss tile floors supporting a claw foot tub. Steam filled the room as the hot water filled the gargantuan bath. Sandra could feel Amanda's muscles relax and Sandra gently scrubbed the grime off of her face. She ran her fingers through Amanda's hair, removing the tangles the afternoon had brought her.

Sandra caressed Amanda's shoulders as she lay in the bathwater. It was taking all of her power not to burst into sobs. No girl, especially Amanda, should have to go through that. She continued cleaning. Amanda eventually closed her eyes and faded off to sleep. Sandra leant forward and kissed her on the forehead. Amanda would need clothes, hers were ruined. Sandra got to her feet and went to find something she could wear.

She opened the bathroom door to find a footman standing outside, as if he were about to knock. *"Ah Madam...'* began before Sandra placed a finger to her lips gesturing to Amanda sleeping. *"Apologies ma'am."* The footman whispered. Sandra stepped into the hall and gently closed the door behind her.

"What is it?" she asked.

"It's the marshals Madam." the footman answered. *"They're arriving."*

"So?" Sandra questioned *"What does that have to do with me?"*

"Well Ma'am...." the footman replied *"What do we do with them?"*

"I don't know." Sandra stated *"Why are you asking me?"*

"Ma'am it's just..." The footman started his voice getting shaky. *"His Majesty is gone, so is the Lord High Chancellor..... And you are... ummmm."* he was starting to shake.

Sandra took a deep breath. *"Just take me to them."* she said. The footman bowed and led her down the hallway. *"Oh."* Sandra said, *"And have someone get Ama... Ms. Beasley some clothes."*

"As you command Madam." The footman replied, continuing down the hall. The Footman led her to the main staircase that led to the great hall. Near the front doors Madame DuBois, and the other marshals, Stevenson and Samerson were waiting. They were all dressed in black, nervously whispering to each other. The footman stopped Sandra at the top of the stairs. He stomped his foot to get the marshals' attention and then gestured for Sandra to descend the staircase as he scurried off to find clothes for Amanda.

Sandra descended the stairs. The marshals at the bottom ceased their conversations and dipped their heads in her direction as she did so. Their heads remained bowed until she reached the bottom of the stairs and approached them.

"My Lady." Samerson said, taking Sandra's hand and kissing her Imperial ring. The other two shortly followed suit.

"Please don't do that." Sandra said, withdrawing her hand. *"What do you guys want?"*

"We're here for you Ma'am." Madame DuBois said. *"To take you to the funeral."*

"What?... I..." Sandra stumbled. *"What?"*

"I know..." Madame DuBois answered. *"It's a little quick. But it's how we do things."*

"I can't leave." Sandra replied. *"I have to stay here with Amanda."*

"She's coming too." Samerson interjected. *"The Footmen will bring her behind us."*

"No, out of the question." Sandra said. *"She's in no condition to go anywhere tonight. And I'm not leaving her."*

"We understand how you feel." Stevens said, *"Believe me we do."*

"But we are the leaders of the Empire." Madame DuBois cut in. *"We have to be there to show unity. The people need to see it."* she cleared her throat. *"Amanda survived the attack that killed Sylvia. They need to see her.... And they need to see you."*

"Why?" Sandra asked.

"To see that the Empire is still intact." Stevenson explained. *"That we are only wounded but not beaten."*

Sandra exhaled trying to process all of this information. The three marshals stared at her in silence awaiting her answer.

"Wait a second." Sandra finally said. *"Where's Harold?"*

"He's arriving separately." Samerson answered awkwardly, *"given the circumstances."*

"Fine." Sandra said, *"Then Amanda is coming with me.... Given the circumstances."*

The three marshals looked toward each other, shrugged and nodded in agreement.

"As your Ladyship commands." Samerson said.

"Please stop saying that." Sandra reiterated.

"I think we're at a point where you're probably just gonna have to get used to it." Madame DuBois replied respectfully. *"We'll wait here while you two get ready..."*

Sandra quickly found a black gown for herself and tied her hair up into a bun. Amanda surprisingly was easier to convince than Sandra had thought.

"No... I want to go." She told Sandra *"I have to. For Sylvia."*

Once they were ready Sandra took her downstairs to the marshals. Samerson was talking to one of the footmen, Madame DuBois and Stevenson were whispering to each other. They all stopped when they saw Sandra and Amanda.

"You're one tough kid." Madame DuBois said to Amanda. *"No wonder he took such a shine to you."*

"Let's just go." Amanda answered, clutching onto Sandra.

The group stepped outside into the night and the fleet of cars that were waiting for them. Sandra looked out over the tree line of Reginridge, to the cityscape in the distance. Among the normal lights of Colonna, she saw a bright red beam of light shooting miles into the air.

"What on earth is that?" She asked.

"That's ours." Madame DuBois explained, *"It's a beacon.... Calling all the children of the Empire home."*

Everyone filed into their respective cars and the convoy left Reginridge for the city. Sandra was in a car with Amanda and Madame DuBois. Madame DuBois reached into her garter and withdrew a flask. *"I know you don't drink."* she said before taking a big swig. *"But you may want it."* She offered the flask to Sandra who turned it down, then to Amanda who gladly took a swig. As they entered the city Sandra looked out the window to see small crowds forming around the street. Clusters of people all walking in the same direction they were driving. As the fleet of cars drove past the crowds would stop and bow their heads, until the cars passed, then continue their pilgrimage.

The journey ended at the museum. The red beam of light Sandra had seen was emanating from the attached Amphitheatre. Silent crowds were filing into the amphitheater as the cars parked along the street. The cars stopped and so did the crowds. Hundreds of people turned to face Sandra, every single face solemn. The driver opened the door and helped Sandra, Amanda, and Madame DuBois out of the car. Stevenson and Samerson were waiting as well.

The crowd of people around the amphitheater dispersed on either side, creating a path for the marshals. Two of the Emperor's footmen approached the group from the crowd. They were carrying violet banners bearing the Emperor's Sigil, torches attached to the top of the banners to light the darkness. They took their positions at the front of the procession. *"Kurt and George in front."* Madame DuBois whispered to Sandra, *"You and Amanda behind them, and I pull up the rear."* The five took their places as the amphitheater sound system began playing a solemn march. The procession walked slowly into the arena, the crowd on either side dropping their heads as Sandra passed by. She kept her eyes front, trying to tune everything out.

Inside the arena a large cluster of seats had already begun to fill. All rose to their feet, and the procession of the marshals entered the grounds. The entire amphitheater was lit by scores of torches placed around the perimeter. In the center was a large platform with a slew of chairs positioned on either side of a large central throne. Directly on either side of the large central throne were two more thrones, scaled down. One of these was occupied by Harold, slumped in his seat, alone. The chairs were directly behind a large pile of wood, at least two feet tall, neatly arranged in a block shape. Harold stood up as the procession approached the central seating. One by one, the marshals offered condolences to him. When Amanda got to him, she reached out to give him a large embrace. *"I am so sorry."* Amanda said to him, *"I don't even know what to say."*

"It's not your fault." Harold replied, his voice hoarse. *"Those animals are gonna pay for this..."* he fell back into his chair. Sandra took the small throne opposite of Harold and Amanda sat next to her. Once they sat the entire arena crowd followed and the remainder of the mourners filed inside. For a few moments the hundreds of people inside the arena sat in silence. But then the sound system began again with slow violins. The marshals rose to their feet and Sandra followed, as did the crowd. Headlights came into view as the Emperor's limo rolled through the main gate and onto the arena ground. The crowd bowed their heads and the marshals bent down onto one knee. The limo stopped just inside the Arena, some 50 feet from where Sandra was. The driver hurried around the side of the vehicle and opened the door, a team of footmen ran to assist him.

Out of the car first was Cody, the violins still playing on the speaker as he took his position beside the car. Sandra looked on as the Emperor emerged next from the limousine. He planted his cane into the dirt as the team of footmen began reaching inside of the limo. Together they slowly pulled out Sylvia's corpse and raised it above their heads. Upon seeing his fallen wife Harold collapsed to the ground in grief, Stevenson reaching down to console him. The footmen slowly carried Syvia's body across the arena ground, her flowing dress still billowing in the night wind along with the torch flames but now it was cold and joyless. The Emperor and Cody followed marching in step with the footmen. They reached the center of the Arena where Sylvia's body was gently placed on the center of the wood pile. Now that they were closer, Sandra could see, Sylvia's eyes were still open.

The Emperor and Cody walked onto the platform and took their positions. The Emperor in the center, and Cody along the wing next to Amanda. Cody gave Amanda a hug and whispered something in her ear Sandra could not hear. The Emperor kept his eyes toward the crowd. He did not look at Sandra once. The music died down. The Emperor raised a hand high into the air and the crowd took their seats, those on stage doing the same.

"Today." The Emperor began, speaking into a microphone. *"Today the Empire bleeds. She mourns for her fallen daughter. She cries out in agony as her brightest spirit has been stolen from her."* he began to pace back and forth across the platform. *"The enemy has struck a deep and terrible wound right into the heart of that which we hold dear!"* He removed his hat and looked at Harold, still sobbing at the sight of his wife. *"We all come tonight with broken hearts."* The Emperor continued *"Yet our brother has been subject to the brunt of the enemy's wrath."* He placed a hand on Harold's shoulder. *"Fear not my beloved friends.... For tomorrow the enemy shall pay tenfold what they have taken from us this day!"* The crowd began to yell in approval. They worked themselves up

into a frenzy screaming and chanting. The Emperor held up his hand and the arena fell silent again. *"Tomorrow they will pay.... But tonight... tonight we strike all anger from our hearts."* He walked back out to the front of the platform and looked at Syvlia's body. *"Tonight, our hearts will know only love. Love for she who fell in service to us all."* He picked up a nearby torch and turned his gaze to the sky.

"LORD!" He screamed up into the air. *"I have failed Sylvia Jones, Marchioness of the Empire! I allowed the swine to take her from those who love her dearly! I beseech thee merciful God.... take better care of her than I have done."* with that he tossed the torch onto the funeral pyre and Sylvia's body was soon engulfed in flame. The Emperor turned toward Harold, knelt down and wrapped his arms around him. Soon the members of the crowd began embracing either other in turn. Sandra turned toward Amanda. She was holding Cody tight, staring at the flame. Sandra held the two of them. This was the first time she could remember seeing Cody cry.

"Are you alright?" Sandra asked him.

"I'll be fine," he responded. *"I knew Sylvie for a long time, that's all. Her, Harold and I have been in it together since day one."*

"I'm so sorry." Sandra said *"I can't even imagine."*

"Just please..." Cody said, *"Keep an eye on him. He's not handling it well at all. Something snapped when he saw her body tonight."*

"I'll do my best." Sandra replied. She turned around and went toward the Emperor. He stood up and faced her. His eyes, blood red. Fire from the funeral pyre raging behind him. She went in to hug him but he held up a hand to stop her.

"Come with me." he said sternly, grabbing her by the arm. *"Lord Chancellor ride home with Amanda."* He said to Cody "Have Amanda *stay at Reginridge tonight, I'll call on you before the night is out."* Cody nodded in understanding as the Emperor dragged Sandra away toward his limousine. Sandra turned and took one last look at the arena, the red beacon had been turned off, replaced instead by the flames of the pyre, shooting off into the night.

"Where are we going?" Sandra asked as the Emperor's Limo sped down the Colonna city streets. The Emperor had said nothing since they got in the car. He sat silently beside Sandra, caressing his watch. *"I have a witness."* He finally said, looking out the window.

"A witness?"

"Yes." The Emperor solidified. *"A beggar that frequents an alleyway near the attack site."* He tapped his cane on the floor of the limo *"And he's going to tell us what he saw."*

"Well." Sandra said, stretching in her seat. *"At least a beggar will be easy to bribe."*

"No bribes." The Emperor said, shaking his head. *"Not this time...."*

"Why not?" Sandra asked. *"It's pretty effective."*

"Because it's time for people to make a choice." The Emperor said coldly. *"They are either a friend of the Crown or they are an enemy..."* The Limousine pulled into a parking spot along the street. *"Wait here."* The Emperor said to the driver as he climbed out of the car, with Sandra following behind.

The Emperor led her down the street and into a nearby alley. The alley led into a secluded area of pavement behind the various buildings. There were two of the Emperor's inquisitors clad in all black, standing over a shriveled hobo. The hobo was in a fetal position, he looked scared, but from what Sandra could tell, unharmed. As Sandra and the Emperor approached the guards did a bow.

"Thank you, gentleman." The Emperor said sternly to the guards. *"You may leave us now."* The guards did another bow and followed their king's command. Disappearing into the city fog. The Emperor used the tip of his cane to gently direct Hobo's head toward his own. *"Now my friend."* The Emperor said softly. *"I think you have something to tell me."*

"Listen man." the hobo quivered. *"I don't know what this is about.... I was coming back to my corner after a long day of working and your goons grabbed me."*

"You saw the attack that happened here today." the Emperor snarled. *"Don't lie to me."*

"I ain't lyin'!" The hobo shot back. *"Yea I hang out around here but I didn't see nothing 'bout no attack."*

"Hmmph." The Emperor grunted. *"So that's the game?"*

"What game?" The hobo said, *"I told you I ain't seen nothing!"*

"LIAR!" The Emperor growled, smacking the Hobo on the head with his cane. *"You saw what they did! They paid you not to speak!"* He smacked the hobo again who was now shielding his face. *"YOU!"* smack, *"WILL!"* smack, *"TALK!"* smack. Sandra winced.

"I swear to God man!" The hobo said, covering his face with his arms. *"I swear to God I saw nothing!"* His cheek had swollen from the Emperor's blows; it began to affect his speech. Sandra winced at the sight, the first time in a while that had happened.

The Emperor bent down and seized the hobo by the scruff of his shirt, and hoisted him to his feet, now they were eye to eye. The Emperor threw him against a nearby wall, pinning the hobo in place with his forearm.

"You think your friends can protect you now?!" he spat at the hobo. *"You have one last chance."*

"Come on man you gotta believe me." the hobo whimpered. *"I ain't got no friends, no one gave me nothing and I didn't see nothing."*

"Alright then... the hard way." The Emperor said, dropping the hobo. The Emperor pulled the head of his cane brandishing the blade hidden within. A jab to the ankles sent the hobo back to the ground, faint eeks of pain coming from the hobo.

"You gotta believe me..." the hobo repeated, his strength fading.

"If you won't give me the answer I want. I will cut it out!" he lined his blade up to the Hobo's femur. Sandra had had enough. The Emperor raised his blade to strike.

"Now hang on!" Sandra said. The Emperor froze before twirling around.

"What?!?" he snarled at Sandra.

"You need to calm down." Sandra said calmly. *"Have you ever considered he may be telling the truth?"*

"I am supposed to believe that this cur, wretched and filthy, was conveniently at work during the attack?" The Emperor questioned. *"He saw what they did, he saw it and he's protecting them. He dies!"*

"I don't know about the rest of it." Sandra stated, desperate to keep her composure, *"but it's very plausible he genuinely saw nothing. He could be innocent."*

"Whose side are you on?!" The Emperor shouted.

"I'm on your side, you idiot!" Sandra shouted back. She stopped and took a breath. *"Where were you really today?"* she asked the hobo.

"Okay Okay you're right." the hobo said groveling at Sandra's feet. He found a burst of energy now that his life had a chance to be spared. *"I wasn't at no job I was trying to score. But I wasn't here, I didn't see nothing!"*

"We have no reason not to believe him." Sandra said. *"That makes him innocent. Now please let him go."*

"*Innocent, pfft."* the Emperor spat. *"Just look at him, who's to say he didn't sell Sylvia out for a dimebag of crack."*

"Do you hear yourself?" Sandra said *"This is not the man I know. The man I know is cruel, but he's at least fair..."*

The Emperor made no response, he stood staring down on the hobo, his head lost in thought. Sandra approached him. *"You're grieving..."* she said, placing her hands on the Emperor's shoulders. *"You aren't thinking straight. Please let's just go home."* She could see tears welling in the Emperor's eyes. She nuzzled her head into his chest. *"Please..."* she said again.

"NO!" The Emperor yelled, shoving Sandra to the ground. *"He DIES!"*

"You have no right!" Sandra screamed at him as she got back to her feet. *"He did nothing to you!"*

"I have EVERY RIGHT!" The Emperor roared. *"It's time the enemies of the Empire learned true fear!"*

"I won't let you!" Sandra shouted, she was running on autopilot now. This had to stop, any affections aside, *"I won't let you do this to yourself."*

"You can't stop me." The Emperor snarled. He raised his blade once more as Sandra pulled a pistol she had hidden in her dress.

"Edward Von Drac!" she yelled, he recoiled at the sight of the gun. *"My name is Officer Sandra Blewens and I am placing you under arrest for attempted murder. Drop your weapon and raise your hands above your head!"*

The Emperor stood stunned. He did not move nor did he drop his weapon. *"officer..."* he whispered to himself. *"officer..."* he repeated.

"Drop your weapon and place your hands over your head." Sandra said again.

"I need to see it." The Emperor growled finally, still unmoved, Sandra took one hand and reached into her breast, procuring her badge. She tossed it to the Emperor. He studied the badge intently. His gaze shifted back and forth between the badge and Sandra herself. He tossed the badge back.

"Now surrender." Sandra said. *"It's over."* The Emperor nodded numbly in agreement. He peered into Sandra's eyes and raised his blade to be level

with his stare. Sandra gripped her pistol tighter. *"Don't make me do it."* she pleaded, a tear rolling down her cheek. *"I don't want to, but I will."* This standoff lasted for several moments, Sandra moved her finger from the trigger guard to the trigger, ready to fire.

The Emperor, however, dropped his blade, the metal clanging on the concrete as it hit the ground. Without saying a word, he kicked the blade over to Sandra's feet. He raised his palms in surrender as he walked toward Sandra. He walked forward until his chest touched the barrel of her gun. Still silent, and without breaking his gaze he slowly removed his Imperial ring from his index finger, and dropped it next to his blade on the pavement. He then outstretched his arms and presented Sandra with his wrists. *"Go on then, dog of democracy."* he said coldly. *"Do what you must".*

Chapter 20: Amanda

"CODY! Get in here!"

"What... What's wron... Holy shit."

<u>BREAKING NEWS</u>
Local Millionaire philanthropist Edward Von Drac was exposed tonight as underworld boss operating under the moniker "Emperor" ... Arresting Officer Sandra Blewens pictured above...Commissioner Helming cited saying arrest will lead to a cessation of increased gang activity in recent days.... More to come... Emperor... Arrested.

A mix of rage and sorrow created a tidal wave within Amanada, yet it was all washed out by fear. What in hell are they supposed to do now?

Chapter 21: Sandra

"Excellent work Blewens. I knew you had it in you."

"Thank you, Commissioner, sir."

"You alright? You're pretty quiet for someone who just bagged the biggest criminal in the city."

"Fine sir... just tired, it's been a long assignment."

"Right. Right. Well go get some rest. You earned it."

"Yes sir. Thank you."

Sandra's stomach was in knots. By God what had she done?

Chapter 22: Amanda

Day 1

Dead: 0

Wounded: 1

Arrested: 2

Day 2

Dead: 2

Wounded: 3

Arrested: 1

Day 3

Dead: 5

Wounded: 10

Arrested: 6

Day 4

Dead: 7

Wounded: 2

Arrested: 1

Day 5

Dead: 4

Wounded: 2

Arrested: 2

Day 6

Dead: 4

Wounded: 8

Arrested: 0

Day 7

Dead: 0

Wounded: 0

Arrested: 0

Day 8

Dead: 13

Wounded: 0

Arrested: 0

Day 9

Dead: 1

Wounded: 2

Arrested: 2

Day 10

Dead: 3

Wounded: 10

Arrested: 8

Day 11

Dead: 5

Wounded: 16

Arrested: 5

Day 12

Dead: 10

Wounded: 6

Arrested: 6

Day 13

Dead: 10

Wounded: 14

Arrested: 0

Day 14

Dead: 13

Wounded: 8

Arrested: 0

A bloodied hooker hobbled back into the warehouse. She collapsed as Amanda and the girls rushed toward the doorway. She had no bullet holes; she had been beaten. Coughing on her blood Amanda held the girl's hand as she passed. The Empire lay scattered, and leaderless. The marshals issued no orders, or maybe they did but Amanda was without a marshal, and without an Emperor. She hung her head.

Chapter 23: Sandra

Day 1
Officer Casualties: 0
Civilian Casualties: 0
Arrests: 2

Day 2
Officer Casualties: 0
Civilian Casualties: 1
Arrests: 1

Day 3
Officer Casualties: 1
Civilian Casualties: 6
Arrests: 6

Day 4
Officer Casualties: 0
Civilian Casualties: 4
Arrests: 1

Day 5
Officer Casualties: 2
Civilian Casualties: 5
Arrests: 2

Day 6
Officer Casualties: 1
Civilian Casualties: 10

Arrests: 0

Day 7
Officer Casualties: 0
Civilian Casualties: 0
Arrests: 0

Day 8
Officer Casualties: 1
Civilian Casualties: 15
Arrests:0

Day 9
Officer Casualties: 2
Civilian Casualties: 6
Arrests:2

Day 10
Officer Casualties: 0
Civilian Casualties: 10
Arrests:8

Day 11
Officer Casualties: 1
Civilian Casualties: 8
Arrests:5

Day 12
Officer Casualties: 1

Civilian Casualties: 10
Arrests:6

Day 13
Officer Casualties: 0
Civilian Casualties: 12
Arrests: 0

Day 14
Officer Casualties: 3
Civilian Casualties: 11
Arrests: 0

All Sandra heard these days was gunfire. Skirmishes ran the street as the Empire and the Republicans vied for control. The future of the city's criminal world was at stake. With such a prize on the table, the police were a secondary thought. And both sides greatly outgunned anything the department could hope to muster. Arrests were made, but it made no difference. There was no control, not even an illusion of control, everyday people were dying, and it was all her fault.

The royal family are a focus of patriotism, of loyalty, of affection and of esteem. That is a rare combination, and we should value it highly

-Margaret Thatcher

Act 3:

His Majesty's Most Loyal Government

Chapter 24: Amanda

Amanda sat alone in her room. She leaned against her desk, spinning her ring atop its surface. She had lost three girls in the attacks following the Emperor's arrest. The ones that were left had gotten so scared she could barely get them to go out at all, not that she even wanted to.

Sylvia was dead, the Emperor was gone, The Republicans had pushed the Emperor's people out of vast swaths of the city. No Emperor meant no protection so arrests from the police were more frequent every day.

She reached under her desk and pulled out a small lockbox. She entered the combination and slid open the lid. Inside was two hundred thousand dollars cash, she shifted the money aside and dug a postcard out from the bottom. It displayed a scenic beach view but was now worn and frayed with age. She looked at the postcard and again at the money.

She got up from her chair and walked to the door, opening it slightly she peered out at the room below. Everyone sat solemnly, no one was speaking. The guards sat at the door loaded rifles in hand. The girls sat at their beds, almost frozen, just waiting for hours to pass.

She opened the door wider and cleared her throat. The crowd below turned and began congregating beneath her. Once they had gathered Amanda spoke. *"I know you're scared."* She said plainly, *"I'm scared too."* her audience stayed silent. *"But we have to do something."* she continued *"I don't know about you guys, but I like what we've built here."* There was a collective murmur of agreement. Amanda, feeling more confident, strengthened her tone.

"And do we give it all up?" She asked, *"Just because some thugs are waving guns in our face??"* The crowd agreed again, getting more worked up. *"Do we just bend our knee to anyone??"* She asked loudly, a large unified "NO" bellowed from below. *"I say we FIGHT!"* Amanda declared to cheers.

"Yea!" Tiffany roared from within the crowd. *"We've got this girls! Give the boys hell!"* The crowd applauded. Chants of "FIGHT! FIGHT! FIGHT!" rang out.

"Arm yourselves girls...." Amanda said scornfully once the crowd had settled, *"We're hitting back... tonight."* the cheering continued as Amanda went back into her room. She closed her eyes, took a deep exhale, and ripped the postcard in two.

The plan was daring. There was a Republican lieutenant who oversaw their movements in Amanda's territory. Amanda was going to lead a small team out to the city once it was dark, and execute him. That wasn't the hard part. The Republicans had gotten cocky since the Emperor was arrested, they didn't put much energy into defending themselves. The hard part was the retaliation that was sure to come. Amanda's crew had spent the day turning their warehouse into a fortress. Large barricades were placed in front of all entry points; small holes were smashed into the walls for people to fire out of. Amanda watched the construction efforts and thought how proud the Emperor would be if he could see it.

Her crew had pulled all sorts of scrap materials for the creation of the warehouse's defenses. Amanda looked to the pile and had one of her guards pull out a long metal pipe. She ran to her room and grabbed a bedsheet. Using some paint she found lying around, she painted on top of the bed sheet a large crown, covering a sword and trident all enclosed within a laurel wreath. It was nowhere near as extravagant as the banners at Reginridge, but it would do the job. *"Put this up outside."* Amanda commanded, *"We aren't hiding anymore."*

Night had finally fallen; Everyone was as ready as they were ever going to be. Amanda handpicked a team to go with her into the city. Three girls who could handle themselves quietly. This part of the plan relied on stealth. She left her guards in charge of the warehouse until she got back. The quartet had made their way out into the city proper. It was eerily quiet. Activity had slowed in Colonna as average people became more and more scared of the carnage that was ever increasing around them. The group kept to alleyways but did not go to great extent to make themselves inconspicuous.

As they marched into the night, Amanda saw a bakery that had been the scene of an attack a few days ago. One of the Republican thugs had tried to rob one of her girls but the girl held firm. By the time Amanda's guards were patrolling the area had heard the commotion and reached her, the girl was lying dead in a pool of blood. They shoved her through the display window of the bakery, and the glass shards tore an artery wide open. The bakery window was still broken.

Amanda forced the memory from her mind and led her strike team onward. The Republican lieutenant hung around a nightclub a few blocks farther. The Republican's first move once word had gotten out about the Emperor's arrest was to hit the local businesses. The ransacking was horrendous until the message was clear, the Empire isn't protecting anyone anymore. More and more places stopped paying their protection money to the Crown and instead began funding its enemies. This nightclub was one such place.

As they got closer lights and music began to break through the dark and barren alleyways. The nightclub had come into view. Amanda and her crew confidently approached the bouncer. He held up his arms blocking the door.

"Woah ladies, not so fast." he said, *"$300 cover charge for hookers."*

"Christ." One of Amanda's girls replied. *"That's freakin' robbery."*

"What you been livin' under a rock or something?" the bouncer questioned. *"Been some changes around here lately."*

Amanda shrugged casually and withdrew a wad of cash from her breast; she gently kissed it and rubbed it atop her cleavage before handing it to the bouncer. *"That should cover it."* she said with a wink. Too easy. The bouncer stepped aside and let the girls enter into the club.

"How do we know for sure which one's him?" One of the girls asked Amanda as they were walking in.

"Something tells me we'll be able to figure it out." Amanda answered. *"Let's split up and see what we see."* the team dispersed into the nightclub floor. The music was loud and the strobe lights were flashing incessantly. It reminded Amanda of the parties the Emperor would allow his men to throw at Reginridge, while his Majesty hid upstairs doing God only knew what. How far away those days seemed.

There was a large crowd of people inside and Amanda wasn't one hundred percent sure exactly what she was looking for. She maneuvered her way through the crowd to reach the bar. She ordered a drink to maintain appearances and began scanning the area. No one was particularly standing out. She shifted to the other end of the dance floor to get a view of the booths lined up along the back wall.

There. In one of the booths there were two men sitting whispering to one another, both in silk suits and with an obnoxious amount of gold jewelry. *"Only an enemy of the crown could present themselves in such a tacky manner."* Amanda heard the Emperor's voice in her head. Two other men stood on either side of the booth, obviously guards by their stance, backs straight and arms crossed.

Amanda surveyed the room again, until she locked eyes with one of her girls. She thrust her jaw in the direction of the lieutenant's table. The girl nodded in understanding and found the rest of their companions. The four rendezvoused into a huddle near the wall.

"Alright." Amanda began *"We're gonna do this... just follow my lead."*

"*Mandy,"* one of the girls protested, *"No disrespect but it's been awhile since you've been out there... maybe let one of us take the lead?"*

"Whatever." Amanda conceded quickly *"I don't care, let's just be quick."*

"Relax." one of the others chimed in *"We've got this."* Together they all approached the lieutenant's table. One of Amanda's crew cricked her neck as they walked up, adjusted her bosom and

flashed a big, faux smile. As they got close the lieutenant and his men turned to face them.

"Heyy boys." One of Amanda's girls said, leaning forward on the table, *"You wouldn't happen to have room for us to join you?"*

"Shit." The lieutenant said with a licentious smile, looking around to his men *"I think we can squeeze you in right fellas."* Two of Amanda's girls took up with the guards standing on either flank, caressing their chests and batting eyelashes. Amanda and the remaining girl sat down at the booth. Amanda next to the lieutenant and her remaining girl next to his friend.

"So beautiful." the lieutenant said, placing a finger under Amanda's chin, moving her head to provide a better view of her cleavage. *"What brings you guys to this part of town?"*

Amanda placed a hand on the lieutenant's thigh. *"Why you did of course."* she said haughtily, leaning down with her face close to the lieutenant's groin. The lieutenant's eyes widened in excitement and placed a hand on Amanda's lower back. While in her current position Amanda slipped an unseen hand into her boot, grabbing hold of her pistol.

She jumped back upright and brandished her weapon in the lieutenant's face. He was slightly taken aback but clearly still aroused. Her crew pulled guns of their own on their respective partners. The lieutenant looked around the table, assessing the situation. The music and lights were distracting enough that no one else inside the club had yet seen what was going on.

"Woah woah ladies..." the lieutenant said lightheartedly. *"There's no need for all this, if you need some money, you could have just asked."* He reached a hand into Amanda's inner thigh, *"I'm sure we could work something out..."* he said greasily. The rest of the group froze, waiting on Amanda to make a move.

Amanda lifted her leg to position it on top of the lieutenant's lap. The lieutenant had a smug grin on his facing thinking he had just disarmed her with his charm. Amanda leant in close yet again, lowering her pistol. *"Long live the Empire..."* she whispered into the lieutenant's ear.

"Uh oh..." The lieutenant managed to get out before Amanda squeezed the trigger. *BANG!* A round went right into his waist. Before his men could react three more shots rang out in quick succession and they fell limp to the ground, each with a bullet hole in their head.

The gunshots had alerted the crowd of the nightclub to what was happening and panic ensued. The crowd screamed and began rushing for the exit. A perfect opportunity to slip away unnoticed. The girls rushed to the exit with the crowd, but Amanda stayed behind for just another moment. *"You'll die for this bitch."* the lieutenant said through gritted teeth, clutching his wound. *"My people... they'll find you...*

they'll rape you... they'll take whatever's left and throw it in the river!"

Amanda did not reply. She raised her gun to be square between the lieutenant's eyes. *"For Sylvia..."* She pulled the trigger again.

Sprinting through the city, the prostitutes turned assassins made it safely back to Amanda's warehouse. Once inside they hurriedly shut the main entrance as Amanda's guards placed a barricade to bar the way. The first phase of the mission was a success. Now all there was to do was wait.

However, they did not have to wait long. Soon light shone through the firing ports that had been bashed into the exterior walls. The sound of engines tore the silence. Amanda looked through one of the holes and saw multiple SUVs assembling outside of the building. Everyone was in position. Amanda's small army of hookers manned the walls, armed with rifles provided previously by Madame DuBois. Her guards manned the barricaded doors, ready to repel any breaches. The engines outside shut off, and once again it was dark and silent. Amanda took cover. The entire warehouse was still.

RATATATATATATTATATATATATAT Machine gun fire smashed into the side of the building. Everyone ducked as the bullets poured in. The wall was holding but the occasional round would come in through the portholes, bouncing around the open space as it ricocheted. The wall began to vibrate from the bombardment, but it held.

Soon the cracking of gunfire turned into soft clicks. The assailants were out of ammo. *"NOW LADIES!"* Amanda shouted and her working girls placed their guns into the makeshift embrasures and returned fire. Amanda picked up a shotgun and manned a station herself. Outside she saw at least twenty men fleeing for cover behind the SUVs. Two republican dogs had fallen so far, she had lost no one.

As munitions got low she directed girls stationed at other walls to cycle in with those facing the enemy. This allowed for continuous suppressive fire. This cycle lasted for no more than five minutes when Amanda saw one of the gas tanks on the SUVs had been punctured. She ditched her shotgun and picked up a rifle with iron sights. Sighting in the puddle of fuel forming beneath the SUV she inhaled deeply and pulled the trigger.

BOOM! The vehicle went up in flames. She counted three bodies fall, engulfed in flames while the remainder of the Republican thugs fled from the scene of the firefight. Cheers erupted from within the warehouse at the sight of the retreat. Amanda's crew began hugging each other and exchanging shouts of victory.

"Stop!" Amanda shouted angrily. *"They know what they're up against now... reload and get ready for them to come back!"* The celebration stopped as Amanda's forces began once again bolstering their defenses. Guns were reloaded and barricades were reinforced.

One of Amanda's girls walked up to her slinging a rifle. *"Mandy, I was thinking..."* she said, *"What if we took the mattresses and stood them up around the floor? They could absorb any loose bullets bouncing around."*

"Not a bad idea." Amanda replied, *"use some of the barricade pieces to prop them..."* Amanda became distracted by a small red dot appearing on the girl's temple. *"MOVE!"* Amanda screamed as she tackled the girl, just in time as a sniper shot soared through the window and grazed Amanda's shoulder. Before anyone had time to react two more shots rang out and two girls fell dead.

"Away from the windows!" Amanda shouted, *"Stay by the walls!"* Another beam of headlights could be seen in the distance, but only one. It grew brighter and brighter. The guards manning the main door jumped clear just in time as an SUV smashed through the door and got lodged in the barricade. The barricade held but now there were cracks, exposing them to the outside. Amanda snapped her fingers, pointing at the gaps and two rifles plugged the hole emptying their magazines into the SUV.

"I got him, he's dead!" one of the guards at the barricade declared. *"But we may not take another hit."* Amanda surveyed the situation around her. The two girls that had been killed by sniper were on opposite ends of the warehouse. The enemy had surrounded the building. She crept to one of the firing positions and ever so slightly peeked outside, she could see men off in the distance. Way more than before, armed and walking in the direction of the warehouse. She gestured for someone on the other side of the space to do the same. They confirmed her fears. The next attack was coming from all sides.

"Alright." Amanda said trying to keep her composure *"As of right now they can't get in. Which means we're safe."* She took a deep breath. *"We see headlights, aim for the tires. They cannot break through the doors no matter what."* She looked outside again, the Republican soldiers were getting closer, almost in range. *"Stay strong!"* she ordered. *"We have the upper hand; we can bleed them out. Wait for my signal."*

Everyone took positions. Amanda moved to another hole in case a sniper had seen her. She looked again. Almost there, just a few more seconds and they would be close enough to shoot. From her new position she could see the makeshift banner she had placed outside earlier in the night, it was tattered but still flapping in the night breeze. The Republicans marched closer to the building. Now they were in range.

"FIRE!" Amanda yelled and everyone took to their portholes and unleashed lead hellfire into the advancing army. Girls fell as sniper fire retaliated into the building. As one fell another would file into place. Smoke from the guns had begun to obscure her vision but Amanda could still see the men outside dropping like flies to their maelstrom of bullets.

"Check the rooftops!" Amanda barked, *"Find those snipers!"* gunshots continued deafening the warehouse. As the enemy got closer, they began returning fire. But the walls were holding. Outside the bodies began to pile up as the men advanced without cover. She just had to hold out. There's no way the Republicans could sustain these losses, they'd have to give it up eventually.

Then without warning flaming lights flew into a few of the windows. Molotov cocktails. As the bottles smashed on the warehouse floor fire spewed in every direction. It began to bellow so much smoke it was hard for Amanda to breathe. Clusters of her crew rushed to put the fires out but they were spreading too fast, catching the pieces of old wood used for the barricades. The air grew denser as the firefight continued. Amanda could barely breathe.

"We can't stay in here!" Someone shouted *"We'll choke to death!"* They were right. Amanda looked around. Her forces were still firing but they were getting visibly weak.

"Alright, new plan." Amanda said, *"Tear down the barricade by the back door. We open the door*

and shoot off everything we have to give us a window. Get out and find cover ASAP."

"We'll all be killed!" One of her guards argued.

"No we won't." Amanda retorted. *"We get out and we disperse into the city. We took enough of them out, they can't chase us in every direction."*

Since no better plan was available, everyone agreed to Amanda's idea. A team began congregating around the rear barricade and started dismantling it, while the others kept up the suppressive fire. Once the barricade had been taken down everyone moved toward the door.

"Once that door opens we only have a few seconds." Amanda reminded them all. *"Find cover and get out. We'll reconvene later."* This was suicide. But there was nothing else to do. Amanda placed a hand on the door handle. She flung it open as every weapon unloaded into the doorway. Amanda charged out into the open with her battered crew behind her. Gunshots came in all directions. She stayed low and found a concrete divider to cover behind. Luckily the smoke from the burning warehouse obscured their movements.

"Go!" Amanda shouted, waving the girls on. *"We have to punch a hole!"* They were completely pinned down. There was no getting out. The Republicans moved closer in and now it was Amanda's people being mowed down. There was nowhere to run. The plan had failed.

Through the smog Amanda saw more headlights enter the fray. A fleet of cars bashed into the line of men advancing on their position. Swerving vehicles and gunshots created chaos within the attackers. Men jumped out of the cars and Amanda recognized them. She had seen them at Reginridge before. The Emperor's inquisitors.

Spirits renewed by this turn of events Amanda led another charge to link up their forces. She fired into the Republican lines as she led her crew toward their saviors. The Emperor's men had punched a sizable hole in the Republican line, and the Republicans had scrambled to reorganize themselves.

Amanda heaved a sigh of relief as she saw Cody barking orders to the Emperor's men, situating them into a defensive ring. Amanda sprinted to him and flung her arms around his neck. *"Thank God you came."* she said to him.

"Are you insane?!?" Cody yelled back through the gunfire. *"What we're you thinking starting a fight like this?!?"*

"I... I..." Amanda stammered.

"It doesn't matter." Cody cut her off. *"You're safe, that's what's important."* He continued ordering his men around as Amanda's remaining people fell behind the safety of the Imperial lines. *"There's a*

fleet of vans over that way." Cody pointed. *"Take your people and get the hell out of here. We can buy you some time."*

"I'm not letting everyone die just for us." Amanda argued. *"We stay with you."*

"Just GO!" Cody roared, shoving Amanda in the direction of the vans. *"We got this now, your guys have fought enough. I'll see you at Reginridge."* He turned away from Amanada and gave his attention back to his men, who had positioned their cars to provide cover as they began returning fire on the Republicans. Amanda led her group to the vans and helped file everyone in. Once she was sure everyone had made it out she climbed into a van herself and slammed the door shut. The fleet of vans began to pull away from the battleground, carrying Amanda and what was left of her crew to safety. The last thing Amanda saw as the vans carted them away was her makeshift banner, still billowing victoriously above the smoke.

Chapter 25: Sandra

The Commissioner's office was droll. Filing cabinets, stacked papers, fluorescent lights. A beat-up rug and a desk with scratches. Sandra could only imagine what the Emperor would say if he had ever seen it. The Commissioner was standing facing a corkboard which had a large map of the city planned on it. Red pins dotted all over the map marked locations where recent gang attacks had taken place.

"What a nightmare..." The Commissioner said, studying the board. *"What are we gonna do, people?"*

The Commissioner's task force sat around his office. The first time they had all assembled since Sandra had planted herself inside of the Empire. They had been discussing an attack on what looked like a brothel last night. Scores of deaths, countless wounded. The Commissioner was livid. Sandra was worried. The city officials were still combing through the bodies and had not yet released the names of any deceased. If Amanda's name was on it she would never forgive herself.

"We need to start cracking more heads." Keith suggested, lounging in his chair, *"These dicks need to realize they aren't in charge."*

"New flash genius." Trayvon responded, *"We've been doing that. It's not working."*

"I agree." Greg chimed in *"brute force isn't going to solve this issue."*

"It would if they were scared of us!" Kieth shot back. *"But they don't see us as a threat. We're a joke to them, all of them."*

"Blewens." The Commissioner interjected from behind his desk *"Once again you've said absolutely nothing... care to join in?"*

Sandra shifted uneasily in her chair. *"Keith's right,"* she said. *"You know I was in there for months, and I don't think I can remember the police being mentioned even once."*

"Yea but we got their boy." The Commissioner argued, *"Once we threw that freak behind bars all the political protection went with him."*

"I know." Sandra sighed, *"But it seems like all we did was create a power vacuum..."*

"Elaborate" the Commissioner ordered.

"Well if one side goes underground to avoid the police." Sandra explained, *"The other side gets control of the city. So we have become a secondary problem."*

"Gangs do not control this city, Blewens... The law does." The Commissioner corrected.

"Commissioner with all due respect." Sandra began *"Up until two weeks ago a gang did rule this city... we upset that balance... now look what's happened."*

"Oh so we do nothing?!?" The Commissioner griped. *'We just let thugs rule the streets and mug and harass innocent people while we sit on our asses?!?"*

"The Emperor's men don't mug sir." Sandra said, *"He forbids them from any kind of stealing."*

"They are CRIMINALS!" The Commissioner argued back. *"We are not tolerating any more criminals in this city."*

"I understand you sir." Sandra said shakily. *"But maybe..."*

"Maybe what?" The Commissioner asked, pounding his hand on his desk.

"You don't mean we should be working with these people?" Greg inferred. Keith scoffed at the suggestion and Trayvon eyed Sandra nervously.

"All I am saying," Sandra eked out. *"Is this city is turning into Bedlam with each passing day. We need to explore every avenue to restore order to the streets as soon as possible. The people don't care how it gets done, just that it gets done."*

"Oh my God." The Commissioner said, walking toward Sandra. *"You sound just like him."* He was towering over her now. *"You've been mingling with the wrong people too long, Blewens, I'm placing you on suspension until you get your priorities in check."*

"Sir you need me to..." Sandra began but the Commissioner cut her off.

"I don't need any of your noble vigilante nonsense. You wanna consort with criminals, you won't do it wearing one of my badges." he held out his

hand. *"Your badge and gun,"* he ordered. Sandra handed her effects over and left the room.

Sandra couldn't sleep. She had been lying in bed for hours wondering if Amanda was okay. It had to have been her that killed that guy sparking the raid last night. Who else would have that gumption? She felt so powerless. She rolled onto her side and looked at her nightstand. On it sat the Emperor's ring, she recovered it the night she arrested him.

She picked up the gaudy silver band and ran her finger along the sigil embossed on its surface. Her mind ran through the countless interactions she had with His Majesty. The spark of life that would flicker in his eye when he watched people walking through his museum, or the deep sadness that would well in them when he saw his people in pain. She remembered giving Amanda shooting lessons, how Amanda looked up to her like a toddler to their mother. She could feel her own eyes tearing up. She hadn't felt powerless then. That goddamn idiot. Why did he have to go too far? She placed the ring back on the nightstand and laid flat on the bed. Definitely no sleep tonight.

The next day brought little solace, with the city for all intents and purposes on lockdown, there was nowhere Sandra could go to distract herself. The few businesses that stayed open in the wake of all the recent violence were seedy to say the least. And almost certainly in league with the Emperor's enemies. She sat in her apartment and turned on the news. More skirmishes between the Empire and the Republicans. Nothing else ever seemed to happen anymore. She turned off the TV.

She tried to find peace looking out the window. That didn't help. For months she had seen the sprawling grounds of Reginridge and the Emperor's vibrant prized lavender bushes. Now all she could see was the vacant street of a city that had died. She was almost relieved that the Commissioner had suspended her. What was there left to protect? They had already lost.

She stared deeper out of the window; her gaze focused on an apartment building opposite hers. She could see inside of the unit's windows. There was a family inside. Children running around inside the apartment, the mother desperately trying to keep them from destroying the place. The father reading the paper solemnly. The kids kept gravitating to the window, but the mother hurriedly pulled them back. Sandra saw the strain in the mother's face as she presumably was explaining to her children they could not go outside. It was too much. Sandra groaned to herself and snatched up her car keys.

The Colonna City Jail was just two miles outside of the city proper. Sandra hurriedly parked her car and walked into the visitor entrance. Inside she found the visitor's check-in desk and approached the receptionist.

"Who are you here to see?" The receptionist asked in a bored fashion.

"Edward Von Drac." Sandra answered.

"Inmate Von Drac has stated he isn't taking any visitors ma'am." the receptionist replied in kind it was apparent this was not her first time delivering that news. *"I'm sorry. Have a nice day."*

"Um." Sandra said, the receptionist groaned. Sandra ignored her. *"Could you tell him Sandra Blewens is here to see him?"* No point in lying about her name now, *"I think he'll see me."*

"He's turned everyone else away honey." The receptionist said again. *"He won't see you."*

"Could you just ask?" Sandra pressed, tapping her fingers on the desk.

"Fine." The receptionist exhaled, annoyed. She picked up her phone and relayed the message to whomever was on the other end. It took a moment to wait for the response, but Sandra saw the receptionist be taken aback as the voice on the other end spoke.

"Well, look at you." The receptionist said to Sandra, hanging up the phone. *"Go through that door and an officer will direct you to the visitation room."*

"Thank You." Sandra said as she followed the instructions. Inside of the next room a correctional officer escorted her into a private meeting room. Inside there was just a table and two chairs.

"Have a seat there." the officer said. *"They're bringing him now; it'll just be a minute."* He shut the door behind him.

Sandra sat down nervously. Her palms began to sweat. She wasn't sure how this reunion would go. She wasn't even sure exactly what she was going to say. She just knew she needed to talk to him. She tapped her foot anxiously on the ground while she waited. She heard footsteps coming in her direction. She took a deep breath as the door cracked open.

The Emperor was escorted in by another correctional officer. He was in an orange jumpsuit and handcuffed at the wrist. When he walked in the room his face was completely blank. The second he locked eyes with Sandra however he jumped to life.

"God as my witness, I had to see it to believe it." He said as he took the seat opposite Sandra. He looked back to the officer standing behind him. *"It would seem that Judas Iscariot has ventured to Golgotha.... Hoping to cast eyes on his handiwork."* He lifted his arms to better show his handcuffs and rattled the chain that joined them. The officer chuckled as he unlocked the Emperor's restraints.

"I gotta say." Sandra said cooly, it was like they had never been apart, *"Comparing yourself to Jesus may be the craziest thing that's ever come out*

of your mouth, which is no small feat." The Emperor grunted. *"And anyway"* Sandra continued, *"I'm pretty sure Judas killed himself before Jesus was crucified."*

"Such a student of the Bible." The Emperor remarked patronizingly, *"yet you have completely forsaken it's message."* Sandra made no response, instead glanced up at the officer.

"Officer Leefort, would you be so kind as to give us the room for just a moment." The Emperor said politely to the guard. *"Officer Blewens and I have some catching up to do."* The Officer nodded and saw himself out. *"Being Emperor does still have its privileges, even in exile."* The Emperor noted boastfully as Leefort left the room.

Once the guard had left the room the Emperor folded his hands together on the table. *"So what do you want?"* he asked coldly.

"I needed to see you." Sandra replied.

"I am much the way you left me." The Emperor said dismissively. *'Still rotting in here just as you would have it."*

"Look." Sandra said sharply. *"I don't apologize for what I did. If I could go back I'd do the exact same thing."*

"Treason." The Emperor muttered.

"Salvation." Sandra snapped back. *"All this time you were in here I thought you may have done a little self-reflection... Clearly that was too much to ask."*

The Emperor eyed Sandra angrily but made no response.

"Hate me, I don't care." Sandra continued, annoyed. *"But this city is suffering."*

"So I hear." The Emperor snarled. *"A royal bloodbath the papers are saying."*

"So what do we do about it?" Sandra asked.

"We?!?" The Emperor chortled. *"WE do nothing. I have been deposed madam, by your own hand. I have no power to exert."* He relaxed his shoulders and settled into his chair. *"It's not my problem anymore."*

"So you're just giving up?" Sandra asked.

"Uhhh yea." he stated flatly.

"They're dying." Sandra shot back, *"the ones that aren't dead are in total fear."*

The Emperor froze *"I know."* he said quietly, he looked away from Sandra. She finally hit a nerve, *"I failed them."* The Emperor whispered hung his head. His thin veneer of cockiness had completely vanished into regret, *"Good for one thing and I failed..."* he whispered to himself.

"So, this is all that's left." Sandra said mockingly, *"His Gracious Glorious Majesty... reduced to a sniveling wimp."* The Emperor said nothing. *"At least Amanda still has some balls..."*

The Emperor's head perked up. *"What do you mean?"* he asked sharply.

"I mean," Sandra explained, *"While you've been sitting in here sulking. Amanda killed a*

Republican lieutenant. There was a huge gunfight two nights ago, I'm surprised you didn't hear the shots from here."

"I... but..." The Emperor stammered. *"Is she alright?"*

"I don't know." Sandra said softly. *"But I tell you one thing that girl needs you to come back."* She took the Emperor's hand. *"I need you to come back."*

"You put me in here." The Emperor growled recoiling his hand.

"I put a monster in here." Sandra argued, forcefully taking his hand again. *"Let me get the Emperor out... his people need him."*

The Emperor returned Sandra's grip, he eyed the table between them. He eyed Sandra. *"It'll get in the way of my brooding..."* he finally lamented.

"Somehow I think his Majesty can multitask." Sandra said with a smirk.

The maniacal spark flickered back into the Emperor's eyes. He jumped up from his chair in excitement. *"By God I have another fight left in me!"* he shouted.

"So many sire..." Sandra replied slyly.

"No box can hold his Imperial and Apostolic Majesty!!" The Emperor shouted louder. *"BY DIVINE PROVIDENCE I AM KING!"*

Sandra hastily shushed the Emperor, but she was relieved at the return of his vigor. *"So... what's the plan?"* she asked.

"Plan?" The Emperor asked. *"You mean to tell me you came all the way here and you didn't have a plan??"* he let out a hearty laugh; The man she knew was coming back to her.

"I wasn't really thinking." Sandra said awkwardly. *"I just..."*

"Tsk tsk tsk..." The Emperor scolded sarcastically. *"How unlike you Sandra Blewens... I assume I can call you that now?"*

"I'd rather you did." Sandra replied.

"Well then I'm afraid for now this is goodbye." The Emperor said. He approached Sandra and ran a hand alongside her face. He reached up to brush her hair. His hand on her cheek sent a quiver down her spine. The moment, however, did not last as Sandra felt him pluck a bobby pin from her hair. He gave her a wink as he slid the bobby pin into his sleeve. He walked to the doorway and knocked sharply on the metal door.

Officer Leefort opened the door. The Emperor jiggled his handcuffs and extended his arms to the officer. *"I'm sorry my dear but I really must go."* he said, *"I have laundry duty at 8 PM sharp... and Officer Leefort can testify how foul my mood becomes when my shirt is not pressed."* Officer Leefort snorted and nodded in agreement. *"Laundry... 8 PM"* the Emperor again mused aloud, *"Ahhh what a life."* As Officer Leefort escorted the Emperor back to his cell Sandra could hear him whistling down the hallway, mimicking the violins that typically played when he entered a room.

Sandra returned to the prison at a quarter to eight. She entered the parking lot with her headlights off to avoid attention, carefully she found a cluster of cars that appeared to be staying overnight and she waited. At ten minutes to eight she saw a light emanate within the prison gates as a door opened. Men began filing out of the doorway pushing large laundry carts. The Emperor's sign must be close. He hadn't given her specific instruction, yet subtlety was never his Majesty's strong suit. She had a feeling she would know it when she saw it.

The laundry men continued with their work. Gradually they loaded a multitude of laundry carts into a van. The van was enclosed completely in a steel fence. All the prisoners working were monitored by armed security. What was the Emperor's plan? Was he going to seize the van? No, there was no way to get it out without being caught. It was now five minutes to eight.

Sandra shifted around nervously in her chair. Maybe she misread the whole thing? He said 8 PM twice, that had to have been a clue. But she saw nothing. The prisoners continued their work under close watch from the guards. It had turned 8 PM. Nothing.

The prisoners had finished loading the laundry van three minutes past eight. They were all escorted back inside by the guards as the van's ignition sprang the vehicle to life. Slowly the gate was opened to allow the van to leave.

BOOM

An explosion rocked the wall near the van's location. Sandra jumped in her seat at the sudden sound. A huge hole had been torn into the side of the prison. Smoke and dust billowed from the blast site. Soon hordes of prisoners in orange jumpsuits poured out of the open space. Sirens began to wail around the prison and searchlights illuminated on the growing mob.

Prisoners ran in every direction as guards from around the prison scrambled to contain the situation. Sandra could see scores of prisoners bolting too freedom, but she was too far to distinguish their faces. Where was he? She turned her own car on but kept the headlights off. Guards had begun firing at the escaping prisoners, Sandra instinctively ducked upon hearing gunfire. She peaked out over the dashboard. There in the sea of orange was one escapee, walking as the others ran, back rigid and marching full of purpose. The Emperor.

He began surveying the parking lot. Sandra laid on her horn exposing her position. The Emperor spotted her as she pulled her car from its parking space to get closer to him. He began a brisk run to her location. He was close to her car now. Before reaching the door, he stopped. Sandra laid on the horn again, but he waved her off. He turned back toward the escape in progress. *"Remember children!"* He shouted, *"The Emperor's mercy grants you freedom! Waste not this second chance!"*

His speech was met by gunfire in his direction from the guards. He fell in shock as bullets rattled against the van. Sandra rolled down a window. *"Shut the hell up and get in!"* she yelled. The Emperor fumbled back up to his feet and opened the door. As he climbed into the vehicle, another shot rang out. The Emperor grunted and clutched his lower abdomen. He began to fall out of the car, but Sandra grabbed him by the collar holding him in his seat as she sped away.

The emergency roadblock began rising. Sandra clutching the Emperor with one hand and steering with the other steered toward the exit. She cut the wheel hard enough to force the passenger door shut, securing the Emperor in the vehicle. He moaned as blood began pooling in his abdomen. Sandra floored the gas pedal on a straight path to the exit. She just cleared the exit as the roadblocks rose into position, smashing the rear of her car as they ascended. The car fishtailed onto the connecting street as Sandra worked the steering wheel to regain control. She managed to straighten the car out and began putting as much distance between them and the jail as possible. She looked at the passenger seat and its occupant. The Emperor was gritting his teeth, placing pressure on his abdomen, but he was conscious.

"Away from the city." The Emperor grunted *"Need... strength..."* he began to fade in and out.

"Oh no!" Sandra said angrily. *"You son of a bitch you aren't dying now!"* The Emperor's strength was failing. His hand fell from his wound. Sandra reached over and placed one hand over his stomach and began applying the pressure for him, his warm blood seeping through her fingers. She continued speeding into the night.

"Where am I going?!?" Sandra asked as she drove, in her current position it was hard to both steer the car and hold pressure. The car veered back and forth.

"No time..." the Emperor gasped, *"pull over..."* his breathing was becoming very labored. Sandra found a nearby patch of grass and pulled the car over. She quickly jumped out and ran to the other side. Flinging open the passenger door she placed her full weight on to hands to cover the Emperor's wound.

"cauterize..." the Emperor said between increasingly weaker breaths. *"It's the only way..."*

Frantically Sandra moved the Emperor's arms to cover the wound. *"Hold on."* she said as she felt him using his remaining strength to hold the pressure. She ran to the trunk and snatched the lug nut wrench from the emergency tire kit. There was an old towel in the trunk as well. She grabbed it and created a makeshift handle for herself on the wrench.

Running back to the front of the car she lifted the hood, the motor was still running, leaving the engine very hot. She placed the tip of the lug nut wrench against the engine.

Leaving the wrench she returned to the passenger seat. The Emperor was fading fast. Quickly Sandra tore a piece of her bloodied sleeve off and balled it up as much as she could. *"I'm sorry about this."* she said as she shoved the wadded fabric into the Emperor's mouth. She ran back to the front of the car and carefully used the towel to pick up the searing hot wrench.

Back to the Emperor she used the bullet hole in his jumpsuit to tear open his clothes, exposing the torso. She was surprised to see it was already covered with scars and lacerations. She stood in shock at the sight of the Emperor's mangled body before he grabbed her wrist. Unable to speak with his mouth gagged, his eyes emulated pure desperation. Carefully Sandra moved his hands exposing the bullet hole in his abdomen, blood began oozing once more once the pressure was released. Sandra positioned her arms so the Emperor could grab her forearm, she lined the heated wrench up as the Emperor braced, and she plunged the scalding metal into his skin.

The Emperor's muffled cries were bad enough. But the smell was worse, Sandra pressed the wrench harder against his abdomen as the searing skin crackled and blistered. The aroma of rotting flesh filled her nose. The Emperor bit hard on the fabric, writhing as Sandra pressed. The bleeding finally stopped. Sandra threw the wrench into the grass and took the Emperor by the shoulders. She leaned in close to his face, she could feel slight breathing. He had made it.

Feebly, he reached up and placed a hand on the back of Sandra's neck, pulling her closer. *"0537 Hunter's Lodge Road..."* he whispered, *"Exit 24... key under doormat."* with that his strength left him and he fell limp into the seat, but still alive.

Sandra followed the directions the Emperor gave her and found the exit off of the highway. The Emperor groaned in his seat. Writhing back and forth, his eyes barely open. The exit ramp led to a fork in the road to which the Emperor flung his arm toward the right. Sandra followed his instructions as their surroundings became increasingly more rural. Soon they were enveloped entirely in trees.

Sandra continued on as the Emperor groaned in pain. She saw the sign for Hunter's Lodge road. She took the turn and the asphalt beneath them turned to gravel. The car began bumping on the gravel street, causing the emperor to wince. Sandra slowed down to smoothen the ride. They passed through a multitude of houses. At the end of the street was number 0537, a derelict run-down shack that had to have been abandoned for at least a decade. The lawn had long died, and the entire foundation of the house was bowing in the middle.

"Is this the place?" Sandra asked, the Emperor nodded meekly. Sandra parked the car and walked to the passenger side. She opened the door.

"You're gonna have to walk." she said looking down onto the crippled Emperor. *"I can't carry you, you're too heavy."* The Emperor let out a feeble laugh though it clearly pained him.

"I am monarch of a great empire." he choked out. *"If Alexander can bring the Persian horde to heel, I can walk,"* He began to push himself out of the car and Sandra helped him onto his feet. She slipped underneath him and rested his arm around her shoulders. Together they trudged to the front door of the shack. Sandra helped ease the Emperor against the wall as she found a beat-up spare key under the doormat.

"How do we know this place hasn't turned into a drug den?" she asked.

"Because." The Emperor heaved *"Who would dare touch the Emperor's birthplace...?"*

Sandra unlocked the door and opened the house. The inside was completely empty; there was no furniture to speak of. Just a heap of empty rooms and ruined appliances. Dust and cobwebs littered the entire structure. Sandra helped the Emperor into the main room of the house where he directed her to lie him on the barren floor.

"Move your hand." she ordered once she laid him to the ground. *"I've got to see it."* the skin around the Emperor's injury had turned to hues of yellow and green. Infection was already setting in.

"It's fine." The Emperor grunted meekly, Sandra noticed large beads of sweat forming at his forehead.

"Look at you, no it's not." she replied, exacerbated. She glanced around the house; it was entirely empty. She ripped off a piece of her own shirt and used it to wipe the sweat from his face. She brushed his cheek with her hand. *"You have to hold on until the morning."* she said. *"I can find you help then."*

The Emperor tried to sit up to no avail; he writhed back and forth clutching his wound. *"I will endure,"* he said. *"But please... please don't leave me tonight."* desperation rang in his voice. Sandra laid down next to him. His breathing slowed.

"I'm not leaving you." Sandra said softly. The Emperor leaned in and placed his head in the crook of her shoulder. His eyes were closed now, *"Sandra Blewens..."* he coughed. *"First you saved my soul... now my body."* he let out a deep exhale and faded off to sleep.

Sandra looked at the Emperor's sleeping form. Despite all they had been through that evening his face was one of genuine peace. *"Edward von Drac,"* she whispered to herself. *"You have opened my eyes..."* She placed her head next to his and together the pair slept through the night, atop the cold and drafty floor.

Chapter 26: Amanda

Amanda had never seen Reginridge so disheveled. The grand halls and opulent rooms were stripped bare as makeshift cots were filled up all throughout the mansion. Tables were pushed aside, furniture was piled in heaps, even some of the paintings had been moved from the walls. It was not just her and her girls that were seeking safety here but refugees all throughout the city that had nowhere else to go. Her girls thought it was the most magnificent thing they had ever seen but Amanda was disheartened at the state of the Emperor's palace.

When the fleet of vans Cody sent brought them all back to the house, medical staff had seen to the girls that were injured and the footmen showed them all to their temporary living quarters. The Emperor's inquisitors in their trademark black suits patrolled the manor and the connected grounds. Amanda sat with her girls in what was formerly the Emperor's library, now a makeshift campsite for his retreating forces.

Her girls were bruised and bandaged, their clothing was torn and crusted blood, both personal and foreign, coated their skin. Their spirit, however, was far from diminished. Collectively they all sat, admiring the grandiose house, sharing stories from the battle they had all just partaken in. Despite the absolute catastrophe that took place earlier in the evening, pride showed through on their defense of their territory and the casualties they inflicted on their enemy. *"God we were such badasses!"* one said. *"They thought we would be some pretty pushovers... fuck 'em!"* The rest of the room held similar sentiments. Together both Amanda's girls and her security thugs commended one another on their bravery. Amanda heaved a sigh of relief.

Her relaxed feeling came to an end when she saw from the window another fleet of cars came down the long driveway. She rushed from the library to the main entrance out to the on comers. Medical staff again were there taking the wounded reinforcements into the house to begin treating their injuries. Slowly they filed in, but Amanda frantically looked for one in particular.

Finally, Cody emerged from one of the cars, appearing unscathed. Amanda sprinted over to him and threw her arms around his neck. He recoiled in surprise but quickly relaxed when she planted a giant kiss on his lips, he pulled her closer and returned her affections. The crowd of Imperial soldiers laughed and cheered for Cody, pumping their rifles in celebration.

"That was so dumb of you." Cody said to her once they separated. Guilt washed over Amanda's face.

"How bad was it?" she asked.

"We lost a lot of good guys." Cody said, *"not to mention your people..."*

"Oh Jesus." Amanda said. *"I know I shouldn't have but..."*

"Well." Cody cut her off. He couldn't hide his smile anymore. *"They lost about four times as many."* He quickly spun Amanda around and held her arm up in the air for everyone to see. *"Gentlemen!"* he shouted to the surrounding soldiery. *"Here she is... Amanda Beasly, Hero of the Empire!"* The crowd cheered again this time shouting Amanda's name. She looked up to the library window and could see her people cheering as well. The shouts of Amanda's name filled the sky, and she imagined the echoes made it all the way back to the city.

"You gave them hope." Cody told her. *"Your stunt showed everyone we aren't beaten yet.... Thank you."*

"It wasn't just me." Amanda replied. *"Every one of my people fought like hell, and it still wouldn't have mattered if you didn't come to save us."*

Cody nodded and led Amanada into the house. As they crossed the threshold a footman rushed up to greet them. *"Lord Chancellor, we are relieved you returned safely,"* he said to Cody. *"We've made the arrangements as you requested and are finding room for all the new additions."*

"Good." Cody replied curtly. *"We're gonna need more room soon so keep it going, every square inch of this place needs to be turned into something functional."*

"Of course sir." The Footman answered. *"We will do our duty."*

"I need someone to send a message to all the other marshals." Cody continued. *"I want them all here within an hour."*

"As you command sir." the footman said.

"Thank you." Cody replied. He began to lead Amanda upstairs before the footman cleared his throat. Together they turned back toward the footman. *"Is there something else?"* Cody asked.

"Just a question for Ms. Beasley." the footman explained. *"It's just that before her departure, his Majesty procured quite a wardrobe for her ladyship, and I thought you may wish to make use of some fresh clothes."*

Amanda's face turned sour at the mention of Sandra. *"No, I don't want those."* she responded coldly. *"In fact, burn them."*

"As you wish ma'am." the footman replied before scurrying off to attend to his duties.

"It was a shock for all of us." Cody said as he led her up the stairs. *"I never would've thought she was a cop."*

"She was a liar." Amanda spat, her face flushing red, *"She lied to him, she lied to you... she lied to me. All of us."*

"Luckily," Cody said, pulling Amanda close to his side. *"We're used to being lied to."*

"No." Amanda replied, separating herself. *"Not like that, not the way she did it."*

"Well...." Cody said, as they reached the top of the stairs, in an awkward attempt to segway, *"There's someone else who hasn't been taking this well."* he led her down the hallway to the Emperor's bedroom. *"I was hoping maybe you would cheer her up."*

He opened the door gently. Amanda was relieved to see that the Emperor's room hadn't been touched. His large desk still planted firmly in place. Portraits of historical figures imposingly large along the various walls. Amanda had never been inside, but it looked exactly like she imagined it did. Cody led her inside and directed her to the Emperor's bed.

On top of the bed was Edwina, her bright white plumage contrasting sharply to the deep violet blanket. She was sitting almost motionless on the bed with her head drooped. Amanda reached a handout to pet her, which Edwina lazily brushed up against before returning to her slumped position.

"What's wrong with her?" Amanda asked.

"No matter what I do she won't move." Cody said, he gestured to a bowl of fruit on the floor near the bed. *"I've tried seeds, fruits, even worms,"* he explained, *"and she won't even get up to eat."*

"She's depressed." Amanda observed as she scratched the top of the Peacock's head. Amanda noticed feathers falling out as she did so. *"She's had*

one friend her whole life and he's gone... she misses him."

"I know." Cody lamented, *"I thought maybe seeing another familiar face might cheer her up, but I guess not."*

Amanda reached down to the bowl of fruit and plucked a slice of pineapple, she held it to Edwina's beak. The bird looked at the fruit momentarily before turning her head away from it. Amanda sighed as she scratched the bird's head once more. *"We miss him too girl."* she whispered before giving the peacock a gentle kiss on her forehead.

Cody had all of the marshals meet in Reginridge's dining room. Luckily the table there was still in place giving the residents somewhere to eat so it could double as a conference space. Despite her protests, Cody insisted that Amanda sit in as Sylvia's temporary replacement, citing her leadership prowess in the events now affectionately being called "The Battle of the Brothel".

Harold sat at the table angrily tapping his fingers on top of the surface. His eyes had sunken in since the funeral. Madame DuBois was seated next to him, wearing a headscarf as opposed to a wig, her makeup sloppily done. Stevens sat with his chin resting on his hands and Samerson was frantically wiping his forehead. The great Marshals of the once mighty Empire of Colonna, an absolute wreck.

"*Gentlemen.*" Cody said as he took his seat, "*Ladies... Thank you all for coming.*" his audience made no response. "*After tonight's events I am sure Amanda needs no introduction.*" Cody continued gesturing towards Amanda. "*I asked her to come sit with us to represent the interests of our prostitution division.*" Again, there was no response, but Harold did give Amanda a polite smile which put her somewhat at ease.

Given the continued silence Cody cleared his throat and changed tact. "*Alright everyone here it is.*" he said, losing his professional pretext. "*We hit hard tonight but we all know they're going to come back harder.*" This did not come across as news to anyone in the room. "*We got them tonight.*" Cody continued, "*but they still outnumber us. So, I want everyone to move all of their people here ASAP so we can dig in.*"

"*Excuse me.*" Samerson said accusatorily, cocking his head.

"*What?*" Cody asked, "*What's the problem George?*"

"*It sounds like you're giving us orders.*" Samerson answered. "*What gives you the right to boss us around?*"

"*I'm not bossing anyone around George.*" Cody replied defensively. "*But I am the Emperor's deputy and...*"

"The Emperor's deputy?!?" Samerson scoffed, cutting Cody off. *"What have you EVER been besides his glorified secretary?"*

"George, what are you doing?" Harold interjected angrily on Cody's behalf. *"Why are you being so hostile?"*

"Because..." Samerson continued. *"Nowhere did we concretely establish a chain of command if the Emperor was... incapacitated."*

"Well, I was closest with his Majesty..." Cody offered up.

"So freaking what?" Samerson mocked. *"If the Emperor was here and heard what just came out of your mouth he would smack you! Nor would he approve of this blatant power grab."*

"Well he's not here, is he?!" Cody shot back, *"Believe me you piece of shit the last freaking thing I want is to be in charge of this mess, but someone has to hold it all together!"*

"George is being a little dramatic, I agree." Madame DuBois cut in. *"But he does have a point, I think we should all discuss our next steps as a collective. Even his Majesty always took the time to heed our advice."*

"Thank you Steven." Samerson offered, Madame DuBois rolled her eyes.

"Alright then." Cody said defeated. *"What do you all think we should do?"* he threw his arms at the table.

"We do nothing." Samerson answered. *"Cody, the game is up man. We don't have the muscle; we don't have the political protection. We have nothing."*

"Nothing??" Cody repeated angrily. *"I think tonight we showed the world that one of ours is worth twenty of theirs."*

"Cody please listen to reason." Samerson pleaded, *"Okay you took a bunch of people out tonight. You still lost the warehouse. If we pull everyone back here. Where are we gonna run to once this place falls?"*

"So we just give up!?" Harold snapped, *"Everything we built we just throw it all away?"*

"What choice do we have?" Samerson asked, *"Let's say even for the sake of argument we go out in some magical blaze of glory and we win.... Two seconds later the police are gonna arrest every last one of us."*

"Kurt you've been quiet..." Madame DuBois observed, *"Where do you stand on all this?"*

Stevens tugged nervously at his collar, *"well...."* he said sheepishly, *"It's not my intention to upset anyone but I agree with George."* Harold threw his hands up in the air.

"Without the Emperor's connections..." Stevens continued, *"There's no way we can conduct business like we have been. Maybe it's better if we all cut our losses and parted ways."*

"I cannot believe what I am hearing!" Harold exclaimed, jumping to his feet. *"These pricks came*

onto our turf and killed our people. And we're just going to turn the whole operation over to them??"

"You have every right to be upset Harold." Samerson interjected. *"No one has forgotten your tragedy.... but we have to be rational."* Arguments ensued back and forth as the room devolved into chaos. The Marshals had now all risen from their chairs and were shouting at each other. The vitriol had grown to such an extent Amanda couldn't even comprehend what anyone was saying anymore. It all got to be too much for her. Unsure of how to gain control of the room she turned to Cody. He met her gaze and understanding its meaning he withdrew a gun from his jacket and fired it into the ceiling.

BANG

The room went silent. *"Go ahead Amanda."* Cody said calmly as everyone retook their seats. Amanda cleared her throat anxiously.

"I don't know everyone here very well." Amanda began, *"But if I had to guess I am almost one hundred percent sure that everyone in this room got to where they are because of the Emperor."*

"Of course we did." Samerson agreed, *"No one here is doubting his Majesty's leadership but..."*

"If you'll just let me." Amanda said, holding up a hand. *"For most of my life the Emperor didn't know I existed."* she continued. *"Me, and a lot of people like me, fell through the cracks. I know what it's like to live in a world without the Empire. And I am sure you all remember from your own time as well."* the table

collectively agreed. *"The Emperor personally went out of his way to give us all a fighting chance at dignity in this world."* Amanda said, *"he showed me I wasn't alone, I wasn't helpless, and that I have a voice... don't we owe that to everyone else? Don't we have an obligation to give everyone else the opportunity that he gave us? I know for my people, turning ourselves over to the thugs means abuse and destitution, and I can't do that to them. So regardless of what is decided here today... We're going to keep fighting."*

The room silently mulled Amanda's words. Most were emotionless but Cody's face was one of immense pride. Harold swished his tongue around his cheeks while he tapped the table, finally he broke the silence. *"They killed Syliva..."* he said, *"They die no matter the cost. Me and my guys are with you."*

Madame DuBois came next, *"I am and will always be a member of his Majesty's loyal government."* she said. *"The Empire has given me and mine a whole lot, we will defend her to the death."*

The table now collectively looked at Samerson and Stevens, the two were in a heated but hushed conversation. When it appeared the two had reached a consensus Samerson rose from his seat. *"It's suicide."* he said finally, Amanda was wash with disappointment. Without everyone on board there was no chance of them winning. *"But..."* Samerson continued, *"They're going to hunt us down either way so we may as well die with some balls."* Stevens nodded in agreement. *"On one condition...."*

Samerson stipulated. *"We'll follow you through this Cody, but when it's done we all sit down and figure out how we reorganize the command structure. If by some miracle we survive."*

"You have my word." Cody promised, *"Just until this mess is settled."*

"Alright then." Samerson said, satisfied. *"We're in."* Everyone at the table took a big exhale. Relief should have been the feeling of the Imperial Council; however, a grave melancholy filled the room, in anticipation of the monumental task ahead of them.

That night Amanda and Cody lie in bed together. They had taken the room the Emperor gave to Sandra during her time in Reginridge. Amanda wasted no time throwing any personal effects of Sandra's that remained out into the hall. They both sat upright in bed unable to sleep.

"Can I ask you something?" Amanda pondered to Cody.

"Yea." Cody answered

"She really genuinely seemed to care about him." Amanda thought aloud. *"Like REALLY sold it."*

"I know." Cody agreed. *"Like I said earlier we were all fooled. What's your question?"*

"Well..." Amanda started, *"how do we know that one of us isn't gonna hurt the other like that?"*

"Stacy-Sandra, whatever her real name was." Cody explained, *"She was a cop. Cops don't care about people like us... They look after their own and we look after our own."*

Amanda pondered this for a moment. *"That's not true."* she eventually answered, *"Plenty of cops look out for us... and people like us don't always look after our own."*

"Well you and I do." Cody retorted. *"That much I do know."*

"You're right." she said, popping up out of the bed. Quickly she rushed out of the door and into the hall.

"Where are you going?" Cody called after her.

"Looking after our own!" she shouted back from the hall. She returned a few moments later, carrying a lethargic Edwina in her hands. The bird made no motions, rather just accepted her fate. Amanda laid her gently on the bed between her and Cody. Cody affectionately stroked the birds back as she lay on the bed and Amanda climbed back in.

"I know we aren't as good as him." he said to Edwina, *"But we'll take care of you the best we can."*

"We'll love you even when you're sad." Amanda said, affectionately brushing the bird's wing. Edwina still did not move. But Amanda could hear a faint cooing emanating from the peacock. It made her smile.

"Cody, I need to tell you something." Amanda said, still brushing the bird's wing. *"Do you remember*

the night Syliva died and you asked what happened to my wrists?"

"Yea." Cody answered, shifting in the bed to face her. *"What about it?"*

Amanda took a deep breath and recounted her encounter with Frankie following Syvlia's death. As she relayed to Cody the story of her attack, he listened intently. His face curdled as Amanda described the attack in detail by brutal detail. When she had finished Cody took a moment to process the entire story.

"I wish you had told me". He said finally.

"I told the Emperor." Amanda said, *"I thought that was enough."*

"Well, why tell him and not me?" Cody asked again. *"I mean you know I care about you."*

"I know you do." Amanda said, nuzzling closer to him in the bed. *"I don't want you feeling like you have to protect me."*

"*Oh but he can protect you?"* Cody inquired, his feelings appeared to be hurt.

"It's different." Amanda meekly offered. *"I don't know how to describe it."*

"Can you try?" Cody asked.

"Well to the Emperor, I'll always be the scared girl he plucked from a brothel." Amanda explained, *"To him I'm a responsibility."*

"Okay" Cody nodded, *"So what am I to you?"*

Amanda pushed herself away so she could be upright. *"I want us to be equals."* she said, *"I want you to look at me and see strength....*" she gave a halfhearted at the irony forming in her head. "*I want you to look at me the way the Emperor looked at Sandra.*" she muttered before her face soured, "*at least that's how I felt at the time.*" she glared angrily at the bedsheets.

Cody leaned over and reached a hand out to Amanda, he recoiled slightly at first but then proceeded to brush her hair from her face. "*We aren't them.*" he said, "*I don't look at you and see strength...*"

"*What do you see then?*" said Amanda, she felt embarrassed.

"*I see peace.*" Cody said, brushing Amanda's chin.

Amanda felt more relaxed after that answer. "*Peace?*" she asked.

"*I don't know if you've picked up on it yet.*" Cody said sarcastically, "*but this life is stressful as hell.*" Amanda giggled at his sarcasm. "*I mean no wonder the Emperor is batshit crazy,*" Cody continued, "*I've been halfway in charge for just a few days and I already wanna blow my brains out. Even before that it's just endless headaches and misery and you get to a point where you wonder why you keep doing it.*"

"*So why do you keep doing it?*" Amanda asked.

"*Because I didn't have a reason to stop.*" Cody answered, "*There was nothing else out there for me.*

Until I met you." he took Amanda's hands into his. *"Then I started picturing a house, a normal house, not this castle, a dog, maybe some kids... peace."*

Amanda smiled at the vision, *"I dreamed about running once, leaving it all behind."* She envisioned her postcard of the beach; she could hear the waves crashing into the sand. *"But then I met you, and the Emperor, and Sylia, and everyone else."*

"Amanda, this is no way for people to live." Cody said, *"Look at it... everything's falling apart around us. Don't you think you deserve to be happy? Haven't you been through enough?"*

"Of course I deserve to be happy." Amanda replied.

"Then run away with me." Cody pressed, *"We could go right now. By the time anyone realizes we're gone we'd be a hundred miles away from all of this."*

"No." Amanda answered curtly, *"I can't."*

"Why not?" Cody pressed, *"We've both done our part. It's time for us to have our life."*

"Those people downstairs are scared." Amanda said, *"Their whole world is crashing like you just said, we can't leave them, not now."*

"Why not?" Cody asked again, *"What did they ever do for you?"*

"They put their faith in me." Amanda replied almost instantly. *"And tonight, the marshals put their faith in you... that means more than any amount of money or favors."*

Cody fell flat on the bed exhausted, *"you're just as bad as he is."* he sighed. *"Why I listen to either one of you I don't know."*

"He's taught me a lot." Amanda mused, *"but you love him, don't you?"* Cody nodded silently. *"I love you too..."* Amanda said. She gave Cody a gentle kiss before curling back into his arm and together the pair drifted off to sleep.

Chapter 27: Sandra

"God damn this festering thing!" The Emperor grumbled as he prodded his infected wound, *"An Empire on the brink of disaster and I'm saddled with this pestilent affliction."*

"Well at least you have your temper back." Sandra noted jokingly, *"that's gotta be a good sign."* She was relieved the Emperor had made it through the night, but as morning came, she realized their decrepit accommodations had very little in the way of medical supplies, much less any food.

"You need to eat." she said standing over him, *"you're still weak."*

"Weak?!?" The Emperor scoffed, sitting on the floor against a wall. *"The only sustenance I require is the blood of those rebel heathens who are too cowardly to face me in the open field!"*

"I know." Sandra said with a smile, *"I tell you what... you stand up and walk five feet, I will drive us back to the city right now."* The Emperor made no response, just glared at her angrily. She met his stare, squinting into his soul. He eventually conceded defeat and turned his head away.

"That's what I thought." Sandra said, *"Now... first thing's first, we need to get food in you then we need a doctor."*

"Just hang me now and be done with it." The Emperor groaned.

"Aw come on." Sandra said, kneeling down to meet him eye level. *"Where's that fighting spirit you had two seconds ago?"* She gave him a playful jab which made him wince, Sandra let out a small laugh at his agony before reassuring him he would be okay.

"I'm coherent now." the Emperor said, *"How bad is it?"*

"Well, it's definitely infected." Sandra answered, *"That's why we need a doctor."*

"Oh for God's sake, all this time and you're still inept." The Emperor scolded, *"Not me... the fate of the crownlands... how bad is it?"*

Sandra took a deep breath. *"It's bad."* she said. *"There's a lot of people dead, and if I understand correctly, the Republicans have pushed everyone either out of the city or underground."*

"Damn them." The Emperor growled. He closed his eyes and massaged his forehead, *"Master Chesley would recall them all to Reginridge."* he said to himself. *"That's where they'll make their stand."*

"But if they lose there..." Sandra surmised,

"That will be the final nail in the coffin." The Emperor confirmed. *"We'll need to gather reinforcements."*

"Well..." Sandra continued, *"I am the most hated woman in Colonna city at the moment, so the hearts and minds game is your job. And we can't do that if you don't get better."*

"There's a bar not far from here..." The Emperor began to detail.

"I'm not giving you any alcohol." Sandra sharply interjected.

The Emperor hung his head and massaged his temples. *"If you would allow me to finish."* he said annoyed, *"There is a bar not far from here, it's called Jack Mezzos. Go there and ask for Brenda..."*

"Whose Brenda?" Sandra interrupted again.

The Emperor took a deep dramatic breath through his nose. *"Madam I may be incapacitated physically but my faculties are still present, just allow me to speak!"*

"Sorry sorry." Sandra offered up with a lazy concern *"go ahead."*

"Brenda is the proprietor of the bar in question." The Emperor explained, *"Go there, find her and tell her where I am. She will take it from there."* Sandra gave the Emperor a puzzled look but did not say anything. *'What is your question?"* the Emperor sighed.

"Is this Brenda a doctor?" Sandra asked.

"No." The Emperor said with a patronizing tone, *"She owns a bar... but she will get us in contact with the proper channels so can you PLEASE just do as I ask?"*

"Yes I can." Sandra replied curtly. She crouched down again to the Emperor's level. She flicked his wound which made him jolt and wince in pain. *"That's for being rude."* she said, *"I'll be back."*

She stood up and got herself ready to leave, out of the corner of her eye she could see the Emperor smiling as he sat half-alive on the floor of the shack. She walked out the door with a grin of her own. She didn't quite realize how much she had missed his company.

The bar the Emperor described was easy enough to find. Tucked away in the town center of this secluded suburb was a building with a sign bearing the name Jack Mezzo's. Sandra parked her car in the almost empty lot; she straightened her hair in the visor mirror before exiting the vehicle and walking inside.

The inside of the bar was nothing of amazement, beat up wooden floors hosting a small seating area of handmade wooden tables, behind which was the bar itself. The building smelled of sweat and mildew. Yet, it held that quaint small-town charm, one Sandra had seldom experienced in a life lived completely in Colonna City.

To the building's rear, at the actual bar were three patrons, all wearing biker vests, they all shared one similar patch depicting a horse with steam pulsing from its nostrils, the words "Charging Cavaliers" stitched around the image. Nothing out of the ordinary for early in the day. A soft hum of country music played over the building's speaker system. Behind the bar was a lone bartender. A young woman with long dark hair, conversing with the bikers to alleviate her boredom.

"Hey, how are ya." The bartender said as Sandra approached the bar. She had a friendly face as she placed a disposable coaster in front of Sandra. *"What can I get for you?"*

Sandra took a seat on one of the barstools. The bikers gave her a halfhearted wave before resuming their conversation. *"Ummm. Just a water for now."* Sandra answered.

"A water?" The bartender asked, she snickered slightly which caused the bikers to laugh. *"Babes, you know this is a bar right?"*

"I know sorry." Sandra responded jokingly, *"I actually came here looking for Brenda."*

"Brenda?" The bartender repeated as she poured Sandra a water from the fountain gun behind the bar. *"Is something wrong?"*

"Nononono... oh thank you." Sandra said as the bartender gave her a cup of water. *"I just came here on business."*

The bartender shrugged, *"I'll go get her, I'll be right back."* she said politely, *"Gary, watch the place till I get back, will ya?"* One of the bikers lifted his cup in acknowledgement. The bartender scurried off through a doorway which presumably led to the back. Sandra took a sip of her water. No one gave her a second thought.

The bartender returned very shortly. Behind her was a woman, bleach blonde, middle aged, rubbing her hands with a towelette. The bartender pointed Sandra out to the woman and she approached Sandra's stool.

"Hi there." The woman said with a friendly smile, outstretching her hand to Sandra. *"How can I help you?"*

"You're Brenda, I take it." Sandra said politely as she took the woman's hand and shook it. The woman nodded in affirmation. *"A friend of yours asked me to come see you."* Sandra explained.

"In this business darlin' I make a lot of friends." Brenda laughed heartily, *"You're going to have to be more specific."*

Sandra cleared her throat nervously, *"ummm, the Emperor."* she whispered. Brenda gave her a look of utter confusion.

"Excuse me?" Brenda asked, *"I don't understand. Who are you talking about?"*

Sandra began to grow anxious; she wasn't sure exactly how much she should divulge here in this barroom. She took another sip of her water to buy herself some time. *"I'm from the city."* she tried again.

"Sweetheart you're losing me." Brenda said again. *"Are you feeling alright?"* Brenda seemed genuinely to not understand what Sandra was talking about, however Sandra did notice the nearby bikers had stopped their conversation and began to pay more attention to her. One of them got up and moved over to the exit, blocking the path out. Great.

"Brenda." One of the bikers said, *"She's talking about Eddie."* Brenda's eyes widened at the realization.

"Ohhhh EDDIE." she said her face lit up for a moment, but then quickly turned somber. *"I thought he was in jail."*

"So did we." the biker replied. He got up from his stool and walked in Sandra's direction. *"I saw it on the news.... And I saw the cop that took him down."*

"Oh you mean..." Brenda said, addressing the biker but pointing to Sandra, the Biker nodded as he eyed Sandra skeptically.

"Alright." Sandra said calmly, instinct beating out fear, *"Just everyone take a deep breath."*

"Listen lady... whoever you are." Brenda said coolly, shooing the biker back with her hand. *"We don't want any trouble with you or with the police. But we aren't interested in testifying against anyone so it might just be better if you left."*

"You misunderstand." Sandra said as she stood up from her seat. *"He asked me to come find you."*

"Why in the hell would he send you here?" Brenda asked, *"You gotta realize how crazy that sounds."*

"Look." Sandra said turning toward the biker, *"Clearly you know him... is crazy really out of the ordinary?"*

The biker looked stunned, caught off guard by her question. *"What do you want?"* The biker asked.

"Hang on." Brenda interjected, *"Stormy go lock the door."* The bartender darted over and did as she was asked, switching the sign on the door to say the bar was closed.

"I'm really not looking for a fight." Sandra reiterated,

"Neither am I." Brenda stated, *"But whatever this is it feels like it should be private."*

"Edward..." Sandra began, that felt too weird to say, *"The Emperor... he's with me."*

"Okay now you're really not making any sense." Brenda said. Everyone was standing around Sandra now.

"It's a long story that I don't have time for." Sandra pressed, backing away to give herself some space, *"He's with me and he's hurt, and he sent me here to find you to get him help."*

"Brenda, I think she might be telling the truth." one of the bikers said, the tension in the room was relaxing, *"that's a weird ass thing to lie about."*

"That boy," Brenda chuckled, *"leave it to him to win over the cop that arrested him."* The comment caught Sandra by surprise, hearing the Emperor referred to as a child was strange to say the least. But that didn't matter now.

"It wasn't like that." Sandra fumbled, *"I... can you help me or not?"*

"Uh no I can't." Brenda said, *"But they can."* she gestured to the bikers.

"Where is he?" one of the bikers asked

"This old house... I can take you to it. It's not far from here." Sandra answered. The bikers all looked at each other and nodded. They left some money at the bar and gathered their things, ready to leave.

"Tell him I said hi!" The bartender called out to Sandra as she turned toward the exit, it made Sandra turn back round, curiosity getting the better of her.

"How do you guys know him?" she asked.

"Oh he used to work here." Brenda answered, *"Now go on, you just took three customers from me. I wanna open back up."* she waved Sandra and the bikers out of the door. Sandra exited the building and got back into her car; the bikers mounted their nearby motorcycles. From the bar entrance, Brenda gave them one last wave as she flipped the sign on the door back to open.

Sandra pulled into the driveway of the old shack. Behind her the bikers had parked their bikes and dismounted. They followed her up to the door as she walked into the house. The Emperor was right where she left him, seated on the floor with his back propped up against the wall. He shot his head in the direction of the doorway when he heard it open, still clutching his abdomen, he was visibly happy at Sandra's return.

His joy increased when he saw the bikers behind her. *"Fellas!"* he exclaimed as they all entered the shack. *"It does my heart good to see you again. You'll excuse me if I don't rise."*

"Jesus Christ." one of the bikers said, *"Eddie Drac... how long has it been."*

"Too long I know I know," The Emperor coughed out, *"But Harold keeps me updated on all your news, babies, weddings, the essentials."* The biker snorted.

"What the hell happened to you?" the biker asked, noting his injury.

"Casualty of my early release I'm afraid." The Emperor sighed.

"How'd you even get out?" another biker asked.

"Ahhh." The Emperor heaved, his breathing had increased, the conversation was taking much of his energy. *"My associate, the divine Sandra Blewens."* He reached a hand up to Sandra *"Formerly of Colonna City's finest, now a true Lady of the Empire."* Sandra took his hand. *"She is the architect of my liberation."*

"I'm lost..." the biker said, *"I thought she arrested you?"*

"Nevermind that." The Emperor said sharply, *"We have more pressing matters to attend to."* He moved his hand and showed his stomach; the infection had clearly spread and the blisters had

begun to ooze. The bikers made a disgusted face at the sight of the abhorrent lesion.

"There's a bullet in here." The Emperor explained, *"I need it removed if I am going to reclaim that which is rightfully mine."* He squeezed Sandra's hand tightly.

One of the bikers knelt down to take a closer look. He ran a finger across the burn scar. *"It's gonna hurt like hell,"* he said to the Emperor. *"If you can hang on a little while longer I can scrounge up something for the pain."*

"No pain is greater than the cries of my people under attack from mindless brigands." The Emperor stated, *"Do it now."*

"Your call man." the biker shrugged *"I have to get the pliers from my bike, you guys lay him down."* He stood up and walked out the door as the other two helped lower the Emperor flat onto the floor.

"Hang on just a second." Sandra interjected, everyone stopped. *"What exactly are you going to do?"*

"I'm gonna get the bullet out." The biker said, confused why she was asking.

"And you can just do that?" Sandra pressed.

"I was an Army medic for ten years." the biker said, *"so... probably."* He left the house for his bike.

The Emperor sniggered at the biker's joke. *"It's our only option,"* he said, *"I refuse to believe God means for the Emperor of Colonna to die here in this damp ruin of the past.... It will be fine."* The biker returned with a pair of pliers and pulled a pocketknife from a case on his belt.

"Alright boys hold him down." the biker said. The bikers got on either side of the Emperor, one pressing down on his shoulders and another on his ankles. *"He's secure."* The Emperor eyes Sandra nervously. She rushed to his head. Coming down to her knees she placed the Emperor's head gently in her lap.

"If you die I will never forgive you." she said, looking down on the Emperor's face and cupping his cheeks. *"I threw my whole life away for this."*

"Have you ever known me not to repay a debt?" the Emperor replied sweetly. *"I wouldn't dream of it."*

Sandra again ripped part of the Emperor's jumpsuit and stuffed it into his mouth. He closed his eyes and braced for what was to come. Sandra looked to the biker and nodded. The biker placed the knife's blade on the cauterized skin.

Sandra held the Emperor's head tight as the biker performed the impromptu surgery. The Emperor's muffled screams piercing the wind in the drafty shack. He writhed slightly but the two assisting bikers did a good job holding him in place. Slowly and delicately his abdomen was sliced open again. Blood began pouring from the opened skin. One of the bikers holding him to the floor placed a knee on the Emperor's stomach attempting to cut off the flow, the bleeding slowed enough for the work to continue but

Sandra could see the last bit of color begin to drain from the Emperor's face. They had to be fast.

Sandra watched the initial stage of the operation but had to turn away once she saw the pliers plunged into the Emperor's belly. She pressed her forehead onto his and squeezed his face tightly. The pliers were pulled back out, clutching a squashed 9mm shell. Quickly the pseudo surgeon pulled a cigarette lighter from his leather vest and used it to reseal the wound. Though she had done the same thing not twenty-four hours prior, the smell of burning flesh still made her queasy.

The Emperor was now breathing extremely heavily through his nose but had stopped screaming. Yet again he had somehow pulled through. Sandra's grip loosened. God this man refused to die. The bikers restraining the Emperor had let go as well. One of them had a water canteen which they poured slowly over the Emperor's new burn. The Emperor's eyes rolled back into his head as he passed out, but he was still breathing.

"He's gonna be out for at least an hour or so." the biker told Sandra as he wiped his hands clean, *"I'll be back tonight to check on him."*

"Are you sure he's going to make it?" Sandra asked. The biker just shrugged.

"60/40" was all he could offer her. *"Stay here with him though. He needs an eye on him at all times. Keep him calm."* The biker tossed her a canteen.

"Keep that wound clean, I'll bring more stuff when I come back."

"Thank you." Sandra said she got up to walk them to the door. *"Really... thank you."* The biker said nothing. Him and his cohorts left, and Sandra and the Emperor were once again alone in the shack.

It took a little over two hours for the Emperor to regain consciousness. He let out a gentle moan that caused Sandra to rush back to his side. Slowly his eyes fluttered open and his head swished from side to side.

"Can we please be done with you almost dying?" Sandra asked gently as she caressed his face. *"At least for now?"*

"Madam, when I die it will take much more than a bullet." he coughed in reply, reaching up to wipe a tear from her eye. *"Where did they go?"*

"They'll be back." Sandra reassured, *"Just take it easy for a second, get your strength back."*

"That's why I need them here." The Emperor said, *"To get my strength back."*

"I never meant for this to happen to you, you know." Sandra said, turning away from the Emperor's gaze. He pulled her face back, forcing her to face him.

"What do you mean?" he asked, *"You didn't shoot me."*

"No but this whole thing is my fault. I thought if I took you in, you would make bail and be back in a

few hours" her eyes swelled with tears *"pull some strings with the DA I don't know. I just wanted you to calm down. Now all these people have died, you almost died twice and it's my fault."*

"Your fault?" The Emperor croaked, he tried to laugh but it pained him too much. *"No it's not your fault."* He pushed himself up to a seat position and Sandra sat next to him. *"Had I killed that man..."* he lamented, *"I would be no better than those from which I seized power all those years ago, the same as those who seek to usurp me now, everything I worked to build would have been a lie in one single instant... You madam saved the Empire."* He took a deep breath and massaged his new scar. *"What I don't understand is why you came back for me."*

"I don't know." Sandra said, *"People were dying, civilians, the police weren't making any meaningful headway, you seemed like the only person who could stop it."*

"You mean restore order." The Emperor clarified.

"I guess." Sandra replied.

"What do you think of me?" The Emperor said after a brief pause, *"As a man?"*

"I think you're a man who judges people wholly by their actions." Sandra answered, *"And a man who is desperate to have people look up to him."*

"Do you look up to me?" he asked her.

"No." Sandra said, *"You're not a role model to me.... But I do admire you."*

"Funny." The Emperor contemplated.

"What?"

"I admire you too."

Sandra scoffed playfully, *"Okay I'll bite."* she said, *"What do you think of me, as a woman?"*

"I think many people cater to my eccentricities." The Emperor said, *"Usually out of fear or a desire for money... But you never did; not really."*

"So what does that tell you?" Sandra asked.

"You have a strength about you, an independence that a gross amount of the population desperately lacks." The Emperor observed. *"Yet I have only ever known you to use that strength in the service of others... Even to save the Emperor from himself."*

"I think you're supposed to say something about me being pretty too." Sandra joked, *"That would be polite."*

"Oh yes how foolish of me." The Emperor grinned. *"The blood loss must have affected my manners."*

"Well." Sandra pressed, *"Go on, I've never known his Majesty to be at a loss for words..."*

The Emperor paused for a moment, his eyes whirred in thought until his eyebrows propped up in victory. *"If one thousand angels wrote one thousand songs"* he began *"and Aphrodite herself sang the chorus, it would pale in comparison to thy radiance."*

"That's pretty corny Majesty." Sandra giggled, *"but I'll take it."*

"I'm glad her Majesty likes it." The Emperor sighed.

"What was that?" Sandra inquired, *"What did you call me?"* She scooted away from him so she could look at him properly.

"Nothing... sorry" The Emperor corrected. He tensed up. *"I'm lightheaded from our recent misadventures... It's a conversation for later time."*

Sandra said nothing for a moment. Together they sat in awkward silence. There was no mistake in the Emperor's intentions. Fondness was one thing, but this was another. Her mind suddenly began racing a thousand miles a minute. Buzzing with thoughts of all she had seen of the disheveled convict sitting next to her. She could barely process it all until her mind seemed to stop abruptly on one memory in particular. Her teaching Amanda to shoot in the fields of Reginridge, the Emperor standing behind them gleefully watching the whole affair.

"Yes." she whispered, finally breaking the silence. *"Yes, I will marry you."*

"Really?" The Emperor asked, genuinely surprised *"You would?"*

"But not now..." Sandra insisted, *"We have a job to do first."*

"Oh, I quite agree." The Emperor acknowledged his muscles relaxed again, *"If there is to be an Empress, there must be an Empire for her to rule."*

"God help me..." Sandra muttered, *"Before long I'm going to be as weird as you."*

"You're already well on your way." The Emperor chuckled as he scooted closer, so they were touching. *"Sandra Von Drac.... Imperatrix Regina.... Long may she reign."*

Chapter 28: Amanda

Amanda looked out the window of Cody's bedroom, The entire occupancy of Reginridge was hard at work turning the Emperor's palace into a military installation. It made her efforts at the warehouse appear like child's play. Deep long trenches were dug on either side of the long driveway. Barbed wire was being placed all along the perimeter of the house. There was a crew of people, some her own, some not, creating nail strips that could be used to incapacitate oncoming cars. Sandbags had been brought in and were being piled to form pill boxes at strategic locations along the sprawling grounds. At the wood line, tripwire was being placed and it seemed Madame DuBois had managed to get her hands on some landmines that were being placed in the Emperor's lavender garden. If the Republicans were to take the Empire's last vestige, it would cost them dearly. But that wasn't an option.

Cody entered the room as Amanda surveyed this massive feat of engineering. He walked next to her and observed the construction for himself. *"I hope everyone gets here in time."* he said checking his watch. *"This is it."*

"They'll come." Amanda said, mostly to reassure herself. *"They have to."*

Cody made his way to a table in the room, on top of it was a map of the property that he used to plan out the home's defenses. He began analyzing the map, mumbling to himself as he recited all the preparations he had made. He ran a finger across every trench line, traced the extensive perimeter with his finger.

"Amanda come here." he said, *"Check this again and make sure we didn't overlook anything."* Amanda studied the map intently. *"Look hard."* Cody ordered, *"everything depends on it."*

Amanda pushed him away *"I know I know."* she said, *"let me look."* The map had marked all potential avenues of attack, the main driveway was of course the largest, but even areas where the woods were less dense and a large volume of men could push through were circled. *"Maybe if we moved another sniper from the south facing line to the western one, we could take a group of those troops and reinforce the center."* she offered, *"But even that is just an idea. We're going to have to adapt as it happens."*

"I guess you're right." Cody said, running his fingers through his hair. *"God, I have no idea how to do any of this stuff. Meanwhile the Emperor waited his whole goddamn life for it and he's not here."*

"I know." Amanda said, placing her head on Cody's arm. *"But this is where we are... and you managed to put it all together. All we can do is hope for the best."* There was a knock at the door.

Amanda opened it to reveal Samerson standing in the doorway. *"The army is arriving."* he said, *"The other Marshals are already on the balcony... it's time."*

"Right." Cody said as he straightened his tie.

"Don't you think it's silly." Amanda said, *"We're all about to be fighting for our lives and were dressed for a dinner party."*

"One hundred percent" Cody answered, *"But the Emperor would say men only respect officers who are well dressed or some dumb line like that. And he got us this far."* Amanda nodded in agreement. Samerson cleared his throat.

"Right," Cody said again, *"Alright George we're coming."* Cody took Amanda's hand and together they followed Samerson down the hallway and to a doorway that led to the outside walkway. Samerson opened the door for Cody and Amanda as they stepped outside. The other three marshals were already out there waiting for them.

Madame DuBois said nothing but just pointed to direct their attention to the main driveway. As the finishing touches of the defenses were put into place Amanda could hear faint drumming in the distance. It grew louder and louder and soon she could hear trumpets. As the trumpets sounded a massive procession could be seen coming down the drive.

The entirety of what remained of the Empire was marching in perfect unison down the path. Hundreds of people, drug dealers, prostitutes, loan sharks, gun runners, and bookies all marching side by side in columns twenty to thirty people deep. They had no uniform and their shouldered rifles were all mismatched, yet every section bore a large violet banner with the Emperor's sigil. As they marched, fife and drum kept them in step. It was an awesome spectacle. *"Jesus he woulda loved to see this."* Cody whispered to Amanda as the Grand Imperial Army marched to the Empire's last stronghold.

"His Majesty's forces are assembled." Madame DuBois announced to the marshals on the balcony. *"The Crown and Empire stands ready to defend her people, and the marshals rally behind you, the Lord Regent, in his Majesty's absence."* Madame DuBois dropped to one knee as the other marshals did the same. *"We await your orders sire."* The procession had reached the mansion now. Amanda looked out to find them all on one knee, as well as those who were already there. All eyes were on Cody. Amanda began to drop to her knee but Cody stopped her before she made it down.

"Rise please my friends!" He shouted out to the crowd. *"You need not kneel before me for I am not your king!"* The crowd rose to their feet, still all looking to Cody for direction. *"Soon our enemies will make one final assault against us!"* He yelled shakily, *"Here is where the Empire will either live... or it will die. The duty falls to us to ensure that all his Majesty helped us to build endures here today!"* The crowd let out a cheer which helped boost his confidence. *"I say let the enemy come!"* he roared, *"Let them come and*

see the true strength of our resolve!" Another resounding cheer from the crowd below.

"FOR THE CROWN!" Cody shouted

"FOR THE CROWN!" The crowd replied in unison. They all began dispersing and taking their positions. Trenches began to be filled, pill boxes were manned, snipers began climbing to vantage points. Cody turned back toward the Marshals.

"Well guys.... This is it." He said to them, *"I may never get the opportunity again so I just gotta say, we had a great run."*

"Look at this place." Harold responded, *"Ain't no way we lose."*

"If we do..." Madame DuBois offered, *"There's no other people I'd rather die with."*

"I made a lot of money over the years." Stevens cut in, *"I guess now we will see if I actually deserved it."* Samerson nodded in agreement. The marshals gave Cody a curt bow and left to join their respective forces.

"It's time for me to go too." Amanda said, *"They're waiting for me down there."* Cody leaned in to kiss her, but she pulled back. *"Now you have to live."* she said slyly, *"you can kiss me after we win."* he gave her a smile as she left him on the balcony.

The Prostitution Corps was manning the eastern quadrant of the defensive work. There was a little over two hundred of them, most of which Amanda had never met before. As she approached her forces Tiffany came up to greet her. *"Whadda say general?"* She said in a faux military voice with an overly dramatic salute. *"A good day for killin' eh?"* Amanda laughed as she hugged her friend.

"How are they?" Amanda asked, *"Are they nervous?"*

"Nervous?!? Are you kidding me?" Tiffany shot back, *"They get to be under Amanda Beasley, the badass who took out a Republican lieutenant and single handedly killed twenty men in one night. They're probably the calmest ones here!"*

Amanda chuckled at the title. *"Well alright let's get to work then..."* Amanda proceeded to direct all the girls to their stations, filling the trench lines, manning the pill boxes, showing them where the mines and other traps were so they knew to avoid them. She pointed out the weak spots in the nearby woods to make sure they monitored them extra closely. The defensive lines formed a semi-circle around the eastern wing of Reginridge and at its center was a small command center set up for Amanda to monitor the battle. She was given a handheld radio that was tuned to the same frequency as radios held by assigned group commanders in her Corps so she could give them orders as needed. Tiffany remained with her at the command post with a pair of binoculars to help Amanda keep an eye on things.

"Oop" Tiffany said looking through the binoculars *"A large concentration of hunks headed our way general. I better go investigate."* Amanda

turned to see what Tiffany was talking about and saw a group of men headed in Amanda's direction.

"Stay here." She said to Tiffany *"I'm gonna see what they need."* Tiffany looked disappointed. Amanda walked over to the group of about twenty men and stopped and saluted as their commander stepped forward.

"Colonel Rodriguez Ma'am" he introduced himself, *"His Majesty's 5th Narcotics Regiment."*

"A pleasure to meet you Colonel." Amanda said, shaking his hand, *"What can we do for you?"*

"Marshal Jones thought you ladies could do with some additional sniper coverage." he explained, *"Me and my boys are the best shots in the Empire."* Amanda peered over to where Harold was standing, he gave her a brisk wave before going back to organizing his own troops.

"Well thank you Colonel." Amanda said politely, *"It's a pleasure to have you with us."*

"The pleasure is all ours ma'am." The Colonel replied, *"We were all fond of the Marchioness ma'am, protecting her legacy is the highest honor."*

"So it is." Amanda nodded, the thought of Sylvia made her sad for a moment. The Colonel gave her a salute and then directed his men to various vantage points along the east wing of Reginridge. Amanda returned to her command post. There was too much to do to be sad.

"You know Mandy..." Tiffany said, *"You better not die."*

"Why's that?" Amanda asked,

"Because" Tiffany replied, *"I never forgot about that numbers job you promised me."* The two girls shared one last laugh as everyone finalized their positions. Everything was in place, now all that was left was to wait.

The snipers shot the first volley of the day. A hail of bullets soared from their scoped rifles from both the eastern and the northern lines. It did not take long before a mass of Republican soldiers came from the wood line and down the main drive. Amanda ordered her people to open fire and chaos began.

The attackers advanced sporadically at first, testing the resolve of the defending Imperial legions. The entrenched positions provided perfect cover to mow anyone who left the safety of the woods and entered the open fields. Amanda's girls unleashed lead hellfire in the direction of the enemy as bodies began littering the field in front of them. The sound of hundreds of rifles all firing together was deafening. From the woods, Republican assault rifles sent rounds of suppressive fire towards the house, Sandbags exploded dust and sediment into the air as they were hit but the bulwark remained solid.

Amanda turned to the north where both sides fought over control of the driveway. The attacking forces there were much more concentrated and had assumed prone positions to hold their gains against

Harold's stiff resistance. In the East where her forces were, the Republicans began to retreat to the safety of the wood line. She ordered her girls to continue firing into the woods until every last Republican had disappeared into the trees. Casualties were low, for now.

The Northern section of the grounds were still under heavy fire as the Republican's auxiliary forces reorganized for a flank to the south this time. Tiffany had spotted their movements and warned Amanda, giving her crucial time to alert her snipers to refocus their efforts in covering Samerson and Stevens. As the advance came from the southern front, assailants now lobbed grenades at the trenches, shrapnel exploded, tearing the Empire's bookies and money lenders to pieces. Screams now rang out along with the gunfire as limbs were ripped from sockets and blood filled the front-line trenches.

"They're wearing us down little by little," Amanda observed to Tiffany, a stray bullet grazed by causing them both to duck. *"If they break one part of the ring it's. over."*

"We have to tighten up then." Tiffany surmised. Amanda nodded in agreement. She looked back to the north, the front line there had changed very little as the fighting raged on.

"Pull back our two front trenches!" Amanda shouted into her radio, *"Get over to the south. Find sandbags... stay out of the trenches."*

Amanda's vanguard followed her orders, abandoning their posts. They propelled themselves out of their trenches and bolted south to reinforce the lines. She gave signals to the snipers to cover their movements. Consequently, her remaining forces pulled back closer to the house, tightening their formation.

Back to the North the Republicans had ramped up their assault. Two vans came barreling down the driveway. The obstacles in place did their job, spike strips caused the tires to blow as both vans spun out of control and crashed halfway down the drive. Relief in the trap's success turned to terror as the Vans exploded in the field. The immediate shockwave took out two rows of Imperial force, while flying debris and vehicle parts peppered the remaining lines with flaming death.

"Son of a bitch!" Tiffany exclaimed witnessing the explosion. *"Should we send people over there?"*

"No." Amanda ordered, *"We're too thin as it is. Madame DuBois will have to help them."*

Almost on queue, a squadron of Madame DuBois' soldiers moved from the western theatre to reinforce the tattered northern lines. The west had yet to fall under heavy attack, so her troops were fresh and full vigored. They were able to hold back the newest wave of Republicans attempting to seize the driveway. Again, the lines held, but his Majesty's forces were thinning fast. The banners of the Empire were torn and holes littered the fabric, but they had yet to fall.

Cody hadn't checked in with Amanda. She looked to the balcony on Reginridge's third story. There he stood guarded by snipers on either side, surveying the battle. His surveying caused their eyes to lock. For a brief moment the battle paused for Amanda. The world came to a standstill, for just a moment it was just the two of them, and everything was alright.

The bliss was cut short by two rockets smashing into the roof of Reginridge, the explosions sent vibrations all through the building and into the field below. The blast caused two snipers to be flung from their vantage points and fall to their deaths. More rockets came behind; each one bore a new hole into the Limestone walls. Debris from the blast came crashing down, indiscriminately killing Republican and Imperial alike.

There was no reprieve for the Empire's forces to regroup. Immediately following the rockets two more Republican vans attempted to break through the main driveways various barricades, again they were rigged to blow, causing massive explosions once the defensive traps had incapacitated them. Bodies flew into the air. The contested ground in the North was now completely coated with a layer of corpses. Cadavers were piling on both sides, the Republicans had reserves, the Empire did not.

More rockets came from the trees as men with rocket launchers emerged from both the east and west. Amanda ordered all fire be directed on these makeshift artillery pieces. The prostitutes quickly gunned the grenadiers to the ground, but the explosions created a thick cloud of smog around the building, it was quickly becoming impossible to aim.

"Shit." Tiffany blurted from the command post, *"I can't see anything!"*

"I know." Amanda agreed, *"this is bad."* She switched on her radio.

"Cody what can you see, it's getting too thick down here."

"I can see absolutely freaking nothing." Cody's voice scratched back through her radio. *"We're gonna have to pull back."*

"Pull back to where???" Samerson's voice rang out. *"They're coming from all sides now."*

"They've gotta be almost spent." Cody answered, *"Pull back to the house and force them to take it... room by room!"*

"We're just delaying our deaths if we do that." Madame DuBois voice chimed on the radio.

"Exactly." Cody said, *"We either die now or we die later."*

Seeing no favorable alternative, Amanda slowly began pulling her sector back, until their backs were practically to the walls. Slowly small groups filed inside while the rest of her army group provided suppressive fire. The once green fields of Reginridge had now been washed red with blood as his Majesty's tattered armies assumed their final defensive posture. The inside of the house was torn apart by the battle. Smoke billowed through the windows, the paintings that adorned the regal halls had fallen out of place. The grand staircase and hallways were cramped as the remainder of the Imperial Army scrambled to make their last stand.

Amanda pushed her way to the staircase and charged to the second level of the house. Another barrage of rockets shook the walls and caused everyone to stumble. Amanda trudged on and worked toward the balcony where Cody was positioned. When she reached the top of the stairs, she heard a loud bang as Republican soldiers breached the main door and a firefight broke out in the entrance hall. She grabbed a rifle from a fallen comrade and began unloading a magazine into the invaders filing in through the doorway. The Republicans falling in the doorway created a makeshift barricade of flesh, making it harder for reinforcements to enter. That would hold them at bay for now.

She rushed to the balcony and found Cody there with a small contingent of guards all taking cover behind the stone balustrade. She quickly dropped to her stomach as automatic rifle fire began chipping away at the stone. Slowly, she crawled to Cody under the maelstrom of bullets.

"Thank Christ you're safe." he said as she joined him behind cover.

"I don't know if safe is the word." Amanda replied back with a smirk *"but I'm here."*

Cody peered out to the battlefield, Amanda peeked her head through the railing as well. Large swaths of the fields were on fire, burning trucks littered the driveway. Over a hundred Republicans lay dead in every direction, yet scores more were still pouring into the house. They had mounted a good defense, but it wasn't enough.

"It's over." Cody said as the Republicans began filing into the house at every entrance. The battle outside was fully and totally lost, the gunfire died down outside as the fighting inside picked up. Muffled sounds of battle could be heard coming from the first floor. The enemy had stopped firing on their position from below, there was no point. They would be upstairs soon enough.

Cody's soot covered hands were resting on the railing, Amanda placed her hand atop his. The pair was covered in dried blood and bruises. Their clothes were torn and scuffed from the battle. They said not a word, instead stood silently together side by side and waited for death to take them.

"Lord Regent!" a voice rang out on Cody's radio. *"There's a large movement of people coming this way."*

Cody buried his face in his hands; he began laughing out of exhaustion. *"They already won and they're sending more!"* he exclaimed, *"what a mess..."* he looked up to the sky. *"YOU WIN!"* he yelled to the clouds, *"YOU MADE IT CLEAR! YOU'RE ON THEIR SIDE NOT OURS!"*

"Lord Regent..." the voice rang in the radio again, *"They're coming into range... should I fire."*

"Who are they?" Cody asked into the radio,

"It's hard to see sir." The sentry replied, *"But they look like bikers."*

"Bikers?" Cody snapped up to attention, *"negative soldier. Hold fire and wait for my orders!"* A small twinge of hope broke through his previously shattered morale.

"What's going on?" Amanda asked, alarmed at Cody's rapid change in mood.

"I don't know for sure yet." He answered, he brought a pair of binoculars up to his eyes and was focused on the long driveway. *"May be good, may be bad."*

Amanda could hear the rumbling of engines now. Dust began to billow through the trees and at the end of the driveway suddenly a horde of motorcycles became visible. They were too far away for Amanda to see clearly but they numbered at least over fifty. She turned to Cody who was solely locked on the new arrivals to the fray. They reached the edge of the driveway but stopped and waited. The battle inside the house came to a standstill as everyone became distracted by this development. Amanda could see a massive grin spreading across Cody's face as he looked through his binoculars.

"What?!?!" Amanda asked, *"Who are they?"*

"Lemme just ask you one question." Cody replied, *"How many men do you know that wear a cape?"*

Chapter 29: Sandra

"Ha." the Emperor scoffed as he peered through his telescope.

"What is it?" Sandra asked, standing dutifully by his side. The bikers had snuck into the city and procured clothes that were more fitting to the Emperor's aesthetic. The Emperor looked upon his ravaged home, standing tall in boots, a suit and a large black cloak with a violet lining. He handed the telescope to Sandra as he adjusted his hat. Sandra was given an elaborate gown with draped sleeves and matching heels. Riding a motorcycle in heels had been absolutely torture but his Majesty was insistent.

"The children are alright." The Emperor noted. He pointed to a balcony on the second level of the house and Sandra lifted the telescope to see Cody and Amanda staring back at them through the smog.

One the bikers walked up to the Emperor and Sandra as they surveyed the field. *"The boys are ready."* he said to the Emperor, *"We move when you say."* The Emperor patted him on the shoulder and turned to address the bikers.

"My Friends!" He exclaimed, *"Never once have I asked you to bend thine knee and call me king."* He took a pause, *"Yet the crown has always been able to maintain a mutually beneficial relationship with our more rural allies."* He pointed down the driveway. *"These dogs seek to disrupt our peace!"* he yelled, *"And to think they would honor any*

arrangement you have with the Empire would be folly! For there is no honor among thieves! Now let us drive these demons back to the fiery pit!" A large cheer emanated from the mass of bikers as the Emperor mounted his motorcycle. He withdrew his old sword that Sandra had kept. Sandra mounted her own motorbike and slung her sawed-off shotgun around her shoulder. Behind them the bikers loaded clips into their submachine guns.

The Emperor turned toward Sandra. *"Do try not to die,"* he said with a wink. Sandra blew a kiss in his direction, *"As your Majesty commands."* She said sarcastically.

The Emperor raised his sword; the bike engines began revving. The Emperor spun the sword above his head, *"Cuirassiers.... ADVANCE!"* He shouted and thrust the blade forward. He took off on his bike. Sandra and the rest of the bikers followed close behind. The Emperor's cape billowed in the wind behind him as they rode full speed to the house.

They had come in so fast, the Republicans at the perimeter of the house had no time to properly react. The bikes smashed into the cluster of Republicans attempting to push into Reginridge and bodies flew into the air in every direction upon collision. The Emperor leapt from his bike and jumped into the fray, pressing around the now disorganized Republicans hacking and slashing his way through the crowd. Sandra dismounted her own bike and held her shotgun at her hip and sent countless lead shells into the crowd, mowing down the invaders.

The Republicans moved to regroup but the bikers had already smashed a hole in their line, they began pushing out as they retook the northern sector of the house. The Emperor pranced along the perimeter, gracefully slicing Republican soldiers as if he were doing a dance. Sandra pumped more and more lead into the fleeing enemy. Before long, the outside of the house was secure, but a large contingent of enemy troops still was inside the Emperor's palace.

"Come with me." The Emperor said, grabbing Sandra by the wrist. *"We can flank the dogs."* As the bikers pushed in through the main entrance the Emperor led Sandra to the outside of the east wing, feeling along the base of the house he pulled aside a faux piece of wall that revealed a secret passage, he took Sandra down a ladder that led to the dungeons beneath the house.

"This way." The Emperor said charging through the dank halls under his home. *"We'll catch them in the ballroom."* Sandra rushed behind him. It was hard for her eyes to adjust to the darkness in the Emperor's cellar, but the Emperor moved from memory and Sandra kept close behind.

The Emperor turned a corner which led to the final hallway before the stairs to reach the main level of the house. Sandra stopped abruptly as the

Emperor swung his arm out to block her path. In between them and the stairwell stood Mr. Charteris, his chains draped down to the concrete floors as he hunched over. The Iron casing over his head was dented and cracked, likely a casualty of the blasts that hit the house. He had a pistol in his hand and pointed it at the Emperor.

The Emperor halted but seemed unphased, he stood cooly beside Sandra, his eyes locked onto his monster that blocked their way. *"Well well"* The Emperor scoffed. *"Look at you."*

Mr. Charteris moaned in reply but held the gun firm.

"You want to do it don't you." The Emperor said mockingly, *"You must've been dreaming of this moment for ages."* Sandra lifted her shotgun, but the Emperor gently pressed the barrel back down toward the ground. *"Come closer you wretched beast. That far back you may miss your shot."* Mr. Charteris did as the Emperor bid, the gun still trained squarely on the Emperor's face.

"You probably think I deserve it." The Emperor continued to mock, *"That this is just good and true revenge."* Mr. Charteris gurgled and moaned.

"But you see." The Emperor carried on, *"Either way I win... Shoot me now if you must, but every time you look in the mirror, I will still remind you of your sins."* His face contorted into his characteristic wicked smile; he took a step toward Mr. Charteris. The wretched man hunched over at the

Emperor's approach but held the gun firm. Slowly the Emperor reached his hands out into a crack in the Iron mask. He pulled away the piece of dislodged metal which caused the entire mask to loosen and fall to the ground.

Sandra covered her mouth at the grotesque sight. He had no nose, large chunks of his cheeks were missing, his jaw was dislocated and part of his lip was gone, exposing his lower gums and teeth. He had no eyebrows and only loose individual strands of hair clung to his head. The flesh around his lacerations had infected and scabbed giving what remained of his face an overall uneven shape. The Emperor slowly traced one of the scars with his knuckle.

"Look at you." He whispered with a sickening sweetness. *"Such a pretty boy."* He grabbed Mr. Charteris by the jaw and turned his head toward a piece of shattered glass so he could see his own face. *"Kill me now but this is your forever..."* he scolded. He shoved Mr. Charteris back, causing the walking zombie to stumble.

Mr. Charteris caught his footing and pointed the gun again at the Emperor. Keeping the gun pointed at the Emperor, he turned again to face the shard of glass. He traced his various deformities with his finger; this must have been the first time he had actually seen his face since the Emperor caught him all those years ago. He tried to speak but only managed his usual unintelligible gurgles. Quickly he turned the gun on himself and pulled the trigger.

BANG

Mr. Charteris fell limp to the floor, blood pouring from his now opened temple. The Emperor smiled triumphantly over his slave's cadaver.

"You're sick." Sandra said, shaking her head.

The Emperor merely nodded in agreement and charged down the hallway and up the stairs.

The stairwell led to the ballroom, it was vacant, but Sandra could hear gunfire coming from the main hall through the doorway opposite where they emerged. Together they crept to the door. The Emperor placed a hand on the doorway and locked eyes with Sandra. She nodded, indicating she was ready, and the Emperor threw the door open. In the Main hall the last bulk of the Republican attackers were making their final push. A small group of them manned the front door to hold back the incoming bikers while the rest pushed deeper into the house.

Because of the commotion of battle no one had noticed the Emperor and Sandra's entrance into the flank. The Emperor picked up a machine gun lying nearby and Sandra readied their shotgun. Together they unleashed one final barrage of bullets into the unsuspecting Republicans from their left flank. As the Republicans fell in droves the remaining combatants realized they were exposed. That was the end. Completely demoralized the Republicans broke and began to route en masse. Giving up their assault they fled from the field as the bikers mounted their motorcycles once again to rundown the fleeing soldiers. The battle was over, and the Empire, once again, was victorious.

Cheers rang out as the Emperor entered the main hall of Reginridge. Clapping and shouting, the people heralded their king's return. He moved to the various crowds, shaking hands and embracing his subjects as they rejoiced in their victory. Sandra decided to stand back. After all, to most of them she was still just the woman who threw the Emperor in jail. The Emperor, however, had other ideas. He leapt over to Sandra and dragged her to the forefront. Grabbing her by the wrist he thrust her arm high into the air. The crowd cheered for her with matching vigor. It appeared any trespasses were forgiven. Sandra looked around the hall, basking in the glory the Empire was bestowing on her. Then she saw someone who wasn't clapping.

At the top of the grand staircase behind the masses of adoring subjects. Amanda and Cody stood. Silent. The Emperor soon became aware of their presence as well. He looked up at them, his face beaming with pride. As the crowds all became aware the celebration died down. Everyone parted to make a path from Cody and Amanda to the Emperor. Slowly they descended the staircase and made their way to where Sandra and the Emperor were standing. Cody was carrying in his hands a laurel wreath made of gold. They reached the Emperor and stopped.

"I kept it safe for you, your Majesty." Cody said.

"That you did, master Chesley." The Emperor replied respectfully. *"I wonder if you might be more worthy of it than I."*

"Your Majesty flatters me." Cody said, *"But there is only one true Emperor."* He handed the golden crown to Amanda. Cody then took a step back and dropped to his knees. The surrounding crowd followed suit. The Emperor softly eyed Amanda. She looked happy at his return but very purposefully made no acknowledgement of Sandra. Subtly the Emperor jutted his head in Sandra's direction. Finally, Amanda looked at her, and her face soured. The Emperor placed a hand on Amanda's shoulder and gestured again in Sandra's direction. Reluctantly Amanda handed the crown over to Sandra and assumed a kneeling position beside Cody. Amanda clearly hated her. It tore at Sandra's chest, but she couldn't blame the girl.

Sandra took the Crown into both hands. She stopped closer to the Emperor as he dropped his shoulders and lowered his head. She placed the laurel wreath on top of his head. With his crown returned The Emperor stood tall once more. Sandra began to kneel, but the Emperor caught her. *"You stand with me now."* The Emperor whispered, *"Wholly and fully."* Sandra looked out to the kneeling subjects of the crown. They all looked to her and the Emperor, desperate for guidance on what to do now.

"You all have fought admirably." The Emperor said addressing his people. *"The enemy has been repulsed but they still control our lands... Tonight we lick our wounds, but tomorrow we retake that which is ours."*

Two sentries burst into the main door interrupting the Emperor's speech. They were dragging a prisoner whose head was covered with a hood. They threw him at the Emperor's feet. *"Forgive us your Majesty."* One of them said, *"but we thought you'd want to know right away."*

"I don't understand," the Emperor said, *"What is this?"*

"A traitor your Majesty." The sentry replied. He ripped off the hood exposing the prisoner's face. Sandra saw Amanda recoil at the sight of him. He had a large strip of cloth tied from his jaw to the top of his head. Cody and the Emperor's eyes both simultaneously blazed with fury. Sandra didn't recognize him. The Emperor pulled off the cloth strap and as he did the prisoner's jaw came loose and dangled from his face. The Emperor just snarled, seeing the prisoners deformed jaw had provoked him. *"Out."* The Emperor said softly, no one but Sandra heard him. *"I SAID OUT!"* He said again, screaming this time. Everyone quickly scurried away. Only Sandra, Cody, Amanda, and the prisoner stayed in the room.

"So Franklin...." the Emperor said as he walked around the man kneeling before him, his cape trailing the floor behind him as he paced. *"Fitting you should join the rot."* He bent down and picked the man up by the scruff of his shirt. *"Give me one good reason I shouldn't throw you to the dogs."*

The prisoner began to make a sound but the Emperor grabbed his loose piece of jaw and tugged at it. He let out a scream as the Emperor threw him to the ground. *"You dare to try and defend your abhorrent actions!"* The Emperor snarled. *"Get her out of here!"* he barked to Cody who proceeded to lead Amanda away from the room.

The Emperor ran to the wall and grabbed an axe that was hanging nearby. He marched back, dragging the axe behind him. *"Now vermin..."* he growled, *"The time has come for your penance."* The prisoner lay shaking on the ground but offered no resistance.

"Who is he?" Sandra asked, *"I've never seen him before."*

"Amanda..." Was all the Emperor offered, his focus was unbroken.

Sandra was confused at first, then she remembered the last day she had spent with Amanda. Washing out her hair as the girl's tears filled the tub. The despair that was on her face. The memory began to fill her with rage, until her eyes were burning the way she had seen the Emperor so many times before.

The Emperor lifted the axe high above his head. He began to swing down but Sandra stopped him. *"No."* Sandra said, *"My turn."* She snatched the axe from the Emperor's hands and lobbed it into Frankie's calf. The Emperor watched in curiosity as Frankie began meekly attempting to crawl away and Sandra proceeded to dismember him little by little with each axe swing. First his feet, then his knees. Frankie dug his fingers into the floor to try and drag himself away. Sandra swung the axe and chopped the fingers of his left hand off, then his right. Blood spurted in all directions covering both the Emperor and Sandra.

Curiosity turned to wicked glee as The Emperor watched Sandra mutilate the sexual degenerate. Frankie made one last attempt at life by rolling onto his back and pleading with Sandra, though his deformed jaw made the words unreliable. Sandra answered his pleas with one final swing, lodging the axe into Frankie's skull. He fell dead while Sandra stood over top of him, heaving her hands still on the axe handle.

The Emperor stepped closer to her, placing a hand on her waist. She spun around and the Emperor caught her hand opposite his. *"Madam"* he said softly, *"If you would do me the honor."* He took one step back and Sandra followed his lead. Her heart was still racing at what she had just done. The Emperor's movements didn't calm her per say, rather they synced into her radical emotional state.

Together they began a magnificent waltz around the ballroom. Caked in blood, they spun and strutted around Frankie's dismembered body. The dance was graceful and the steps came naturally to Sandra.

The waltz continued for what felt like hours. Sandra had yet to see the Emperor's passion put in positive force like this. He held Sandra close as he spun, his head leaning back and forth in tune with an imaginary symphony. His muscles were completely and totally relaxed, moving on instinct alone. Sandra's heels clicked on the stone floors as she spun in the Emperor's arms. She didn't even know she could dance, but the steps came to her.

Sandra bones quivered at the feelings she had just liberated within herself. Anyone who touched her loved ones would face a brutal death like the pig she had just slaughtered. She would keep them safe. Now she held the man who took a similar vow years before her. The waltz culminated in three dramatic spins and following their execution, Sandra grabbed the Emperor by the face, pulling him in for a kiss. This time he did not recoil and instead returned such intensity that Sandra's veins pressed against her skin. She pulled his head into hers with every ounce of strength she could, and he did not resist. The world around the pair faded away as the two kindred souls finally interlocked. God she really did love him.

Finally, he pulled away but left his forehead pressed to hers. *"So, what now?"* Sandra asked.

"Now..." The Emperor mulled the question, *"Now I regain my lost lands. And together we will rebuild a shattered Empire, so a new stronger one can rise from the ashes."*

"And everyone will be safe." Sandra added,

"Yes." The Emperor nodded, *"Side by side we will keep them prosperous."*

"Good." Sandra answered, releasing the Emperor from her grip *"Let's get to work."*

A knock came at the ballroom door. The Emperor walked to the door and swung it open. He let out a giddy shriek as Amanda stood in the doorway; Edwina wrapped in her arms.

"MY DARLING!" The Emperor exclaimed as the bird hopped from Amanda's grip and reunited with her master. The Emperor knelt to scratch the underside of the peacock's head while she affectionately cooed and nuzzled the Emperor's leg. *"My sweet little baby."* The Emperor cooed, brushing out the bird's feathers, *"Oh I promise we'll never be separated ever again."*

"She's missed you so much." Amanda explained, *"I figured you'd want to know she was alright."*

"And I missed her." The Emperor replied, fiddling with Edwina's beak, *"she's my oldest friend, no one knows me better than she does."* Edwina nuzzled the Emperor one more time before trotting

over to Sandra. She gave Sandra an affectionate nibble to which Sandra scratched her head in return. The Emperor stood up and smiled to see the bird's love for Sandra as well as himself.

"Let me have a look at you." The Emperor said, turning back toward Amanda. He brushed her face softly and firmly gripped her shoulders. *"So strong."* he said, his face beaming with pride. *"So brave.... I bet that lieutenant you gunned down soiled himself when he saw you."* Amanda chuckled. *"Oh my girl,"* The Emperor continued, *"I am so proud of you."* Sandra felt a similar pride. She remembered the timid girl she met at the gala all those months ago. The warrior that was before them now was at least partly her doing.

"Can I see him?" Amanda asked, The Emperor nodded silently. He led Amanda to the center of the ballroom. Sandra stepped out of the way as Amanda eyed her cautiously. Together the Emperor and Amanda stood over Frankie's body. Amanda's face showed little emotion.

"Good." She spat, leering down at the cadaver. *"He got what he deserved."*

"That he did." The Emperor commented his eyes wandering off into space, *"He won't be pestering you or anyone ever again."*

"Thank you, your Majesty," Amanda said. She reached out to hug the Emperor, but the Emperor stepped back.

"Actually..." The Emperor interrupted, *"You'll want to direct your gratitude that way."* he gestured to Sandra. Sandra locked eyes with Amanda. Amanda again showed no emotion, more so she was contemplating how to proceed. She must hate Sandra, of course she did. The poor girl finally found a father after all these years and what did Sandra do but take it away?

Sensing the tension the Emperor stepped between them. *"It wasn't her fault."* The Emperor said, *"It was mine."*

"Your Majesty." Amanda exhaled, *"I know you have feelings, and you want to defend her."*

"My dear," The Emperor cut her off, his voice becoming stern, *"I have done many things in this life better men might condemn. But I do not believe I have ever lied to you for my benefit."*

"Of course it was her fault!" Amanda yelled, *"She lied to you! She lied to all of us..."*

"We lie to the police a lot, my child." The Emperor remarked sternly, but still composed, *"We can't be mad if they occasionally lie to us."*

"She locked you up." Amanda argued, *"This.. ALL OF THIS is because of her."*

"Now that's not fair." The Emperor countered, *"The greed and arrogance of fools are to blame for this insurrection."* He explained.

"You'll make any excuse." Amanda sighed. *"But I'll trust you for now."* She passively extended a hand to Sandra. Sandra took it earnestly. She tried to

speak but Amanda pulled away before you have a chance. *"I'm glad you're back, sire."* she said to the Emperor, giving him a bow. *"Ma'am"* She said to Sandra with a curt nod and she walked out of the room.

"She'll come around." The Emperor offered to Sandra as they walked Amanda leave the room.

"Don't act like you didn't enjoy that." Sandra said, rolling her eyes.

"Maybe just a little." The Emperor smirked. *"But for now I have territory to regain, I hope the map room is still intact...."* The Emperor straightened his cloak and marched to the door and out of the room. Sandra stood alone in the ballroom. Edwina trotted over to her and laid at her feet, cooing softly. *"At least somebody else missed me."* Sandra lamented as she scratched the bird's head.

The Emperor poked his head back through the doorway into the room. *"Aren't you coming?"* He questioned.

Sandra, Cody and The Marshals all huddled around the Emperor as he peered over a map of the city. He ran his fingers along the map occasionally tracing circles of various buildings. As he silently studied the buildings, streets, and landmarks Sandra could tell his mind was whirring with a multitude of attack plans. *"The key ladies and gentlemen"* he finally said, *"Is strongholds."* He held out a hand and

Cody gave him a pen. The Emperor proceeded to draw large "X's" across one building in each of the city's seven districts. *"Large complexes we can project power across each district."* Switching back to his finger, he traced lines between each of the buildings, starting again to change the order.

"I'm thinking we split our forces into two army groups." He said scratching his chin, *"One to strike east and the other west."* He murmured to himself as the plan formulated in his head. *"I will lead the eastern assault and seize key points here, here, and here."* He drew arrows connecting three buildings, forming a semi-circle around the eastern half of the city. *"Lord Chancellor, you will take the western theatre seizing these."* He now made marks connecting the western half of the city. *"Once we rejoin each other, we slowly constrict them inward..."* He drew arrows from six of the strongholds he had named and pointed them toward the center. *"Until we make them pop."* He drew a large circle around his museum positioned in the city center. *"There is where we will snuff out their flame... rather poetic don't you think?"* He smiled smugly to himself as he looked to either side, giving his Marshals a chance to speak.

"We'll need to send scouts out ahead of time." Harold offered up, *"See where they're the most heavily fortified."*

"Normally Marshal Jones I would be inclined to agree. However, we have severely battered their

numbers today. They are disorganized and they are looking to regroup. We cannot give them that chance, we strike fast and we strike hard. We march on the city the day after tomorrow."

"Why wait that long even?" Samerson asked, *"Why not just go tomorrow."*

"Because" The Emperor explained, *"I am going to give that old fool Helming one last chance to do the right thing.... Will someone take a letter?"*

Cody nodded and grabbed a sheet of paper and a pen. He situated himself at a table while the Emperor began to pace and dictate.

Commissioner Marcus Helming,

I can only imagine the frustration you feel at my recent departure from your custody. Where the circumstances better I would be inclined to gloat yet there is a grave errand that awaits the both of us. Though we disagree on the method, we both have always been paragons of order for our respective sides of law. You know I cannot tolerate these scum to lord over my lands and you know I must take actions to restore order. It will be a gruesome affair, the kind which civilians should not be privy to. I therefore appeal to your sense of humanity and ask you to evacuate Colonna until such a time as my forces can do what is required and the streets can be made safe for the families we both yearn to protect. I know this will come as a wound to your pride but please remember my sole goal is the safety of the city, as I hope yours is as well. Please think of the people, you have Twenty-Four hours before I begin my assault.

Your Faithful Ally,

Edward Von Drac
Imperator Rex Colonna City,
All Honorifics etc. etc.

Cody gave the Emperor the letter who reread it before neatly rolling it into a scroll. He tied it with a ribbon and handed it back to Cody. *"The city is too dangerous for you."* he said, *"Find a courier those democratic demons won't recognize and have them drop this at City Hall."* Cody gave the Emperor a bow and left the room.

As he left the room Sandra noticed two men standing outside in the hall, each of them on either side of a large, wheeled clothes rack covered in a black shroud. They peeked inside the room as the door was open, which caused Madame DuBois to shake her head. *"Not the time boys!"* She shouted out to the door. The Emperor raised an eyebrow.

"I apologize, sire." Madame DuBois explained, *"It' s a couple of my guys... They like to sew and they made something, it can wait."*

"No, by all means." The Emperor said, He walked over to the door and gently opened it again. *"I*

always love a good distraction." He waved for the two men to come into the map room as the Marshals eyed them inquisitively. They rolled their covered rack into the room and dropped to their knees at the Emperor's feet.

"Your Majesty." They greeted the Emperor. One grabbed the Emperor's hand and kissed his Imperial ring.

"Please rise gentlemen." The Emperor said, lifting them to their feet. *"Tell me what is this work of art you wish to show me."*

"Sire a great many of us had faith that you would return to save us." One of the men said.

"And we know how much you appreciate refined fashion." The other added.

"My contemporaries might be inclined to disagree." The Emperor said, straight faced. His lips then curled into a smile. *"Fortunately, I have no contemporaries."*

"Well we thought it would be appropriate if the Emperor reclaimed the city in attire befitting his station." One of the men continued.

The Emperor's eyes grew wider, *"May I?"* He asked excitedly, reaching for the black sheet covering the rack.

"We would be honored, sire."

The Emperor tore the sheet off exposing a mannequin adorned with a uniform that can only have been created for the Emperor. A black suit bearing a violet sash with gold trim. A large black cape draped across the shoulders with a gold chain held on by fasteners in the shape of the Emperor's sigil. The cape's interior was violet to match the sash again with gold embroidery and a gold sigil in its center. The ensemble was crowned with a large, plumed hat, and of course the feathers had been died violet. The Emperor's face lit up upon seeing it. *"Absolutely magnificent."* He said, caressing the cape. *"Vulcan himself couldn't forge a finer piece of armor."*

"So you like it sire?"

"Like it?!?!" The Emperor scoffed. *"It's perfect! Though I do wonder how fast can you two work?"*

"As quickly as your Majesty needs." They said in unison, a twinge of relief sounded in their voice as they learned of the Emperor's approval.

"I wonder if you might..." the Emperor proceeded to whisper to the two tailors. As he spoke to them, they eyed Sandra up and down. Nodding as he described what he wanted.

"Of course, your Majesty." They responded to the Emperor's request. *"Though maybe something a bit more modern, yet complimentary."*

"I'll leave it to your judgement." The Emperor agreed, and walked them to the door, closing it behind the two tailors as they left. *"Now."* He said, *"Does anyone have questions about our proposed course of action?"* The room stayed silent. *"Good."* The Emperor concluded, holding his hands behind

his back, *"The final battle approaches, and may God grant us victory."*

Chapter 30: Amanda

The Emperor's armies were amassed. In a procession befitting the Emperor's style, the forces of the Emperor marched from Reginridge to the line of Colonna City. Banners flew in the wind and the Emperor's home staff created a music brigade among their ranks. The fife and drum pierced the air announcing the Emperor's return to the city.

The Emperor led the procession himself. Wearing the uniform that Madame DuBois' tailors had made for him. He marched so precisely that his cape covered his movements, making him appear to merely float through the roadways. Behind him his forces marched in rigid step, all sects of the Empire united as one formidable force, ready to retake their home. He halted the army at the city line, procuring a telescope from his jacket, he surveyed the city.

"What do you see sire?" Amanda asked him.

"To be frank, not much." The Emperor said plainly, keeping his focus on the city.

"Well" Madame DuBois pondered, *"With your Majesty at the helm we are sure of victory."*

"Oh, I am quite confident we will win the day." The Emperor said, collapsing his telescope. *"The enemy is in disarray and finally it is the crown that holds the advantage once again."* He turned to face the mass of soldiers behind him. At the front of the columns were the standard bearers. *"Alright my children!"* The Emperor coyly announced, *"It is time*

to unleash the Empire's wrath! Let the rebels know they shall receive no quarter!" The musicians started up again. Drums beating shook the ground as the imperial banners and were replaced with solid red flags.

"You all know the plan." The Emperor said, *"Army group west, Godspeed. Army group east, With me."* The Emperor's army divided itself into two. The Emperor's group marched east and Cody's west. The Emperor stood in the middle, lifting his hat into the air, wishing them all well as they began to depart.

"I guess this is it." Amanda said to his Majesty. *"Wish us luck."*

"You won't need it my child." The Emperor replied confidently. *"Time and time again you've proven yourself an apt commander... Relish in the final victory."* He took her cheeks into his hands and kissed her forehead, *"Now run along... we have heathens to slaughter."* She gave him one last hug.

"I'll see you soon." She said, The Emperor shot her a wink in reply. He turned toward Sandra. The tailors had made her a dress to match the Emperor's. A long violet gown with a golden shawl draped across her shoulders, of course embroidered with the Imperial Sigil. Her hair had been done up in rigid curls with pearls and gold strands woven into it. *"Come along darling."* He said, leading Sandra away. *"I yearn to smell sulfur and death in the air again. Enemies of the Empire beware. For his Majesty approaches..."* He stormed off with his army to begin

their campaign. Cody came up to Amanda and together they watched the Emperor leave.

"It'll be nice when this is all over." Amanda mused, *"And we can get back to normal."*

"I agree." Cody said, *"So commander, what's our move?"*

"Excuse me?" Amanda questioned, *"you're in charge here."*

Cody handed Amanda the ceremonial sword the Emperor had given him. Shocked, Amanda took it reluctantly. The blade felt heavy in her hand. *"We're at your command ma'am."* Cody said politely.

"Well...." Amanda said, turning to face the troops. *"We can't let his Majesty win the war without us. Let's begin to advance."* Her own music corps started their drums. The rattling kept time for the hundreds of imperial soldiers marching into the city. Amanda led them, Cody, Harold, and Samerson at her flanks. Raising the sword high Amanda led the band of hookers, drug dealers, and money grubbers into battle, hopefully their last one.

The reconquest of Colonna was a bloody affair, but not an entirely tense one. The Emperor was right. The Republicans were scattered and disorganized following their defeat at Reginridge. They had yet to set up any sort of meaningful defense. Instead of a grand battle of epic proportions it consisted mostly of small skirmishes. Once the fighting started and Amanda realized how the campaign would play out, she divided her army group into small independent corps, tasking them each with seizing various buildings along the path. Their first major goal was the exchange building in the city's financial district. Strategically it was important because the old Greco-Roman building was surrounded by skyscrapers, giving easy access for sentries to defend it. Its central location allowed for easy troop deployment anywhere in that district of the city. The small squadrons of Republicans actually in the street posed little threat and Amanda easily swept them aside. They were a block away from the exchange building when Amanda halted the advance and ordered her people to take cover behind nearby structures. This would be the day's first actual challenge. She used a pair of binoculars to survey the exchange and the surrounding skyscrapers. Her suspicions were confirmed when she saw snipers posted in the surrounding skyscrapers.

"Harold." she said, studying the sniper positions, *"If me and my girls give you a window to cross the street can you take those three towers."* she pointed at the buildings she was referring to.

"You got it." Harold replied confidently. *"My boys will take 'em"*

"Alright." Amanda said, *"How long do you need once you're inside? If those snipers fire on us charging the building we're all dead meat."*

"Five minutes." Harold answered, *"Wait five minutes then go in for the kill. We'll make sure the path is clear."*

Amanda nodded and directed the Empire's prostitutes into position. Armed with submachine guns they laid down a flurry of suppressive fire into the skyscrapers surrounding the exchange. Immediately Harold and his drug dealers charged the three points. Entering the building with very few casualties, once they made it inside Amanda and her squadron returned to the rest of the army behind cover. She could hear the muffled gunfire from the buildings, but no screams, and no crowds running into the street. It looked like the Commissioner had done his part and evacuated the city.

"So..." Cody said as he maneuvered over to Amanda, *"What's the plan once we charge the building?"*

"Nothing." Amanda shrugged, *"We clear the building to make sure it's empty. Then leave a small group behind to defend it and we push forward."*

"Simple." Cody remarked playfully, *"I like it."*

Amanda looked at her watch. It had been five minutes; she heard the gunfire becoming more and more sparse as well. *"You ready?"* she asked Cody.

"Right behind you, general." Cody said with a lackadaisical salute. *"Let's kick some ass."*

Amanda moved to the center of the mass of troops. *"Okay everyone here we go...."* She said to the army. She turned to face the exchange. There was a small contingent of Republican soldiers beginning to file toward the front but nowhere near enough to stop them. She lifted her new sword high into the air. Those holding the red banners filed tightly behind her. *"CHARGE!"* she screamed as she thrust the sword forward.

A mass of the Emperor's fury stormed the street and into the exchange building. The Republicans had tried to hold them back but the advancing imperial horde and support from Harold's men in the surrounding towers quickly broke their meager resistance. The inside of the building was primarily the large trading floor. Some Republican troops had barricaded themselves behind various bits of cover, but they couldn't do much. It didn't take long for them to disappear either through the exit or courtesy of a soaring bullet. By the time it was over Amand had lost less than ten soldiers and her forces spread out and began to clear the building, a swift and total victory.

"Well, that was fun." Harold announced as he walked into the exchange building. *"I left a few of my sharpshooters up there, but the rest are gathering back outside."*

"Good." Amanda said, *"Let's hope everything else today is this easy."* She stormed outside with her hookers following behind her. She gradually got the army reorganized for a further push deeper into the city, leaving fifty behind to hold the exchange. Their

next target was the entertainment district, and the Colonna Royale Casino.

George Sammerson was the secret weapon for this phase of the assault. He was a part owner of the casino, and it was a crucial piece of the Empire's money laundering network which he helped oversee. *"There's bound to be more resistance there."* Samerson said as the army marched across the city streets toward the entertainment district. *"I left so much money behind in that safe they wouldn't want to be anywhere else."*

"What do you suggest?" Amanda asked him.

"There's a security room in the back." Samerson explained, *"They won't be able to get into it, it's locked by fingerprint, only myself and the Emperor can open it... it's for discrete cash relocation and such activities."* He straightened his tie, proud of his statement.

"So, what does that do us?" Amanda asked bluntly.

"Well..." Samerson cleared his throat, seemingly annoyed at Amanada's lack of admiration at his importance. *"We can access it from the alleyway, sneak fifty or so people in and take them completely by surprise."*

"Now we're talking." Amanda's face lit up at the realization of the plot. *"That will do perfectly."* Samerson smiled smugly to himself and brushed his lapel. They were getting close to the casino now.

"Gather your men." Amanda commanded Samerson, *"You go in and when we hear the fighting start we'll hit the main entrance and flank them."*

"My men?!?" Samerson sputtered in protest, *"Ma'am my men are bookies and card sharks, you don't want them leading the fight."*

"They know this place." Amanda explained, *"They're the best ones to do a sneak attack."*

"I don't know." Samerson eked out, nervously scratching his neck. *"I don't think it's a good idea..."* He eyed his men who looked equally nervous.

Annoyed, one of Amanda's girls threw back her hair and angrily marched over to the cluster of Samerson's men, without warning she pulled down her blouse enough to expose her bare breasts. *"Freebies to anyone who goes in and comes out alive."* A few other of Amanda's girls followed suit. Eye's wide with excitement a generous amount of Samerson's men quickly volunteered to take part in the surprise attack.

"Nice work." Amanda said, giving the hooker a high five.

"You're welcome" The hooker replied, covering herself again, *"Sometimes they just need something to fight for."* The comment made Amanda laugh.

Cautiously, Samerson led his Squadron down the alleyway to the casino's security door. He placed his thumb onto the scanner and the door unlocked.

As they filed inside, Amanda led the rest of the Army around to the front of the casino where they waited. Unlike the exchange, the casino was the largest building in the area by far so sentries were less of a worry here. It wasn't long before Amanda again heard the increasingly familiar sound of muffled gunfire, Samerson had engaged the enemy. Amanda again led the assault on the casino's main door. This time her sword was holstered, and she bore a carbine rifle. The Empire's forces kicked in the main doors of the casino to see the Republicans blasting Sammerson's men with relentless gunfire.

They held their position well and the main bulk of the Army was able to completely catch the Republican's off guard. Again, they dealt with a large open room, but the various gambling machines and gaming tables left a lot of potential cover for the Republican defenders. The initial wave came as a shock, but the Republicans were able to regroup and corner themselves in the back end of the casino. Amanda directed her troops to spread out and press the enemy's flank. Amanda herself led the push on the right flank firing bullet after bullet into Republican guts whenever the opportunity presented itself. The defense here was much stiffer than the exchange but ultimately it was to no avail. Amanda broke the right flank of the Republican perimeter getting in close enough that she ditched her rifle for her sword. Once the other Republicans saw Amanda frantically slashing at their compatriots they engaged in a full retreat, turning the casino firmly into imperial hands. Losses were heavier, almost thirty this time, but still the field was won. One final objective to go, then the battle was won.

The last stronghold Amanda needed to seize was a park in the residential district. Tactically it held little value, it was wide open with not much cover, but Amanda suspected the Emperor had chosen it in case the Commissioner did not heed his request to evacuate the city. It was well removed from all the apartments. Nevertheless, Amanda and her army approached the final landmark.

Everything so far had proceeded to plan, the Republicans were in full retreat, but now there's little left to retreat to. The Emperor may have written them off as aloof thugs, but they were not completely oblivious to what his Majesty's forces were doing. Should they lose this battle, the Republicans would be completely encircled spelling their doom.
The enemy strength was gathered, all retreating forces convened at the park to make their desperate stand. Amanda's numbers had dwindled, leaving people behind to safeguard the already captured strongholds. She still held the numerical advantage, but it was much slighter than the previous two engagements. The park presented a wide-open field, no cover to hide behind, just carnage. Amanda surveyed the park with her binoculars, The

Republicans knew she was coming, they had created a layered defensive ring. They brought in cars to hide behind; surprise would not serve her here.

"You're nervous." Cody observed as Amanda silently tried to come up with a plan.

"Of course I'm nervous." Amanda shot back, *"Look at it out there... it'll be a bloodbath."*

"Yes." Cody agreed, *"But we can win."*

"I don't think that matters to the tons of our people who are about to die." Amanda argued.

"You're right." Cody conceded, *"But everyone picked a side when this all went down, we knew the risks."*

"Jesus Christ!" Amanda exclaimed, *"Thank God you put me in charge, you woulda just led them to slaughter."*

"And that's why I put you in charge." Cody said, *"So how are we gonna do this?"*

Amanda peered through her binoculars again, *"I wish I had those bikers"* she observed. *"We could use them to smash the flank; they'd be too fast for the Republicans to react."*

"Then ask him." Cody advised, *"He'll send them over for you."*

"He needs them." Amanda responded curtly.

"He doesn't need anything," Cody argued, *"and you know it."*

"I'm not going to take away forces from him just because I can't figure this out."

"Amanda." Cody said, taking her shoulders. *"Have I ever lied to you?"*

"No." She replied.

"And I know you're close with him... but whose knows him longer?" Cody asked.

"You have."

"And I say he will give you what you need.... It's kind of what he does."

"Fine." Amanda conceded, *"just because I don't see a better way."*

"Thank you." Cody replied. Kissing her on the forehead. *"I can deliver the message personally if you want."*

"Might as well be someone I can trust." Amanda answered, *"I'm gonna plan around it."*

"Don't even worry." Cody said, *"next time you see me I'll have a whole motorcycle club at my back."* With his last comment, he dashed off into the east, to find the Emperor's forces. Amanda began to plan her attack.

Chapter 31: Sandra

The day had progressed about to The Emperor's expectations. As they approached the various cells of rebel forces guarding the city, they fled in terror at the mere sight of him, marching in full regalia, an army at his back. Those that did stand and fight only served to show the objectivism of those who fled. His Majesty was not in a merciful mood. With raw fury he slew any who stood in his path. Waves of gunfire supported his advance, but it was his Majesty's insanity that broke the will of his would-be usurpers. In a matter of a few short hours army group east had achieved all three objectives and completed their encircling maneuvers.

The Emperor set up camp in the industrial district. He had named Harold's drug manufactory as the stronghold for the district. He personally ran the Imperial standard up the flagpole when the building was secured. He sat at a desk, wiping the blood from his sword, Sandra close beside him.

"Your Majesty has once again demonstrated his uncontestable power." Madam Dubois said with a flourish as she approached the couple. *"Victory is yours sire."* She gave the Emperor a respectful bow.

"Yes, the day is won... on our end." The Emperor replied, rising to his feet. *"But what of the Lord Chancellor... does he fare as well as us?"*

"Master Chesley is more than capable," Sandra offered, *"Have faith."* The elaborate dress she

was wearing made it easier to talk like the Emperor. The Emperor looked at her and smiled briefly but said nothing. He walked over to a window *"We're so close."* he mused, *"Then this will all be over."* His face soured.

"What is this?" Sandra asked, walking close behind the Emperor, *"You were in such a good mood earlier."*

"The thrill has worn off." The Emperor exhaled, *"Now all I see is a field of corpses, loyal soldiers who gave their lives for the Empire... but who won't reap the benefit."*

"They believed in the Empire..." Sandra said, trying to quell his concern. She stood behind him and propped her chin on his shoulder *"They believed in YOU."*

"And it cost them their life." The Emperor scolded. He nudged Sandra off of his shoulder. *"It all used to be so simple."* He paced around the room, *"Follow my rules and I'll keep you safe.... Now they're dead."* He rubbed his hands along his neck as he began muttering nonsensically to himself. Sandra rushed to comfort him but Madame Dubois intercepted her.

"Try this my lady." Madame Dubois said as she thrust a flask of whiskey into her hand.

"You know I don't drink...." Sandra said as she took the flask.

"Oh honestly." Madame Dubois groaned, *"If I am going to have to call you Empress someday soon,*

you're going to have to be more perceptive than that." She pointed in the Emperor's direction.

"OH!" Sandra exclaimed as she put it together, *"Sorry I feel dumb now."*

"Just go!" Madame Dubois laughed as she shoved Sandra in the Emperor's direction. *"You can thank me later, my lady."*

Sandra handed the Emperor the flask, he stopped his tirade long enough to down the entire thing and hand it back to Sandra. *"Thank you."* he said with a calm exhale. Sandra looked back toward Madame Dubois who slyly tapped her nose in reply and backed off.

"You can't control everything." Sandra said to the Emperor, *"And trying is only going to drive you crazy."* The Emperor eyes her suspiciously. *"You're not crazy."* Sandra assured, anticipating his comment, *"A little too performative and prone to anger, yes. But not crazy."*

Their conversation was interrupted by Cody bursting into the room. The Emperor was shocked to see the Lord Chancellor in front of him and scurried over.

"What's wrong?" The Emperor asked, *"Why are you not leading your forces?"*

"Amanda was selected to lead in my stead Majesty." Cody explained, *"We're beginning our assault on the park but resistance has stiffened, she needs reinforcements."*

"Oh." The Emperor acknowledged, *"So that's where the scoundrels ran to.... The bikers then..."*

"Our thoughts exactly, sire." Cody agreed.

"Madame DuBois if you would be so kind." Madame DuBois gave the Emperor a polite bow and left the room. She returned a moment later with one of the bikers accompanying her.

"What's up?" The biker asked, folding his arms. Sandra noticed the slight wince the Emperor gave at the lack of reverence, but he made no comment about it.

"It seems Army Group West is facing a last desperate defense by the enemy." The Emperor explained., *"Master Chesley will be taking you and your men to return the order of battle to our advantage."*

The biker just shrugged, *"Just as long as you don't neg on our deal."* He said.

"Half price in perpetuity of all weapons and narcotics sold to our friends the Charging Cavaliers." The Emperor repeated, *"I have not forgotten nor do I intend to dishonor my promise."*

"Alright then let's roll." The biker agreed, *"I'll gather the boys, we'll be ready when you are."* he left to rally his men.

"Strike hard and strike fast my friend," The Emperor instructed Cody, *"With surprise on your side the enemy will quickly route."*

"Actually Majesty..." Cody said awkwardly, *"I don't know how to ride a motorcycle."*

"Is that so?" The Emperor questioned, *"Nevermind."* he waved the situation off, *"Lady*

Blewens and the Marshals can keep things in hand here... I'll go with you."

Sandra now felt the time was right to insert herself into the discussion. *"Actually sire,"* she said, *"I was thinking maybe I can go in your stead."*

"You?" The Emperor recoiled, *"Why?"*

"I'm just worried about your safety." Sandra answered flatly. She was lying.

"No you're not." The Emperor quickly countered, *"Something else is going on here."* He peered at her inquisitively, *"What are you playing at?"*

"I already said," Sandra answered, unamused.

"You're a bad liar." The Emperor challenged. Damnit.

"I seem to remember being an undercover cop right under your nose for months." Sandra shot back. Cody's eyes widened at the mention of the sore subject, but the Emperor's expression remained unchanged.

"So you are lying then?" He pressed. His eyeballs whirred as he ran the possibilities through his head.... *"AH!"* He exclaimed shortly after, his face lighting up as the dots in his brain connected. *"You want to save her... and make her love you again."* He smiled with smug triumph at his hypothesis.

"So what?" Sandra asked, *"What's wrong with that?"*

"Nothing at all." The Emperor shrugged, *"I won't stand in your way... provided my Lord Chancellor approves."* Both of them turned to Cody.

"Honestly Majesty," Cody began, *"I'd rather hold onto her hips than yours."* He chuckled nervously.

Both The Emperor and Sandra gave Cody a disgusted look.

"Sorry," he muttered, *"bad joke...."* The Emperor merely rolled his eyes.

"Be careful my darling." The Emperor said, turning back to Sandra. He pressed his forehead against hers.

"We haven't been apart since I sprung you from jail." Sandra noted, *"don't miss me too much."*

"I miss you when I close my eyes." The Emperor said sweetly, kissing her hand. *"But there is work to do.... Go get our little girl."* He left Sandra and Cody behind and left the room to do God knows what. *Our little girl.* The line repeated itself in Sandra's head over and over.

The bikers were assembled; his Majesty's mercenaries revved their engines as they prepared to launch the assault. Sandra started her bike. Cody positioned himself behind her. *"Don't be mad at her if this doesn't work."* Cody said to her.

"I'm not mad at her," Sandra replied, annoyed, *"Don't hold my hips too tight."* Cody blushed. The Emperor emerged onto the concentration of motorcycles to bid his farewells.

"Gentlemen." He announced to the bikers. *"It is time to redeem the charge of the light brigade! Show the enemy the meaning of swift terror. God be with you."* He walked over to Sandra's bike. *"Look out for yourselves,"* he instructed, *"The war nears its conclusion... I'd hate for you to miss the final curtain falling."* He placed a hand on Cody's shoulder and the two friends nodded to each other. The Emperor paid Sandra no attention, instead storming back to the company of Madame Dubois. Madame Dubois gave Sandra a friendly wave.

"Good luck!" She shouted. Sandra waved back in response. Sandra twisted her wrist and her motorcycle shot forward. She felt Cody's hands dig into her sides as she accelerated, a legion of bikers behind her. Together they tore through the city, pushing west until they reached the park.

As they reached the park an intense firefight was already underway. The roar of the motorcycle engines was eclipsed by gunfire. The republican line got steadily closer as the motorcycles advanced on the battle. Amanda was right to call them; Army Group West definitely held the advantage but this shock attack on the Republican flank would prevent countless Imperial losses.

Much like at Reginridge, by the time the Republicans realized the bikers were there it was too late to mount any sort of effective defense. The bikers, with Sandra and Cody at the head, smashed into the Republican's left flank. The bikers fired their machine guns but ultimately running down the enemy proved more effective. With the Republican defenses now in complete chaos, Sandra saw Amanda thrust her sword forward and lead an all-out charge on the remaining defensive positions.

After Amanda's charge, the Republicans lasted mere minutes before they engaged in a full retreat. Cheers erupted from the Empire's ranks as the final stronghold fell firmly in control. The bikers chased down clusters of fleeing Republicans mowing them down. The battle was now truly won; the Republicans had no escape.

Sandra pulled her bike up to Amanda who was talking to some of the Empire's soldiers. As Sandra and Cody dismounted, the soldiers Amanda was talking to bowed deeply and dispersed. Cody ran up and hugged Amanda while Sandra held back. *"Congratulations!"* Cody exclaimed, picking Amanda up and spinning her around. *"You did it!"*

Amanda seemed happy as Cody flung her around, but when he set her down, she stepped back. *"We'll catch up later."* She said politely, *"Can you give us a sec."* She eyed Sandra which made

Sandra stand straighter. Cody looked back at Sandra as well before nodding in understanding. He gently kissed her cheek before joining the celebrating soldiers.

"Thank you for coming." Amanda said coldly as she walked up to Sandra, still it was a start.

"I'll always come when you need me." Sandra replied. *"Anything I did... it was to protect you, whether you realize it or not."*

"I want to believe you." Amanda said, they were standing close together now. *"I just don't understand."*

"You don't have to understand it." Sandra replied curtly, *"It was between me and him... what you do have to understand is I would jump in front of one hundred gunmen to protect you."*

"Don't you realize all of this is your fault?" Amanda asked, gesturing to the battlefield around her. *"You gave them the conditions to attack."*

"I did what I thought was right." Sandra said bluntly, *"I didn't really plan to have this much influence over people's lives. Just like I don't think you did either, when you killed that lieutenant."* She cut her eyes at Amanda.

Amanda's gaze fell to the ground as she contemplated Sandra's words. Since Amanda did not respond Sandra continued, *"The point is... I'm on your side. Always."* Her eyes began to fill with tears, *"I was fuddling through life but now I have a purpose."*

"What's that?" Amanda asked, her voice began to quiver too.

"To keep that maniac in check and to keep you safe." Sandra answered, smiling down on Amanda. *"You and him, you give my life meaning."*

Sandra watched as Amanda contemplated her statement. Amanda repeatedly ran her fingers through her hair as she thought. Sandra said nothing, giving Amanda all the time she needed to process...

Now it was Amanda who had tears swelling in her eyes. Amanda closed her eyes, she sniffled as she wiped her tears from her cheeks, desperately trying to maintain composure. *"Still you..."* she choked through her tears. She couldn't finish her thought.

"Let me ask you something." Sandra sweetly said, *"If it was as simple as that, why didn't he fight the charges?"*

"What... what do you mean?" Amanda said, gently wiping her eyes.

"The Commissioner has been hounding the Emperor for years. Never once has he been convicted. What was different that time."

"You mean he wanted to be in jail." Amanda whispered to herself.

"All I'm saying is it's complicated." Sandra said, brushing her hand through Amanda's hair. *"It's not because I betrayed him, and I would certainly never betray you."*

Amanda lunged herself at Sandra and took her in a giant hug. Sandra jolted in surprise at first but quickly relaxed and returned the embrace. *"I missed you."* Amanda said as Sandra felt a tear roll down her breast. She placed her chin on top of Amanda's head and began to stroke the back of her head. Her mind recalling the night leading up to the Emperor's arrest, her brushing Amanda's hair in the bathtub.

Sandra held tight to Amanda until Cody came up to interrupt them. *"I'm sorry. To ruin the moment."* He said as he cleared his throat. *"But we're not done just yet..."*

Chapter 32: Amanda

Amanda led her army to the Emperor's museum, nestled near the city's center, it was the last refuge of the Republican rebellion. As they approached the Emperor was already there. Madame Dubois standing dutifully beside him, his forces had already surrounded the perimeter of the complex. Imperial banners proudly blowing in the wind and trumpets and drummers in full swing the Grand Imperial Army once again was reunited into a force of magnificent splendor. The Emperor stood tall, raising his hat to Amanda and her procession as they filed in to strengthen the Empire's encirclement. Amanda, Sandra, and Cody broke ranks to approach his Majesty. He was locked in hushed conversation with Madame Dubois. As the trio got near, Madame Dubois gave a respectful bow and excused herself.

"I am glad to see you all made it safely." The Emperor said in jovial spirit, *"The moor is surrounded in Grenada,"* he gestured to the museum *"and the Reconquista reaches its final stage..."*

"So what's the plan your Majesty?" Cody asked, *"We never actually discussed how we're going to handle this part."*

"Never fear." The Emperor said coolly, *"Preparations have been made."* A twinge of wicked malice briefly flickered across his face. Cody eyed Amanda nervously but she just shrugged. *"Now!"* The Emperor exclaimed, clapping his hands together,

"Amanda my sweet child, you must return to your soldiers." He took her by the shoulders and turned her around, he gently pushed her in the direction of an area where all of the Marshals, save Madame Dubois, had congregated. The Marshals all gave Amanda a friendly greeting. They made space for Amanda to stand next to Harold, who gave her an affectionate smile. *"We did it."* he said.

"What's he planning?" Amanda asked, but Harold had no answer. Amanda watched as the Emperor stood inside of the circle of his army. He directed Sandra and Cody to either of his flanks, two steps behind him. He turned in the direction of the sharpshooters and gave them a signal with his hand. Immediately they lifted their rifles and trained them on the various windows and doors of the wall the Emperor was facing. The Emperor held his arm out again, one finger outstretched, then two, then three. He pointed at the music brigade who began to play a military march on their trumpets, the fife and drum soon joined in. As the music played the Emperor with Sandra and Cody in tow, approached the building. He stopped about ten feet from the wall, the music slowly died down. No one exited the building, conversely it appeared empty, but the Emperor knew better. He jabbed Cody with his elbow.

Cody took a deep breath and cupped his hands around his mouth, *"Now announcing the arrival of his Regal Imperial Majesty!"* he shouted, *"Edward Von Drac, Imperator Rex Colonna City.*

Anointed Master of the Imperial Convocation. Crowned Lord Protector of the Seven Districts. First Counselor of the Imperial Diet. First Admiral of the Imperial Armada. Grand Defender of the Street and of the Sea. In his presence, may you bow your heads in unmatched reverence or fall to your knees in repentant shame!"

Everyone watched on but no movement came from within the museum. The Emperor looked up impatiently. *"Rebels!"* he shouted, *"Dissidents! I give you one chance to plead for your lives! Would you not take it?!"*

Slowly a figure emerged onto a balcony above where the Emperor stood. Amanda was taken aback at the sight of the familiar face. He rested his hands on the balcony, he was missing a pinky. On his face there was a large bandage, covering the spot where most people would have a nose.

"Majesty." Pump Nasty said, his voice was changed, likely a result of the lack of a proper nasal passage. *"We meet again."*

"You?" The Emperor sneered, *"I remember banishing you."*

"You did sire but —-"

"*Do not refer to me by my regal homages."* The Emperor interjected. *"You are not my subject nor am I your king... I owe you no such protection."*

"It's funny you should say that Edward." Pump replied, The Emperor's nostrils flared. *"Because these good people have elected me their president."*

"President?!" The Emperor giggled, he chuckled softly at first but it soon devolved to a full hearty cackle. *"Sexual misconduct and abuse of power... then they elect you president..."* he cackled again with such force he began to tear up. *"All we need now is Linda Tripp and a tape recorder..."* he belted out another laugh. Pump eyed the Emperor confused but Cody chortled through his nose at the Emperor's comment. The Emperor regained his composure. *"So tell me Mr. President."* he began sarcastically, *"What is it you ask of me?"*

"I'm smart enough to know when I'm beaten." Pump explained.

"Apparently not." The Emperor shot back dryly but Pump paid him no attention.

"There's no way we win this." Pump continued, *"We're out numbered, outgunned, you win."*

The Emperor flung his finger in a quick succession of circles, directing Pump to get to the point.

"You are known for being a cruel man. But not an irrational one."

"Thank you." The Emperor beamed, *"but flattery will not avail you, especially when its source is so repugnant."*

"Your position is secure." Pump explained, *"We can't pose any real threat to you... Why waste any more of your people's lives just to kill us off... Let us leave and you can have your city back."*

"The lives of my soldiers?" the Emperor asked. He knew what Pump meant but was clearly toying with him, savoring the moment.

"We both know this place is a fortress." Pump expounded, *"You will in the end but we will fight to the last man. Or you can let what's left of us go, and you lose no one."*

"It's true the museum is quite easily defendable.... I did design it." The Emperor agreed, his wicked smile spreading across his face once again, *"But as always you drug addled pervert, you have failed to consider a crucial variable."* He gently raised a single hand into the air.

"What variable?" Pump asked, The Emperor's face filled with glee at the question.

"FIELD ARTILLERY!" The Emperor shouted back, his raised hand closed into a fist and he brought it crashing down to his side. Suddenly Amanda heard distant whooshing sounds. They were quickly replaced by screeching from the sky. She looked up to see a trail of smoke arching towards the museum. The Emperor sprinted away from the building, Cody and Sandra panicking, rushed to follow him. The smoky arch collided with the museum and erupted in a massive explosion. Four other explosions followed in quick succession. The blast made Amanda uneasy on her feet. Fire shot out every direction from the impact. One of the shells hit the balcony before Pump had a chance to retreat. He came crashing down with the stone, his body

immediately motionless on impact. More shells came crashing into the museum. The fire quickly spread and Amanda could see windows shattering from the internal pressure. She turned around to locate the source of the blasts to find Madame Dubois and a handful of her gun smugglers manning mortar tubes, firing them into the museum.

"Watch the doors!" The Emperor commanded, the continual shockwaves made his cape billow behind him. He held his arm up to shield his face from the heat. *"Kill any man who dares try and escape the Emperor's wrath!"*

Guns were trained on the doors, but they were unnecessary. Any republicans who did manage to get out were already lit on fire, succumbing to the flames before they made it so much as a yard. Mortar shells kept hitting the building, large chunks of stone and wood crashed around the flames as the demolition ensued. Fire was protruding from almost all the windows now. The situation inside the building was so bad Amanda watched as men jumped from the windows of the higher levels, choosing a fall to being burned alive. The worst part was the smell. The odor of burning flesh was so pungent Amanda barely heard the screaming. She held her hand up to her nose. The Emperor's army all collectively retreated a few yards to avoid any debris, but the Emperor did not move. Standing alone inside the circle he watched as shell after shell tore down his museum, until finally the roof caved in completely and the massive building was reduced to flaming ruins. Only then did the shelling stop.

Chapter 33: Sandra

It was eerily quiet. By the time the mortars had stopped firing, any one left inside the building had been long dead. Now the Emperor's armies stood silent yet victorious surrounding their sovereign and the smoldering ruins. The Emperor stood alone, staring into the fire. He made no movements and gave no orders, just staring.

"What do we do now?" Cody asked the marshals. None answered, all of them hoping he was the one with an answer.

"Let me handle this." Sandra said to them, *"Give me just a minute."* She marched from the circle to the Emperor's side, the train of her violet gown dragging behind her. When she reached the Emperor's side he turned his face slightly away from her. He was massaging his pocket watch. He said nothing.

"You're Majesty." Sandra said softly, taking his hand from his waistcoat pocket and into hers. *"The people need to know how to proceed."*

"I need just a moment." The Emperor exhaled. He bent down and picked up a small piece of stone that had been flung from the building. He studied it intently, rotating it in his fingers, before looking back at the flaming remnants of his museum.

"I'm sorry my friend." He whispered, clutching the stone close to his chest and closing his eyes. He tossed the stone into the flames.

"We'll build a new one." Sandra offered, *"A bigger one."*

The Emperor finally turned to face her and he smiled. Without saying a word, he turned back toward the fire and rested his head on her shoulder. *"Perhaps a memorial."* He suggested, *"For all those who fell in this ungodly conflict."*

"Maybe the Mayor will commission a giant statue of you." Sandra joked, *"Edward Von Drac, savior of the city."* The Emperor laughed quietly.

"Well." he exhaled again, *"This is no way to celebrate a victory."* He shook his head back and forth repeatedly before springing to life. He jumped around to face the men and women of the Empire, eagerly awaiting his words.

"Today we have restored order!" The Emperor exclaimed, raising his hands high in victory. *"We lost many friends in the struggle, but when the citizens return tomorrow, they shall come home to safe streets and good honest criminal enterprise!"* A large bout of cheers and applause emanated from the Imperial legions. He waved his hands to get the crowd to settle down.

"The amphitheater is still intact!" He announced, pointing to the large arena that connected to the museum. *"Return to Reginridge, get all the food and libations you can carry! Tomorrow we begin to rebuild, but tonight we shall celebrate with the fury of a thousand GODS!"*

The party was everything the Emperor had promised. Everyone raved about the amphitheater dancing and drinking. Someone had even found an old case of fireworks in the bowels of Reginridge to shoot off into the night sky. Large tables of food were hastily set up, allowing people to eat whenever they wanted. A faint smell of Marijuana pervaded the air. The music was loud and wholly not to the Emperor's taste. Sandra almost felt bad for him knowing he likely would have preferred to lock himself in a room with his phonograph, but there was no chance of that tonight. Luckily someone had thought to scoop up Edwina and brought her to the party so his Majesty and the peacock could sit and disapprove together.

Sandra, on the other hand, fully embraced the gaiety of the evening. She danced, shimmying with all of the men and women of the Empire. The three glasses of champagne she consumed helped her in this effort. As she danced, she noticed Harold sitting in the stands off to himself, he appeared sulky.

Tactfully she maneuvered through the hordes of partiers over in his direction. Emerging through the dancing area she marched over to him.

"Oh ma'am I didn't see you" Harold said, springing to his feet.

"Shut up with that for a second." Sandra said lightheartedly, *"It's okay he can't hear you."* She made

Harold sit down as she took a seat beside him. *"What's wrong?"* She asked.

"Nothing..." Harold lied lazily, *"It's just that I'm at the biggest party in the Empire's history and she's not here."*

"We all miss Sylvia." Sandra said empathetically, she gave Harold a friendly pat on the shoulder, *"She could light up a room like no other."*

"She woulda loved this." Harold said, his tone bittersweet.

"I think she would be heartbroken that you aren't having fun." Sandra argued, *"Come on."* She took Harold by the arm and lifted him to his feet. As she led him to the dance floor, she caught him giving the Emperor a nervous glance at the other end of the arena. The Emperor merely raised his glass and smiled.

Harold danced lazily at first. But Sandra insisted on keeping her energy up. She spun around him and forced him to sway to the upbeat music. Slowly but surely, Harold loosened up and began to match the atmosphere of the party. Once Sandra had him moving, she thrusted him onto a cluster of Amanda's girls. *"Keep him moving."* she ordered, *"I won't have anyone sad tonight."*

"As you wish for your ladyship." The prostitute replied with a grin. Sandra waved her off as the girls surrounded Harold and began dancing with him. She maneuvered across the dance floor once again. This time she headed in the Emperor's direction. He had

positioned a large chair for himself. Amanda and Cody sat in a chair next to him, Amanda on Cody's lap. The three of them were engaged in friendly conversation while Edwina waltzed around them and cooed.

"Alright you kids, go have fun." Sandra said as she walked up to them, *"I'll keep him company."*

"Do you wanna dance?" Cody asked Amanda, looking up into her eyes, the innocent way he asked it made Sandra smile.

"Let's go!" Amanda agreed, bending down to kiss Cody on the lips. Together they stood up and prepared to join the party. Amanda stopped for a second and turned back toward the Emperor. *"Yell for me if she tries to arrest you again."* she said completely straight faced. Sandra's face went white, but the color soon returned when both Amanda and the Emperor shared a laugh at the awkwardness.

"Run along, go enjoy yourselves." The Emperor grinned shooing them away *"you've earned it."* Amanda gave the Emperor a peck on the cheek and hand-in-hand with Cody they strolled off to the dance floor. Sandra watched them run off as she sat in the chair next to the Emperor. She saw the Emperor smiling as he watched the party, even tapping his foot to the beat.

"Look whose chipper." She observed out loud. *"If I didn't know better, I'd say you're enjoying yourself."*

"I'm relishing our victory." The Emperor replied, *"Don't overthink it."* Sandra said nothing, instead she placed a hand overtop of the Emperor's and together they sat and watched the party. They partially focused on Amanda who had let loose, spinning and twirling like a girl should as she danced with Cody.

Madame Dubois' voice rang out on a loudspeaker. *"Alright everyone settle down for just a minute."* She said, the party died down slightly but not nearly enough. She raised a pistol into the air and fired it, *BANG "Just a minute you jackals!"* She shouted this time, everyone laughed but listened this time.

"Thank you." She said sarcastically, *"I know we're all having fun... but I was thinking we would be so lucky if their majesties would grace us all with a dance."* She outstretched her arm in the Emperor's direction and the dance floor parted on either side to make a path to where the Emperor and Sandra sat. Everyone clapped heartily to sway the Emperor's opinion.

Sandra stood up first, *"Come on you."* she whispered to him, *"It's time to show your Empress off to the world."*

"Not until we step foot in a church." The Emperor replied, *"But in the meantime I can show*

these mongrels the meaning of poise." He took Sandra's hands and rose to his feet.

Together they walked, hands interlocked at shoulder height, down the aisleway the people made for them. Sandra and the Emperor reached the middle of the dance floor and the crowd backed off, giving them plenty of room. She looked around to see hundreds of eyes all on her. It would have been daunting, but she caught a glimpse of Amanda and Cody, Amanda shot her a thumbs up, that gave her all the confidence she needed.

Sandra placed a hand on the Emperor's shoulder, her other hand in his, holding up the spare fabric of her dress. The Emperor placed a hand on her waist. *"Maestro!"* Madame Dubois shouted, pointing to the DJ, *"Something nice for their majesties!"* The DJ gave Madame Dubois a salute and began to play a song. It started off with low long violins; The Emperor slowly began a waltz keeping pace with the music. Sandra followed his lead; their eyes locked onto each other. Flutes entered into the fray, fluttering around the deep strings. The Emperor sped up slightly, until an oboe slowed him back down. They spun in grand circles, never once looking away from each other. Sandra began to feel dizzy, the rest of the world was a blur of motion, yet the Emperor's eyes kept her steady. Two steps forward, one step left. Sandra's heart beat hard into her chest as the Violins accelerated. They spun faster and faster. The Violins crescendoed and drums entered for the grand finale.

The music was pulsing through her now. She could feel the Emperor's pulse rushing through his hand along with hers. The violins were lighting and the drums thunder. It all became too much, poise be damned. She took the Emperor's face into her hands and kissed him as the orchestra reached its final notes. The Emperor pulled her in at the waist and cupped her cheek in his other hand. The crowd erupted into applause, but Sandra didn't hear them.

"I love you, you wretched monster." She whispered to him.

"And I love you, you insolent shrew." He whispered back before pulling her chin up to his, kissing her again.

Chapter 34: Amanda

The sun beat down on Amanda's face, forcing her to wake up. Most everyone had fallen asleep on the ground of the amphitheater following the party the previous night. She wiped the sleep from her eyes. Her head was pounding but she fought through it and started to move. Cody was lying next to her still sound asleep. She nudged his disheveled hair out of his face. He looked so peaceful, more peaceful than any of them had looked in a long time.

Amanda got up slowly so as not to wake him and stretched herself to consciousness. Most people were still asleep. She tiptoed around her sleeping comrades over to The Emperor. He was still asleep too. Sandra slept next to him, using his chest as a pillow. Edwina was nuzzled at his side.

Sandra must have felt Amanda's presence because she woke up not long after Amanda walked up. *"Sorry I didn't mean to wake you up."* Amanda whispered.

"It's all right." Sandra yawned as she cracked her neck to wake up fully, *"Do you need him."*

"It can wait." Amanda said, *"can you let me know when he wakes up."*

"Just a second." Sandra laughed, she jabbed her knee into the Emperor's ribcage. *"Wake up!"* she shouted. Amanda couldn't help but think it was funny.

"I WON'T KILL SARASTRO!" The Emperor blurted as he jolted awake, *"Wha... What's happening."*

Both Sandra and Amanda looked at the Emperor dumbfounded, *"You are so weird."* Sandra said to him.

"And what does that say about you..." The Emperor shot back. *"What do you want?"*

"Not me... Amanda" Sandra answered.

"Oh.. sorry dear I didn't see you." The Emperor said to Amanda, he got himself up to his feet. *"What can I do for you?"*

"I apologize your Majesty. I didn't mean to wake you."

"I'm sure you didn't." He smiled before he shot Sandra a nasty look, she just grinned.

"Anyway..." Amanda continued, *"I've been meaning to talk to I have this friend Tiff—"*

"Hang on." The Emperor interrupted holding a finger up to his lip. *"Do you hear that?"*

They all listened silently, but Amanda heard nothing.

"I hear it." Sandra confirmed, *"What is that?"*

"It better not be what I think it is." The Emperor grumbled. He fumbled around his jacket pocket until he found his telescope he marched over to the arena wall and used the instrument to look at the sky. Amanda listened again, she could hear a very faint whirring sound.

"GOD DAMN THAT MAN!" The Emperor screamed, *"DAMN THAT FOOL TO THE FIERY PIT!"*

His screaming began to wake people up. The whirring sound was getting louder.

"Get everyone up!" The Emperor shouted, *"They've got to get out of here."*

"Why?" Sandra asked, *"What's going on?"*

"The Commissioner's come." The Emperor said coldly, *"He's brought the national guard."*

Amanda looked to the sky. She could see a multitude of helicopters racing in their direction. Their whirring blades growing increasingly louder. Amanda could hear sirens now too. The Emperor was making as much noise as possible to wake everybody up.

"Disperse my children!" He shouted, *"This fight we cannot win! Run underground, await orders!"* People began waking up in droves. Panic ensued as they heard the desperation in the Emperor's voice. Everyone frantically ran for their lives as the helicopters closed in, Police cars close behind them. It was utter chaos, uncontrollable.

"Amanda!" Cody shouted, *"Amanda, where are you?!"* He tore through the crowd until he found her. Wrapping her into his arms. *"We have to get out of here."* He said.

"I know but where?" Amanda asked.

"Come with me." The Emperor growled, charging ahead, Edwina and his cane scooped in his arms. Cody, Sandra, and Amanda all frantically

followed him. He led them through the chaotic crowd to an interior hallway within the arena. He pulled at a loose piece of flooring which exposed a trap door. *"Go!"* He shouted. As Amanda climbed down the ladder to the bowels beneath the arena, she could see the helicopters hovering over the main arena, national guard soldiers rappelling down into the dispersing crowd below.

The Emperor was the last to enter the trap door, securing a lock as he shut the door on top of them. They all filed down. The ladder led to a long metal tunnel, lit with fluorescent lighting, it had an industrial feel with long pipes running across the rounded walls.

"Come on." The Emperor commanded, pushing forward, *"No time to waste."* He delved deeper into the tunnel; Sandra and the others close behind. It seemed to go on forever. Amanda didn't even know where they were going. What the hell was happening? Ten minutes ago, everything was perfect. She held tight to Cody as they all rushed down the tunnel.

"Not too much farther." The Emperor said, *"just keep going."* His panic had turned to determination. He picked up the pace. Poor Edwina bouncing in the Emperor's clutches. They rushed through the winding tunnel. Rushed until the Emperor halted in his tracks. The Commissioner was blocking their path.

Chapter 35: Sandra

"Well what do we have here?" The Commissioner snarled. He stood alone blocking the way.

"No backup Commissioner?" The Emperor questioned, *"Wherever are your goons?"*

"They're rounding up yours. I don't need them to take you in." The Commissioner answered. *"Now if you would all please put your hands behind your back."*

"Rather cocky." The Emperor mused.

"The governor declared martial law." The Commissioner explained, *"There's no running this time Edward."*

"I don't run from the likes of you." The Emperor spat. He turned around and gently placed Edwina into Amanda's arms. *"Take them to the docks."* The Emperor instructed Cody, *"Wait for me there."*

"No one's going anywhere." The Commissioner interjected, pulling his pistol from its holster.

"Oh but they are." The Emperor said, responding with a pistol of his own. *"It's me you want, they're of no consequence to you, certainly not worth your life."*

The Commissioner took a moment to assess the situation, *"she stays."* he finally said, jutting his chin at Sandra.

"Deal." Sandra replied before the Emperor had a chance to object. Commissioner Helming waved off Amanda and Cody, both of whom continued further down the tunnel.

"Now." The Emperor said calmly, *"Why not sheath our weapons and talk like civil men."*

"There's nothing civil about you." Helming snapped, *"You've had this city under your thumb for too long, it ends now."*

"Is that so?" The Emperor asked, *"You don't think I can win over a jury."*

"I don't need to." The Commissioner said, *"You're going to plead guilty."*

"How do you figure that?" The Emperor laughed.

"Because if you don't I throw her in jail." He turned his gun on Sandra, and the Emperor immediately stepped in front of her.

"You couldn't," The Emperor argued.

"Oh yea, people have so much sympathy for cops who get involved in organized crime." The Commissioner sarcastically remarked, *"And organize jailbreaks."*

"Fine." The Emperor said, *"It'll take one call to the DA's office, and this will be over so do you worst."*

"Oh no." The Commissioner said, *"When I tried to arrest former officer Blewens she resisted..."*

"What are you talking about?" The Emperor asked confused,

"She resisted arrest. I had no choice, I was in fear of my life..." he waved his gun around.

"That's why you didn't bring anyone." Sandra said, *"You didn't want any witnesses..."*

"You bastard." The Emperor growled, *"How the mighty have fallen."*

"I was thinking the same thing." BANG.

The Commissioner's shot missed, instead ricocheted off one of the pipes causing steam to hiss in the tunnel. The Emperor charged Helming and tackled him to the ground. Sandra tried to yelp in protest but it was too late. The Emperor had the Commissioner on the ground and was beating him relentlessly.

"What are you doing?!" Sandra yelled, *"He is the police Commissioner! You can't hurt him there'd be no going back!"*

Sandra distracted the Emperor long enough for Helming to shove him off. Helming wriggled his way free. He grabbed one of the loose pipes and ripped it from the wall. He swung the pipe at the Emperor. The Emperor jumped back to dodge the swing. Quickly he unsheathed the blade hidden in his cane and raised it to the Commissioner's eye level.

"This is not going to end well." Sandra said to him through gritted teeth.

"I quite agree." The Emperor said before swinging at Helming's cheek.

Helming used the pipe to block the Emperor's attack. He returned with a flurry of swings, his Majesty effectively parrying each one.

"Marcus...." The Emperor pleaded, *"This is your last chance to see reason."*

"I am seeing reason..." The Commissioner snapped back, *"Finally for the first time."* He lifted the pipe over his head and brought it down hard. The Emperor pushed the pipe out of the way with his sword before it cracked the Emperor's skull. *"I'm gonna kill her... and you're gonna watch. This is my city, not yours."*

"So be it." The Emperor exhaled, *"Perhaps this is long overdue."* The Emperor thrust his sword toward Commissioner Helming's chest. Helming jumped back. Helming attacked again. He swung high, low, high, high again. The Emperor stayed light on his feet, jumping back to lessen the impact as he used his blade to block each attack.

The Emperor grabbed his cape and flung it forward. The fabric tangled itself with the pipe the Commissioner was using as a weapon. The Emperor tugged hard and managed to pull the pipe out of Helming's hands. It hit the ground with a giant clang echoing through the tunnel.

"It's over." The Emperor said, again raising his sword to the Commissioner's eye level, *"Submit."*

The Commissioner pulled out a radio, *"This is Commissioner Helming, I have suspect Edward Von Drac in the tunnels beneath the Amphitheatre, requesting back up."* A muffled "*10-4*" rang back through the radio.

"There." The Commissioner said, *"Backup comes, they see a bloody Commissioner and two guilty parties. You're done."*

"Bravo." The Emperor sneerily conceded. *"This is quite a pickle."*

Sandra was now beyond worried. She didn't see a way out of the situation that didn't end in absolute disaster. The Commissioner eyed his gun lying on the ground.

"Don't try it." The Emperor said, *"You'll lose."*

"They'll know it was you." The Commissioner muttered to himself, *"They'll have to throw you both away forever."*

"Don't." The Emperor repeated.

The Commissioner dove for the gun, but his Majesty was faster. The Emperor swiftly intercepted Helming, driving his blade deep into the Commissioner's gut. Sandra watched as the last bits of breath left her former boss' body. The Emperor twisted the blade to ensure the job was done, and then using his boot, pushed Helming's limp remains off of the blade. The Commissioner let out a final gasp on the ground, and it was over.

The Emperor put his blade back into its sheath. Heaving a defeated sigh as he did so. He looked down on Helming's corpse and shook his head.

"We have to get you out of the city." Sandra said.

"Agreed," The Emperor replied, together they pushed further down the tunnel.

Chapter 36: Amanda

Cody had led Amanda through the long tunnel and out the other side. It emerged near the city's waterfront. To both of their surprise there were no authorities they had to avoid. The Commissioner must not have told them where he was going. They didn't have to wait long before Sandra and the Emperor came running behind them. The blood stains on the Emperor's boots told her what had happened in the tunnel.

The Emperor approached them, Sandra looked solemn, The Emperor, determined. He gently took Edwina back into his care and whispered something into the bird's ear. The Emperor led them through the waterfront. Sticking to alleyways to avoid any potential national guard patrols that may be nearby. The faint sounds of gunfire could be heard from further within the city.

The Emperor took them to a small enclosed private berth along the water. The outside appeared like a rickety wooden shack, dilapidated and abandoned. The door was padlocked with a combination. Hastily the Emperor entered the combination and freed the padlock from the latch. Swinging the door open showed a narrow U-Shaped walkway surrounding a thin waterway. Floating in the water was an old, decommissioned military submarine.

"There she is." The Emperor beamed at the rusted vessel, *"The pride of his Majesty's navy...."* On the nose of the submarine in intricate black lettering was painted, *"The Royal Margaret."*

"What's happening?" Amanda asked as the Emperor bustled about the berth, opening a secret panel that revealed a variety of large suitcases.

"What's happening my dear is I must go." The Emperor explained. *"The Empire has finally at last been dismantled.... It seems in the end, we still lost."* He began tossing the bags onto the submarine. Amanda tried to reply but she was too stunned to speak.

"You're Majesty..." Cody began *"Surely there's some other way."*

"Not this time my friend." The Emperor turned to Cody. He reached into his shirt and withdrew a key that was hanging around his neck. He shoved it into Cody's hand. *"Get to the counting house in the Industrial District."* He commanded, *"behind the portrait of Napoleon you'll find a vault... Don't let my fortune fall into the hands of those corporate drones. God only knows what they'll waste it on."*

"Your Majesty, I can't," Cody protested.

"Spread it as best you can..." The Emperor commanded *"My parting gift to the people who served me so well."* He loaded the last bag onto the boat. Lastly, he picked up Edwina once more. *"Well little one... looks like it's you and me again. Just like the old days."* The bird cooed softly back at him. He

gently placed her in the submarine through the entrance hatch.

As the realization of the situation hit Amanda she began to tear up. *"Oh don't cry darling."* The Emperor said, returning back to her. *"This isn't goodbye forever. We'll see each other again."*

"You're lying." Amanda replied, sniffling. The Emperor didn't respond, instead just giving her a warm hug. She returned it with all of her strength.

"You don't need me anymore." He said kindly as he gently pulled away. He wiped a tear from her eye. *"You're going to create a life all your own and it's going to be grand."* He walked over to Cody and the two joined in a final embrace patting each other on the back. *"We had a good run, old boy."* The Emperor told him, *"We truly did build something magnificent."*

"Yea we really did." Cody agreed. *"I'm gonna miss you man."* They squeezed each other one last time before separating. Finally, the Emperor turned to Sandra.

"You took this from me once." he said, removing his Imperial ring from his finger. *"I wonder now if you might keep it as a gift... a reminder of what we once shared."* He extended the ring toward her.

She looked at it confused, *"What are you talking about?"* She questioned while shoving the ring back to him, *"I threw everything away for you... I'm coming with you."*

"I can't let you." The Emperor said somberly, *"There's no life I can provide to you anymore, take your share of my treasure and move on."*

"I don't need you to provide me with anything." Sandra shot back, annoyed, *"We're going to build a new life together."* She pushed him out of the way and jumped onto the submarine. *"Well, are you coming??"*

The Emperor looked back at Amanda, confused, but she just tearily waved him off. He had to go. And Sandra had to go with him. He boarded the boat and took Sandra by the hand. *"And give me that!"* Sandra scolded, reaching into his waistcoat and ripping out his pocket watch. She hurled it into the water.

They stood over the entrance hatch. Together they turned back to Cody and Amanda, still standing on the dock, Sandra gave them one last wave. The Emperor kissed his fingertips and then held his hand out to them. Together Cody and Amanda gave them one last goodbye. Cody stood behind Amanda wrapping his arms around her as the fallen King and Queen climbed into the submarine's hull. The diesel engines roared to life and the vessel slowly pulled out from its berth and into the wide river. *"God save you, Your Majesty."* Amanda whispered to herself. Tears in their eyes, they watched the craft make for open water, creeping slowly beneath the ripples, never to be seen again.

The End

Acknowledgments

When I started scribbling down the original rough draft of this story over four years ago, I never thought I would actually get to this point. Even though I had one heck of a time chronicling the misadventures of his Majesty the Emperor, It would never have been possible without all of the wonderful people in my life and the support they provided every step of the way.

That being the case, I would love to extend a huge thank you to my friends and family for consistently putting up with my crackpot nonsense and allowing my creative insanity to flourish.

I'd also like to share my personal gratitude for anyone who bought this book, because of you I am officially a professional artist. I hope you had as much fun reading it as I did writing it.

www.ingramcontent.com/pod-product-compliance
Lightning Source LLC
LaVergne TN
LVHW090544110826
845146LV00001B/17

* 9 7 9 8 9 9 5 3 9 3 0 0 9 *